Au... Lasts

The L... of London Series

Meghan Hollie

First eBook and paperback editions April 2023.

Book Cover by Coffin Print Designs Ltd.

Developmental edit by Amy @ Amy Edits Ltd.

Copy and line edit by Sarah Baker @ Word Emporium.

Formatting by Atticus.

Published through KDP Publishing Amazon.

Contents

Playlist

Taylor Swift – Wildest Dreams
Ruth B. – Dandelions
Ashe, FINNEAS – 'Till forever falls apart
Jenna Raine – See you later (ten years)
Ellie Goulding – Still falling for you
John Legend, Gary Clark Jr. – Wild
Emily Watts – La Vie En Rose
Megan Thee Stallion, Dua Lipa – Sweetest Pie
BORNS – Electric Love
Laica – Nobody else but you
Forest Blakk – If you love her
JVKE – Golden hour
Clinton Kane – I guess I'm in love
Suriel Hess – Little bit more
Maren Morris, Hozier – The bones

Foreword

Please be aware there are a few sensitive topics discussed during this book.
Content warnings:
Drug addiction/use & Alcoholism (side characters).
Childhood trauma & healing.
Sexual content intended for 18+ audience and explicit language.

This book is also written in British English (hopefully not a trigger)

Dedication

For all the women who need a sweet boy, a filthy boy, and a big boy.

Part One

1

Jessica

Jess: Are we still on for milkshakes after school? No taksies backsies everyone has to be in.

Nora: Yesss! I need a milkshake today. Science was awful.

Liam: Order mine for me? I might be a little late. I have to swing by dad's office first. You know my order x

Jess: Hurry though, I won't be able to stop myself from drinking yours too.

Liam: You wouldn't.

Jess: I so would.

Nora: Stop arguing now, kids.

Jess: Who you calling kids? We're all the same age. Also hurry up! I'm dying from a milkshake deficiency.

Liam: Always with the drama.

Nora: I'm two mins away. Quit your bitching.

My foot taps the ground in quick succession as I wait for Nora to meet me in our spot outside school. The cool springtime breeze whips my hair around my face as the sunshine peeks through the few lingering clouds. It's a rare dry day in London; we've had almost a whole week of rain and right now I'm grateful for the break in the weather. Damp shoes are not the one.

"I'm here, I'm here," Nora hollers as she drafts around the corner with all her schoolbooks in tow, like she's just robbed the library, her brown eyes widening as she spots me.

I lift an eyebrow. "Why do you have all that?" I ask, gesturing to the books she's about to drop.

"I need to study before the exam next week and I don't have these," she says, trying to adjust the strap of her backpack by shrugging her shoulder.

"You're such a geek, Nor. You definitely have that one." I point to the books, making her scowl at me as they wobble slightly in her arms. "And that one too."

"Hey! These are different editions so…" She pokes her tongue at me whilst scrunching her nose.

"Like I said… geek. You're lucky I love you."

"I think you'll find you're the lucky one because I'm buying shakes tonight."

"In that case, need help with your books?" I say as I smile, flashing my teeth.

"Thought you'd never ask." Three heavy books drop into my open palms as I exhale a quiet grumble upon impact. She's lucky she's my best friend because I wouldn't do this for anyone, milkshakes or not.

I place the books into my backpack, and do my best to ignore the extra weight pulling on my shoulders as we walk the mile and a half to the milkshake shack near Chelsea Road. This place is our favourite because the owner always gives us extras and the shakes are to die for.

"Hey girls, I thought you weren't going to make it tonight. This is late for you two." The owner, who we call Shake - his real name is

Sam, but we've taken him under our wing as our resident and favourite shake maker, so nicknames come with that territory – says to us.

"You can blame this one and all her books she's forced me to carry." I hike a thumb over my shoulder, gesturing to Nora, who swats my arm in response.

Shake's shoulders bounce gently as he chuckles at us. "Liam not coming tonight?"

Just as my mouth opens to reply, Liam flies up next to us panting like he just ran the London marathon. His dark hair is dishevelled, and his eyes are watering from sheer exertion.

"I... am... oh, God... here." He folds over, gasping.

Ignoring Liam's dramatic entrance, I turn my back to him and smile sweetly at Shake.

"Shake, we'll have our usual please and it's on Nora tonight." I push her, jolting her forwards.

Liam exhales deep, wheezing breaths next to us.

"Jeez, you need to do more cardio." I snipe at him.

"Is this hangry Jess talking or regular Jess? Because I think I can see a glimmer of hangry Jess in there." He waves his finger around my face, and I pretend to bite it. Pretty sure I growl a little too. *Maybe hangry Jess is here.*

Liam chuckles lightly and removes his finger. "Now, now, biting is saved for boyfriends, remember?"

My face flames at his words, heat creeping up my neck and settling right behind my ears. Thank God he's turned to talk to Nora, and he doesn't see me light up like a tomato.

Liam and I have this flirty banter that is new. It doesn't happen all the time, but it's happening more and more lately. It's like we both want to push boundaries with our friendship to see who cracks first. Nora noticed it and has bets on me giving in first, but she's so wrong—I'm far too stubborn.

I won't lie and say I don't like him; I do. I probably like him more than I'll admit to myself. He's cute with his messy brown hair and sparkly hazel eyes, and he has the body of a rugby player, which, as it happens, is his sport of choice and my personal favourite to watch. Boys with thick thighs, tackling each other on a field in, *oof*, those short shorts.

Off the pitch, Liam wears his school clothes so well, too. There's something about the white shirt, blazer and trousers that just screams Nate from *Gossip Girl*, you know? It's completely unfair he looks this good. Even now, with his crumpled shirt and undone top buttons that are framed by the tie that hangs loose around his neck. My head tilts, watching the sliver of his exposed chest as he speaks... *yeah, not fair.*

"Three shakes for my three favourite kids. Jess yours has extra whipped cream, and Liam yours has none. Nora, I've not forgotten your extra sprinkles."

I make my biggest heart eyes at him. "You're the best Shake. I love you." I lift the straw to my mouth and slurp the sugary goodness, groaning at the way it melts on my tongue.

Liam scoffs next to me. "He gets all your good moods and I get snarky Jess?"

I slurp my milkshake and crunch down on the sweet, delicious brownie chunks hidden inside. "He makes me amazing shakes and you just, well, you're..."

I can't think, not when there's this much sugar rushing to my head and a hot boy standing in front of me.

"I'm what?" Liam raises an eyebrow, wearing a smirk on his face that I'd quite like to knock off with a punch.

Reserving my anger, I decide to focus on the sweet treat in my hand. "Nothing," I huff. "I was going to be mean, but you're lucky that my blood sugar levels are back to normal, so hangry Jess has disappeared. You can thank Shake for that." I wink at Liam before turning to walk away.

As I turn, I manage to crash straight into a wall of boy. Specifically, the boys from Liam's rugby team. All of them stand, grinning at me, but Dan, who plays second row, leans down, and grabs my hip before I topple over.

"Woah, Jessie girl I've got you." His fingers dig into my hip, while his eyes stare straight at my chest instead of my face. *So charming*.

Liam is next to me before I can splutter a word, growling at his teammate. "Hands off, Dan."

My gaze flicks between the two boys as I take them in. Liam has dark hair and light eyes, while Dan is the opposite with light hair and dark eyes. The school's most notorious playboy, with a back catalogue of half the girls in our school, and I have no interest in him at all.

"Oh look, it's your bodyguard, Jessie."

My skin prickles at the nickname. I hate being called Jessie.

"Actually," I say, stepping out of his hold. "It's Jess or Jessica. Jessie is not my name, and you'd know that if you were actually one of my friends."

The boys behind him whoop and make wolf noises at my response, making my nostrils flare, and my jaw clench. "Something you need, Dan?" Liam barks, his fists curling by his sides.

"Maybe I want to ask Jess out. How would you feel about that, huh Taylor?" he says, moving two steps forward, so he's inches from his face.

Oh, good, there's a cock show tonight.

I'm not usually the centre of all this male attention so, I'm less than thrilled that these two idiots have decided now is the time to fight over me. Liam's vein in his neck pops, his lip curling into a warning snarl.

"I'm pretty sure she's busy," he sneers.

Oh, is she now?

I sidestep Liam, glaring daggers at the back of his head. My hip pops out as my arms cross in front of my chest, irritation prickling at my skin. I have very little interest in doing anything with Dan, but I also don't need Liam coming to my rescue. I am completely capable of using my own voice. "Huh... interesting. I said that without moving my mouth, didn't I?"

Dan looks back down at my boobs again because apparently crossing my arms has highlighted his favourite part of me. "Eyes up here, big boy," I snarl, clapping my hands in front of him, but he just has the audacity to chuckle.

My reaction doesn't deter Dan, who steps forward, crowding my personal space again as his eyes fix on Liam once more, holding his attention. "Want to go out tomorrow night *Jess*?" he asks, his voice low and suggestive, making me shiver with disgust. I'm not even a little flattered by this. Even if it wasn't obvious that he is only asking me out to annoy Liam, there's no way I'd want to go anywhere with this twat.

This whole standoff is getting more irritating by the second. And probably the worst part of this testosterone fuelled fiasco is that my milkshake is going all melty. I look between the two boys, shaking my head.

Liam's jaw is so tense I'll be surprised if he has any molars left at this point.

"Okay, am I missing something or is Liam the one you want to ask out, because you aren't even looking at me, Dan?"

No one answers.

The boys shoot lasers at each other, silently daring the other to make the first move. My face burns with frustration. I feel like I'm on the outside of a joke and it's making my blood boil.

"Well?" I growl through gritted teeth.

Dan shifts his attention to me, and I instantly wish he didn't. His stare is smarmy, making my skin crawl as he leers over me. "Liam here said that if any of the boys try anything with you, they'd get their arses handed to them."

He did what?

I'm not really sure how I feel about that. Angry, annoyed, maybe a little bit okay with it because he's trying to protect me from these dickheads? But does he get to decide who I mess around with? Nope, sure as hell not.

Liam steps in front of me again, his chest pushing against Dan's as he hisses, "Back the fuck off... now."

This is ridiculous.

My jaw tics. I don't need him to fight battles for me; I can do that myself. My hands fly up to separate them. "Boys are so unbelievably fucking stupid sometimes," I mumble to myself, the words strained from the effort of pushing their rugby player bodies apart. "I'm going to say it louder in case either of you need help..."

I pin Dan with wide eyes, making sure I've got his attention. "Just because you're a boy doesn't mean you get to act like women are yours to play with." Then I flick my gaze between them both. "Both of you, put your metaphorical dicks away and do yourself and your future girlfriends a favour—grow the fuck up, p-u-lease."

I swivel on my heel, walking away before I bash their stupid heads together. Making my way over to Nora, who must have gotten bored at some point and found us a seat, she's grinning at me like she just figured out a secret.

"What's that look for?" My brow raises in question.

"Oh, nothing." Which, in Nora terms, means *everything*.

2

Liam

I said nothing while we walked home last night, avoiding her eyes because I was worried she'd see how annoyed I was that someone was moving in on her. I know Jess wouldn't entertain Dan and his bullshit, but I hated that he was goading me into admitting that I like Jess more than a friend. If I'm being honest with myself, I've always felt something more with Jess, but I didn't want to act on it and ruin things between us. After last night, I feel differently; I feel like I need her to know how I feel.

"Hey Liam, can you pass me the duster so I can reach up here?" Jess is standing on a stepladder wearing high-waisted jeans and a crop top that makes it hard for me to concentrate around her. Saturdays are the day we clean the offices my dad owns. I guess it's another way my dad likes to make sure I'll definitely be joining the family business. It keeps me busy, but really, it's an opportunity to spend more time with Jess, just us two.

I pass her the duster only to be on the receiving end of one of her devastating smiles, dimple and all. It takes all my self-control not to melt into a puddle in front of her.

Jess is all long brown hair, pretty blue eyes with toned, lithe legs and curves in all the right places. She's only about 5 foot 4 and I'm over

6 feet already. I'd be lying if I said I don't love the height difference between us; it makes her seem pint-sized and adorable. Which is probably the last way she would want to be described because she's fierce too. But I see all of her and she's the most beautiful girl I've ever seen. The fact she could fit in my pocket is just another reason she makes me smile.

We've been friends forever, but lately, things have changed. I flirt, she flirts, but nothing more happens. Until last night, when I may have shown more jealousy than a bear getting his honey stolen.

The thing is, I know her, and I like everything about her, even her grumpy moods. Her absolute favourite things in the world are milkshakes and her best friend (and cousin who she calls her sister because they're so close) Nora, which is why I promised her we would all go and grab a milkshake after work today. Mainly because she complained the whole way here that hers was melted and mushy last night, mumbling about it being my fault. Well, that and I'm weak when it comes to her.

"You okay over there?" Her narrow ocean eyes assess me, and I realise I probably look like a weirdo standing next to her, breathing a little too deeply, lost in my thoughts.

I shake off the rising tension in my neck before it turns into a blush I can't control.

"Me? Oh yeah, I'm fine. Great, fantastic, wonderful." I'm also rambling. I step backwards, rubbing my hands down my jeans, suddenly very aware that I'm sweating like crazy.

I want to tell her that she should go out with me, not a guy from my rugby team, and fuck, that feels scary. I should've done it last night, but I chickened out and now I feel like I'm in way over my head. The prospect of her saying no, or that she doesn't like me like that, makes me feel like I'm standing on the edge of a volcano. About to leap into a hot, fiery, burning pit of lava.

I guess the bigger question is, how do you tell someone you like them when you've been friends for years? How do you tell someone that their existence is the highlight of your day, of every day you get to see her? I can't just lay it on her.

"Surprise! Your best friend wants to go out with you."

No, that's too much.

She'll likely punch me and assume I'm messing with her, but in reality, I'm not. I'm about to change the very fundamentals of our friendship.

Maybe having her as a friend is enough. Maybe I can get over this and still have her in my life... as a friend. That'll be enough. Except it isn't. I know it. I feel it. The foundation we've paved in our friendship has led us here. I know her well enough to know that she *does* like me. It's subtle, but it's there; an invisible string connecting us together.

"Are you okay? You look seriously pale down there." Jess looks at me curiously and this is the problem with liking your best friend—when you are acting weird, they notice... and they care.

"You think you could come down here?" I ask, trying to keep my voice even.

Jess nods, the ladder creaking as she moves. As she gets to the last step, she trips on the lace of her Converse and falls forwards into my arms.

And right now... this moment will forever be etched into my memory as the first time I got to feel up Jessica Scott because I catch her awkwardly. And by awkwardly, I mean my hand flies out before I can stop it and my palm firmly connects with Jess' boob. Her actual boob.

Yeah, the universe saw an opportunity to have a good laugh at my expense.

My cheeks have been replaced by fireballs, an instant flame burning through my face. My hands are still touching her as I fumble over my apology. "Shit... Jess, I'm sorry. Fuck, this is... I-I'm so sorry," I rush, standing her upright and removing my hands from her.

She just laughs... really laughs. I obviously can't because I just grabbed the girl I like by the tit. Just before I was going to tell her I like her.

Fuck. My. Life.

Oh, and to make matters worse, my guy *down there* has decided now is the perfect time to try to stand to attention, because I can still very much feel the imprint of Jess' boob on my hand.

Jesus, that fiery pit of lava feels quite appealing right about now.

"Liam, it's fine. Stop apologising," she chuckles awkwardly before continuing. "Seriously, forget it. Come on, we have to get this place clean for your dad in less than half an hour."

I take a deep breath and force myself to keep cool and not let my raging hormones take over.

The moment is slipping away from me again, so instead of deciding that might be for the best, considering what just happened, I take a deep breath and plunge headfirst into that lava.

"Jess, I... I like you. I *like* you like you. I don't want you to go out with Dan or anyone else. I should've said something last night. But I'm telling you now because I want you to know I think about you... and not just in a friendship way. In the kind of way that has me wanting you to trip over again so I can touch your other boob."

Shit. I said boob. To Jess. I said boob.

Why is it so hot in here?

Her big blue eyes stare at me amused, the sides of her mouth curve upwards into a cute as fuck smile, her skin blooms a pink colour behind her ears. It's the most adorable look I've seen on her to date. Jessica Scott blushing... over me.

I decide to swallow my nerves and be bold because I've already broken the ice, so I may as well learn to swim in cold water, or lava, whatever it is I'm in right now. I hold her hands in my shaky ones, as our bodies meet in the middle, almost touching but keeping a thread of distance between us.

Her eyes shine up at me. I watch her lips roll between her teeth before she smiles the biggest grin. "I win."

My face contorts into a frown. "You win?" My head fumbles through other words that I can't seem to articulate. "You win," I repeat. "I... you... I... huh?"

Jess beams triumphantly at me still, making me more confused. "Yep, I do. Nora had a bet to see which of us would fold first and admit we like each other, and she bet against me, little witch, but jokes on her because I win."

I rub my chin, letting her hand go. "That's a lot to unpack. Nora knows I like you. How... when... I haven't even admitted it out loud until now." My voice rises to an octave, I wasn't sure I could hit.

Jess pulls me closer, connecting our hands again. Tiny sparks of electricity vibrate across my skin from her touch and I wonder if she feels it, too. "Nora sees everything..." Her eyes dip briefly to my lips. "But let's just circle back to the part where you like me because I'd like to see you get all flustered again."

As if on cue, my face heats, and my whole body feels like it might catch alight. The air is sucked from my lungs, and I have an overwhelming urge to tell her exactly what she wants to hear.

"I'd like to try that again... without the boob comment."

I need to stop saying boob.

She nods and lets out a carefree, sweet chuckle. It's one of my favourite sounds.

"I like you, Jess. The way you laugh at my awful jokes, and you flash me that adorable dimple on your cheek... God, you're so cute." I brush my finger across the place where her dimple is, loving the way she leans into my touch, making my pulse thrash wildly in my throat. "I like the way your nose crinkles when you don't like something. Your snarky attitude keeps me on my toes, and I like that too. The truth is, I like a lot about you and I'm tired of pretending there isn't more between us."

My hands are clammy, but she doesn't seem to care, holding on to me tightly. I've never been so open with a girl before. Hell, I've never even been in this close proximity to a girl I like before. It's a wild ride of hormonal turmoil thinking about girls and how to appear cool around them, but everything about Jess feels... right.

A moment passes between us, her eyes holding mine, looking for an answer she already knows. "For the record..." She moves her palm to rest on my chest, the heat from her hand pulsing through my thin t-shirt.. "I only laugh at your jokes when they're really funny. Second of all... I do not have a snarky attitude..."

Before she can continue, I pull her closer, my hands drift to cup her soft cheek. I hold her close to my lips, suspending the air between us as her clear blue eyes soften from my touch. Her vanilla scent invades my senses. We're close enough to kiss and I already know I don't want this moment to be over. Shifting my weight on my feet, I edge towards the invisible line that stands between us. When I thought of this moment, I assumed I'd be nervous and shaking, but I'm not. I realise I've never felt as calm as I do right now with Jessica between my hands, ready to change us forever.

"Let me kiss you, Jessica Scott, please?" She nods her head, air ghosting my lips from her exhale. Our noses touch, softly brushing with one another, charging the air between us. Our breath mixes before our lips finally touch. It's soft and gentle, exactly how I imagined it would be.

I wrap one arm around the back of her neck and the other around her waist, tethering myself to her. My hands grip onto her, holding on for dear life, saying a silent prayer that this never ends.

Deepening our kiss, I push against her and she responds by timidly dipping her tongue to taste me. Having her here, like this, is easily the best thing to ever happen to me. I can't imagine ever wanting to be pressed against anyone else because she feels perfect in my arms.

"Liam," she whispers so breathy and hopeful against my mouth, that it feels like my whole existence shatters in her hands. Our hearts beat as one as our lips collide over and over, filling the need that burns in both of us. She arches into me, letting out a soft whimper that I swallow eagerly. Our lips crash together, hormones raging, until we part, both frantically gasping for air.

Her eyes are closed at first, but when she opens them, I see something new in Jess. Lips pink and plump from our kiss, her eyes sparkling and her cheeks flushed. She looks vulnerable, and it strikes me right in my chest. "So, you *like me,* like me?" she hums, letting her fingers intertwine unconsciously with my hoodie strings.

"I guess so," I reply, shrugging a shoulder, trying to keep a tiny semblance of cool whilst trying not to be distracted by her lips again.

Jess looks down at our hands that have connected again. "How long have you wanted to kiss me?"

I want to say 'since the moment I met you. Since the day we were introduced when we were ten, and you were the cutest girl I had ever seen', but instead I say, "A while."

With wide eyes, her lips part and her tongue dances over them. *Does she want me to kiss her again?* That tiny semblance of cool I have left disintegrates into dust when she looks at me like that. I lean down towards her, my hand on her exposed skin. All of my nerve endings feel raw as our skin glides against one another. I trace a pattern against her lower back, watching as her lips part and a quiet gasp leaves her mouth, making me hard as steel in my jeans. I stop myself from pushing into her, wanting to memorise the kiss for this moment as our lips touch again.

I let her set the pace because honestly, being a teenage boy and kissing the girl who is a regular in my dreams has my head spinning.

But she does everything I'd hoped, and more. She lifts her hands, raking her fingers through my hair, making me dizzy. Her tongue parts my lips, tasting and exploring my mouth, and I know that no one else will ever taste as good as she does right now. She surprises me by biting my lip, my chest making a guttural sound I've never made before, and I pull back, staring at her. "Biting is for boyfriends, Scotty."

Her eyes flare in devilish delight. "So be my boyfriend, lover boy, so I can bite you."

I'm pretty sure I've died and gone to heaven. I lean back into her, smelling her sweetness, letting my nose run along her jawline as she quivers against me. "You might have won the bet with Nora, but you're the one who just asked me to be your boyfriend, Scotty, so I think I win."

Her mouth gapes open and her hands push me backwards so she can see my face. "You made the first move, though." She pouts, and I can't help but lean in to take her lip between my teeth this time, enjoying hearing her gasp at my intrusion, the sound sending heat prickling along the back of my neck.

"Not fair," she grumbles, but doesn't stop holding me close.

"Fine, I'll be your boyfriend. You don't have to beg."

She barks out laughter. "So charming. The *only* thing I'll ever beg for is..."

"Milkshakes, I know," I say playfully, rolling my eyes.

She smiles proudly at my response, and at how well I know her. We've been friends for years, so of course I know her. I'm hoping she'll let me continue to get to know more... as her boyfriend.

3

Jessica

Saturday came around again pretty fast. Since Liam kissed me, my whole world has become a little brighter. School is boring when your body is on fire for the person sitting across from you in science. The stress I felt last week from our exams is only a tiny whisper in the back of my mind now, and studying has become far more interesting when *he* talks about the things we have to learn.

Liam has been incredibly sweet all week, holding my hand in between classes and sitting me on his lap during lunch. Nora threatened to puke if we carry on being so adorable.

I promptly flipped her off and kissed Liam's cheek to prove a point.

And now tonight is our first official date night. He let me pick the film so already we're off to a great start because I'm bossy, which he already knows, so I don't have to hide any part of myself. I'm sure he also said something about more kissing, which sounds pretty good to me because we haven't really kissed since last Saturday. When we cleaned the offices this morning, Nora tagged along so my hopes and dreams for less cleaning and more kissing were squashed but tonight, I get my wish.

Three loud knocks on my door send my body into a flurry. My pulse picks up to Olympic swimmer speed, my breathing rapid, as I smooth my shaking hands down my cream jumper.

A gush of air breezes in as I open my door, immediately greeted by his beautiful, beaming smile. The kind that I've seen a thousand times before, but it hits differently now. Knowing he's here for me because he wants to kiss me and be my boyfriend makes me feel all gooey inside.

"Hi," he says, his voice trembling slightly.

I stare at him for a second, the way his white t-shirt hugs his biceps, which are pretty defined for a sixteen-year-old and his favourite black jeans wrap around his long legs perfectly sends my tummy flipping.

My heart makes a ruckus in my chest as his eyes roam over me too, before his arms reach out to pull me in for a hug. *God, he smells good.* Sweet, fresh and clean.

"Hi," he mumbles into my hair.

I smile into his chest. "You said that already."

He hums happily against me, sending shock waves through me as I tip my head upwards. He towers above me, and I have never been so glad to be short, or more correctly, the perfect size to snuggle into my 6-foot-plus boyfriend. God, *boyfriend*. I might need to say it a few more times, just to make sure.

Green and brown orbs blink owlishly at me. His thumb dusts over my cheek as his fingers fan the side of my head, holding me in place for what I long for. My stomach is filled with a thousand fireflies as he leans in, giving me a small peck of a kiss.

Oh.

Well, that wasn't exactly what I'd hoped for. My disappointment is obviously written across my face, because he grins wickedly at me.

"Ready for milkshakes and movies?" he asks casually, as we step away from my front door.

I frown, trying to figure out if he's messing with me or not. I'm pretty sure he's messing with me. Trying to make me needy for him. Which I obviously am.

"Wasn't there something else you said we could do, too?" I ask, whilst fluttering my eyelashes at him. Two can play this game.

He grins wolfishly, far too pleased with himself for teasing me.

"Oh, you mean this?" His arms wrap around me, pulling my body towards his easily, as if he has done this a thousand times, and presses our lips together. The oxygen evaporates from my lungs so quickly that it feels like it was never there in the first place, but I don't dare breathe in because I don't want this kiss to ever end. I'd happily run out of oxygen if I got to keep his soft, full lips pressing into mine. My whole body grips on to him like I'm on the precipice of a cliff, about to fall at any moment, and maybe I am. But maybe I'm ready to take the jump, as long as it's with him.

This was the kind of kiss I would feel for a lifetime, echoing through my whole body, etched onto my lips forever.

I can't tell you the exact moment when I fell for Liam Taylor, but this, right here, feels a lot like falling, fast and hard. A week ago we were just 'Liam and Jess, friends-who-flirt', but now that feeling is a million miles away, swept away by the presence of someone familiar but also new, occupying every cell in my body as if it were his to take all along.

I pull back to look at him and revel in his warm gaze, casting a spotlight on me. His soft brown hair flops forward and my fingers itch to run a path through the strands. His eyes flutter closed as my nails drag through his scalp, his hot breath skating across my cheek.

When his eyes open again, he beams at me. "Let's go, Scotty. The movie starts in…" He flicks his wrist to check his watch. "Half an hour. You know how much I love the trailers."

We walk hand in hand towards the cinema, car engines purring alongside us, horns beeping in the distance and children shouting and playing in the park echo around us in a distant symphony. A patch of dandelions catches my eye as we turn a corner. I lean down and pick one and hold it up to Liam. "Make a wish," I say, thrusting it into his face.

Liam's eyes crinkle as he smiles at me. I'm sure he's humouring me, but I like that he is.

His eyes close, as he sucks in air then puffs it out, making the tiny little fluffy seeds float around us before getting whipped away with the wind. When I look at Liam, his eyes are on me, like I'm the only person in the world.

"Want to know what I wished for?" he asks, letting his eyes drop to my lips.

I shake my head. "It won't come true if you tell me."

His lips turn upwards as he moves closer to my ear, his warm breath trickling down my spine. "Pretty sure it doesn't matter. You're already mine, anyway."

Liam moves slowly, letting his lips skate over my jaw before locking eyes with me again. I run my hands across his neck and pull him in for another kiss, letting myself relax into him. As he pulls away, he doesn't open his eyes but licks his lips like he's committing my taste to his memory.

At this moment, I know that I will always want to be his for as long as he'll let me.

Liam

Jessica Scott has well and truly put me under her spell. I mean, I've always been there, hanging off her every word, but now I can touch her and show her how much I like her. It's giving me a power trip knowing that I've finally got the girl of my dreams.

"Oohh, what about those two?" She nods towards a couple that must be in their twenties, sitting near us in the coffee shop outside the cinema.

"He's a marine biologist, on a visit from Florida. He met her at the university he's working at and fell for her vibrant red hair. By the way she is playing footsies with him I'm guessing she is pretty taken with him too." I lean in towards Jess to whisper, "What she doesn't know is that he has a foot fetish that would send her running for the hills."

Jess breathes out an amused chuckle. "Maybe that's why she's playing footsies with him? She knows, and he can't resist her that way. She has him right where she wants him."

I nod and laugh in agreement as I scan the room for our next couple. "How about those over there?" I gesture towards an elderly couple sat in the corner.

"Oh easy. They were high school sweethearts, met just before he was sent to fight in the war. He sent her love letters, she wrote to him every day. Oh, he had a little picture of her that he kept with him all the time. When his tour ended, they fell pregnant and had triplets and after they were born, he got a job working for a construction company that he now owns. His three boys now run it whilst they sit and drink coffee together and reminisce about all the time they spent dancing to *Frank Sinatra* or *Billie Holiday* when they were young." She lets out a longing sigh and dreamily stares at the couple as they hold hands, but my eyes are only fixed on her.

"Your best one yet, I think. They are pretty adorable sat over there," I say without even glancing over.

"I want to be like them when I'm old," she let out wistfully.

I want to tell her that if it were up to me, she would be the one I grow old with. She is the one I would spend every day worshiping and adoring. Instead, I lift her hand to my lips and kiss her knuckles, whilst I watch that cherry blush swarm across her neck, smiling like the lovestruck puppy I am.

"Jess?"

"Hmm?" she says, slurping her milkshake.

The words shrivel on my tongue as I lose my nerve to tell her everything I want to say. "You're so cute. Get over here."

She throws her sleeve covered hand to her mouth and stifles a chuckle, the sound floating over to me melodically. Her movement is swift as she climbs into my lap, her sweet scent crawling around me as I inhale. She kisses my face softly, blissfully unaware of how loud my heart beats for her.

On the way home, we talk and laugh about everything and nothing. Our hands are always clasped together, and it brings me a warmth that is bone deep.

As we approach her house, I hear shouting from inside. The familiar sound of her mum's raised voice is something that's become more and more frequent lately, but it's not something Jess likes to talk about. As soon as Jess registers where the noise is coming from, she drops my hand as her face pales. She wraps her arms around her body and freezes, a panicked expression lacing her features as she moves toward the house, her pace quickening with each step.

She doesn't look up at me again, leaving an icy chill in her absence.

"I'll see you at school tomorrow," she mumbles, opening the door and stepping inside before I can protest.

I chase her up the steps and place my hand against the closing door. "Wait, Jess," I say, lowering my voice to a whisper. "Are you going to be okay?" I hold the door open and lean inside to see if I can catch a glimpse of what's going on, but the low lighting in the living room reveals nothing. The yelling has stopped, but I hear the clink of metal, as if something is being kicked further inside the house.

I don't want Jess to go inside with her mum upset, and I'm filled suddenly with the need to scoop her up and take her away. "You can crash at mine if you want to?" I offer, already knowing she won't.

She shakes her head. "It's fine. She sometimes just needs me to help her calm down if she's had a bad day. I'll see you tomorrow." Without letting me reply, she closes the door. I didn't even get to give her a goodnight kiss.

I stand outside for a second to make sure I know she's safe before I walk home. When a few minutes have passed and I've not heard anything from inside, I drop her a text telling her to call me if she needs me.

On my walk home, I flip my phone around in my sweaty hand, unable to stop tapping the screen to check I haven't missed anything from her.

I've been home at least an hour before I hear from her again.

> **Jess:** Mum is asleep now. I'm sorry you had to hear all that.
> **Liam:** Please don't apologise. You don't have to. I'm here if you want to talk about anything, Jess.

My phone rings instantly and her face flashes across my screen. I take a deep breath and school my expression, not wanting to let her see my concern as I accept her FaceTime.

"Hey, Scotty, you miss me already?" I say lightly, removing any concern from my voice.

"You wish," she taunts.

There's an awkward pause before I ask, "You okay?"

"Hold on," she whispers, and I see her move around her bedroom, shadows around her face as the door clicks shut. "I'm okay, I mean... I'm okay now. She's sleeping so, it's fine."

"Have you talked to your Uncle Cam or Harriett about any of this lately?"

She sucks in a deep sigh; I watch her cheeks puff out the air before she speaks.

"Yes, and no. They don't realise how often she gets like this. It just seems like she isn't herself anymore and I can't help her as much as I used to. She's just so different since her accident."

Jess lowers her head. The dim lighting in her bedroom means I can't see much of her face, but I can tell she is worried. I can hear it in her voice. She fiddles with the string on her hoodie, methodically running her finger down the length of it and back up again, lost in her thoughts.

I remember how scared Jess was last year when she got a call from Cam telling her about her mum's accident; how scared we all were. One of us losing a parent feels like all of us because of how close we are. Claire had a car accident that broke her lower back, and it took months of physical therapy for her to walk properly again—and plenty of support from Jess—and I know it's taken its toll on her. I can see on a Monday morning if she's had a rough weekend helping her mum; her eyes don't sparkle and she's quiet, which isn't like Jess at all. But Jess isn't telling me everything that's going on. I know this because a few months ago, she stayed with Nora for a while but wouldn't tell me why and now this. I want her to open up to me but I don't want to push her either. So I take her mind off her mum for now.

"Well, I had a great time today with you. Even if the movie was awful." I say.

The way she looks so small on my screen, her knees all tucked into her giant hoodie, makes me want to protect her and keep her safe from all this shit she's feeling.

"It was not awful." She smiles weakly, but I don't buy it, so my eyebrow raises.

"It was the worst. I'm picking the movie next time." I laugh and she responds by poking her tongue out at me.

We stare at each other for a while through the phone. Just being together. Absorbing everything that's happened recently.

She shifts her body. "Get some sleep and take me for breakfast tomorrow, okay?"

"Wild horses couldn't keep me away, Scotty... Night."

4

Jessica

Liam is so warm; every single one of our limbs are tangled together as we sit on his sofa watching some reality tv show. We haven't left each other's side since he asked me to be his girlfriend two weeks ago.

Nora is losing interest in us, which is probably for the best. She isn't jealous, but it's an adjustment from being with us as friends to now seeing us holding hands and kissing when she's a plus one. I've been trying to set her up with the boy she sits next to in English—he is sweet and definitely likes Nora—and even though she won't admit it, I know she likes him too.

Liam's front door creaks open as his parents walk through, hand in hand.

"Hey, you two," his mum sings.

"Hey Mum. Hey Dad."

Liam waves a hand behind his head, not moving from our spot on the sofa. I look back and say hello too and catch his parents sharing a kiss after they have taken their coats off. It's a small peck, but it's one that shows so much love between them. I let my mind wander for a second with thoughts of what it was like for Liam growing up with two parents, let alone two fully functioning, caring parents who are still so in love.

Mine are none of those things.

I desperately try to ignore the pang of... envy that creeps into my subconscious as Liam's mum walks into the lounge.

"You kids want anything to eat?" Her light eyes gleam as she walks towards us. They're so similar to Liam's, but that's all they share. Looks wise. Liam is a carbon copy of his dad, even down to the scowl they both have.

"I'm good, Mrs Taylor, but I know Liam is always hungry, so I can't answer for him," I reply with a smile, forcing away any lingering negative feelings.

"Oh, Jess, please call me Erin." She smiles warmly, and it suddenly hits me that I haven't seen my mum smile at me like that for months. Maybe a year even. I beg my brain to keep my emotions at bay for now, because the last thing I need is to cry in front of Liam's mum.

"I'm good, Ma. We've had snacks already. Thanks though."

His mum smiles and then leaves us alone again.

I chew the inside of my lip as thoughts of my mum flood my brain. I wish, more than anything, she could be the person she was before her accident. But lately, I never know what I'll get with her. And more often than not, I get the shitty version of her who shouts and gets angry over everything, just like Liam heard the other night.

My chest constricts with embarrassment, and I have to press the heel of my hand to my ribs to ease the pressure building there.

What is she doing right now? Does she need my help? Fuck, I should probably get home.

Liam places his fingertips under my chin, lifting my face to his. "Hey, you okay?" he asks, as though he can sense my panic.

Usually I'd feel secure in the knowledge that Liam knows me; he knows when I'm overthinking, like right now. But this is my family, my problems and I need to handle them myself.

I shake my head to try to clear the fog of worry that's settled there. "I should probably get home."

His face falls and his lips pout. "Right now?" His big puppy dog eyes almost make me change my mind, but I know I have to go before my worry takes over and I'm forced to admit to him how bad things are.

I lean in to kiss him briefly, "I really have to go. Walk me to school tomorrow?" I ask, hoping that'll deflect the questions I can see brewing in his eyes.

I push up from the sofa quickly, picking up my backpack. Liam follows me to the door and wraps his arm around my waist, hauling me into him. "I'll miss you. Let me walk you home?"

"No, I'm good. I could do with a quiet walk alone," I say, feeling feverish and I'm not sure if it's from how close he is, or because I'm desperate to run before he notices how I'm feeling right now.

I don't like this feeling in my chest; it's hot and sticky and makes speech feel impossible. I tell myself this is why I can't tell him how I'm feeling, but I know deep down that it's not the reason at all. Really, it's because my mum isn't his problem, she's mine.

"What if I want to walk you home?"

"I'm fine, honestly. Call me before bed?" I say, deflecting him again.

I slip out from his arms and pull the front door open, hating how instantly I miss his touch as I walk away from him, back to my house.

When I get home, the house is quiet, the lights are off, and my shoulders drop on an exhale as I realise that my mum isn't home. Although, the relief is fleeting because I'm not sure where she is as she didn't answer her phone when I called her on the way home.

The smell of burnt food lingers in the air like a mist as I walk through the hallway and my foot crunches on something as I step into the kitchen. I flick the light on, and my eyes widen at what lies before me. Broken glass covers the floor, burnt food litters the worktop, black crumbs lining the floor, mixing with the crunch of the glass beneath my feet as I walk around the kitchen island.

What the hell happened?

A shuffling noise drifts down the hallway, making my pulse rocket as my mum turns the corner into the kitchen. Her short, dark curls are matted, she's in yesterday's clothes that hang off her slight frame, mascara is smudged under her eyes and her shoulders are slumped, making her appear even smaller than she is.

My mum was always such a confident person. She used to tell me it's where I get my determination from, but the woman in front of me right now bears very little resemblance to the person who raised me.

Her brows pinch when she sees me. "Hey, Jessie, what are you doing here? I thought you were in school?" She takes a step towards me, making me shout out, "Stop, mum, there's glass everywhere. Stay there. You have no shoes on. Let me get the broom."

Her hand flies to her mouth, letting out a quick gasp, as if she was shocked to see the carnage spread all over our kitchen floor. I move quickly to clean it up, all the while she doesn't move from the spot I told her to stay in, her eyes firmly fixed on the mess before us.

"Mum, school finished hours ago." I throw my arms out wide. "What happened in here?" I ask wearily. A part of me isn't sure I want to hear the answer. I'd rather just clean it up like I always do and forget about it.

"I... I don't remember," she says, shame evident in her voice.

The spotlight above her head makes the dark shadows under her eyes even more obvious as she looks around the kitchen curiously, like it might spark a memory as to what the hell happened.

"Well, something happened," I mumble to myself, leaning into the cupboard to get a cloth and cleaning spray. I quickly remove all the burnt food, wipe the crumbs from the worktops and begin filling the sink when I feel her hand rest on my arm.

"Jessie, you don't have to do that. I'll clean this up. I'm sorry, sweetie. I promise I'll do better. I don't know what... I just get so..."

she trails off, lost in her own thoughts, whilst I tiptoe on the edge of tears. I keep my back turned to her. I won't let her see me upset because I need to make sure she knows I'm strong; that no matter what she throws my way, I can handle it.

"Go take a shower, mum, I've got this." I shrug her hand from my arm and throw her a small smile, because that's all I can manage right now. Her mouth opens to say something, but it closes just as fast before she turns and walks away. It isn't until I hear the hum of the shower that I let the first tear fall into the sink full of bubbles.

Then another.

And another.

Letting the tears fall freely until I hear the shower stop.

I sniff and wipe my streaked cheeks on my sleeve, blowing out a deep breath just as she comes back into the kitchen. The dishes are clean, and the bubbles have melted in the dirty water, but I can't seem to move. I don't want her to see that I've been crying, so I stay still, re-washing the same things.

As mum appears in my peripheral, I see she has a packet in her hand that I recognise. I saw them in her bathroom cabinet last week when I was looking for tampons.

The packet crinkles as her hands tremble, attempting to pop out the pills. Her voice is raspy and low as she mutters cruse words under her breath just as one pill springs free from the foil pack.

And then two more.

My heart sinks to my feet. "What are those?"

"They're just painkillers, Jessie. I have a headache. That's all," she snipes.

That's all. *That's all.*

So casual.

Like she didn't just straight up lie to my face.

Like I haven't found other packets of pills in the house before. Not that she knows that. Only Cam and Harriet know what I found a few months ago.

I watch her swallow the pills quickly, without even needing to wash them down with water, her throat bobbing at the intrusion. My eyes blink away the threat of even more tears, as the realisation that I'm going to have to tell Cam and Harriet again dawns on me. But not tonight. I've hit my emotional limit for tonight.

"I'm going to bed," I announce.

"Jessie, wait." The plea in her voice is the only reason I turn to face her. "I'm sorry, sweetie. I know I've not been myself lately, but I swear I'll do better. For you, okay?"

She sounds so sincere, full of promise. I know that deep down she wants to mean the words she's saying. The Jess who was with Liam an hour ago would want to believe her right now, give her a hug and tell her everything is going to be okay, just like I've done a million times in the last year. But the Jess that's here now, fighting back tears, is tired and fed up with not being enough for her to stop this shit.

Which is why I reply with a simple, "Okay, Mum, night."

Because tonight I just wanted to be the girl who could revel in the fact that she was falling in love with her best friend, not the girl whose mother was an addict.

When I collapse into bed, the cool, soft, familiar comfort of my duvet wraps around me like a cocoon. I steady my breaths, not wanting to feel like I'm losing control of my emotions again. Picking up my phone, I notice that Liam has called. A pang of guilt I have for leaving so suddenly earlier hits me square in the ribs. I want to tell him so much; I want to explain that I'm scared my mum is lost in this world of addiction and she'll never find her way back to me.

My whole life, it's just been her and me against the world. She never left me lacking when my father (for lack of a better word) didn't want to stick around. It didn't matter because she was enough; she made everything better until she didn't. And now, my whole world is crumbling slowly and has been for the past year, as I watch her become a ghost of herself. As hard as I try to help her, I can never get it right.

Tears fill my eyes again, but I don't want to cry anymore tonight. There's only one thing I need right now.

Without a second thought, I press his name on my phone, clear my throat and inhale deeply.

He answers on the second ring. "Hey." His warm voice filters through the phone, instantly calming me.

"Hey yourself," I answer back, begging the emotion to stay out of my voice.

"Everything okay?" he asks quietly.

I nod before remembering that he can't see my face. "Everything is... better now that I'm talking to you." It wasn't a lie, but it also wasn't the complete truth... again. If I tell him what I came home to, I know he would insist I stay at his house or at least call Nora, and I don't want to do that tonight. I just want to forget for a second.

"You know you can talk to me, Jess, right?" His words slice through something in my chest. I knew I could talk to him, I just didn't know how. That, and I never wanted to be the girl with 'issues', but I guess that was a pipe dream now anyway because those issues were following me no matter how hard I tried to ignore them. No matter how hard I tried to be the carefree Jess I was last year, my reality keeps smacking me in the face every time I get home.

When Mum broke her back, everything changed and I'm angry about that. Her happy outlook disappeared almost overnight; everyone knows she struggled with her recovery, but they don't know everything.

My pulse picks up at the thought of what would happen if she just never came home one day, or I came home to something worse than what happened tonight.

What if...

What if she...

I stop the thoughts before they plague my mind anymore. My breathing is shallow and uneven when Liam's voice pulls me back into the moment.

"Jess, are you there?"

With my heart beating double time and my fist clenching my bedsheet, I try to grasp onto anything. I feel the weight of the phone in my hand, the soft bed beneath my legs, the smell of the washing powder from my hoodie.

Breathe, Jess.

"I get to keep you, right?"

Fear slams into my chest so hard that I worry I might crack open, but I need to know I've got him, no matter what. In a world where everything can feel big and scary, he does everything to make me feel protected and grounded, even before he was my boyfriend. He holds me in the eye of the storm whilst my world spins out of control around me and right now, I need him to tell me that it'll all be fine.

"You get to keep me, so long as I get to keep you too," he whispers.

His words settle me, allowing me to exhale. I loosen my grip on the sheets and lay back, my heart rate finally returning to its usual rhythm.

"Liam?"

"Yeah, Scotty?"

"Thank you," I sigh.

5

Jessica

"Hey, don't make me come in there, Scotty!"

I playfully splash the blue sea water, that's lapping at my feet, over Liam again with a roguish smirk.

"That's it, you've had it now."

He comes hurling towards where I stand on the beach and throws me over his shoulder, making me squeal as he moves quickly through the waves and dunks us both.

The chill of the sea water hits me like a bucket of ice, coating my skin as I fight to the surface. My teeth rattle when I push out of the water and throw my arms around Liam's neck, licking the salt water from my lips.

"It's freezing." I shudder, my legs wrapping around his waist, searching for his warm body.

He angles his head as he dips towards my mouth. All I can hear is the soft swooshing of the waves gliding past us as our lips collide.

"I can keep you warm." He mumbles against my mouth, making butterflies flutter in my stomach. Big hot, fiery butterflies that ignite for him.

I slap his chest and push away from him. "You are very bad, Liam Taylor." He laughs and splashes me, soaking me with more chilly droplets. My legs frantically tread water, my arms swirling around me, as a flash of pink on the sand catches my eye. The giant unicorn that Liam won for me earlier at the arcade sits proudly on our beach towels. It's obnoxious and it'll be a pain to carry home on the train, but I secretly love it.

Who even am I now? Loving huge soft toy unicorns. Someone save me.

On second thoughts, I'm happy here with this boy and my giant unicorn, with the waves rolling around us and the sun peeking through the clouds.

It's been six weeks of him, of us.

Six weeks of soft kisses, stolen touches, and conversations about everything we can do together when we get older. He makes everything in my life less... noisy, and I'm grateful for that.

Things with my mum are still the same, good days and bad, but I find myself feeling more of the good since Liam and me became a couple. He brings a little bit of sunshine into my life and I love him for that. Not that I've told him that yet.

We took the train today to the beach, and in less than a few hours, we were surrounded by salty air and gritty sand; my happy place. Since school is almost over for the summer, we've made plans to spend most of our time enjoying adventures before we start college in September.

God, school is almost over. It's scary that everything is so close to changing. We're all going to the same college to finish the last two years before university. Liam is studying business; Nora, child psychology, and I'm enrolled in an events management course.

The thought of us all growing up and picking our futures at our age is daunting, but at least we'll have each other still. That's probably why I don't feel like I'm going to freak out about it, in all honesty.

I let my fingers drift over the cool sea water as it sways around my waist. I watch Liam's chestnut hair drips down his face; his skin tanned and golden, the light reflecting off his broad shoulders. I'm not sure he realises how bad I've got it for him. I bite my bottom lip, trying to school my face from the blush I can feel creeping over my skin.

He shakes his head like a dog as droplets of water whip my way, coating my skin in tiny little shocks of ice.

"Liam!" I cry. "You're such an idiot," I splutter, wiping my face as he peppers kisses all over me.

"Yeah, but I'm *your* idiot."

My smile is schoolgirl big because he *is* mine and I like it that way.

I take his hand as we wade through the current as it pushes us forwards, towards our towels. The sea air nips at my wet skin as we leave the water.

"Oh, I saw your mum yesterday," he says casually, whilst I feel anything but casual about that comment.

A feeling of dread sneaks into my subconscious like a heavy weight and I try to act unaffected. My pace quickens, focusing on feeling the sand slipping beneath my feet like quicksand. The light, happy feeling that I felt minutes ago is slipping away faster than I can hold on to it.

"Oh, you did?" I say, trying to keep my voice even.

"Yeah, she was talking to someone on the street. They both looked pissed."

"I don't... I mean, I saw her last night, and she didn't say anything. She looked fine."

I'm lying. When I saw her last night, her eyes were rimmed bright red and within two minutes of being home, she had passed out on the sofa. I hadn't woken her when we left this morning to tell her where I was going, either.

Liam nods, smiling at me, but it doesn't reach his eyes.

I blow out a quiet breath, turning my head away from him, hoping that he doesn't ask any other questions. And he doesn't.

My teeth chatter as Liam wraps his giant beach towel around my shoulders. I cling to the edges of it, bringing it to my nose and inhaling a deep breath, smelling his washing powder, smiling at the soothing fresh scent. I plop my body onto the damp sand and Liam follows, sitting next to me, our shoulders touching. I reach out in front of us to prop up my giant unicorn and a breeze drifts around us, knocking over the giant fluffy toy, causing me to shiver. Liam chuckles lightly.

"Come here. You're always so cold. My little ice queen."

He lifts me under my arms and pulls me into his lap, so I'm straddling him, my towel coming undone. He wraps it back over my shoulders and cocoons his around him too, creating our own bubble of warmth.

His thick legs brush against my inner thighs and I beg my body not to react, but I already know it's futile as I feel that heat spreading over my skin like wildfire.

I pull him close to me, enjoying the scent of suncream and salty water filling my head as he snuggles into my chest. My lips meet the top of his head, then the tip of his nose. He looks up at me, his eyes shining, swirls of green and ochre dancing in the sunlight. My heart bounces around my chest like a space hopper. I have no way of controlling this new feeling I have when he looks at me like that; like I have all the answers to all the questions in the world.

His arm wraps around the curve of my back, his towel dropping to pool around the floor where we sit, letting a brief chill enter our warm space, but he doesn't flinch. He holds me safely against him. His hands continue to slide down to the back of my legs to pull me closer. How much closer I could get, I wasn't sure, considering I was on his lap.

His fingers grip onto my thighs shakily, as he bites his bottom lip, exhaling a long minty breath, he locks his eyes on mine.

"I'm falling in love with you, Jess. I think I've been in love with you for a long time. I mean, I've never actually been in love, but I just know it would feel like this."

He presses his searing hot lips against the skin over my heart, and a thousand goosebumps scatter over my body. The contrast of his grip on my thighs and the soft kisses on my chest makes me delirious.

"Tell me what it feels like," I whisper, placing my hands over his that rest on my thighs, needing to feel his warm skin.

"It feels like I have to be near you—touching you, kissing you, even breathing the same air as you all the time. My skin burns for you. My heart feels like thunder in my chest when you kiss me. And when we aren't together, I think about you all the time."

I lift my hands from where they rest on his and bring them to his face, holding his gaze. "If that's how being in love feels, then I feel it, too."

His hands drift upwards to the middle of my back as he pulls me down. He seals our lips together so softly it feels like a feather brushing over me as my eyes flutter closed. I tilt my head as the kiss deepens, burying my fingers in the short hair at the nape of his neck, making a soft moan fall from his lips. Our tongues moving, gliding, tasting each other, stealing all the air from my lungs.

The world around us has all but disappeared, leaving only the sounds of the waves and our hearts beating against each other.

"I love you, Jessica Scott."

"I love you too, Liam Taylor."

I'm diving, flying, falling and floating, all because of him.

The world slowly comes back into focus, the eternally restless sea softly whispers around us. The seagulls call to one another along the shore. The bustle of people chatting filters back into the moment as I shift from his lap to face the ocean once again.

I love this time of day; the moments before the sun sets. It feels like the world is quieter somehow, like everything stills while the sun takes its last chance to remind people how beautiful it is before it disappears into the horizon.

"Promise me something?" Liam rests his head on my shoulder, so I can feel his breath on my neck.

"Anything," I reply, reaching up to wrap one arm around the back of his neck from behind me.

"Every time you look at the sunset... you remember this feeling between us right now."

I take a deep breath and close my eyes, making sure that I save this moment to my memories, inhaling the suncream and salt on our skin, remembering the lollipop sunshine as it bobs on the horizon, the way the wind dances around us like magic, softly singing to the beat of our hearts. Because this is what it's like to be young and in love and I never want to forget.

"Always." I turn my head to rub our noses together. Admiring the way the sun is glowing onto his face, then I softly kiss the tip of his nose and we sit together watching the last of the sun's rays disappear into the horizon.

The truth is, this *is* perfect. He is perfect. Even my giant pink unicorn toy is fucking perfect. And I can't help but feel like this kind of perfect can't last forever.

Breaking the spell around us, my phone buzzes in my bag, and I see Nora's face light up my screen.

"Hey, Nor."

6

Jessica

One month later

"I don't want to leave." I sigh, looking at Liam's face.

He's so handsome. His perfectly messy brown hair, and big doe, autumn-coloured eyes that always make my knees go weak look just as sad as I feel, making all of this so much harder. His usual confident shoulders are slumped forwards, leaning into me.

This officially isn't fair.

"I know, but we can still talk every day and I can visit when my parents let me." He holds me close to his chest and my body sinks into him, like it always does.

I draw in a breath so deep it starts at my toes, squashing my fears of losing him, and I focus on us right now. I hate the thought of leaving him, but I really don't have a choice.

After that day at the beach, my whole world changed. My worst fears came to light; my Uncle Cam called in to see Mum and found her passed out in the bathroom from an overdose. The pills that I've found in the house were regular, prescribed, strong pain killers, but Cam said that wasn't the only thing she was taking, and I didn't ask any more because, deep down, I knew.

It's hard not to blame myself. The guilt eats away at me and sleeping peacefully has become a thing of the past now. I should've talked to Cam more about everything. I shouldn't have been so far away the day it happened. I should've been there to stop her. Not that anything I've done has worked before. I naively thought I might have been the one to help her quit. I thought that *I* might've been a good enough reason for her to stop.

Nausea washes over me at the thought that I couldn't help my own mum. I tried to involve Cam in the beginning when I noticed things, but that made her angrier, so I stopped telling them everything. What a load of good that did; she's not here. I've lost her, anyway.

His wife, Harriet, found a rehab centre just outside of London, that she was meant to stay at for a month or so, but in the second week, she checked herself out and now we don't know where she is. Her phone is disconnected. She left me.

Since that day, I've been living with my uncle and aunt, Cam and Harriett, Nora's parents. I'm grateful for them taking care of me and that I have Nora. I'm not sure how many times she's slept in my bed with me whilst I cried—too many to count.

Their house isn't far from mine, only two streets apart. I grew up spending most of my time there when we were younger, when my mum would be working late. Their house feels like home. Or it did until it actually became my home. Now it feels like a place I'm living in but where I can't settle. I'm just here, waiting for my mum to come back.

God, I wish my mum could take care of herself. I wish so many things were different right now. I wish I had more than one parent; I wish I wasn't upending my uncle's life; I wish that I wasn't leaving. I wish she fucking chose me and not her addiction.

But I know wishing isn't enough anymore.

It's a childish notion that I need to forget about.

So, today we are moving out of London. Harriett says the reason for us moving two hours away is for a job at an art studio she's been offered in Kent that she can't refuse, but I can't help but feel the timing is very convenient given everything that's happened.

My eyes fill with unshed tears.

"Don't be sad, Jess. I hate to see you cry."

Liam wraps his arms around me again, silencing the tears that I can't stop from falling.

I want to cling to him, for him to never let me go, because the last thing I want is to leave the boy who has been my anchor since the moment he made me his. My ribcage aches from all the crying. My heart is howling at me to stop all this pain, but I can't because it's the only thing I can feel.

"I just... I don't know how to leave you. No... it's not even that. Everything in my body is screaming at me that I can't leave. I don't want to leave." I choke on a sob.

He tips my head up so I'm forced to face him, finding his jaw set.

"Listen here, Scotty, you will never lose me. Things aren't perfect right now, but that doesn't mean they won't be again. I love you, Jessica Scott. This isn't the end."

"How can you be so sure?" My voice breaks on the last word.

"I'm sure of you, Jess. I'm sure that no matter what, we'll figure it out."

I stare down at my hands that are resting on Liam's chest, unable to meet his eyes again because as much as I want to believe his confidence in us, I don't know that my heart can take the distance from him, but I'm also not willing to give him up.

Seconds feel like hours as we stand on the pavement, wrapped in each other, both refusing to let go. Liam traces soft strokes on my shoulders as he holds me close.

I inhale deeply and finally look up at him, kissing his perfectly soft lips.

"I love you, Liam Taylor."

He smiles at me like I put the stars in the sky for him and my heart flutters against his chest. The problem with the stars is they're surrounded by darkness; a darkness I can relate to. But Liam... he is sunshine. He is that magical moment the sun rises and sets, and selfishly I want to feel the warmth of him all the time. Leaving him feels like I might drown in my own darkness.

I glance to my left to see Nora, Cam, and Harriett waiting in the car for me. Nora watches through the window with tears in her eyes. My throat swallows thickly as I tell my brain to put one foot in front of the other and walk towards the car.

My steps are heavy as I move away from Liam.

My body begging me to stay with him.

Tears falling like waterfalls down my cheeks.

One step.

Two steps.

Three.

The distance between us feels like a valley already, and I've barely made it to the car.

I take one last look at Liam. I mouth *see you soon* and he mouths *I love you.*

His words echo endlessly through my head.

Things aren't perfect right now, but that doesn't mean they won't be again.

7

Jessica

My phone buzzes on my bedside table. One eye opens, then closes just as fast, cringing as the light bounces around my bedroom from the slits in my blinds. I let out a groan as I pat around, searching for the noise. When I finally grab it, I silence the alarm and pull the covers back over my head.

Mornings, well early mornings, are *not* my favourite time of day, but I need to get up. I've started running along the beach each morning and, as much as I don't want to get out of my warm bed right now, I know that I need that adrenaline boost from my run.

I drag myself upright, running my hands through my wayward hair and down my face. As I stand, I stumble slightly, still shaking away last night's sleep, as I quickly throw on my running gear.

My feet tiptoe quietly into the kitchen, where I spot Harriet at the counter making coffee. Her dark auburn hair pulled tightly in a bun and she's wearing her 'office clothes' not her 'artist clothes'. *Her words, not mine*. The difference is usually the splodges of paint that cover her artist clothes, so today must be a client day for her.

"Morning, sweetheart." She smiles at me.

"Morning," I reply, yawning.

"I made your water for you already. It's in the fridge."

My lips press together. I'm still not entirely used to people looking out for me as much as Cam and Harriet have. I spent over a year being the one looking after my mum, and I guess I'm still adjusting and finding my feet.

"Thank you," I say shyly, as I grab the bottle from the fridge.

Harriet smiles at me. "I'm off into the office today, so I'll probably be back late. I've got new clients coming in to talk about a few pieces they want me to commission for them. Cam will be working from home today, so you girls just get yourselves to college, okay?"

She moves easily around the kitchen, picking her handbag up and kissing my forehead before she waves goodbye. It's been a month of living here and adjusting and so far, the things I'm finding the hardest are having two parents looking out for me who care and check in all the time. I never realised how good that feels until now.

Taking a deep breath and letting that realisation sink in for a second, I make my way out to Bodega Bay, which fortunately is right on our doorstep, and run. The cathartic thudding of my feet hitting the sand travels up my legs and into my head as I speed past other runners. The breeze waters my eyes as I push myself faster and faster, my body burning with endorphins. When I stop, I fold over on myself, gripping my knees, trying to catch my breath. Checking my watch, I realise it's been an hour and I should probably get home to shower and get ready for college.

After my run, my day flew by in a blur. My shower was rushed, as was my getting ready. I missed my morning call with Liam because I had to scoff breakfast and run out the door. Then I was late to one of my classes and I forgot a book for my other one. Days like this make me crazy because I hate being on the back foot, especially as it all started so well.

I'm just about to walk into the house again after school when I pick up my phone to call Liam. He answers on the third ring.

"Hey Jess, hold on one second." He rushes out. I hear mumbling in the background, a few different voices, maybe even a female one. *Maybe that's his mum.* "Sorry about that, you okay?"

"I'm... okay. Did I interrupt something?"

"No, nothing. I'm just at one of the guys from college, Will's house, and Alex is here, too. We were going over some schoolwork."

He sounds honest, and I have no reason not to trust what he's saying, but for whatever reason, I feel a jolt of jealousy. That people get to spend time with *my* guy, when I can't.

"Jess? You still there?"

I shake my head and my jealousy away. "I'm here. Sorry, distracted."

"I missed you this morning. I think that's the first morning call we've missed. My day felt all off without talking to you."

I let out the breath stuck in my lungs, relieved to hear that it's not just me that felt off today.

"I had a weird day, too. I went on my run, but then after that everything just felt rushed and I couldn't catch up, you know?"

Liam hums in agreement. "So, what's going on? Tell me all the things I've missed."

"Since..." I check my watch, "Twenty-two hours ago?" I laugh. "Not a whole lot I'm afraid."

There's an awkward silence that seems to creep into our conversations over the last week. It makes me feel like there are razor blades in my throat when I swallow. I hate it.

"Have you heard from your mum?"

My jaw tenses. "I'm pretty sure I would've told you if I had," I snap.

"Okay... you're right. Sorry."

"No... it's not your fault. I'm sorry. I think... I'm just tired." I rub the bridge of my nose to relieve the sudden pressure there.

"You know, Jess, you can talk to me about everything that's scary. I'm here for it. I'm here for you. You can talk to me."

I chew the inside of my cheek, not wanting to snap at him again. I'm not sure how I can tell him that I'm struggling to deal with being in

MEGHAN HOLLIE

a household with two adults who care more about me than my own mother ever did. Or the fact that I'm only just realising that the last year of my life was fucking awful living with her. Or even that I feel jealous that his new friends get to spend time with him simply because they all live in London, and it's where I wish I was. Or that he isn't here for me, not how I need him to be. He can't help me sleep at night. He can't chase away nightmares or hold me together when I think I might break because he isn't here. And none of that is his fault, I know that, but it doesn't make it any easier to live with.

I hate myself for thinking any of it because Liam is so good. He's doing everything he can for me. And I don't know why I keep holding back from him. I started therapy last week and I've barely managed to get through a session without sobbing the entire forty-five minutes yet, so I don't feel ready to talk to him about it all.

"I know you are, but I... I need..."

"Time... I get it Jess, but... you know what, don't worry. I'm here when you're ready."

"I need you to understand that it's not just as easy as talking about what we had for lunch." I try to keep the malice out of my tone, but I'm pretty sure I fail.

"I know that. I'm not stupid. I just don't want you to feel like you have no one, especially after she left you."

My chest caves, while the room feels like it's spinning. *He's right, she left me.*

"You're right. Can we just leave it for now? I need to figure out how to make it... how I can stop this fucking pain." I clutch my chest, my breathing uneven and shallow. I almost drop the phone to the floor from how violently I'm shaking. My lungs don't feel like my own, they feel too small for me to take a full breath.

"Jess, breathe. Slow it down, breathe for me." Liam breathes heavily into the phone, trying to encourage me to follow him.

I try to inhale deeply, but I can't.

My world spins around me, my hands tingle.

48

"Jess, I need you to breathe." Liam's voice filters back to my consciousness.

He sounds so far away, so tinny. My eyes burn with tears that overflow, making tracks down my cheeks.

One one thousand.

Two one thousand.

Three one thousand.

Closing my eyes, I push out all the air I can manage and then suck in as much as I can, making a loud gasping sound.

"That's it, slow breaths. In and out." Liam gently coaches me on the phone.

Another deep breath in and out.

My pulse begins to quiet as Liam still murmurs words that I can't hear, but the sound of his voice lulls my panic into submission. My room comes back into focus, my bedsheets crumpled from my panicked grip on them. One more deep breath to try to stop my body vibrating.

"Jess, I'm sorry. I didn't mean to push. I just care about you. It's so fucking hard not being with you."

I swallow thickly. "I know." It's all I can manage to say.

The silence between us is loud and obnoxiously waiting for one of us to speak, but I need it to be quiet for a second, my body still reeling.

I'm not sure how much time passes, but Liam doesn't speak; all I can hear are the quiet puffs of him breathing down the phone.

"I'm going to shower," I say, finally breaking the spell.

"Liam, come on! We have to finish this assignment." A girl's voice that definitely wasn't his mum's drifts into the phone before I hear Liam mumble something back to her.

The rational part of my brain tells me that she's no one and Liam wouldn't hurt me, but the irrational part tells me that he's spending time with other girls and that fucking stings.

"I better go too. I'll call you in the morning. I love you."

My heart stutters at his words, my thoughts laced with guilt, for not being able to open up to him for doubting him for a second. Liam wouldn't do anything like that to me. I want to say I'm sorry, that I love him more than anything and I don't want to lose him, but my stupid, stubborn brain won't let me.

"I love you, too."

8

Jessica

31st October

Jess: Have a great time at the Halloween party
tonight. Wish I was there.
Liam: Me too Scotty x

I place my phone in my bag, locking it and throwing it into
my handbag. Liam and I have had more missed calls than actual
conversations lately.

I worry my bottom lip, trying not to think about the fact that he's
going to a party tonight and there will be plenty of girls swooning
after him, I'm sure, including Alex, who seems to be integral in his
new friendship group. I try to not think about it but some days it's all
consuming.

*Is he giving her all my favourite smiles? Does she like him? How much
time do they spend alone?*

"Jessica?" My therapist's voice snaps me out of my jealous trance.

I stand from my seat in the waiting room, brushing the non-existent lint from my jeans as I raise my hand to wave awkwardly. I've been coming here for almost six weeks now and I still manage to make it weird every time, from all the nerves rushing through my body at the thought of opening up about how I'm feeling I tend to lose all composure.

Joy, my therapist, gestures to my usual grey armchair that's equal parts comfortable and uncomfortable

She smiles. "So, how are you doing today?" Joy asks the same question every session. As though she's hoping I'm going to magically one day tell her the truth from the beginning of our session. I never do. I usually, and unintentionally, make her work for her answer until I'm a crying mess. Yet, today, I feel like being... honest.

I clear my throat. "I'm feeling anxious today."

Joy schools her reaction, trying to hide her surprise that I didn't give my usual *I'm fine* answer.

"Tell me what's happened today. Run through everything and we can pick it apart." She pushes her clear glasses up to the top of her nose as her hands clasp together on her lap on top of her notepad, twirling the pen between her fingers.

"I started the day with a run, like I always do. I usually speak to my boyfriend in the mornings, but he had rugby training, so we didn't catch each other. College was the same as always..."

"...but?"

I sigh. "Liam is at a Halloween party tonight and I think... no... I know that's why I'm feeling anxious. He has a new group of friends and one of them is a girl..."

Joy nods and takes some notes.

"I think it's perfectly normal to feel anxious, but tell me, has Liam ever made you feel like you couldn't trust him?"

My head shakes in answer.

"And do you feel as though you are still close? Do you make time for one another?"

My shoulders shrug, not giving an answer straight away. "We don't have a lot of free time with our part time jobs, school work too. So seeing each other has been tricky, and that's been hard to deal with." I pause, "That and I haven't been able to... talk to him about how I'm feeling, coping or really anything deeper than, *Hey, my day was good, how was yours?* And I overthink everything. Even when I know he would never hurt me, I'm scared." I slump in the chair, feeling the lumpy cushion behind me. I dig it out and place it on my lap instead.

"Why do you think you feel that you can't talk to him?"

"I don't know..." I trap my bottom lip between my teeth as I think about how to say what I'm thinking. "I don't want to lose him, but I know by doing what I'm doing, I'm pushing him away. It's just... talking about my mum is hard. I feel ashamed and guilty and let down and those are only some of the things I'm feeling. If he sees that I'm as broken as I feel, then he might not... he..." The words get stuck in my throat as my eyes pool with tears.

"You think he'll leave you?" Joy finishes for me.

I nod my head and touch my chin to my chest.

She pauses, tapping her chin with her index finger. "I want you to write a letter to Liam. It doesn't have to be long, but it should include some of your feelings you are too scared to say to him. Can you do that for me?"

Can I do that? I honestly don't know, but she's the expert here.

"I want to try." And that's the truth. I really want to try to be better at sharing.

12th November

> **Jess:** I'm not sure that I can make it to London this weekend. Everyone at the hotel had this sickness bug, so I've been asked to work extra shifts. I'm sorry x

After my double shift today, my feet are concrete weights that I drag around my bedroom. Groaning at the strain of getting undressed, I realise I'm completely unable to do it effectively either. My arms are stuck in my shirt as I try to peel it off my body. I squeal before throwing my half-undressed body onto my bed.

"Jess?" Nora knocks at my door.

"Help!" I cry, but the sound is muffled by my complete inability to lift my heavy head from my bed.

"I'm coming in. If you're naked, you've been warned."

I hear my door handle click, and Nora exhales. "Thank God you aren't fully naked."

The bounce of her sitting on my bed almost has me lifting my dead body to see her face, but I quickly decide that's far too much effort.

"What are you doing right now?"

"Dying."

"Oh, okay. I thought it was something serious."

That does make my head lift slightly to shoot her a raised eyebrow, because that really is all I can manage.

"I worked a double shift today. I'm exhausted and now I can't even get my uniform off."

"I don't think I understood most of that, because your head is buried in the bed, but still... want me to take off your shirt and get your hoodie?"

I nod and feel the bed bounce again as Nora stands.

The struggle to get my dead arms out of the shirt is almost not worth the hassle, but once I'm free of my restraints, Nora helps me sit up like a grandma in a nursing home and pulls my hoodie over my head for me.

"There you go, Princess." She pats my cheek, and I refrain from kicking her in the shin as she stands.

"Didn't you start your internship today?" I ask her.

"Yeah, it was... good."

"... But?"

Nora turns to face me. "I think I have a lot to learn still."

"Isn't that the point of college?" I ask, confused.

"Yeah..."

"You can't expect to know everything within six weeks, Nor. Just go with it. Be a sponge, learn as much as you can from this. You'll be a great therapist one day. Hey, I've got plenty of issues for you to practice with." I wink, joking, but half serious too.

"Don't even joke about that... speaking of issues. Did you write your letter to Liam?"

That is a great question. Did I write my letter? Technically, the answer is yes. Has he seen it yet? That would be a no.

"I've definitely made a start."

"You know, I hope your therapist can see right through you because you just lied to my face."

I squeeze my eyes together. "Fine. I've written it but it's still in my drawer. I'm scared to send it."

"What if you sent him a picture of it, so you don't spend the whole time thinking about it being lost in the post or how long it'll take... remove the element that makes you overthink sending it and just do it."

I think for a second. "That's not a bad idea... Except for the fact that I'm scared of the words I've written and what he'll say when he reads it."

"Oh, right... Just send it. If you don't, I will."

"Said Miss future therapist," I tease.

24th December

> **Jess:** Merry Christmas Eve. Nora is making me watch *The Grinch* and I've never related to someone more in my life #hatehatehatedoublehate
> **Liam:** #loatheentirely. I wish I was there with you. *The Grinch* is my favourite Christmas film.
> **Jess:** Six more days xx
> **Liam:** Six more days Scotty x

9

Jessica

New Year's Eve

O ur house looks like a party shop exploded in here. The gold and silver streamers that me and Harriet insisted we *needed* for the party, line every single wall and doorway of the downstairs. It looks like the whole place is covered in metallic rain. The matching foiled balloons float around the conservatory, being bounced around like bubbles, as people sway to the music. The tables are draped in white organza and there are enough sequins floating around every surface that it looks like pixie dust has been sprinkled everywhere.

I scan the room for the one person that makes me feel like my heart might stop and when I spot him finally entering the room, his brown messy hair and shining green and brown eyes, my heart does exactly that. It pauses for a beat. I can't stop the smile that erupts across my face as I rush over to him, throwing myself into his arms with a thud.

"Hi, lover boy."

"Hi, Scotty," he says, nuzzling into my neck.

His fresh scent fills my lungs; summertime and limes. It makes me dizzy because I haven't been able to smell him for four months and now, he's here. It's like a very vivid, incredible dream.

"I missed you," he whispers into my ear.

"You've been with me all day."

"And I still missed you. I have four months of catching up to do."

I missed him, too. So much. Even just walking to the bathroom and back was too long apart from him.

"Jessica, get your cute bum over here." Nora shouts from the other side of the room. I begrudgingly dismount Liam's waist and take his hand, smiling at the fact that he's here and I can actually do that. I drag him over to where Nora is dancing with some of our college friends and make quick introductions and Liam settles into easy conversation with Elena's boyfriend, Mike.

Liam takes my hand when the song 'Electric Love' comes on by Borns, singing into my ear as we sway to the music. I feel every word he sings, my body humming from our contact. His hand holds me against him, burning its place on my skin. I've missed being close to him.

I like the way he moves us with the beat but keeps his mouth firmly next to my ear, singing only to me. Butterflies throw a rave in my stomach that I can barely contain. It feels like they're fluttering over my skin and escaping into the air around us. Our hips move with the rhythm of the beat in our own bubble.

My arms wrap tighter around his neck as he pulls back to capture my lips in a searing kiss that I feel all the way from the tips of my ears to the ends of my toes. Kissing Liam will never not make me feel like I'm simultaneously flying and falling and I'll never be able to get enough of this feeling.

We break apart breathless, lost in each other's gaze.

A loud crash echoes across the room, sounding like it's coming from the hallway. Liam spins around, searching for the source. Booming voices travel down through the crowd, but not everyone has noticed yet. The bass drowning out most of the sound. I swear I heard Cam shouting, which is weird because he *never* shouts.

"Leave, now." Cam's booming voice travels over the sound of the music, although me, Nora and Liam are the only ones paying enough attention, everyone else still lost in the music and laughter.

Nora lifts onto her tiptoes to see if she can see what's going on when Liam grabs her arm with a look that chills my bones. His head shakes as Nora's face pales, her eyes flitting to me for a second but then back to Liam as she nods, the both of them exchanging a silent conversation I don't understand. My temperature rises as the suddenly cool air prickles against the back of my neck.

"What is going on?" I ask a little louder than I'd intended.

Nora looks at me with a pained expression. "Shall we go down to the beach?"

What? My brow furrows and my head shakes at Nora's sudden need to go to the beach.

"Nora, what's going on?" I hold her stare, challenging her to try and brush me off again, but her eyes flick between me and Liam as my jaw clenches. *Fine, if they are going to be telepathic, then I'm going to see what the hell is going on for myself.*

My feet stomp towards the source of the noise. I shoulder past people, dipping in between the few bodies gathered in the kitchen. When I reach the hallway, I see Cam and Harriet blocking the front door. Harriet catches my eye. Her eyes are so full of apology, and I can't figure out why.

What the actual hell is going on right now that has everyone looking at me like that?

Cam spins as I stride past the last of the streamers, making them rustle. I'm instantly met with a set of glassy and bloodshot blue-grey eyes.

"Mum?" I whisper, but it's so quiet I'm not sure if I said it out loud.

Her brown wavy hair is limp and lifeless as it rests on her shoulders. She takes one step into the house towards me, and I can't tell if my body wants to run towards her or away from her. My eyes blink rapidly, making sure I'm not dreaming. *Would this be a nightmare or a dream of having my mother here right now?* My stupid heart betrays me, thinking she's come back to get me.

A gush of air tells me that Nora and Liam are now behind me, although all I can see is her. My arms hang like planks of wood by my side and my legs are rooted in place as she takes a step towards me before Cam blocks the gap between us. His familiar smell of cloves hits my senses and my vision clears, as though I've just been snapped back into the room again.

"Claire, don't do this here. I'll give you money, but you need to leave." Cam's voice is deep, firm and determined. He's protecting me and it makes my eyes fill with tears.

"You don't tell me what to do with my fucking life. I want to see *my* daughter." Her words hiss from her mouth as she steps closer to Cam, poking his chest.

When Cam captures her wrist, she stumbles backwards and struggles to regain her balance.

I only needed to glimpse at the glaze of her eyes when she stumbles to know that she's high, those vacant dull orbs are etched into my memory at this point.

She's not here for me.

"Leave now and I won't call the police," Cam growls.

"Get the fuck off me, *brother.*"

The way she says brother has so much malice that the sound lingers in the room like a bad smell.

"Mum, stop." The words leave my mouth before I can stop them. When her eyes snap to me, her lips tip upwards in a smile that sends chills down my arms and I suddenly wish I hadn't gained her attention. I pray that my body doesn't show how small I feel right now. I push my shoulders back, trying to gain some semblance of strength, even though I don't feel strong right now.

"Jessie, baby, come home with me. You don't belong here, you belong with me."

My heart folds in on itself. I should belong with her; I should feel completely safe with her, but the reality is, I don't and I haven't for a long time. The pain of my reality cuts deep, deeper than I have ever felt. It's as if seeing her has ripped open an old wound that wasn't completely healed, and judging by the look on her face, she's not done pouring salt into it yet either.

The worst part of this is that the little girl inside of me just wants her mum. The one who used to make me pancakes for breakfast and brush my hair every night, before she read me stories, but the woman in front of me is a stranger. One that I can't save anymore.

My heart thrashes, beating against my chest torturously. The faint thumping of the party behind us creeps back into my reality. The last thing I want is my college friends to see her make more of a scene, but I can't focus on anything else around me; it's all blurry and distorted.

"You should listen to Cam and leave... now." My hands shake as I squeeze them into fists by my sides. The hurt inside of me feels like a wildfire that is ripping through me, obliterating everything I ever felt for her, but I can't let her see any of that; I won't give her the satisfaction. Not that she'd remember it when she's sober. But me? I'll be left with the memories for a lifetime.

"You don't mean that, Jessie. Come on. We're leaving together." She brushes off my request as though it was nothing.

She grabs my wrist, trying to pull me forwards, my skin pinching under her fingers, but Cam has her off me before she gets a chance to take me anywhere.

"I'm not leaving." I place my hand over Cam's, silently letting him know that I've got this. He nods and steps back so I can face my mum. "You left me." I try to keep my voice stern, but I fail as emotion digs its claws into my throat. No, I will not let her see me cry. I swallow down all the emotion before I demand, "Leave... now!"

The way she stands in front of me; so fucking broken, a shell of the person I love makes my breath stutter. It takes all my courage not to break down and ask her why she chose something so fucking disgusting over me, why she tarnished all those memories of us against the world, just me and my mum, forever. But I don't. I can't ask her because I'm too scared of the answer. My lips purse as I stare at her, glaring at the ghost of the woman I thought I knew.

She huffs, raising an eyebrow in disbelief. "You know, I gave up everything for you and you do this... choosing my brother over me?" She runs her chipped polished fingers through her hair. "I fucking hate you for that, Jessie."

Her words are bitter and sharp, but she chose her addiction over me, so it feels somehow fitting that she feels the same about me now. We're even.

Except, it was never a game I wanted to play.

She turns to leave, slamming the door. As soon as it connects, the noise echoing through the hallway, I fall to the floor in a heap. My heart shatters into a million pieces, my hands clutch at my throat, hoping that somehow, I can figure out how to breathe again. The silent sobs come hard and fast and I feel Cam scoop me into his arms, but it gives me minimal relief as he tries to comfort me; his voice is distant as he tells me it's okay.

How would he know it's okay? Nothing about this is okay.

I'm broken, forever scarred by someone I love.

I don't remember how I got upstairs to my bedroom, or how long Nora and Liam sat with me because I don't feel like I'm in my own body right now. I'm looking down at myself, sitting on my bed with my two best friends either side of me, wondering how to wake up tomorrow and be okay.

"It's almost midnight," Nora whispers next to me.

My face is crispy from the tears that have dried on my cheeks. My body feels hollow, like there are no more organs occupying the space anymore. Everything feels upside down and backwards as I look at Nora trying to figure out how to say something without sobbing again.

Liam's hand finds mine, and he links our fingers together, brings them to his mouth and kisses each of my fingers. I try to smile, but I can't. Maybe I'll try again later.

The cheers and bangs of distant fireworks tell us that it's officially midnight. Both Nora and Liam stay silent and just sit with me as we listen to other people's joy that erupts downstairs.

The start to a new year.

The hours after the new year disappear as quickly as bubbles melt in a bubble bath. Nora went to her own bed around 1 am. Liam fell asleep in my bed not long after that. As tired as I am, I can't sleep. My brain won't let me.

The sun rises, letting warm light peep through the blinds on my window. I can see the dust floating around through the slivers of sunshine and my focus fixes on how many particles are suspended in the air right now, silently drifting around my room.

I might need some sleep. Obsessing over dust particles has to be a sign of sleep deprivation, or insanity. Either could be true.

Liam stirs next to me. When his eyes open, his head immediately jerks up to make sure I'm still here. When he finds me sitting in my armchair next to my dressing table, he exhales loudly and drops his shoulders.

I give him an empty laugh. "I'm still here," I spit out, not meaning it to sound as harsh as it does, but I don't have the energy to take it back.

Liam sits up, his t-shirt crumpled, and his hair is pushed to one side where he slept like the dead on his face. I've never understood how people can sleep on their fronts. It looks so uncomfortable. *How do you even breathe?*

"Did you sleep at all?" Liam's voice is raspy.

I shrug, avoiding his stare. "I wanted to see the first sunrise of the new year."

It's mostly the truth.

Silence fills the room and I find myself fixated on those stupid dust particles again.

"Come here." Liam pats the bed next to him.

I stand, dropping the blanket from my waist, without really noticing my movements, like a soldier in a line up being told to move because someone demands it. I sink under the covers next to Liam and he immediately pulls me in towards him. The feel of his warm body behind my back is soothing, but it also makes me want to cry.

God, is this just my personality now? Eternally sad girl.

Liam peppers soft kisses across my shoulder until he reaches the nape of my neck. It feels good, like he's caressing something deeper than my skin. My body sinks further into his as his arms tighten around me. He's holding me tight enough that it makes me feel like I might fall into a million pieces if he tries to let me go. I grip onto his arm wrapped around my middle, anchoring myself to him.

"I'm here," he whispers against my skin, as if he can sense my inner turmoil.

That's all it takes for the damn to break. Heart wrenching sobs escape my mouth, my chest stuttering on each exhale and howling for each inhale. My fingers dig deeper into Liam's arm, as my body tries to curl in on itself, but he doesn't let me go, wrapping himself around me, holding me together.

We stay twisted together until my sobs ease and my heart rate keeps a steady rhythm again. I wipe my tears with the backs of my hands, and turn to face him. His face is framed by the sunlight darting into the room, and if it's possible, it makes him look even more handsome.

I trail my fingers across his jaw, feeling the slight scar on his chin from when he fell out of a tree when we were fourteen. I dust across his high cheekbones and smooth over the soft hair of his eyebrows. I trace the slope of his nose. It's regal and perfect as I tap the end of it, earning myself a soft smile from him. His eyes are swarming with more green than brown this morning like they're in motion, the colours gliding over one another like a settling snow globe.

My fingers draw an outline of his lips, whispering across his Cupid's bow and pinching the plumpness of his bottom lip before I quickly wrap my hand in his hair and pull him to me, sealing us together.

His arms instantly wrap around my back, holding me, pushing me further into him. My body ignites like a lighter, fire pumping through my veins, desperate for him to touch me more than he ever has before. There's a dull ache in between my legs that I can't ignore. It throbs and screams for him, as he gently nips and sucks my lower lip.

The noise that falls from my mouth is full of desire for him. I need him closer. I need him to touch me. I need him now.

Hiking my leg around him, I tug him on top of me and he moves willingly, pinning me under his warm body. I can feel every hot, hard inch of him against me and it makes my eyes roll into my head. I am lust, I am dust floating around searching for a surface to settle on and he is my surface, my anchor.

Liam breaks our kiss. "Jess... I..." he pants, flicking his eyes between my wild ones.

I'm not sure if he is hesitating or asking me what I want, so I answer for him without ever hearing the question.

"I need you." I rasp against his mouth. The feeling pooling between my legs for him is consuming me, making me writhe underneath him.

He searches my face for something, but I know all he'll find is my need for him. He kisses me lightly, tentatively, before he grinds himself against my core, groaning against my mouth as he does. My nerve endings zing all over my body as he rubs against my clit, just as I roll my hips into him, searching for more.

He moves his hands to my breast, where he palms it gently before flicking my hardened nipple. His hot mouth trails kisses down to the same nipple as he sucks it through the fabric of my t-shirt, making my mouth fly open and my body buck beneath him. The sensation of his mouth on me is making me dizzy as I fist his hair in my hands, wanting to pin him there against me.

I remove my hands and he hovers over the top of me, pausing briefly before dragging his hands between my breasts and smoothing his thick fingers over my shorts, the heat in his eyes stirring something deep inside me as he rubs over the fabric. It's not nearly enough, it's a light touch compared to what my body seeks.

I lift up and claw at his shoulders, silently begging him for more. When he moves his hands away from my apex my body relaxes briefly before I move my hands between us, fumbling with the drawstring of his jogging bottoms, eager to feel him against me. He keeps his body hovering over me as I push the material down his legs, trailing my fingers slowly back over his tense thighs. His arms shake beside my head as he kicks off his joggers. When I drag my fingers to the waistband of his boxers and run them along the soft skin there, he hisses in approval.

Just as I'm about to dip my hand lower, he stops me and his eyes lock onto mine. "Jess... I think... should we... I mean... it's not that I don't..."

Ice replaces all the heat in my body, except my cheeks—they're burning with embarrassment.

"Oh, I..." I feel anything but okay right now as Liam moves off me, replacing his heat with a chill. I shuffle upwards and tuck my legs into my t-shirt stretching it out, dipping my head to my knees as I hug them.

He runs his hands through his hair and adjusts himself. "I want to, Jess, but I don't think it's the right time."

I squeeze my eyes closed, wishing I hadn't just been so desperate. I clear my throat, "Yeah... right." I nod robotically, staring at the crumpled sheets on my bed.

"Fuck," Liam whispers next to me as he slumps backwards onto the bed. "I don't want our first time to be something we regret... I want you so badly, Jess, but you're hurting, and I can't act on impulse. It doesn't feel right."

"Okay," I answer.

"Look at me... please, Scotty."

I wish my eyes would stop watering on command, but I can't seem to stop it. My gaze snaps to his as frustration pulses in my neck.

"I'm sorry, I love you," he says quietly and I believe him. I know he's sorry.

My mouth twists. "It's fine." I brush it off, metaphorically waving my hand in the air.

For whatever reason, I can't tell him I love him right now. It's cruel, but not only am I heart-hurt, now my pride has taken a hit too. And then the stupid thoughts of him wanting other girls, namely this Alex I keep hearing about, infiltrate my mind, poisoning it. It's barely rational, but I can't help it. So, if I utter those three little words it feels like I might give him the last shred of dignity I have left, and I just can't do that.

"I'm going for a walk." I stand quickly, grabbing my hoodie from the chair in my room and walk out without looking back, eyes filled with tears yet again. I ignore Cam in the kitchen and sneak out the back doors, straight to the beach. It isn't until my feet hit the sand that I realise I haven't got any shoes on.

The sand is cool as it moulds around my toes. I look down at my feet as a tear falls from my eyes. *For fuck's sake, I'm done crying.* I wipe my face with my hoodie sleeve again and walk further towards the ocean.

When I reach the water's edge, I stare intently at the waves, marvelling at the way they list into an arch, floating perfectly before they crash into the sand and disappear. The repetition has me in a trance that is only broken by the feeling of someone behind me. I know it's Liam before I turn around.

He stands next to me without saying a word. My mind races with an apology that lingers on the tip of my tongue. My eyes blur from the unsaid words, ones I know I need to get out.

"Jess, what are you thinking?" he asks quietly.

"I-I... I don't... I don't know what I think actually," I admit, kicking the sand beneath me, barely making a dent in the damp, solid mass, needing to focus on anything but Liam's face right now. "Everything feels so messed up. Summer was so different. I had moments where I didn't think about the shit with my mum. Maybe that was selfish...

that I blocked it out, but it's how I coped and now it's all out in the open and it's not fine anymore... and I don't feel like the same girl I was in the summer." I sigh heavily, looking out at the ocean. "All I want to do is feel like my problems were smaller again."

Liam doesn't respond straight away; He just stands next to me, listening. When he's sure I'm finished, he turns to face me, hoping I'll do the same, but all I can manage is a glance over to him. A glance that lets me see the pity in his eyes, pity I don't want to see right now.

"I'm sorry," he says, regret lacing his tone.

I sit down with a huff. "Everyone is sorry, like that's a magic word that is going to fix everything. It fucking isn't." I dig my hand into the wet sand and watch as the water creeps forwards until the waves hit my toes, encasing them with a chill that is bone deep. I let the sand fall between my fingers, mindlessly watching as is slops back into the sand, disappearing into water.

"Jess, everyone cares about you..." Liam walks towards me sitting next to me, placing his hand on my lower back and I flinch, not sure if I want to be touched right now. He drops his hand with a sigh and tucks it into his hoodie pocket.

I laugh incredulously, "I know, everyone cares *so* much, except the one fucking person who should care the most. She doesn't give a shit about me."

Logically, I know it isn't his fault and I'm not mad at him, but right now I *feel* mad at him because he's here and, like he said, he cares and maybe my pride hasn't fully recovered from his rejection yet. I should walk away before I say something else. Unfortunately, logic isn't something I can fathom right now. It's mostly overshadowed by my rage.

"You know, you should probably go home."

It's low. I know it is. I'm hurting and I don't want to be the only one, so of course I hurt someone I love. Misery loves company, after all.

His head whips around to face me, his mouth open in shock.

"You want me to go right now?" he asks in disbelief.

"I think it's best. I need some time to breathe and figure out... all this shit," I snap.

I know Liam is staring at me. I can feel his eyes burning into the side of my face, but I still can't bring myself to look at him. His puppy dog eyes will, without a doubt, make me change my mind and I'll be begging him to stay.

Liam stands abruptly and paces in a circle, placing his hands behind his neck and looking up to the sky. "I'm going back to the house. I'm not fucking leaving you, Jess, but I'll give you some time."

My pulse rockets. I don't want him to be nice to me. I don't want him to care about me right now.. I don't fucking want it at all.

The pain from my mum, his rejection from this morning; it's all too much. I just need it to stop for a second so I can breathe again. I fist my hands in my hair, tugging at the strands until it hurts.

"I don't fucking want you here." As soon as the words come out, I regret them. I inhale rapidly, wanting to retract the words, but it's too late. The impact of them spreads through me like poison.

I'm retreating from the pain, the pain that is ripping me apart. Ripping us apart.

Liam crouches next to me, while I hide my face because my chin is starting to wobble, and I refuse to cry again.

"I know you don't mean that, but just so you know, that hurt. If the roles were reversed, Jess, I'd need you more than my next breath, but that's just me. Maybe I care too fucking much."

He stands and walks away, and I immediately want to run to him. But I stop myself. I've hurt him and we both need some space.

I realise that all I'm doing is wallowing in my own self-pity and rage. Nothing good can come of this, yet I can't seem to stop. I'm swirling in circles, drowning in shallow water, unable to find my anchor because I'm actively pushing him away.

"Get it together, Jess. Fuck."

I chastise myself for being such a bitch.

It's hours before I manage to retreat back to the house.

I don't apologise to Liam, even though I know I should.

I think about the letter my therapist told me to write and how I never actually managed to give it to him, I guess it doesn't matter now. It's all irrelevant.

I don't tell him I love him.

I just can't, when I feel like I don't deserve to hear it back from him.

When I open the door to my room, Liam is propped up, asleep on my bed. He's discarded his jeans in favour of joggers and a hoodie that's pulled up over his head, his arms firmly crossed over his body. He looks peaceful; I watch him as his lips part and a steady low snore comes from his mouth.

I don't want to wake him, and I'm too exhausted to talk about anything, so I pick up my fleece blanket and snuggle into the armchair.

Alone.

10

Liam

It's been three days since Jess asked me to leave. I ignored her demand because I know she needs me, but she just can't admit it. Things have been quiet; weird and borderline unbearable. She's stopped crying as much, but I can't help but notice how she flinches every time I try and get close to her. She's trying to protect herself from getting hurt again, but what she can't accept is that I could never hurt her. It guts me, the fact she thinks I *might* hurt her. My heart beats for her. When she hurts, I do too. The ache of us disconnecting like this makes me fear that I might lose her.

"Morning." Cam wanders into the kitchen. I've been here since Jess woke up at 4 am this morning, watching her from the kitchen window as she sits on the beach, unmoving.

"Morning," I reply.

Cam watches me, following my gaze out the window and lets out a heavy sigh. "You know, she's going to be okay. It's going to take time, but she's strong."

I nod. "I know."

"I called her therapist yesterday. She has an appointment at 11 am for Jess."

I nod again, not really knowing what to say. I'm not naïve enough to ignore that Jess needs more support than I can give her, so I'm glad she has Cam and Harriet looking out for her and not just her seventeen year old boyfriend. Although she would hate that I've just said that to myself, Jess doesn't need anyone to save her. I know that. But it doesn't stop me worrying about her.

I sigh deeply. "I have to go home tonight," I tell Cam. School starts up again tomorrow and as much as I want to be here, my dad told me I have to come home. *Telling* might be an understatement. The phone call we had last night was him barking orders at me, informing me that if I don't come home, I'll be ruining my own future.

Staying and helping my girlfriend is the opposite of ruining my future. In fact, she's all I can see in my future, so going home is the opposite of what I want to be doing.

"I've got her. You don't need to worry."

I nod again, trying not to let the worry seep into my face. I'm going to worry; I love her.

I thank Cam, wash up my plate from breakfast and head upstairs to pack the last of my things, ready for later.

As I'm zipping my backpack, Jess walks into her room, eyes red and wide as she focuses on the bag in my hands, looking at it like it's offensive.

"You're... you're leaving."

"Not until tonight."

She pales, her eyes darting around the room. I move in closer, but she backs away towards her closed door, her heels knocking against the wood behind her.

"Stop running from me, Jess," I say, a little too harshly. "Fuck," I whisper as I turn, hanging my head.

She doesn't say anything as she walks into her bathroom and turns the shower on. The thrumming sound of the water does nothing to stifle the sound of her crying. My entire being feels like it's being held a hundred feet above a building, suspended, ready to drop when I hear her cry. I want to punch something, scream, rage and swallow down all her pain because she doesn't fucking deserve any of this.

When Jess comes out of the bathroom, her eyes narrow on my phone as it flips in my hands. Her hair is damp, her small frame drowning in the hoodie she wore before her shower. She looks so fucking sad it hollows my chest.

"Jess, I'm sorry."

Her lips form into a thin line, as she hisses through her teeth, "Stop fucking telling me you're sorry. I don't need you to be sorry. I don't need to hear that you're sorry anymore. I don't fucking need you."

Her nostrils flare as she stares at me. I place my phone down on her bedside cabinet and stand so I'm closer to her.

"Stop lying to yourself, Jess. You're just pushing me away. You won't talk to me, you won't open up. You won't even let me fucking hug you after the other day, and I don't know what to do here."

She glares at me. "Nothing, you don't need to *do* anything. I'll... be fine. I don't need saving."

"I'm not trying to save... fuck, I don't mean to make you feel that way. You mean so much to me that it's killing me to see you so sad." I say, twirling on my heels, needing to move my body with all the frustration buzzing through me.

She clamps her jaw together as her brows raise and her eyes water before she steels her expression again. "You can't save me, you can't fix me, so stop trying. You don't need me to be the sad girlfriend. You've got plenty of options back in London. So I'm not sure what the point of all this is anymore."

I squint my eyes at her, praying that she isn't trying to say what I think she's saying.

"What does that mean?" My body stiffens, the organ in my chest thrashing in retaliation of what she's implying.

"It means, when you leave here..." She pauses as her head lifts to meet my stare, her eyes cold. "I want you to forget about me. Shack up with Alex for all I care."

It would've hurt less if she had stabbed me in the heart with a rusty blade. My breath lodges in my throat, suffocating me as the realisation sits heavy. *She doesn't want me.* I raise my hand to my chest to stop the ache that's forming there as I stumble back to the bed, collapsing when the backs of my legs touch the mattress. She wants me to forget about her. The girl I've been in love with since we were ten years old. My best friend . She wants me to forget her.

My eyes fill as I struggle to speak. "You're not thinking straight. I'm not leaving you, Jess."

She scoffs, disbelief marring her face. "*I'm* not thinking straight? Great, so now you think I'm crazy. Even more reason for you to find someone else."

My jaw ticks at her words; anger settling in with my disbelief. "I never said you were crazy. I said you were sad. There's a difference. Why are you pushing me away?" I ask, sounding almost desperate, needing to understand how she could be doing this to me, to us. My hands fist at my sides, pushing into the mattress, my breathing becoming uneven and heavy as I stare at her ocean blue eyes. Despite her words right now, she's still the most beautiful girl I've ever seen and the thought of losing her kills me. I'd rather walk through fire every day for the rest of my life than live without her.

She walks her petite frame to her window, staring at the ocean again. "I don't..." She trails off, not finishing her sentence. I'm about to ask her what she was going to say when she spins to face me. "You're better off without me, and I need time to think. I need space. I need to fucking breathe again and you... you're suffocating me with your puppy eyes and the constant *I'm sorry...* I can't do it Liam."

The air depletes from the room again, leaving me gasping.

She thinks I'm suffocating her?

I search her face; I need her to show me she's lying, pushing me away because it's too painful to hang on. A tick, a flinch, anything and I'll know she doesn't mean it, but her face is flat. She barely looks like my

Jess right now. And still, all I want to do is scoop her up and tell her that I'm not fucking leaving her.

"Jess, I..."

Her hand flies up in front of her, silently asking me to stop.

"No. I don't want this anymore. I need to figure this out alone," she says, her eyes cold and steeled.

She doesn't want this anymore.

She doesn't want *me* anymore, is what she's saying.

My face drains of all its colour. The muscles that were tense are now completely lax and my face feels numb. My palms are damp, my hands tingling, and I feel like I have no blood in my upper body at all. I've been decimated by the person I love the most.

"Is this about the other day when I wouldn't sleep with you? Because that's... I wanted to, Jess, but I'm not going to do it when you aren't yourself."

Her head shakes. "It isn't because of that."

She just doesn't want this... doesn't want me.

I take one more look at her to confirm what I refuse to accept. Her eyes are narrow, unforgiving and determined.

Fuck this.

My feet close the distance between us as I stand in front of her, our toes touching. "I'm giving you one last chance to change your mind... I want to stay and help you through this. You aren't supposed to have all the answers. You're a kid, we're kids..." I pause, raising my hand to her face and this time she doesn't flinch when my palm cups her jaw. "Let me help you. Don't push me away," I whisper.

Her lip trembles as her brows crease and when she finally locks eyes with me, I can feel her pain as though it is my own, assaulting every nerve in my body. Tears spill from her eyes like a waterfall as she squares her shoulders to mine.

"You're leaving anyway, so..." she trails off.

I swallow the daggers that have moved into my throat, as I silently beg her not to say what I know is coming.

Don't fucking say it, Jessica.

"It's over."

Part Two

Ten years later...

11

Jessica

"Jess, we need to get going. There are train strikes again and I really don't like being late!"

Nora hollers up the stairs of our two-bed town house in London. I say ours, it's Harriett's Mother's, but she lives in San Francisco, so for the last five years, we've rented it.

I'm standing in my bedroom, staring at my reflection, wondering how I can tame my nerves for tonight.

"You've got this," I say confidently to myself, smoothing my sweaty hands over my black jeans before grabbing my leather jacket from the bed.

Hurrying downstairs, I spy Nora standing in the hallway. Her shiny black hair tied neatly into a sleek bun and her foot stamps as she fusses with a wayward piece of hair. I quickly reach into my handbag hanging on the banister and walk up behind her, holding out a bobby pin.

"Stay still." I tame the flyaway with ease.

"Thank you. That piece of hair was testing my patience." Nora smiles gratefully at me in the mirror.

"I could tell. You were doing a little dance with your foot there."

She laughs lightly, letting her gaze flick over her petite frame once more in the mirror.

A flutter of nerves erupts through my body, making my hands suddenly clammy again as I think about what we're about to do.

"I'm ready... are you ready?" I say in a rush. "Of course you are. You wouldn't have shouted for me otherwise. Sorry." I shake my hands in front of me, fighting with the pins and needles that are building.

Nora turns towards me, putting her manicured hands on my shoulders to calm me.

"Don't forget to breathe, babe. You can't be this kick ass woman with all these amazing ideas to tell people if you aren't breathing, remember?" Her caramel eyes shine with the strength she knows I need right now.

I inhale and exhale, slowly focusing on each breath.

I can do this.

After a quick speed walk to Victoria Park tube station, Nora and I chatted about anything and everything to take my mind off how nervous I am, we stand on the platform, waiting for our train, as Nora starts nodding furiously.

"We can so do this," she utters, reading my mind like she always does.

"Yeah?"

"Yeah, and listen. You get to decide how much you want me to be involved, okay? I'll be there as much or as little as you want me to be. This is your dream, Jess, but I'm here for you," she says, her smile turning into a wide grin. "Big time."

We managed to miss any delays on the tube and swiftly arrive at Cafe Moretti in Covent Garden, an Italian restaurant that smells like garlic and tomatoes and expensive olive oil and are shown to our seats. The walnut wood of the table contrasts with the light blue booth we sit in and somehow works with the light gold accents that surround us.

Zoey arrives in true Zoey style, rushing and tearing through the restaurant like a tornado. Nothing changes, it seems. Zoey went to school with Nora and I, but we lost touch when we moved. Right now, she might be my new favourite person because she's going to help me tonight.

"Hi, Hi ,Hi, sorry I'm late. It's so good to see you two. God, you're both so bloody gorgeous. Look at you." She waves her hands frantically, gesturing to Nora and me, as we both laugh lightly at her compliments.

"Look at you," I retort. "I love your hair shorter. Really suits you."

She puffs up her short, platinum hair jokingly. "Oh, this old bird's nest? Eh... it'll do." She winks. "It's been way too long, girls. I'm so happy we're getting together now," she adds, sincerity lining her voice.

We fall into easy conversation and chat about what we've been doing since our school days.

"Do you remember when we all got so drunk that Harriett had to rescue us? I'm sure it was your birthday, Jess, and I had snuck some of my dad's vodka. We sat and drank that in the park near my house..." She leans forward, laughing. "And we could *not* remember the way home because we were so drunk." Zoey's blue eyes crease as she sniggers into her palm.

"I definitely remember because Jess and I got grounded for a month," Nora scoffs, as though it pains her to remember the one time she was grounded.

"We're just lucky our parents were mostly good to us for all the shit they put up with." Zoey's laughter sprinkles throughout her words and then her face falls suddenly. "Oh God, Jess, I'm sorry. I didn't mean to bring up anything... shit. Stupid foot always in my mouth." Her hand connects with her forehead. "Forgive me?" she asks with worry in her eyes.

"Zo, don't worry, it's fine," I say, brushing it off, praying that I'm doing a good job at masking the sudden chill coursing through my body. I fiddle with the knife and fork sat on my napkin, feeling the cold metal against my skin, as I beg my emotions not to show me up right now.

Nora glances at me nervously, and I force a smile. I don't miss the way her brows flinch, offering me an apology that she can't voice right now. I haven't seen my mum since that New Year's Eve ten years ago when she showed up at Cam's house, and although I try every day not to think about her, the truth is, being in London reminds me of her a lot. It's just been a while since anyone but me or my therapist have talked about her, and I'm a little caught off guard.

Zoey quickly reads the room and changes the subject, smiling warmly at me. "So tell me about this amazing charity you want to set up."

My shoulders instantly relax, and my breathing evens out as I think about everything I'm here to discuss tonight.

"I want to help children in London who either don't have access to therapy or have been refused help because it's so overburdened. The kids who have been in situations where one or both of their parents have fallen victim to drugs or domestic violence." I take a second to swallow and collect my thoughts as they race through my brain.

"I know not everyone has people who can help them and plenty of kids end up in the system. I was lucky I had family..." I glance over at Nora, who is smiling proudly at me. "So, I want to provide free therapy for extended families who take those children into their homes or foster families who need additional support."

"I want it to be big, big enough that it'll make an impact on the mental health of the children who need it the most and ensure they have access to the tools to help them deal with fractured relationships. Hopefully, we can do this by giving them the ability to form healthy relationships and not repeat the same abusive/addict behaviours they were subjected to. But I need to know the ins and outs of how to set up a charity and I know you've done that with your animal shelter."

Zoey listens intently and then her face softens as she smiles at me. "Jess, this is amazing, you know that right?" Emotion clouding her bright blue eyes. "Sorry, I don't mean to get all... ugh, gross, emotions," she laughs lightly, fanning her face, whilst I try and stop the same tears forming in my eyes too. We lock eyes and laugh at each other. "Anyway, I can definitely help. I'm happy to walk you through exactly what you need to set up the charity itself. I even have a few connections with some foster families because the children they look after volunteer and visit the shelter to see the animals."

I hold her gaze, hoping she knows how grateful I am to have her help. "Thank you so much, Zo."

She waves her hand in dismissal. "What are friends for?" She shrugs, smiling at me. "I'll come by your hotel for lunch, and we can get started then. Does Wednesday work?"

I nod, taking a sip of my water. "Wednesday is perfect."

Nora and I are home and in our pyjamas before 11 pm. The comfort of taking my jeans off and putting on the rattiest, most worn pair of pyjamas is unrivalled.

PJ's over BJ's, I chuckle to myself. Although, it's been a while since I've given one, so PJ's definitely win.

Our soft cream, velvet sofa is far too comfy as I sit, flicking absently through my work emails, my eyes growing heavy. I've manage to set up my to do list for the morning and check some emails for a few prospective bride meetings that are in my calendar for tomorrow.

"Do you want another cuppa?" I hear Nora shout from the kitchen. I shout my "yes" in response, but in reality, by the time she emerges with it, I'm almost half asleep.

"Do you think the hotel will have a space for us to hold the first charity event?" Nora asks, sipping her hot tea and cursing at how hot it is. The Clover is a boutique, art deco style hotel, sitting about a mile from Covent Garden, where I've worked at since we moved back to London. I landed my dream job there as the events manager and I've never been happier.

I yawn loudly, my body feeling heavy as I exhale. "I'll check the calendar tomorrow." I yawn again. "I think there might be an open weekend coming up, but I have no idea how much time we need to

ALL OF MY LASTS

plan something like this. I'm hoping Zoey doesn't mind being a third wheel in all this because I'm going to be blowing her phone up."

Speaking of blowing up phones, my phone buzzes next to me, a familiar face lighting up my screen. I stifle a grumble. I'm tired and want to go to bed but I can't keep ignoring his calls anymore. I glide my finger across my screen, answering him after a few rings.

12

Jessica

Over the next few days after Zoey helped me set up my charity, which was actually embarrassingly easy, and since then, we've been focussed on the first big event we are going to throw to raise money.

I was right, the ballroom in The Clover is free in three weeks' time which is tight, but not impossible. Or so Zoey tells me.

I'm in my element organising it; picking flowers, décor, music, invitations, liaising with companies to buy tables from us. Organising and detailing events is my bread and butter, which is why I made sure I had these jobs on our list. That, and I've had years of experience doing this for work.

Just as I'm sitting in my office at work, I hear my phone buzz.

> **Zoey:** I just met with the chef at your restaurant, who by the way, you have been hiding from me girl. He is all kinds of fine! Anyway, we talked over the menu, and it is all organised. I know you were doing amazing, but I saw on your google list that was an outstanding to do. I hope it's okay that I helped you out xo

Jess: You are a lifesaver, Zoey! Thank you. As for Jake, I can confirm he is single. I will put in a good word for you, but you can't scare him off. He is amazing!

Zoey: He is seriously the whole package, and he cooks! Make me swoon already! I'm hoping to run into him casually again soon so expect to see lots of me at your office xo

I laugh at her reply. I don't know Jake very well yet; he's new to the hotel, but he's made a great impression with his innovative ideas and creative menus. I make a mental note to mention Zoey to him because, God knows, someone deserves to have a successful love life around here.

My afternoon is filled with meeting brides and grooms to be. I'm an expert at selling the space in the hotel for weddings. That happily ever after that can start right here in our contemporary ballroom that boasts 3,200 square feet of space.

Technically, I manage all events here, but it seems the hotel's revenue for weddings has increased 90% since I came on board three years ago, which has meant the staff like to call me the wedding planner. A job title that I never thought I'd be good at. It seems I can sell the idea of forever but can't keep hold of it myself.

In between meetings, I desperately try and tick a few more things from my to do list for the event. I call the florist who we use regularly and order white roses and eucalyptus, then the agent for the live band who also frequents here. As luck would have it, they're in town that weekend and apart from rehearsals, they are available and willing to donate their time and talent for free.

By the time my working day is done I'm about ready to collapse into my bed. But then I remember that I have a date tonight. Evan called last night, and I'd already missed three calls from him. Right now, I realise the error of my ways because I'm exhausted and do not want to go out for dinner. Or maybe it's that I don't want to go out to dinner with *him*. We don't usually go out on dates. We've kept things casual for the last couple of months and we've only ever had one date, which ended up back at his place, anyway. Since then, we've had a few hook-ups but nothing serious.

Story of my life. But I was surprised he wanted to go on a date, surprised enough to say yes.

The black pencil dress I threw on this morning is a bit more crinkled than I'd like it to be for a date, but I don't have time to go home and change. I reach into my handbag and pull out a few make up items, touching up my lipstick and powdering my face again.

That'll have to do. Sorry Evan.

An hour later, I'm walking into one of Soho's fanciest restaurants. Dimly lit for ambience, the tables are lined with the kind of cotton that my bedsheets could only dream of and bottles of Cristal decorate almost every table. The entire place reeks of money and wealth, the smell lingering in the air as I'm ushered to the table where Evan is already sitting. His hair coiffed perfectly and suit crisp as always, he doesn't look out of place in this restaurant, but I certainly do with my crinkled dress and dark bags under my eyes.

"Hey sugar, where you been? I feel like I've not heard from you in forever, I'm surprised you answered my call." His lilting northern accent always sounds a little stronger when I don't see him for a while. He stands and pulls my chair out for me, reminding me of his manners and that he is actually a decent guy. But he's not the guy for me, he's just convenient. I almost hate myself for admitting it, but I'd hate being strung along even more if I were him and that's exactly what I feel like I've been doing.

That being said, I've been on enough dates from stupid apps, that I've since deleted from my phone, to know that men rarely pull out a chair for you.

"Hey, Evan," I say as brightly as I can manage, taking the seat he pulled out for me. I avoid his eye contact initially, feeling bad about ghosting him. In my defence, I've been dealing with the aftermath of an intense therapy session and a crazy work week, and then the charity stuff... it left me feeling overwhelmed and that meant my headspace for anything else was a bit all over the place.

"Sorry... work has been insane this week," I half-lie, all too easily omitting the therapy part and the part where I just didn't fancy seeing him.

"I miss you," he whines, his brown eyes intent on holding my attention.

I already know that he means he misses me in his bed. Because that's what this is, which is probably why I feel so twitchy, sat with my crumpled dress in a fancy restaurant; it's not our usual vibe. I offer him a small smile, shifting my weight in my chair.

"So... how have you been?" I ask, moving my empty wine glass a fraction to the left and then back again, still trying to avoid his unyielding gaze.

"I've been good. Working, keeping busy. You know how it is." He shrugs his suited shoulders. "What's going on with you?" He tips his finger, getting the attention of a waiter and orders us a bottle of white wine before waiting for my answer.

"Same mostly." Evan doesn't know much about my hopes and dreams for the future, let alone the fact I'm setting up a charity, because our conversation usually dries up pretty quickly, hence why 'benefits' work best for us. I haven't shared much with him because he doesn't always ask, and when he does, I don't feel like sharing, which is probably why things have stayed so casual between us.

We order our food; the tiny portioned pretentious kind that makes me roll my eyes, and Evan tells me about his grandma's ninetieth birthday party that his parents are throwing for her. My interest mostly stays fixed on him. He's handsome and easy to look at with his clean cut face, big brown eyes and dirty blonde hair. He could rival most

Abercrombie models with his sculpted physique and he's a great catch, *so why the fuck am I not feeling it*?

"So, I wondered if you wanted to come with me?" he asks, eyes full of hope. I'd zoned out for a second, staring at him but not completely listening, and I'm not sure what he's asking me to do with him.

"Come with you to..." I trail off, hoping it comes off as charming and not me being rude.

He smiles lightly at me. "I'm gonna pretend you were listening and not staring at my smoking hot body, but I'll forgive you either way." He winks all too arrogantly. "Come with me to my grandma's birthday party?"

When I hesitate, he rubs the back of his neck.

"I... um, when is it again?" I ask, squinting my eyes.

"It's in two weeks' time. The last Saturday in September."

Shit, that's the night of the charity event that he knows nothing about. "Ah... I'm sorry, Ev. I can't. I have a work thing that night."

The noise of the restaurant, glasses clinking, waiters shuffling echoes in the awkwardness between us.

His shoulders slump slightly before he recovers, rolling them back and nodding at me. "I get it. It's fine. I just... I want to move things forward with us, Jessica and I want you to meet my family."

Woah, hang on a second.

He wants to move things forward. What is there to move when you're just fucking?

My eyes frantically flick around the room, trying to figure out the nearest exit. My pulse flickers wildly when I feel him assessing my reaction. My mouth forms shapes to speak, but nothing comes out. I'm so confused, I thought we were on the same page here.

"Evan, I... we... this..." My brows are in a permanent crease as I try and figure out where this has come from and how I can diffuse the situation. "Look, I know we've been... seeing each other for a few months but we haven't talked about being exclusive or meeting families. I'm not sure that I'm ready." *Or that I ever will be*, but I don't add that in, salt in the wound and all that.

Evan looks at me cautiously, trying to read what I'm too chicken to say.

"Okay, are you saying we can't have that conversation, or that you aren't interested in having it at all?" His biceps bulge against his formal shirt as he crosses them over his chest, narrowing his gaze again.

He holds my stare, eyebrows raised, waiting for me to speak, as I struggle to look at him. Forcing myself to say the words because I never *wanted* to hurt him and now, I feel like that's a real possibility, I feel shitty about it.

"I thought we were having fun. Meeting your family, that's... that's huge, Evan," I admit shyly. I thought we *both* knew this was fun and casual. I consider the last few months and wonder if I've just spent the whole time misjudging what this was, but I know that isn't the case.

I mean, I don't even know where his office is, let alone his parents' names or quite literally anything other than he is a lawyer and his name is Evan Thompson, who lives in Chelsea. God, that makes me feel even shittier. Was he feeling things I wasn't? I can't take responsibility for that, but I could've paid more attention, noticed and put a stop to it before it came to this.

Evan exhales an unamused sound. "Fun... right. Of course, that's what this is. You know, I really like you, right, Jess?"

I try and keep my face neutral. The fact that I've possibly missed any signals from him baffles me, but more than that, I genuinely feel like this is not what we agreed this was.

"I like you too, but..."

"Please don't. It's fine, let's just finish our dinner." He waves his hand dismissively, not wanting me to carry on, so I don't.

I nod my head and stare down at my plate, suddenly not feeling so hungry, not that there is much on my plate anyway. I worry my bottom lip, thinking that this is entirely my fault for leading on this great, hot guy and I wish it could be different. But he deserves someone who can't stop thinking about him, not someone who ghosts him.

When we say goodbye, he hugs and kisses me. "You know where I am if you ever change your mind, Jess," he says, smiling. My hands grip his arms in a silent apology, but we both know that this is it for us.

When I turn and leave to head to the tube station, I don't look back.

13

Jessica

*R*emember to take it all in. Breathe, and think about how much you've achieved.

My therapists' words stare at me from the piece of paper she wrote them on a few days ago. I may have spent my entire session losing tiny pieces of my mind, and ended up having a panic attack over the stress of worrying that everything was organised. I haven't had one of those for years.

When I managed to pull it back together, taking slow and steady breaths again. My therapist wrote this note and said it would give me something to focus on today just in case I feel overwhelmed again. She suggested I read the note and regain my focus before it slips. It was helping.

This moment has been years in the planning, at least in my head, but in reality, it had taken Nora, Zoey and me two weeks of late nights, rushed phone calls and at least one bottle of tequila between us all, and it's all come down to today.

Every single white rose has been pruned by yours truly. Every inch of the ceiling is covered in white drapes. Every chair is perfectly placed against the white table linens. I spoke to the band an hour ago in the bar and they have sound checked already. The raffle and silent auction are ready to go too.

Everything is set.

I straighten my long dress with slow, nervous strokes, letting my lungs fill completely before exhaling again.

This really is it. The start of something I've been dreaming about since university. Goosebumps rise over my arms and my eyes fill with the enormity of everything I've been able to do and will do in the future.

Nora and I have been fussed over all day by hairstylists and makeup artists. I would've been happy to glam myself up, but Zoey and Nora insisted that we were pampered, and we really have been. I barely recognize my reflection staring back at me.

A long, black satin, figure fitting gown with thin straps that sit on the edge of my shoulders, accentuating my curves. My chestnut hair looks like it has streaks of gold as it tumbles down my back in loose curls. My blue eyes are bright and encased with soft smoky make up.

"Good lord, Jess, you look fucking hot!" Nora's mouth gapes as she looks me over.

I give her a little excited wiggle and smile at my best friend, who looks her own kind of hot.

"Ehh, you scrub up alright too." I wink at her, she barely wears her hair down, usually opting for it to be pulled back off her face. She says it's because when she writes notes with her therapy clients, it stops her hair falling into her eyes. So, right now, with her hair sleek and straight, she looks stunning.

We both look at our reflections once more, contrasting in our black and red dresses. Nora grabs her phone and flips the camera onto us. We pose for a few pictures and send them to Zoey with the caption *Ready for this?* and a winking emoji. Zoey replies almost immediately with a picture of her in a short, black, high neck dress and her caption reads, *Ready for the main event baby!*

I tug Nora's arm and remind her we need to head downstairs before any of the guests arrive.

"Hey, are you okay?" Nora stops me as I press the button to the lift.

I tilt my head. "I'm good. Nervous maybe, but good. Are you okay?"

She nods. "I just want to make sure you know if you need me tonight, if things get overwhelming..." the lift pings in front of us, alerting us of its arrival.

"I'm good, I promise," I say, leading Nora by hand through the metal doors.

As we walk from the lift, through the foyer towards the ballroom, there are people dotted around wearing ball gowns and black-tie tuxedos. It feels like a movie set and my heart stutters in my chest at how real this feels.

"Girls, that picture did nothing to show how bloody hot you are in real life. Come here, let me squeeze you both." Zoey rushes over, wrapping us both in her arms.

"Jessica?" My assistant Kylie gets my attention as she stands in front of the ballroom doors, waiting to let us in to do final checks.

Zoey releases us and looks between Nora and me before squealing, "Let's do this."

I can't hold back my giant smile as I nod to Kylie to open the doors for us.

I saw the room earlier and, I planned everything down to the knives and forks on the tables, but seeing everything like this in front of me, minutes away from it actually happening, gives me shivers.

The Clover's ballroom is beautiful as it usually is, but now... now I'm speechless.

The three-tiered ceiling looks endless as the white, sheer, soft drapes bellow from a height before gently dusting the tops of the glistening chandeliers that line the centre of the room. The art deco framed windows accent each light fixture perfectly, making the room glow softly. The tables are littered with white roses and eucalyptus, the muted green colour balancing out the white tablecloths as each centre piece emulates a waterfall of falling flowers.

It smells fresh and sweet and I inhale deeply, enjoying the scent.

I click my heels on to the white, sparkling floor that looks like it holds a thousand fireflies underneath it. The stage commands enough attention without detracting from the room and I let my fingers run over the edges of the speakers that sit at the front of it before spinning around to take it all in once more.

The cream and gold chairs pick up the gold cutlery and gold stemmed wine glasses carefully placed on each table.

Every single thing is perfect.

Remember to take it all in. Breathe, and think about how much you've achieved.

"Jess..." Nora gasps. "This is..." Her eyes find mine, filled with emotion. We don't say another word; we just nod at one another and take in the moment as her hand squeezes mine.

When we walk back to the front of the room, I tell Kylie to let in the guests.

Within seconds the room is met with smiles, glittering eyes and amazement.

Two familiar faces greet Nora and me first.

"Jess, Nora..." Harriet spins around, her green dress trailing after her as she takes in the room before settling on us again. "It isn't often I'm speechless, but I don't think there is a word to describe how beautiful this place looks and how proud we are of you both." She beams, her eyes filling with tears.

"Now, now honey, don't embarrass these two." Cam pulls Harriet to his side, giving her a reassuring squeeze. "You both look breath taking, and she is right, we are absolutely made up for you."

My eyes fill for the millionth time tonight as they both hug us. "Oh God, I need to get a grip. My make up won't last the night at this rate," I mumble.

Nora laughs lightly, dabbing the corners of her eyes too, sniffing away the tears. "You guys are sitting at our table over there. Number three." She gestures to the front of the room, and they wave goodbye before they find their seats.

Around twenty minutes later, I glance around the room and notice that most people are seated, apart from the few people Nora is talking to at the bar. I see two people gliding over towards me. Checking the list in my hands, I see that these must be the last two for table five.

I don't recognise the woman, but she is beautiful, with red hair and a stunning dark green dress.

As I look to the man whose arm she is linking, the blood drains from my body.

My heart thuds, my throat dries, there is so much white noise thrashing inside my head that I barely notice the vice-like grip I have on the table plan that I'm holding, causing the sides to crumple and tear.

Surely, it's a ghost? Not like the cute Casper kind, either. More like the, '*I haven't seen you for years, ex-boyfriend kind*'.

I'm desperately trying to think about how to flee to the nearest exit. My eyes blink rapidly, trying to see anything but the couple walking towards me but it's hopeless. My tunnel vision is so strong I can't look away and my feet, super glued in place.

Which can mean only one thing: I'm about to come face to face with the man I haven't seen in ten years.

The light blue glow from his phone casts an ethereal shadow onto his face, catching his high cheekbones and the tip of his nose. His lips are the same heart shape that fit so perfectly with mine all those years ago. His hair is a little darker and styled short at the sides, but blends seamlessly with his stubble. *That's new.* He looks older... more defined, and more... *man*. His black tuxedo hugs every inch of his tall, broad frame and his long strides confidently devour the space between us.

Jesus, he is owning that tuxedo.

When they reach me, his date clears her throat, dragging his attention back to her as she passes me their tickets. Liam looks warmly at the woman next to him until finally he turns his head to me and two familiar, warm hazel eyes find my icy blue ones.

A shudder rakes it way from my toes to my knees, settling in my chest.

The air between us is thick, silent, and unyielding. My heart thrashes like a wild stag being hunted. My body is impaled by his stare. My skin on fire as I watch in slow motion as the realisation hits him too. His eyes simultaneously widen and soften, flickering with the same familiar look he gave me so often when we were kids.

I wonder what to say...

Oh hey, ex-boyfriend who was my first and only love. The one who I cried over for months and have never really got over. How's things?

Yeah, nailed it, subtle but direct.

"Scotty?" The lingering silence shatters like glass, and of course he calls me by my nickname. A nickname that I haven't heard for years. Ten years, in fact.

An invisible weight presses against me, robbing me of any breath I'd hoped might help me before he deftly scoops me up to give me a bear hug, the way he always used to do when we were kids. If I had any hope of breathing before, I definitely have none now. I'm engulfed with his warm, summer scent that is stronger now and more grown up. My hands have clenched into fists that are currently squashed beneath this 6-foot-something giant of a man, making it impossible to return the hug, leaving me trapped in this weird twilight moment between past and present.

My mind races. I'm caught in a vortex of emotion as my skin becomes clammy, a bead of sweat threatening the base of my neck. I squeeze my eyes closed, focussing on the note from my therapist. But that isn't helping me, because nothing could've prepared me for seeing the love of my life again.

14

Liam

J ess clears her throat in my ear and I reluctantly put her down.
Her hands fly to her hair, fixing it before running her hands down her sides, highlighting her curves. When her eyes finally meet mine, my heart squeezes in my chest.

We stare at one another, mentally cataloguing changes, or at least that's what I'm doing as I take in the way her brown hair tumbles around her like a chocolate river, and her clear blue eyes that are wide and dilated. She's... stunning. She always was, but she's aged like a fine wine and it's impossible not to appreciate her beauty.

Alex clears her throat next to me, reminding me she's there, and I step away from Jess and back towards her.

"Oh, this is Alex, Alex, this is Jessica Scott. She's an old friend."

Jess and Alex smile at one another, awkwardly shaking hands before Jess fumbles around with our tickets, almost dropping them twice. I've never seen her nervous, not even the first day I kissed her.

Her eyes finally land on Alex. "You're sat at table number five, which is near the mirror to the left. The rest of your table is seated already."

She thrusts our tickets back into my hands, and she hesitates, our fingers brushing just for a second, sending a zap of electricity down my spine.

There are a thousand unsaid words in the air between us, threatening a tornado of emotions, but neither of us can speak. I'm not even sure what I'd say to her. I don't know where I'd start.

"Thank you, Jessica." Alex smiles before she takes my hand, and we walk towards our table.

A snapshot of memories erupts, surrounding me like a fog. I hadn't considered the possibility of crossing paths with Jess again, despite never being able to forget her. I knew she had moved back to London, and I might have stalked Nora's Instagram account a little too much in the past, but Jess rarely featured. I think there was one picture from over four years ago and that is it.

"Erm, Liam? Are you okay?" Alex asks timidly. I hadn't even realised we had sat down at our table, let alone remembered that she was next to me.

"I'm sorry, it's just a blast from the past seeing Jess. We haven't seen each other for..." I stop to think for a second. "Damn... ten years." I lean into Alex, pecking her cheek.

"She's beautiful," Alex says, glancing back over to where Jess stands. "She's *the* Jess?"

I nod robotically. "She is." I'm still confused at how I feel about seeing her, my mind whirling as her sultry voice echoes through the sound system.

"Hi everyone, it is so good to see some familiar and some new faces tonight. Thank you all for purchasing tickets for our very first charity event for 'Giving back'. We're thrilled to have you here and raise some much-needed funds for our therapy programs to help children who have suffered through domestic violence, drug abuse." She pauses for a second, collecting herself before she pushes her shoulders back again.

"We all know how stretched our mental health services are these days so with your help our programs will offer different types of therapy, as well as fun days that will include sports, picnic days, swimming and much more for families and children in need in the UK. So, let's get down to the night's events."

My mind buzzes with the knowledge that this is all her event. She did something that means so much to her and she owns it. I swell with pride for the girl I knew who was so broken by her past, and looking at the Jess up on the stage now, she's anything but. She's a successful, confident, beautiful woman now.

"We have a raffle that Nora will come around shortly to offer you. All prizes are listed on your table. We also have our silent auction and some of the top prizes to bid on include a city break to Paris for two lucky people, an overnight stay in this very hotel in our Penthouse suite, which I must say is exceptional plus dinner and breakfast included, a weekday day trip to our on-site spa and many more. I also can't let the evening pass me by without thanking my boss, Jean-Pierre, for letting us use this beautiful ballroom tonight and my whole events team for putting up with my incessant demands the last two weeks. I've worked here for years now and you have all confirmed why I love it here so much by coming together for us tonight." She swallows thickly before smiling at the table in front of her where I'm guessing her work family is. She clears her throat, searching for others too. "Zoey, Nora, I also know that tonight would not be possible without either of you. I'm more grateful than you know." Her eyes fill again as she inhales and exhales quickly.

"Thank you, everyone for coming tonight. Let's get me a drink before I start crying again, shall we? Enjoy dinner, the band will be on after dessert." She moves to walk off stage but quickly returns to the microphone, laughing. "Oh, and the first one to get Nora to dance wins a drink from me!"

The whole room erupts in applause and laughter. I'm mesmerised as Jess saunters over to her table where Nora is waiting with open arms for her. Cam and Harriet are there too, all bursting with pride for her.

I sit, messing with some loose lint I picked out of my tux, feeling downtrodden, watching them all talk animatedly, when I feel a tightness in my throat. My breathing begins to feel forced, and an unwelcome warmth rushes through me.

"Hey," I say to Alex, swallowing my guilt, jealousy, or whatever the fuck else this is I'm feeling. "I'm just going to step outside for a minute."

"Is everything okay?" she replies, genuine concern forcing a frown.

"Yeah, yeah. Just really warm all of a sudden."

"Oh, okay. Take your time," she says, and squeezes my forearm lightly.

My pulse quickens with every step, jabbing at my tight tux collar as my mind swarms with questions.

Is she married?

Does she live with anyone?

Would we even know each other anymore?

I step outside and suck in a deep breath of cold air, willing my thoughts to chill the fuck out. I have no idea why my brain is running so wild, and I feel like I've unlocked a teenage angst I haven't felt in years; a debilitating mix of anxiety and stimulation that makes my head spin.

Does she think I look good? She looks so fucking good.

I run my hands through my hair and straighten my bow tie nervously.

Fuck, I'm getting nowhere.

I lean back against the wall and then double myself over. I close my eyes and take two deep breaths. I'm having the mother of all meltdowns over a girl I haven't seen for ten years...

"You alright, mate?" Some slightly too drunk guy asks me while swirling some amber liquid in the glass he's holding.

"Yeah," I say, straightening up as I exhale deeply and watch my breath billow in the cold air. "Fuckin' peachy."

"Ha! Been there, my friend. It'll be alright. You need me to get someone for you?"

Great question. "Oh, no. I'm good, thanks."

"Then I suggest booze."

I smile a genuine smile. "Noted."

I can't stop myself from glancing over to Jessica's table through the window. I watch as she throws her head back in laughter at something Nora said. Her whole body is vibrating with happiness and it's my favourite way to see Jess after all these years.

I think back to the last time we were together and my shoulders slump; she was so lost and when she pushed me away, I felt lost, too. I spent a lot of time trying to figure out what I wanted after we broke up. I partied a lot and threw myself into work to keep myself busy. I'm reaping the rewards now because our company is growing and from what I can see, it seems like Jess is happy, too. It's really good to see her happy.

She catches my eye as I slide back into my chair and we stare at each other, lost in a daze for a few minutes, tension leaping around us even from tables away. I don't want to look away from her but when her eyes falter as Nora demands the attention of the room to announce that the silent auction is now open, I know the moment has passed.

I immediately see Nora heading my way after her announcement, and I stand ready for her embrace. "Hey stranger!" Her tiny arms wrap around me, and I let out an *oof* at the contact.

"Hey yourself! Check you out, big shot!"

"Pfft, big shot, hardly." She eyes me, conflicting emotions dancing there as she shakes her head. "I'm sorry, I just can't believe you're here."

I smile at her. "It's so good to see you, Nora. What you and Jess are doing here is... really amazing."

"Yeah, it is, but it was all Jess. You know how she is when she sets her mind to something." Nora's eyes fall to my table as Alex stands next to me.

"Oh God, where are my manners? Nora, this is Alex. Nora is Jess' sister," I say to Alex.

Nora extends her hand to shake Alex's. "It's lovely to meet you."

"You too. What Jessica is doing here today, it's really wonderful." She smiles.

"Thank you. It's been a long time in the planning, but she's doing it."

"She's doing it." I echo Nora's words, smiling.

"I'm going to get another drink really quick. Do either of you want anything?" Alex brushes her hands over my arm before we shake our heads in response and she heads away from us.

Nora tracks the touch between us, but doesn't ask the most obvious question. "So, are you going to bid on anything?" She passes me the list, and I bid on the trip to Paris. I know I won't win it, but I tell Nora that I'd still like to donate, regardless. She beams at me. "We'll have you volunteering in no time. Look, I've got to make the rounds, but see you soon?" I nod before she slips to the next table.

As the evening moves on, I get the distinct feeling that Jessica is avoiding me. I haven't seen her since the meal, and the band is halfway through their first set already.

"I think you should go find her." Alex surprises me, pulling her chair closer to mine, and I spin to face her, resting my back against my chair.

"I... I don't know." I say, rubbing the stubble on my chin.

"I know. This is Jess we're talking about. Come on, we've been friends for years Liam, I might not live in the same country as you and see you everyday, but I know enough to know about her. This is serendipity or fate or whatever." She flails her arms excitedly as she talks. Ever the romantic.

My lips curve into a smile. "You and your destiny shit." I tease her.

"Don't mock me. I haven't seen you in a year and I'm spending the last night I'm in town, watching you pine after your ex. At the very least, make it interesting for me." She grins just as her phone rings.

"Oh, it's Jules. You good for a sec?" I nod as she answers her phone and walks into the foyer.

I sip my now warm glass of champagne, my eyes scanning the room again. Alex is right. I need to find her and at the very least talk to her for longer than a few minutes. I'm not sure about fate or serendipity, but it sure feels like we were meant to be in the same place tonight.

When I spot a tumble of dark hair near the bar, my pulse kicks up to galloping speeds. The new womanly curves of her body give her away, that and her height. But it's the way she stands that catches my attention; alluring, but not flashy. It's a natural sway of her hips as she shifts her weight. It's the delicate toss of her chestnut waves over her shoulder that makes her so fucking beautiful. My breath hitches in my throat and I fight to clear it. Abandoning my champagne, I turn my attentions to who she's talking to.

The group of men in suits are all pawing at her feet, enamoured by the beauty in front of them, and I can hardly blame them, even if my blood is running green right now, watching them all fawn over her. The sound she makes when she laughs is musical. Every note lingers in the air and floats around the room. My head bows slightly as I remember that I used to be the one to make her laugh like that.

The group begins to dwindle, and I head over to talk to her.

I adjust my bow tie as I walk for no reason than needing to do something with my hands. Oxygen is fleeing my body quicker than I can gain it back as I get closer to her.

"Liam!" I hear Harriet almost yell over my shoulder. "You promised me a dance."

"Ah! I did. I wouldn't want to disappoint," I say, incredibly disappointed that I didn't get to Jess, but just as I'm about to retreat to the dancefloor with Harriet Jess' eyes land on mine. "Later?" I mouth.

"Later," she mouths back, offering me the most fucking gorgeous smile.

The white dancefloor sparkles beneath mine and Harriet's feet, and the ceiling drapes cloud above us as the band croons a classic Frank

Sinatra number. We fall into an easy step, letting the slow rhythm control our movements.

"How are your parents doing?" Harriet asks.

"They're good. Dad still works too much, but Mum keeps herself busy volunteering. They're happy."

"And you?"

I glance down at Harriet as mischief dances in her eyes, filled with things she isn't asking directly. "I'm happy. I work in Dad's upper management team, securing the big clients."

Harriet hums under her breath. "I knew you'd go far," she says, as we dance quietly for a while longer.

The song changes and Harriet breaks our hold.

She eyes me for a second. "She's not seeing anyone, you know."

"What?"

"Oh, you know. I might be old, but I'm not stupid."

I look at her and she winks at me knowingly and it takes all my energy to stop myself from fist pumping the air right now and scream *yes!*

"Go on, you. I won't keep you all night."

"It's been a pleasure, Harriett," I say, and kiss her on the cheek.

I walk over to the bar again, searching for Jess but coming up blank.

15

Jessica

I catch Nora and drag her out to the small terrace at the back of the ballroom. When we reach the fresh air, I manage to inflate my lungs to full capacity, not realising how stifling it was in there. My eyes close as the cool air lashes around me and I'm grateful for the cool evening for once, especially as my skin has been at least a hundred degrees hotter than usual since I saw him.

The hustle and bustle of London buzzes in the streets beneath us; in the distance a siren wails, people laugh and wander along the pavement across from us, the smell of car and bus fumes float in the atmosphere. It's a mild distraction from the way my body feels, but one I'm grateful for.

"Are you okay? Did you talk to Liam? You know, of all the gin bars, or however it is that saying goes..." she laughs.

"I... it's strange seeing him again..." I exhale, wishing I could run my fingers through my hair. but then I remember how long it took earlier to make it look like this, so I refrain. "He looks fucking gorgeous, doesn't he? I'm not just looking at him with rose tinted glasses, right?"

Nora shakes her head. "You're far from wrong. He looks hot. So do you though. I think he'll lose his cool when he's around you. I can see it in his eyes." Nora winks at me like that'll calm the nerves taking flight in my belly. Honestly, I feel like I'm travelling on a freight train about ready to jump off every time I try and rationalise what is happening tonight.

"I don't know. This is weird. I'm awkward. He's ridiculously hot. And, that makes me..."

"Hot?" Nora replies, smirking at me.

"Yes. Definitely." I exhale loudly.

"I'm not sure I see the problem, apart from this little freak out. Which, by the way, is highly entertaining for someone who usually loves control as much as you do. I think you should talk to him some more."

"The problem is the beautiful, red-haired goddess he brought with him. Her name is Alex. I think it might be the same Alex from before... when we were at college. Maybe they've been together this whole time." Jealousy blasts into my brain like a shockwave and I try desperately to ignore it and rationalise my thoughts. "I mean, I haven't asked him, but what are the chances, right?"

"Oh, right, I spoke to her. She's really nice too. And gorgeous," Nora sighs.

I want to kick her, but my dress is tight enough that I wouldn't be able to do it well, so instead I scowl and huff like a child because that's not what I want to hear.

"I know. It's shit timing... story of my life." Something else has been bothering me for the last hour though, "I think... I can't help but feel like I need to apologise for being so awful to him, though. The way things ended with us..." I mumble, knocking my heel against the concrete floor.

"Talk to him, explain. You might feel better then. You're only talking. No harm done, right?" Nora hugs me, and it makes me feel marginally better. "We better get back; I can do the end of the night speech. Go find that lover boy." She pokes me and just as we turn around and I'm about to tell her that he isn't *my* lover boy, I slam into a wall of muscle, then I hear a familiar voice; one that makes me instantly hot and needy.

"Lover boy, huh?" His low, husky voice permeates the doorway we are wedged between. My hands rest on his chest from where we collided and all I feel is strength... a lot of it.

My face burns crimson as Nora laughs out loud, makes excuses, and leaves us to it, shouting, "Bye, lover boy," as she walks away, as though she isn't abandoning me right now.

He moves past me and settles down in one of the small outdoor seats before gesturing for me to sit opposite him.

"Talk to me, Jessica Scott. Tell me about you. What has happened in ten years? Please tell me your love for milkshakes hasn't died because I might be physically wounded." His hand clutches his chest and a look of genuine concern flashes across his face as I sit in the chair opposite him, perching on the edge.

"Are you kidding? Of course, I still love milkshakes. I don't have them as much anymore. That kind of makes me sad. When Nora and I moved, we never found anyone who measured up to Shake Sam." I push my lip out to pretend a pout face and Liam chuckles lightly.

"Yeah, he was the best, wasn't he... How long did you guys stay in Kent for?" I try to focus on his face, but that's near enough impossible to do when his broad shoulders are wider than the chair he's sitting in and his thick thighs are flexing underneath his black suit trousers. I briefly clear my throat, pretending I wasn't just checking him out.

"Well, Nora and I stayed in Kent for university after we finished college, and then we both moved back here. I've worked in this hotel in the events management team since moving here, and Nora is a therapist not far from our town house, over near Victoria Park."

"Hm, that's great. Sounds like you're both doing amazing things." He pauses, taking a sip from his cut glass tumbler filled with an amber liquid. "Did you guys buy the town house?"

He acts so casual, like he doesn't even realise he looks like sex on legs whilst he just *sips his drink*.

I internally berate myself for staring again before answering him, "It's Nora's grandmother's house. We wouldn't be that lucky to live in that area if she didn't let us live there. We pay her rent, but it probably isn't even close to what she would get with actual tenants. You'll have to come by and see it sometime. I mean, that is, if you wanted to or weren't busy. It's fine if you are busy, that is. Everyone is busy these days, so I get it. I'm always busy. Busy busy," I rush out.

Liam laughs and smiles a boyish grin. "I love it when you ramble... I've missed it." He takes a sharp inhale as he breaks our eye contact. "I'd love to come by and see you and Nora."

I internally deflate.

Me and Nora. Of course, he wants to see both of us. We were all friends for years.

Fuck, his girlfriend is here, and I'm sitting here having heart eyes over someone else's boyfriend.

His gaze returns to me. My whole body shivers and vibrates with heat simultaneously from his gaze. It's almost too much to handle tonight... him, us, him looking at me like *that*. So, I force myself to talk to distract from the hurricane silently thrashing around my body as I try to remember that he has a girlfriend. "So, what have you been doing for the last ten years?"

His throat clears. "Working with Dad. Mum doesn't really work anymore; she volunteers at our old school. You know he always wanted me to join his business and I love it. I think I'm ready for him to step back a bit though. The company needs a freshen up and he's reluctant for me to take more control, but I'm wearing him down. I hope. I'm trying to take the business internationally too. We have clients who sought us out from the states so we'll see where that goes too." He beams.

I remember our job we had for his dad, cleaning his office properties. We spent so much time together back then, but I've almost forgotten what it was like. I let the memories creep back in. It was always a lot of fun, not a lot of cleaning, but a lot of fun, especially after we got together. We would clean, kiss, clean, kiss and then forget about cleaning altogether and just kiss until it was time to leave.

"I miss your mum. She was always so sweet..." I pause, hoping he doesn't ask about mine and then I change the subject. "It sounds like things have expanded a lot since the days we used to mess around in that one place over in Kensington."

"Oh yeah, I remember that place alright." Hesitation flickers across his face before he holds my attention, taking me prisoner with his warm gaze, leaning forwards his elbows on his thighs as his fresh scent weaves its way around me. "I remember how nervous you made me. All the time spent around you... it would take all my self-control not to touch you. It was fucking torture that day you goaded me with almost dating Dan from my team, so when we finally kissed..." He rubs his five-o'clock shadow and smiles at me, letting the tension between us speak for itself.

He's cute and I'm screwed.

I laugh nervously. The silence between us is thick, syrupy and for a split second, I think he is going to move closer to me, but he doesn't.

Is it wrong to feel disappointed? Yes, Jessica it is. Stop it.

"My mum would lose her mind if she knew we were here together, right now... have you... ah, never mind, actually." He stops himself from continuing. Panic rises in my body for the fear of him asking about the one person I still don't want to talk about. Even after all these years and the therapy, I still can't bring myself to talk about her.

"What?" I ask before I can stop myself, praying that my nerves keep quiet.

"I was going to ask if you were seeing anyone or if you had found someone to spend your life with. Then I realised it isn't my place to ask."

I pause for a second to think about Evan. I can barely call that a relationship but I suppose we were seeing each other for a while. Other than that, my history with men has been pretty diabolical and there has definitely been no one I wanted to spend my life with.

"No, I haven't... no one ever loved me the way you did." I mumble the last part because that is one hell of a statement for a casual catch up on the terrace. My throat thickens and my lips part searching for air that doesn't come.

Fuck, why did I say that. Fuck.

"Jess," he breathes, his warm hand is covering mine where it rests on my knee. The zing of contact burns through my skin and directly sizzles into my bloodstream.

I roll my shoulders to ease the tension building at the back of my neck and fold my arms across my body, moving away from his touch. Even that was a little much for me to admit to Liam and I can't stop my body from going into protection mode.

"But you, where is your date?"

My question breaks the spell and Liam physically recoils, as though remembering something he should have never forgotten. Neither of us speaks. I can barely bring my eyes to look at him, but I know he is looking at me. I can feel it. I'm grateful when I hear Nora's voice fill the room at the stage, announcing the winners of the silent auction. We both stand, making our way back into the ballroom.

Even though my stomach is in knots right now, I force myself to act unaffected. I smile when I see the elderly couple win the penthouse suite; I clap on cue and to the outside world, I look like I'm not having a complete meltdown in my head.

The last auction was the trip to Paris. Liam and I have a clear view of Nora as her eyes shuffle around the room, flicking around a little before she announces the winner.

16

Jessica

"Liam Taylor, your bid was the highest at £25,000 and you have won the trip to Paris for two."

My mouth gapes, practically hitting the floor as I turn to face Liam. I'm not entirely sure I'm breathing; all the clapping and applause turns to white noise around me.

Liam's cheeks are pink, his smile is coy as he stands to move back inside and write his cheque to Nora for £25,000.

£25,000!!

God, I'm not ever going to be over that.

The band resumes their final few songs, and people start to crowd the dancefloor again when I realise I'm still sitting outside on the terrace alone, the cold evening air nipping at my skin. My arms instinctively wrap around myself as I brush off the chill and head back inside.

"I can't believe you bid that much on the Paris trip, Liam. You can back out if you want to." I hear Nora talking to Liam quietly as I walk up behind them both. Neither of them noticing me yet.

"I wanted to donate more, actually. I didn't think my bid would win; I thought I would lose to one of the bigwigs in the room, but I'm glad I won. It means something to give to your charity. I want to help where I can, and this is a good start." His honesty slices through my defences and I feel a warmth spread across my chest.

"I'm guessing the lucky woman you came with tonight will be going with you to Paris?" Nora asks tentatively. I clear my throat and Liam does the same.

"Ah, who knows. Maybe... We'll see."

I want to scream, *take me, take me, I will happily go with you*, but I don't. I keep my cool. Somehow.

Nora looks at me over Liam's shoulder. "Can you believe this guy?" she asks incredulously.

I shake my head, forcing a smile before Nora makes her excuses and leaves us alone.

Liam links our hands together when he turns towards me, and he leans in to whisper, "Dance with me?" Not giving me an option to say no, he whisks us towards the dancefloor.

It's on the tip of my tongue to ask about his girlfriend again, but all of those thoughts suffocate as soon as I'm pressed against his hard chest, with his arms wrapped around my back and arm.

He's so familiar, yet we haven't seen each other for such a long time that I barely know him. Except I can feel him. Like the way you can feel a storm coming, or the first snowfall in winter. My heart used to beat for him; for his smile, his touch, the way he would look at me, like I was the girl who was made just for him. My mind swims in a sea of memories, and the life we could have lived. *Until I pushed him away.*

Guilt lays heavily in my stomach as I think about the way I handled everything. I was so hurt and lost, grasping for control over anything, so when he was ready to go back to London, I couldn't handle another loss and I stupidly pushed him. It's not something I've ever forgotten and I've regretted it every day for the last ten years.

"Liam..." I pause, looking at him. "I'm so sorry."

He frowns, "For what?"

I swallow the lump in my throat. "Everything. For pushing you away. For not recognising what we had. Just... everything."

Liam squeezes my back where his hand rests, never letting our gaze break. The corners of his mouth lift into a smile. "I appreciate you saying that. I really do. Losing you," he pauses, lost in thought, "it was rough. I went through a lot of emotions; I hated you, I loved you again, I missed you, but I never, ever forgot you, Jess. The timing wasn't right for us back then."

I observe every line that has settled on his face, especially the smile lines that have formed around his eyes. I want to touch them to understand the emotions that put them there. My eyes drop to his lips, starting at the curve of his bottom lip and moving to his perfect cupid's bow. I used to kiss that cupid's bow because it was my favourite part of his lips. His eyelashes flare across his lids like a peacock's tail, full and dark, yet masculine, framing his eyes.

During my assessment of him, I hadn't noticed his eyes scan my face as though he is trying to figure out what I'm thinking. Without a single warning, he spins me out, making my dress twirl around me like a fan, whilst the kaleidoscope of the room blurs in my vision. The laugh that erupts from my lips is light and airy, as I spin back towards him and my body nestles perfectly between his arms again, like it belonged there.

As soon as I'm steady on my feet, he dips me backwards, tipping the world upside down. And it makes me realise that this is exactly the theme of the night; everything that was up is now down. I can't stop another bubble of laughter that spills from my lips when he rights me. Our noses are centimetres apart, our breath mixing as we both lose all our playfulness. His eyes darken and, in a second, it's replaced with clouds.

"Do you remember much from back then?" he asks, emotion lacing his voice. It catches me off guard. My palms twitch and heat tingles along my spine.

"Of course I remember. You were my best friend, Liam.." When he doesn't answer, I continue, "Do you think about it?"

"More than you know, Jess." We stare at each other longingly, the tornado of desire and longing, heartache, first kisses and last goodbyes swirling between us. When his eyes dart to my lips, I forget everything, my mind overwhelmed by his proximity. *We shouldn't be this close, we shouldn't kiss, but just for a moment, I wish we could.*

Suspended in time, trapped in this globe of past and present colliding together, it feels like we're the only ones in the room. It's not until something catches his attention and he looks beyond my shoulder. His brows furrow as he stares, and I can practically hear his brain contemplating something. His body stiffens the moment he makes the decision, and his hands loosen his hold on me.

"Is everything okay?"

"Yeah, yeah."

I turn my head and see Alex looking on, her face unreadable.

"I'm sorry, Jess. I have to go."

"Oh yeah, of course." I drop my arms quickly and try my hardest to ignore the sheer level of disappointment brazenly thrashing through my veins.

He walks away from me then before calling back.

"Scotty?"

"Yeah?"

"You really do look beautiful."

17

Jessica

I wake up in a fluster. My heart pounds, my breath is sharp and sweat sticks to my skin. I force myself to look around the hotel room, remembering where I am.

I'm in The Clover hotel.

With Nora.

I'm safe.

I take several deep breaths, calming my racing pulse as Nora stirs next to me.

"Morning. You were moving around a lot last night. You sleep badly?"

"I had that nightmare again." I rub my face, trying to wipe away my dream.

"You haven't had one in a while; do you want to talk about it?" Nora pulls the pillow and tucks it under her chin.

"I don't know, it was just the same as always."

"I think maybe seeing Liam again made you think about the past."

"Probably." I shrug it off, not feeling like going over everything, especially given the way he left so quickly last night.

"You don't have to talk about it right now, but you should consider bringing it up to your therapist again. She'll help. But for the sake of my profession, I have to say I can tell you're shutting down right now and I need you to remember that you aren't the reason she left, okay?"

I knew she was right, but believing it has always been hard for me. The two people that I had loved the most were no longer in my life, and that's something I've been learning to overcome. Therapy helps, but when things happen that feel out of my control, like seeing Liam last night, then I struggle. I'm envious of Alex getting to take Liam home, even though I have no right to be feeling that. I'm still reeling and adjusting from seeing him at all and filtering through the emotions that are linked to him and my mum... it's just a lot sometimes.

I turn to face Nora, knowing I need to give her a reply or she'll lock me in this room until I crack. "I know, but I'm trying here. I don't know how you're so calm all the time. Teach me your ways, oh wise one, but do it after breakfast, 'kay?" I fake a smile at her and leave the confines of the cosy bed, favouring a shower instead.

I know I'm quiet during breakfast. The beady eyes of my family assessing me tell me as much, but I just need a minute to process some thoughts. I'm on my second cup of coffee, and it doesn't seem to be shifting the haze left from an awful night's sleep.

My eyes sting as I stare into space and the only thing that breaks my trance is my phone ringing as the screen lights up telling me 'Lover boy' is calling.

God, stupid nicknames. I'd forgotten he was saved in my phone. What are the chances that we'd both have the same numbers as ten years ago?

"Hi," I answer quickly as I duck away from the table.

"Good morning. How did you sleep?" His voice is rough like sandpaper. It sounds like he's just waking up and it should be illegal to sound so sexy this early.

"Yeah, okay, I guess. I'm just having breakfast with Nora, Cam and Harriett. Can I call you later?"

"Oh, okay, sure. Sorry, I didn't mean to intrude." He sounds deflated.

"You aren't. I just. Shit. Okay, I'm grumpy this morning. I didn't sleep very well and I'm a bit of a bear when that happens."

His guffaw carries through the phone a little too loudly. "I definitely remember, I also remember snarky Jess and hangry Jess.—she really didn't like me—but you don't poke the Jess-bear in the mornings."

"Wow, you really make me sound like a dream," I chortle sarcastically.

"Ooh, snarky Jess. Okay, well, I can handle you. I can help make you feel better if you want? I know a great milkshake hut that might help. It's no Sam Shake's, but it's really good."

I pause, my teeth latching onto my cheek.

"What is this, Liam?"

Another pregnant silence drips over the conversation.

"I-I'm confused," I admit, urging the conversation on.

"About what, Scotty?" he asks innocently.

"Last night. You. Alex. Dance. '*Hey Scotty, you're beautiful.*' Walk off into the distance. Close curtains."

"I think your Liam impression needs work." He pauses, taking in a breath. "But in all seriousness, that's why I called."

"Okay..."

"Last night was amazing."

"O-kay." My brows meet in the middle and my nose scrunches up in confusion.

"I don't want to wait another ten years to see you."

"Okay." I say again robotically, trying to pick apart what he's implying but coming up blank.

"Scotty?"

"What?"

"Go out with me?"

I let out a disbelieving laugh. "Two women? Very brazen of you."

"There's no Alex."

"There's no Alex?"

"Exactly."

"There was definitely an Alex last night. Please don't tell me you…"

"Jess, you are infuriating," he interrupts. "I could do this all day. But as I was saying. I know a great shake place."

"What do you mean there's no Alex?" I ask again, ignoring the fact that he knows the way to my heart with milkshakes.

"I mean exactly that. She lives in America, on her way back home right now, actually. Alex and I have been friends for years. She got tickets for your event last night, her last night in town, and trust me when I say, I'm not her type." He laughs, and it just makes my anger rise.

Heat prickles my back, making me sweat. I honestly think he's just messing with me now.

"O-kay… will you stop with the cryptic stuff?"

"Alex is a lesbian. She was my date last night *as a friend*. We've been friends since college, but being on opposite ends of the world, we don't see or talk that often anymore. Last night was just two friends catching up."

Oh.

"Why did you make me believe that she was your girlfriend?"

Liam huffs out a reply, "I… I don't know. I'm sorry, I should've said something. I guess I didn't realise how it looked."

"Yeah, no shit," I mutter under my breath.

"I don't want to play games with you, Jess. I'm sorry about last night. That's why I'm calling… to set the record straight."

My anger dissipates as quickly as it rose. My skin cooling to body temperature again. I exhale a breath that's long and purposeful.

I let the silence fill the call for a second before I add, "Here I thought you were calling with the promise of milkshakes."

His laugh rumbles through the phone speaker, making me smile. "Does that mean you'll go out with me?"

"Well, that depends. Thing is, I have lots of men fighting for my attention. You know it might be tricky to squeeze you in," I lie.

"It doesn't surprise me that I'd have to fight for you, but exactly how burley are these other guys? Just need to know how many press-ups I should be aiming for at the gym."

I smirk at that thought because Jesus that would be hot. Sweaty Liam, pumping iron at the gym... yeah, okay, that's spicy.

"Well, let's see. I'd say that most of the men are gym bunnies, in fact, I'm sure one of them is into boxing too. Jeez, looks like you will have your hands full." If teasing was a sport, I'd pretty much be an Olympian.

"I'll be living at my gym from now on then and if anyone asks why I'm there, I'll tell them I'm in training to fight off all men from a beautiful woman I want."

Bold. I like it.

"I guess I could move some of them around. Don't tell anyone, but none of them can handle snarky Jess like you can," I whisper-shout down the phone.

"Is that a compliment, Scotty? I'm flattered and a little put out still that you are considering rearranging these guys and not just sacking them off altogether."

"I'm loyal, you know, Liam. I don't like to let people down. Plus, this one guy has a huge—"

He interrupts me before I can finish my little white lie, "Lalalala, don't tell me."

My laugh falls freely through the phone. "I'm free Tuesday after work around eight. Come to our house for dinner? We can get milkshakes another time. No guys will be there to fight you either, just Nora, who arguably you might want to be more scared of."

"Finally, she lets me have a date. Eight is perfect. Ping me your home address. Oh, and I'll have you know that I can and will be the only guy for you by the end of the evening."

"So confident Mr Taylor. I guess we will have to see... Bye, lover boy." I catch myself grinning like a school kid at my phone.

He's managed to change my mood and I'm not mad about it.

18

Liam

M onday morning comes too slowly, and I'm grateful for the distraction of work again. I cut across London's rush hour traffic in my black Tesla Roadster, silently careening over lanes to reach my office.

The sky is dark and bruised with clouds promising rainfall as I pull into the underground car park.

I forced myself to be busy on Sunday after I coached my Little League rugby kids, because if I didn't, I would've been over to see Jess in a heartbeat.

For the last ten years, I've unintentionally become a serial dater. Sometimes I really think I'll try and make it work with a woman, but I never feel how I want to feel, so I end things before they turn serious. My work has been my biggest achievement and the most time-consuming part of my life, so when I need to keep my mind off my spiralling love life, I throw myself into work.

I breeze into the office to see Helena sat at her desk waiting with my usual black coffee in hand.

"Good morning, Liam. Here's your coffee. If you have a minute, we need to catch up on some of your meetings, as some have changed since Friday." She checks her computer. "Oh, and your mother would like you to call her." Helena is the type of PA that is dedicated to her job. She's worked for my father since I was a teenager and we all know who the real brain behind this operation is.

"Thanks, Helena. I saw that Jonah has rearranged in Chicago. Is that the change you were talking about?"

She nods, standing and tucking her grey hair behind her ears as we walk in sync towards my office.

"Let's get another date in with him asap. I want to get that meeting in before the end of October. I wonder if he'd be okay with me coming to Chicago?" I think out loud. "I'll call him. Also, can you arrange to have a bunch of white roses delivered to Miss Jessica Scott at the Clover Hotel, please? I'd like the card here so I can write it before they are delivered."

Her eyebrows shoot to her hairline as her heels immediately stop clicking next to me. "Jessica... as in sweet little Jessica, who you were in love with when you were kids?"

I give her a knowing smile as I turn and push my office door open with my back. "Don't be so shocked, I do have a heart, Helena," I joke as I walk towards my office, leaving her to ponder that.

I drop a text to my mum, telling her that I'll call her tonight. I try to go to my parents a couple of times a month for dinner. I'm curious to see how she will react when I tell her I bumped into Jess again.

Thirty minutes later, Helena arrives with the card for Jessica's flowers and I think about what to write for way longer than I probably should. I even practice writing it on my notepad next to my desk.

> *Just in case all those other men forgot to send you flowers.*
> *Your lover boy x*

I jump straight into work and take five calls back-to-back until 1 pm. Mostly mergers that needed reviewing with my father, but a couple of calls to discuss staffing needs for the next quarter.

My intercom buzzes loudly, Helena practically squeaks with excitement through it when she speaks, "I have Jessica on line one for you."

"Thanks, Helena." I press the button to merge the call to Jess. "Hello, Miss Scott. To what do I owe this pleasure?"

"Mr Taylor, you shouldn't have sent me flowers at work. You're ruining my credibility of being an ice queen." Her tone is playful and makes me smile.

"You're welcome. Also, I'm sure you are just as formidable as you were before the flowers. Everyone needs a weakness; just so happens I might be yours."

"So sure of yourself... maybe I've got you right where I want you."

Yeah, she does.

"That, Scotty, is exactly the truth," I laugh. "Do you need me to bring anything for dinner tomorrow?"

"Not a thing, just yourself."

"That I can do. I'll see you tomorrow."

"Thank you again... Bye, lover boy," she sings songs before hanging up.

My pulse has picked up, and my palms are sweaty at just the sound of her voice. I need to get a handle on these emotions, otherwise I'll end up being the biggest loser around her tomorrow night.

"Mate, you about ready for that beer?" My friend and work colleague, Grayson, rounds the corner and stands in the doorway of my office. I look down at the clock on my desk, not realising the time.

"Yeah man, just let me fire off this email and I'm good to go."

Grayson has worked for us for around five years, and we've been friends just as long. As well as working closely together, we both coach the rugby team on Sundays, arguably spending way too much time with each other. He's a huge pain in my arse some days, especially with his womanising ways, but most of the time he's alright.

I turn off my computer, pick up my jacket, and we walk out into the cold September evening. Those rain clouds from earlier are still lingering, making me thankful for my jacket.

We amble into the pub not far from the office; the walls are lined with old fashioned wallpaper and the carpets are red and gold. Mahogany furniture lines the space, and the smell of stale beer lingers in the air as we find our usual table.

"Two pints, please," Grayson orders.

I shrug out of my jacket just as our beers are placed on the bar. Grabbing the chilled glasses, I make sure not to spill the fluffy foam floating on the top as we walk to our table.

Grayson eyes me as I take my first sip. "You seem... I don't know. You haven't smiled this much since I've known you, mate. It's freaking me out a bit."

I rub my face and realise he's right; my shit-eating grin just won't go away.

He eyes me again and gives me an eyebrow whilst he sips his beer. "You've met someone?"

I'm still smiling when I respond, "Do you remember that charity event last week?"

He nods and sucks the foam from his beer off his top lip.

"Well, I bumped into someone I knew when I was growing up and... fuck me, she's grown up. She's even more stunning than I remembered." My mind flashes back to how she looked that night as a prickle of heat crawls down my spine.

"She must be something else. She got any sisters?" he winks and laughs.

"She is something else." I pause for a second. "We dated when we were kids, but things were... complicated back then."

Grayson takes note of my tone. "You wanna talk about it?"

I do want to talk about it, but I want to talk to Jess. Hearing her apologise the other night, well, I didn't realise how much I needed to hear it. I need to spend time with her again to see if the feelings I had are even valid anymore. We're adults now and a lot has changed. So, for now, I shake my head. "I'll talk to her first before I get ahead of myself. I'm seeing her tomorrow night." I take another cold sip of my beer. "What about you, ponyboy? Got any women putting notches in your bedpost?"

"You know me man, I don't talk endgame, I don't let women stay over. Same shit, different woman. Every. Damn. Week. I like it like that." He shrugs and takes another drink. I see something passing over his face, but as soon as it's there, it's gone again and I don't push.

Jessica

"Nora?" I call as I walk through our hallway, but coming up blank. I spot her in the garden, pruning her vegetable patch. I swear that woman lives for those vegetables some days.

Our garden is narrow but long and Nora has made it a little haven where we often sit outside and eat dinner.

Solar lights weave across the fences, reaching all the way down to where the patio meets Nora's vegetable patch. There is a narrow pathway between two small patches of grass further down and the opposite side to the patch is an array of flowers that Nora plants, that are currently all in bloom, looking like a rainbow dancing in the breeze. I sit on the outdoor furniture and watch Nora as she swans around, trimming this and pruning that with her headphones in, humming a tune, completely lost in her own little world.

She eventually turns her head as she spots me, just before she loses her balance and ends up in her lettuce patch. The laughter that leaves my body is obnoxious and loud as I curl over, gasping for breath.

"Oh my God, Jessica! Come and help me or you will be eating these lettuces with an imprint of my bum on them." I hurry over, still giggling, and grab her hand to pull her up.

She playfully pushes me once she has found her feet and tells me to grab the basket full of tomatoes and bring them inside.

"Tell me those flowers are from Liam." She points to the white roses that are now sitting in a vase on the kitchen table. I nod and smile, regaining my composure, letting a sneak of a blush settle in my cheeks, heating me from the inside out.

"He sent them to my office today. He is coming here for dinner tomorrow night, remember? I'm cooking but..." I hesitate, knowing what I'm about to say will have her cackling at me, "I need you to be a no sex buffer for us."

Nora whips her head around to face me. "Sorry, you want me to stop you two from having sex? Oh, honey, that will *not* happen. That's like asking me to stop the rain," she cackles just like I thought she would, and continues pottering around the kitchen.

"Seriously, Nora. I just need you to be there with us. Then he'll go home and that will be that. No sex," I beg.

I almost have to convince myself here, because the truth is that all I have been able to think about since the charity event is Liam. Being trapped underneath his warm, hard body would be an absolute dream, but I can't. I'm not ready. But I can't *think* around him, and I need to be able to think if I'm going to go there with him.

Sometimes what you really, really want isn't what you need.

Fuck, it would be good, though.

"I'll do my best but I'm no miracle worker... Saying that, it would be good to catch up, the three of us, like old times. What are you going to cook? You can use these tomatoes if you like?"

"I was thinking meatballs and pasta with a salad. I'd love to use those tomatoes for the sauce, if you don't mind? Do we have basil in the herb garden?" I look out the window to check, not really sure what I'm looking for.

Nora nods and points to the huge basil plant outside, giggling at my attempt to know which plant is which. Nora suggests she pick up some of our favourite wine and I agree. This is going to be easy, the three of us, like old times.

Easy.

Dinner, drinks.

Sex.

No, no sex. Absolutely none.

Nora steals my fleeting attention. "I spoke to Zoey this morning about our next event, and she is happy to help again. She said we nailed it last time." Nora's voice is laced with pride.

We really did nail it. Raising over £185,000 is insane for our first event. It means we can get started on the therapy programmes straight away. Nora has already outlined several ways we can help some of the children we already know, and I'm planning some of the activity days. The biggest problem we have right now is having enough hands to help us.

"Do you think Zoey would help us with the activity days?" I ask out loud.

"Yeah, definitely... I think Liam would too, if you want him to, that is. I also asked a couple of my friends from the gym and they'd love to help. Do you remember Jill and Iris? The sweet ladies at my Zumba classes? They're fully invested already."

This is what I love, organising all of this, knowing we are going to make a difference. It makes my whole body sizzle with purpose.

"Oh, before I forget, Jean Pierre said we can use the pool for an afternoon if it works, but I'm not sure about the nightmare of risk assessing that one. Can we look into Victoria Park for other events? Picnics maybe. Then maybe therapy space... do you think your office would let us rent a room a few times a month?" I watch Nora as she dries the tomatoes on a piece of kitchen towel as my mind buzzes with the excitement of all this coming to life.

"I think we could probably use my office. I'll talk to Phil and let you know. Maybe we should look at the cost of a small unit somewhere that we can use for sessions because they will become regular, I'm guessing."

"Great idea. I bet Zoey will know people."

"Come to think of it, Liam might know somewhere that could work, too." She looks at me. "Would that be okay? He said at the event he wanted to help as much as he can." She shrugs casually. I hadn't thought of that. Of course him and his dad's business is property, so it makes sense.

I nod. "Yeah, we can ask him."

"So, what time is he coming over tomorrow?"

"Around eight."

Nora turns to face me. "You're okay about it?"

Laughter explodes nervously from my mouth. "I'm..." I bite my lip. "Nervous about diving headfirst into something I'm not ready for."

There's no point in lying to Nora about that; she would see right through me if I brushed it off, and it has actually made me feel better by saying it out loud. I feel my shoulders relax for the first time today.

"Okay... I understand that. We'll take it slow. I'll be your buffer if things get too weird and then I'll leave when I know you've got it under control."

I nod my head.

Even as my heart races and my chest tightens again. Everything... is... completely... normal.

19

Jessica

"**A**nd you're sure you don't mind closing the event tonight?" I ask Kylie, who I know is more than capable, even before I asked the question.

"Really, Jess? I've closed a thousand events. I know you're my boss, but you're insulting me right now. Go. You never leave early. Enjoy it."

I nod anxiously. She's right, I'm being annoying. "Okay, I'm going. Thank you again. Oh, and don't forget—"

She interrupts me before I turn around. "To tell Jake to turn *all* the lights off in the kitchen. I know, he's the worst at remembering."

Shit, she really has got this. I smile and she waves me goodbye, basically shooing me out of my own office.

As I make my way home on the underground, I listen to the screeching of the trains, the bustle of the people coming and going, the whip of cold, musty air as my train approaches that makes my hair fly around my face and when I can't find a seat, I stand and open my phone to scroll through the recipe for later, mentally prepping everything in my head.

At home, I quickly shower. As I step underneath the hot water, my mind wanders to Liam. I wonder how much he has changed from the kids we were. From what I've seen so far, he's still him. Everything used to be so natural between us that I never gave much thought about being compatible with him. We just were. And I can't help wondering if we still are.

My relationships since him have been... scarce.

Commitment isn't a word I'd use to describe my love life. Not that I haven't had boyfriends, I have, but I guess I've been less than available for the guys I've gone out with.

I quickly wash my hair, realising that I've spent far too long in the shower. I throw on a pair of jeans and a pretty floral, sheer top, moisturise my face, pop on some mascara and leave my hair slightly damp as I rush back downstairs.

As I hit the bottom step, Nora comes in through the front door. "Hey." She drops her bags in the cupboard and toes her shoes off in the hallway.

"Hey, babe, I'm just about to start dinner. Liam will be here in half hour or so."

"I'm going to shower quickly and I'll come and help you. Give me ten minutes."

In the kitchen, I combine all my ingredients into a bowl and start mixing the meatballs. As it comes together, I make individual balls and place them into my hot pan. Once they are cooking on low, I start to boil some water and grab the salad ingredients, just as Nora comes into the kitchen.

"Let me do the salad. You finish your sauce." She gestures to the other ingredients.

Just as I mix the meatballs into the sauce, the doorbell rings. My soul near enough leaves my body and Nora places her hand on my shoulder. "Want me to get it?"

I shake my head, faking a calm smile. "I've got it."

I take a few slow steps towards my front door, passing the mirror in the hallway. I glance over and straighten my outfit, run my hands through my wavy, still damp hair before placing my hand on the door handle and exhaling a quick breath.

The motion of the door opening wafts his scent towards me, and I feel as though a thousand little fireflies are surrounding me, carrying it to me. It is masculine; warm and fresh... so familiar. I have to fight to keep my eyes open because all they want to do is close while I bask in it. Just for a second.

When our eyes connect, the zap of energy that I felt at the hotel is back as we stare at each other. I watch the corners of his lips quirk upwards into a signature Liam-Taylor charming smile that makes it hard to look away. He pushes off my doorway–which seemed so much smaller with him near it—his large arms are framed with a long-sleeved, white t-shirt that tappers down his sculpted body. When he steps forward into my house, the air disappears, as though my body is suddenly fighting to acclimatise at the top of Mount Everest. Then, when one strong arm pulls me into a hug, before I can form another thought or utter a word, I definitely stop breathing altogether. I'm trapped in some sort of warped dimension where this giant version of the boy I used to love ten years ago, is hugging me and I'm confused as hell because my muscle memory has kicked in and it remembers Liam very well.

It's only when he finally releases me that I suddenly decide that maybe air is overrated anyway and I'd much prefer to suffocate in his arms.

"You look fucking beautiful, Jess." His gaze scorching and devious as he scans over every inch of me.

I suddenly feel the need to make a joke to shake off the rising heat at the back of my neck. "I showered. Are you proud?"

"So proud," he chuckles.

As steps forwards, he hands me a dandelion.

My body freezes, holding the soft stem in my hand.

You get to keep me if I get to keep you.

"You know how hard it is to not have the little fluffy things fly everywhere?" He kisses the top of my head and there's that muscle memory kicking in again. My stare flicks between him and the dandelion, then him again, my mouth dropping open, but nothing actually comes out. It's probably for the best, because anything that does come out of my mouth might resemble a sob, anyway.

Liam steps into my space again, but this time, wrapping himself behind my body. His big hands splay my waist. He tucks his head in the crook of my neck and quietly says, "Make a wish, Scotty."

Make a wish. Such a simple term, yet filled with so much expectation. Making wishes when I was younger was something I did because I still believed they'd come true. Like the time I wished for a blue bicycle for my eighth birthday or the time I wished for some new Nike Airs that everyone was wearing when we started secondary school. But as time went on, my wishes were ignored more and more, so I only made them when I felt like I needed to be reminded that magic *could* exist. I suppose I could make a wish now.

I shuffle a step with him moving behind me, leaning out of my front door. I close my eyes and think. *What do you want to wish for, Jess?* The thought tightens the walls of my throat as I swallow to try to clear it.

I inhale deeply, then puff out the air quickly and watch the fluffy seeds explode and settle like snowflakes on the concrete steps. I turn to face Liam, as his head tilts towards me, the million-pound question on the tip of his tongue. I can practically hear his brain thinking it.

"I'm not telling you," I say, walking backwards into the house with him still wrapped around me.

He visibly deflates, but nods and smiles anyway. "I know. I don't expect you to."

The softness in his eyes tells me he really wouldn't expect me to, and that affects me more than I care to admit.

"Liam!" Nora squeals before hurling herself into him.

"Nor!" He releases his hold on me and squeezes her tightly before letting her go and looking between us both. "It's good to see you both. I hadn't realised how much I'd missed you girls."

"Not girls anymore Liam, we are women!" Nora exclaims just as a loud timer buzzes in the kitchen. "Oh, I have to check the food, come in. Jess shut the door, babe. It's cold."

I turn to close the door and Liam follows Nora through the hallway into the arch of the kitchen, whilst I pause to catch my breath for a second.

When I walk into the kitchen, Liam bends over the counter, his hands gripping the counter firmly and my mind instantly wanders to how they'd feel on my body.

God, Jessica, stop!

He leans in to spy the food and inhales deeply, locking his eyes with mine. "Did you make this? It smells insane. I'm starving." I nod, tucking my hair behind my ear as he looks at me and winks. My brain malfunctions to catastrophic levels because its equal parts sexy and charming, which makes it completely disarming. Especially when he lets his eyes linger on me, like he's doing right now. Is he really starving for food? Orrrr...

As if he hears my thought, he leans into my ear and says, "It's you, I'm hungry for you."

I'm dead.

Well, maybe not dead. Just passing out from the blush that's shot so fast to my cheeks it's stopped my heart on the way up. I rub the hot spot on my face, hoping it'll disappear as we enter into a silent staring competition with one another.

"You guuuuuuys. It's been two seconds, and he's already whispering dirty things in your ear. Come onnnn. Give a girl a minute to serve the food, will you?" Nora whines and stamps her feet when neither of us listen to her. "Right, sit down over there, Liam, away from Jessica for now and don't even think about playing footsies with her underneath the table or so help me..." Her stern gaze catches his attention this time and Liam gulps playfully and I can't help but hum, amused at watching him.

"See? You've missed us, right?"

"I missed you both, but I forgot how fucking terrifying Nora can be when she's bossy," he whispers to me.

"Heard that," Nora shouts back from the other side of the room.

Dinner is a raging success. I'd forgotten how much Liam could put away, so I'm glad we made extra. Liam leans back in his chair opposite me, kicking out his long legs underneath the table. When he rolls his sleeves up to reveal his flexing forearms, the temperature of the room increases by at least fifteen degrees, or maybe it's just the fact that my body seems to *really* appreciate being around him again.

"So, what's next with the charity for you guys?" Liam asks, placing his knife and fork onto his plate. *There goes those muscles again... God, mind out of the gutter, Jessica.*

I clear my throat, hoping my thoughts aren't plastered across my face in a giant red sign, "Actually, we were wondering—"

"Yes," he interrupts.

"You don't even know what I'm going to ask yet."

"Listen, if it's for you two and your charity, I'll do it." He looks directly at me, speaking quieter, "And if it is for you, Jess, I'll definitely do whatever you ask of me."

Someone get me some ice, for the love of God.

If Nora wasn't sat right there, I'm pretty sure that would be the end of table manners for us both. *How does everything he says and does affect me this way?*

"Liam Taylor. Behave," Nora scolds.

I cringe with laughter and Liam just laughs. "Sorry, Nor. I don't know what came over me." He winks that heart stopping wink before he adds, "Seriously though, I will help you guys. No strings attached. I can even rope in my mate Grayson, too."

"Thank you. We were hoping you could volunteer at one of our activity days. We haven't put dates to them yet, but we'll let you know as soon as we do," Nora says, clearing the plates from the table.

Liam locks his gaze with mine again. "I'm in, whatever, wherever."

My insides turn to mush, liquified in a nano-second as I try desperately not to overthink if what he meant had a double meaning.

We all drink the remainder of the wine at the breakfast bar and I quickly discover that watching Liam talk about anything is my new favourite pastime. He's so... confident. The set in his jaw, the cock of his head, the broadness of his shoulders. Liam was always confident growing up, but something about him now is more direct, but he still has this softness about him that makes you want to cuddle into him and *that* is a very dangerous combination for me after a few glasses of wine.

"Okay, I need sleep. It's..." Nora checks the clock behind her that reads 10:30 pm. "Fuck, it's not even that late and I'm exhausted. I don't even care. I need sleep."

I give her a wide-eyed look and she stares directly at Liam and says, "If you can try and not make her scream too loudly tonight, that would be great. I don't need to hear you both going at it, because it just reminds me how sad my own love life is right now." Nora's eyes twinkle with amusement as she pats Liam's back and gives us both the peace sign as she walks out of the kitchen.

My mouth hits the floor and Liam is the one who places his finger underneath it to close it with a low laugh that vibrates throughout the now quiet room. It's the kind of quiet that's suggestive and waiting like a loaded weapon. The air feels simultaneously heavy and too thin as I try to fill my lungs discreetly.

Liam stands from his chair and with one hand effortlessly twirls my bar stool, so I'm facing him. He edges between my legs, nudging them apart with his thighs as he leans in closer, his hands surrounding my body like a cage, flexing and gripping the worktop behind me. His scent suffocates me in the most intoxicating way and I find myself searching for it, needing it more than I need actual air. He smells like summertime; the warm, soft summer evenings where your hair is messy and your eyes are sparkling because you've spent all day in the sunshine. I smile as I let it wash over me, coating my skin in him... only him.

One thing I know for certain right now is that I don't trust my body. She betrays me all the time by blushing and pulsing whenever he is near. Like right this second, I'm trying to keep things PG, but I can already feel the heat prickles sneaking up my neck, threatening to make my body burst into flames.

The look in Liam's eyes is deep, dark, and full of want as he gazes down at me.

"I really want to kiss you." He pauses, his eyes locked on my mouth, his thighs flexing between my own as his hot breath drifts over my lips. "But I have to go home and pack because I have a client meeting in Chicago for the next few days and if I start kissing you..." He inhales sharply. "I won't be able to stop." He lifts his hand and runs his thumb over my bottom lip, making the disappointment I'm feeling that much harder.

"Chicago?" I ask, hoping he doesn't notice the wobble in my voice.

"Yeah, one of our new clients is based there and he couldn't make a meeting yesterday, so I offered to fly out instead. I want to move things internationally in the future, so it seems like a good idea to show that the company is willing to do more for our clients, too." His hand now firmly cupping my face.

"Yeah, that makes sense." I swallow thickly, watching the way his lips move as he talks.

I want to ask him when I'll see him again and if we're going to talk whilst he is away, but I already know that makes me sound needy.

"You should probably get going then..." He doesn't move, so I continue, "You should've said. I wouldn't have minded changing tonight if it didn't make sense for you with work." I brush my hair out of my face, and he takes the opportunity to place his hand on my opposite cheek, staring at me with his eyes still full of desire, but I see an inner battle there too. *Maybe he's just as affected by me as I am by him.*

"Can we talk when I'm away? I want to talk to you again and see you when I'm home. The trip is only a few days."

"I'd like that," I whisper on an exhale. His eyes flare with excitement and I catch another glimpse of that teenage boy I fell desperately in love with all those years ago. I barely hesitate as I whisper, "Kiss me." Within a fraction of a second, he pulls me towards his lips, his hands in my hair gripping the back of my neck.

He's so close to me as he leans in slowly, slow enough that it would look like he's not going to kiss me at all, making my nerve endings scream for him. My pulse threatens to burst right out of my neck, and his eyes flicker to the thumping underneath where his fingertips rest. He strokes the skin, and I watch as a small smile lifts the side of his mouth. His eyes soften, showing tiny, faint lines wrinkling the edges.

My fingers ache as I realise I'm gripping his t-shirt so fiercely that I feel like I might float away without him. As if he reads my mind, he moves impossibly closer, erasing the tiny sliver of a gap left between us. His head lowers a fraction, as our lips touch for the briefest of moments, sending a zing across my lower lip. My body betrays me yet again, as a tiny mewl of pleasure escapes my lips. I open my eyes to find him watching me, his eyes stormy and lustful, before he drops his gaze to my lips again. I absent mindedly flick my tongue over my lower lip, while he stays waiting for me to give him access to my mouth.

I tip my chin towards him, granting him access as he lowers his lips to mine again. This time there is no tentative, fleeting kiss. This time it's purposeful and demanding. His lips are still the softest things I've ever felt, like a blanket, wrapping me tightly in its embrace. He slides his tongue and tastes my mouth like he's been starved and suddenly found the only thing that will fulfil his appetite. My heart falters as he moves his hands to my lower back and pushes us together, kissing me deeply that my toes curl with want.

I remember so much about Liam, memories have been hitting me all night, but right in this moment, with him being so close to me again. I couldn't even tell you my own name.

The room around us has disappeared. I'm not sure how long we kiss for; it might've been minutes. It felt like eternity because the last time I felt this way was the first time Liam kissed me ten years ago.

"I really don't want to go to Chicago right now," he whispers against my lips.

My sated eyes open. "I'll be waiting for you when you get back," I say with a playful sigh.

"It's only a few days, I suppose, and you know what they say: absence makes the heart grow fonder, and all that…" I brush his lips with mine, lightly, like a feather, and he inhales sharply.

"Jessica Scott, you do something to me." The way his nose brushes against mine and the hard press of him against my leg sends my body signals my heart isn't ready for yet. "Will you tell me what you wished for now?" he whispers into my ear.

I smile, knowing exactly what I wished for. I press my mouth to his ear, "Now that's a secret, lover boy."

20

Liam

Chicago

I turn my phone on after landing in Chicago to see a text from Jess. I've thought about her and that kiss in her kitchen last night endlessly, like listening to my favourite song on repeat. That moment is etched into my brain like Groundhog Day, and I can't get enough.

> **Jess:** I hope you landed safely. Well, not you, your plane.
> **Jess:** Well, maybe you on the plane. Okay… going to overthink this text for the next seven hours. Byeeee x

I start laughing at her message and type my reply.

> **Liam:** Seven hours is a long time to overthink that. Both plane and me are in Chicago safely though, fyi x

I glance at my watch; I've got an hour to get across town to the hotel, change and be at my meeting downtown.

I hail a taxi and hope that traffic isn't too bad and won't leave me rushing. Another text from Jess comes through as I climb into the back seat.

Jess: Overthinking is pretty much a full-time job, but I'm glad you and the plane are safe. Mostly you x

I like that she thinks about me. I like that she's been on my mind so much lately. The grin that spreads across my face is inevitable when I think of her. It always has been.

Jeremy Presser is the man I have come to woo in Chicago. His company has an opportunity to branch into London and we want to secure the contract that provides his company with the properties he wants. If I can land this, it'll help the move into international waters in the future, but also show my dad that I'm willing to expand his business further than he might be able to right now.

The time between the taxi ride and me sitting opposite Jeremy flies like the passing of a moment. One minute I'm daydreaming, thinking about Jess, the next I'm sitting opposite a middle-aged Yank who doesn't know that he's not the reason I'm sweating so much.

"I really appreciate you coming out here, Liam. The situation at work meant I couldn't leave, but I'm glad we could arrange a time for this. How is your father doing?"

"He's doing well. He sends his regards to you and your family." I smile genuinely.

"You must come out for dinner tonight with my wife and me. Let us show you more of the city."

"I'd love to. Chicago looks like a wonderful place. Shall we get down to business?"

He nods and tells his assistant to get us more coffee. Honestly, another one and I might be a bit too jittery, but I nod and smile politely.

"So, the market right now is prime for you to make the move into London and we have several properties we think would be perfect." I pass him the printed details I hand-picked for him. I already know which one he'll choose based on his current offices, but choice here is key. "I think many of these would suit your needs, but have a look and see which catches your eye."

He browses through the five options and I see his eyes glimmer as soon as he finds the one I knew he'd like the most

"I see that look... that's my favourite, too. State of the art offices near canary wharf, perfect access being in the centre of the city. The entire ground level is the foyer and security offices, the basement is where all the tech servers would be. There is a gym and a creche option if you would like to offer that to your employees on the second floor. All other floors are offices except the top two, which are reserved for your upper management team and can only be accessed with a code. Oh, and the rooftop has a bar that is partially sheltered. With a company as successful as yours, I think this building is a great fit."

Jeremy nods thoughtfully as he processes my sell. "I think you're right. Our company has gotten so big overseas that we need this space, and the location is perfect." He looks up at me, "Mr Taylor, you are a very impressive young man. Where do I sign?"

Fuck me. I've just landed the biggest international contract my dad's company has ever had.

I extend my hand for Jeremy and he shakes it firmly and without hesitation. "I'll have my assistant email the contract to yours within the hour. Thank you, sir. You've made the right choice."

He waves me off, laughing. "Sir is what my father was called. I'm not that old yet, son. You made that very easy for me. I'm grateful..." He glances at his watch. "I have another meeting in ten minutes, but I'll have my assistant give you the details for dinner tonight and I'll show you more of our beautiful city before you head home tomorrow."

I nod and gather my paperwork. "Excellent. I look forward to it."

It takes all my strength not to fist pump the air right now and jump around the office. I'm buzzing. I just landed a deal that will rocket our company's worth by at least fourteen million pounds. I fire off an email to Helena to make sure the contracts get there asap.

The first person I want to share this moment with is my dad. So, I take a moment in the enclosed office, and I call him.

"Hi, Dad."

"Hi, Liam. So, tell me, has my son landed the biggest deal of his career yet?"

I pause for dramatic effect. "I fucking nailed it," I grin into the phone.

I can hear my father clap and laugh on the other end of the phone, and it sends a jolt of pride through my chest. "Knew you would. You're your father's son, after all."

"Pretty sure it was my charm and sparkling personality that did it."

He laughs and pauses for a second. "I…" He clears his throat before continuing, "I'm proud of you, really proud."

"Tell me you aren't crying and I'm not even there to rinse you for it."

He sniffs. "I have no idea what you're talking about."

I let out a laugh when he sniffs down the line again. "Whatever, old man. I'm going to crash at the hotel for a bit before dinner, so I'll talk to you later. Tell mum the news for me?"

When we hang up, I know the next person I want to share this with is Jess. I drop her a text and she replies, telling me she is just about to go into a meeting but will call when she's home in an hour.

After my nap, which was arguably one of the best naps I've ever had because… jetlag, I tap my phone to see I've got a missed call from Jess.

I've got a while before I need to leave before dinner with Jeremy and his wife, so I call her back on video.

"Hey." Her face fills the screen of my phone; she hasn't got any make up on and her hair is in a low ponytail, off her face. I know I saw her twenty-four hours ago, but fuck, she's beautiful. Even more so when she looks like this.

I can't help the huge grin on my face at seeing her. "Hey, Scotty. It's good to see your face." I settle against my headboard and put one arm behind my head.

"Meh, your face is okay too, I guess," she smirks. *There's that snarky Jess I know.*

I mock a hurt expression. "Ouch... I'm wounded. So, is this hangry Jess or snarky Jess? I can't get a read on you over the phone."

She huffs a breath, her eyes narrowing playfully. "You don't know me." The way she says it is like she doesn't want me to know her as well as I actually do.

I shake my head. "Some things never change. Okay, I'm thinking you are snarky Jess. What's got your knickers all twisted?"

"Thinking about my knickers, lover boy?" She winks and licks her lips. I'm not sure if she means to be as sexy as she is, but I'm already at half-mast right now just looking at her.

"Thinking about taking them off, honestly," I mumble quietly, adjusting my body to sit upright on the bed.

"What was that?" Her cheeks redden, and I mirror her emotion, embarrassed that she heard that little slip of the tongue. As she shuffles on her bed, her oversized hoodie slips off her shoulder for a second, showing me her soft, glowing skin. The sight of her looking so beautiful has my temperature rising.

Damn, do I wish I was in London right now.

"Nothing. Tell me what's up." I shake my head of any and all dirty thoughts because that's not why I called her.

"I'm really okay. I just had a stupidly long day with a bridezilla who was looking down at me the whole time. I hated it. I felt repressed for not actively telling that woman to go the fuck away," she rushes out. "Hazard of the job, though, I guess."

"Well, I happen to like snarky Jess... I like all versions of Jess."

Her smile widens at my words. "How was your day?"

"I managed to secure my first international contract, and it's the biggest one we have on our books to date. I'm pretty sure my dad cried when I told him."

"Liam, you should've led with that! God, that's amazing," she beams.

"It's pretty big, hm?"

"I'm so proud of you." Her smile beams from her.

"Thank you. Hey, give me two seconds." I stand and remove my work shirt because I need to grab a shower in a minute before dinner. That and it's boiling in here, even with the air conditioning on.

I pick my phone back up and see Jess' beautiful face again. "Hi," I say, as her eyes dilate and her throat swallows heavily.

"Hi," she squeaks back and then giggles.

"Sorry, it's boiling in here and I need to shower soon anyway, ready for dinner."

Jess tilts her head. "Dinner?"

"Yeah, with the CEO and his wife. They wanted to take me out after signing the contract today."

She visibly exhales. "Oh, that's nice." It's cute that she looked worried for a second, but the truth is, Jess has filled every spare thought of mine since I saw her again, and I don't plan on letting that change. I'm desperate to spend more time with her, to see where this goes again. I know we've got some things to work through, but there's this magnetic pull to her that I can't ignore.

"Hey, can I ask you something?"

She nods, so I decide to go for it.

"Do you speak to your mum after all these years?"

I see the moment her whole face lilts at the mention of her mother, her shoulders drop, and she immediately nibbles her lip. "I... um..."

Her hesitation speaks volumes. Maybe she's not ready to talk about that yet. Fear seeps into my subconscious as I think about how she hated talking about things with her mum before she moved. What if she still won't let me in? "Hey, we don't have to talk about that if you don't want to."

Her eyes flit around her room as she bites the corner of her nail. "It's not that. I'd rather talk about that when we're together, you know, face to face."

I nod my head. "Will you let me take you out on a date when I'm home?"

When her eyes snap back to mine, they're wide and surprised, but I see the moment they soften as a smile creeps over her face again. "I'd like that."

"Friday night?"

"Friday night," she replies.

We stare at each other for a beat. I take in her soft pink cheeks, her full lips, her chestnut brown hair, and the way it's shoved on the top of her head just makes her all the more appealing.

"Jess?"

"Hm?"

I want to tell her that I miss her. That even though we're talking on the phone, I still miss her. I've spent longer than I care to admit missing Jessica Scott and I'm having a hard time processing all the feelings for her again. I want to share more with her, but she isn't ready yet, so I decide to keep it to myself.

"Do you like pizza?" I ask.

She scoffs lightly, "Uh, is the Pope catholic?"

I smile. "I'm taking you out for pizza for our date, then."

Her grin broadens, and her dimple pops, stealing my breath.

I exhale, resting my chin on my hand as I stare at her. "That dimple of yours... it's the sweetest thing."

I watch her head bow and her cheeks flame, my favourite colour creeping across her perfect skin. I can't help my dopey smile as I settle in to stare at her a little longer.

21

Jessica

I stand in the hallway of our town house, focusing entirely on a tiny corner of the wall that paint has chipped from it. I can't stop staring. The chipped paint is grounding me, giving me something to focus on, aside from my beating organ that is currently bouncing around my ribcage. My palms are sweating, my chest is tight, and I can't help that feeling of fight or flight. I'm pretty sure I would fly really far away from this feeling I have right now. I can't remember a time I've ever been this nervous, especially not with Liam.

Growing up, it was simple. Now it feels like a big deal. Our first date. No, our first grown-up date.

I've checked my phone at least a dozen times after Liam sent me a *'I'm on my way'* message, which is why I'm currently trying to keep calm but failing miserably.

God, I'm scared.

What if he doesn't like who I am now?

What if I get stage fright again and can't answer the questions that he asks me?

Nora comes into the hallway and grabs my arms. "Will you stop! Everything will be fine. Why all the nerves? It's Liam."

Exactly.

"Ohh, I don't know... maybe because the only person I have ever loved is coming to take me on a date after ten years apart and I don't know if I'm wearing the right thing, if I'll say the right thing or if my big, stupid mouth will ruin it all." *And breathe.* "Oh, and now I'm sweating too."

I fan my reddening face whilst I look at my reflection. My deep blue eyes are a little wilder grey blue than usual. "Do you think he'd like me even if I'm a jumbled Jess-mess?" I slump onto the velvet chair near the door and Nora follows me, her eyes soft and accepting.

"He'll still like you, even if you are a jumbled Jess mess. You know that you and Liam have always had a natural chemistry, and yeah, okay, things might be a little strange to begin with, but that's normal for all relationships. You'll find your rhythm again," Nora says lovingly, kneeling in front of me to meet my eyes. "Listen, you need to accept that you'll say something that will make you cringe–it wouldn't be you if you didn't. But Jess, you've got this. You are a strong, fearless woman who can do anything. Get up, go out, and charm the pants off Liam *fucking* Taylor."

God, I wouldn't be able to function without Nora. My brain immediately settles, and I take a big relaxing breath out.

I squeeze her hand, stand, and push my shoulders back as Nora smiles at me knowingly. In the mirror I pucker my lips and apply my pink lip stain and as Nora tells me I look hot, there is a knock at the door.

My heart leaps out of my chest as I drop the lipstick to the floor.

"You've got this, remember," Nora reminds me as I bend to pick it up.

She disappears into the lounge, and I stand behind my closed door, needing to take one more deep breath.

As the door opens, Liam's tall frame comes into view. He is wearing a crisp white shirt, faded black jeans and tan Chelsea boots, all pulled together with the casual dark leather jacket. His hair is perfectly styled and I can guarantee he spent no longer than five minutes on it because he's that lucky.

God, he looks hot.

He smells fresh, but with an undertone of something warmer, darker and intoxicating. My senses are ruined by this one moment. Never going to recover and I don't even want them to right now.

"Hi, Scotty." He smiles, and my chest almost explodes again.

Hey Siri, Add this mental image to 'fave pics of Liam' folder.

"Hi." I do my best to stifle a giggle because if I laugh out loud, I fear it'll be more of a snort and that wouldn't be recoverable... in any way.

"What's so funny?" He nudges past me and walks into the hallway.

"Nothing..." *Just you being insanely hot.* "I'm just nervous... like a lot nervous."

"Truth time? Me too, but tonight, I'm going to wine and dine you and..." He pulls me closer to him, our bodies touching everywhere. "...then I have plans for you later..." He pauses his gaze. licking over my entire face and body, "Damn it's been a long couple of days," he confesses with dark eyes and I decide that I need to get him out of the house because if he kisses me right now, I don't think I'll ever want him to stop while he's looking at me like that.

Our kiss has been on replay in my head for days whilst he's been away, but I don't tell him that, even although all I want to do is drag him upstairs and kiss him again and again.

"Woah there, lover boy, let's get going. We don't want to be late for dinner." Pushing him away, I open the door, ignoring the way my body is protesting loudly. I chuckle as he groans, stomping his big feet behind me. "Turn that frown upside down, Mr Taylor."

I turn, grab his chin and kiss his cheek, which earns me a smile.

He just looks so fucking good. He's always looked good, but tonight, he has his dating grown up game on and that is attractive as hell. Even the way he walks over to his car, with so much ease and natural swagger, has my insides melting and my body pulsing, I need to rein it in.

"This is what you drive around London?" I raise my eyebrows at him and his ridiculously expensive matt black Tesla and he just... shrugs.

"Most of the time. It's small enough to fit into tiny car parking spaces in the city, plus it's fast and I like it. It was my first car I bought myself, so it's my baby."

"A very expensive baby," I retort light-heartedly.

He opens my door for me. Our hands brush and sparks continue to fly between us.

The inside of the car is just as impressive as the outside, all dark leather and shiny surfaces that contrast the matt exterior. It's sexy as fuck... just like him.

Liam

Fuck me, she looks hot tonight. I'm not sure how I'm going to keep my hands off her for much longer. It's no exaggeration that I've been dying to kiss her again. I almost had her in her house. I was so close, but she dodged me, leaving me high and dry. Although, it was probably for the best; one taste of her again, and there's a chance I wouldn't have been able to keep my gentlemanly side in check.

I round my car and get into the driver's side. Once I silently pull away, Jess chuckles to herself beside me. "What?" I ask.

"Nothing, just.... nothing." Her eyes twinkle with mischief.

The whole drive to the restaurant, I have to fight to stop my hands from drifting over the centre console of the car to touch her. In the end, I lose the battle and rest my hand on her thigh and gently squeeze it. I love how she feels under my palm and how her breath hitches for a second, then I turn my hand upwards in the hope that she places hers in mine.

Jess doesn't disappoint. Her fingers intertwine with mine and I clasp our hands together, not wanting to let this feeling go.

We arrive at the restaurant on London's south bank. The views from this place are incredible, or so my parents told me. My mum insisted that I try this place soon, so I'm hoping it's as good as they say.

"Do you have a reservation?" the waiter asks, not looking up.

"Yes, Liam Taylor, for two," I say, keeping my hand firmly on Jess' back. When the waiter finally looks up, he nods, leading us through the restaurant.

The place is airy, and open, with tables positioned around the glass windows. The lights of London are winking as we walk to our seats. The dark blue lighting casts a glow over the white tablecloths and when the waiter stops at our table, the views of the River Thames go on for miles.

"Thank you," I say, pulling out Jess' seat for her.

"Here is the wine menu. Roscoe will be your waiter for the evening, and he will be over shortly with the specials for tonight."

Jess' eyes are fixated on the view of the river and London bustling below us. "Liam, this is..." She pauses to look at me. "Stunning."

I look at her over the glow of our table lamp. "*You're* stunning," I return her comment and am rewarded with a dimple pop and a blush. Both of which are becoming two of my favourite things again.

"I thought we were having pizza, though?" she asks. "This place is way fancier than pizza."

"This place is the best pizza place south of the river or so my parents tell me. They have a fancy menu too, if you'd rather have that?"

Her head shakes. "Pizza is good."

I lean over the table. "So, how are you still single, Jessica Scott? I thought for sure someone would've snatched you up by now."

"I don't know... work got busy, I suppose. Then, I didn't look for anything serious because I was busy. I actually haven't had an official boyfriend in a really long time." I note the blush on her cheeks as she admits that last part, but she shrugs it off easily. "What about you?"

"Yeah... I haven't had a boyfriend in a long time either."

Jess barks a laugh.

"I guess no one has given me a reason to settle down yet..." I eye her knowingly. "But you, you're a catch."

"I hate to disappoint you, lover boy, but I'm not that much of a catch." She fiddles with her napkin.

"Whoever told you that you weren't a catch was obviously not looking in the right pond, because you, Jessica, are my favourite catch... *a-a-and* now I've said that out loud it sounds really fucking weird."

I frown at myself and rub the back of my neck, disappointed that I left my charm at home tonight.

She makes my favourite noise, a light, easy laugh, *yes* with her dimple and then she wrinkles her nose, and I might need to lie down because she's insanely beautiful. My poor heart can't take much more, and the night is still young.

"Do you still play rugby?"

"I do, but it's more for fun now. I haven't been a part of an adult team for years, but I do coach a Little League team on Sundays with my friend Grayson. He's mostly hungover and I'm mostly exhausted from being up so early, but I hope we do a decent enough job. The kids are great."

Jess groans. "Oh God, of course you teach tiny humans rugby... do you have any idea how many brownie points you get for that?"

I lean in and catch the scent of her sweet perfume. I'm not sure who was meant to be resisting who, but I definitely don't want to anymore.

My restraint is fraying by the second. "Maybe that was my plan all along. Coach the kids for brownie points with Jess."

"Cute." She narrows her eyes at me and laughs softly.

The evening moves too quickly; we both devour a woodfired pizza each ,that was arguably the best pizza I've had in years. I make a mental note to thank Mum and Dad for recommending this place. Picking up my napkin, I wipe the remnants of any pizza sauce from my mouth.

"Do you want dessert?" I ask, already knowing the answer.

"What do you think?" She raises an eyebrow.

"I think I could probably order for you."

"Okay, if you think I'm still *so* predictable, go on then." Her arms cross over her body and her lips purse, reminding me how badly I'd like to kiss her again.

I signal the waiter and order a chocolate fudge cake with extra hot chocolate sauce and vanilla ice cream.

"I'm impressed."

"How can I forget your favourite dessert? Harriett used to make it all the time when we were kids. That cake is etched into my memory."

Jess' eyes soften at the mention of us as kids. They shine and dance with swirls of blue and hints of grey, like bioluminescence in the ocean. "So, I don't know if I've told you tonight yet, but you look ridiculously beautiful. Even that doesn't feel accurate enough to describe you." I hold her hand over the table and lift it to kiss her knuckles.

A charming, shy look crosses her face as she looks at me. "I'm not used to these compliments, Mr Taylor. You make a girl blush." She really is the sweetest shade of pink right now, and I love it.

"There are other things I could do to make you blush, you know..."

Shit, that might have been a bit forward. I freeze and try to gauge her expression.

Please, don't think I'm a creep. I'm really not. I'm just having a hard time keeping some of my fucking filthy thoughts to myself around you.

Jess' eyes darken for a second, our hands still together, thankfully, so I don't apologise for thinking out loud... not yet anyway.

"Oh yeah? Care to elaborate?" There's a swell of anticipation around us, and I wonder if the other people in the room can feel it. I focus on her lips, my mouth dries, like I haven't had a single drop of liquid touch my mouth for days. I want her and I want all of her. I need to taste her soon or I might explode.

"Well, what would you say if I wanted to kiss you right now?" I ghost my finger around the inside of her wrist and she lets out a small gasp, only loud enough for me to hear, and it lights a fire deep in my chest.

"I might not be able to stop you."

Just as I shift my weight to move over to her side of the table, our desserts arrive, and we both look at each other and know the moment has passed... for now.

Cockblocked by cake. *Excellent.*

The cake is sweet, rich and warm and we both devour every crumb. I do my best to hold back as Jess groans and hums in appreciation of the cake. But I can honestly say that I've never wanted to hear those noises more in my life... just somewhere more private.

On the way out of the restaurant, I ask her to come back to my house for a night cap and to my surprise, she agrees. She reminds me it is just a night cap, and we will only be talking.

I shake my head and laugh.

She's cute when she thinks she's in control.

I bring out two glasses of caramel rum over ice and she purrs in appreciation when she tastes it. Those damn noises are back again, testing my limits, only it's worse now because she's in my house, in my space.

She moves over to the dark oak cabinet, and I follow her instinctively. The way she lets her fingers absentmindedly run over the curves of the wood has me mesmerised. Watching her caress every curve of the cabinet, seeing the sway of her hips as she shifts her weight from one foot to another.

Yeah, all those filthy thoughts are back from earlier and they brought friends. Lots of them.

She looks beautiful as I watch her move her body achingly slowly around my living room. Her perfectly curved hips are hugged by those impossibly tight jeans that frame her petite legs flawlessly. She has such elegance when she moves, it's feline and completely spellbinding.

For days now, I haven't been able to stop thinking about her. Wondering what noises she makes when she falls apart—although if the chocolate cake was a preview earlier, I'm only more eager for the real thing. I want to know how she tastes, I want to worship every inch of her body the way she deserves. Except now she's here, I want nothing more than to slow down time to savour every second I have alone with her.

Her eyes flicker to me as I let my gaze lick every inch of her. My skin prickles with her being so near so I don't hide my feelings this time. I slowly stalk over to her, placing my glass down on the ledge of the cabinet next to us. My shoulders roll as her breath hitches. That noise goes straight to my core like a shockwave. The ripple of anticipation is back and is rolling between us like the waves in the ocean.

I cage her in, my arms resting on the wall behind, but she doesn't move.

She doesn't even flinch. *Good girl.*

I listen to her breathing shallow. I can practically feel her warmth radiating from her body as it betrays her, showing me the sweetest shade of pink bloom from behind her ear and down her cleavage, leaving a small glisten of sweat in between her breasts. I let my eyes follow the trail hungrily and she shifts from the attention. Her scent surrounds me when she moves, until it fills my head with her, teasing every nerve ending in my body.

She licks her lips and I bend closer to her ear, silencing my desire to lick her neck. "Do you know how badly I want you?" I let my breath caress her neck, staying close to her. She smells like oranges; warm, sultry, and fucking intoxicating. "Can I kiss you?"

When I eventually look up into her clear blue eyes, I cup her face and run my thumb over her cheek while she closes her eyes and leans into my touch, letting out a small noise that I want to swallow.

"Say yes, baby. Let me taste you."

She whispers *yes* and releases another quiet whimper, one that I dive into and eagerly swallow this time, as it leaves her perfect mouth.

My tongue touches her bottom lip and just like that, she opens, inviting me in. She tastes like chocolate, sweet and addicting. Our tongues meet, dancing, exploring, possessing, driving the desperation I feel straight to my cock as I push her further into the wall behind her.

I move my hands freely over her body, tracing every curve, the dip of her waist and arch of her back and committing it all to memory. Her skin feels like silk under my hands, reacting to every touch.

Jess becomes just as desperate, her hands dropping to my chest, her touch leaving a scorching imprint that makes my head fall backwards and a groan slip from my lips. She's awoken a need, a longing for her that I can't control anymore. I don't think she understands how badly I need her, and unlike the last time, I won't be stopping unless she tells me to. I want to own her, devour her, and leave her begging for more. Every moment I've controlled myself around her comes hand in hand with every moment I've wanted to strip her bare and make her body sing for me.

She kisses my mouth and then bites my bottom lip, and that last little thread snaps. I lift her legs and wrap them around my waist, revelling in the feel of her warm centre against my stomach and her arms around my shoulders.

"Biting is for boyfriends, Scotty, remember?"

Her whole body shivers at the memory, her nipples peaking against my chest. I bury my head into her breasts, gently biting and teasing, taking full advantage of her reaction to me. Her hands dive into my hair, pulling me closer. *I'd happily suffocate between her breasts. What a way to go.* My cock aches, angrily straining against my jeans. My hips buck against her, rubbing against the heat of her, sending a urgent moan tumbling from my lips.

I stride over to the sofa and sit down with her straddling my lap. Her lips are swollen and bright pink from our kiss, her blouse has a wet spot right over her nipple from my mouth and the sight of it has me feeling possessive over her body. I lean down to bite her pebbled nipples again, and she yelps as she throws her head back, thrusting her chest forward into my mouth.

What the fuck happened to being a gentleman?

22

Jessica

*W*hat the fuck am I doing?

    I look down at Liam and there is so much desire in his eyes I might actually combust.

He feels so good beneath me, and it isn't my head making decisions anymore; my body has taken over, and she is hungry for Liam Taylor.

It's been years since I touched any part of him. It's like my body has woken from a slumber when he kissed me this week and now I'm ravenous. I want to have all of him and experience everything that we didn't do as teenagers.

"I want you." I breathe out the words like it's the last thing I will ever say.

Woah, what is happening? Brain meet mouth.

"I can't believe I just said that out loud."

"I love hearing it, because I want you just as fucking much as you want me." He winks at me, wryly smiling, as he takes off my blouse, his scorching mouth devouring me within seconds, making my body bow and my brain fog.

What was I just saying?

I realise now that accepting the nightcap was a fully loaded invitation and I've walked into the den of the viper. I can tell myself that I didn't mean to, but despite my common sense that tries to drag me away from being lured and bitten, here I am, wanting it.

'Biting is for boyfriends, Scotty.'

The memory hits me full force and a wave of nostalgia sends me spiralling. There was plentiful, playful teasing back then, and it ignites a desire for something more, something I've always wanted. *I hope he bites me, then.*

I wrap my arms around his neck, feeling his broad shoulders beneath my arms. He smells so good; so warm and spicy I can almost taste him. On cue, my mouth waters at the thought of actually tasting him.

One thing at a time, Jessica!

Liam pulls his head back to look at me, his eyes shining bright with arousal, pupils blown with desperation, his breath heavy and erratic and I've never felt more wanted. Blood pumps around my body at a torturous temperature, and the residual heat is pooling between my legs. Liam is looking at me like he wants to ruin me, and I can't wait.

"You, Miss Scott, are wearing too many clothes."

He moves me off him with ease and sits me on the sofa to kneel in front of me, slowly taking off my shoes, softly kissing the inner part of each ankle as he lowers my feet agonisingly slow. Despite the softness of his lips, the searing heat they leave behind is blindly travelling all over my skin. My body responds to him like thunder to lightning. If seeing Liam Taylor on his knees before me wasn't enough, it sure as shit is enough to send me over the edge now.

He leans back on his heels and takes off his shirt one button at a time. Each button that he undoes with his strong, careful fingers sets off another firework of arousal in my core. I watch him eagerly and as the material falls away from his skin. He has an insanely sexy body that he obviously works hard for, and every inch of it is screaming for me to touch him. I run my fingers across his masculine, corded forearms, watching him flex under my touch.

His hands lower to me, until his fingertips reach the buttons of my jeans, but his eyes never leave mine, full of hot desire. The sizzle of his touch on my hips so close to where I need him to be. I push my hips forwards as he peels my jeans off, leaving me in just my black satin thong. He stifles a groan as he lowers his head to kiss the top of my thigh as he inhales.

I may as well be pure liquid now because I'm fucking so far gone for this.

Nipping my inner thigh, he triggers a squeal from me. Standing quickly, he removes his trousers, revealing his thick thighs and toned stomach, the outline of his cock bulging against the cotton.

Fuck, he looks edible.

"You have no idea how much I want you, how long I've imagined this happening, how many times I've fucked my hand thinking of you. I want to taste you, lick you, fuck you, and make you come until you can't think straight." His voice is low, gravelly, and laced with lust as he leans to me again. "Fuck," he says desperately. "Do you want me to stop?"

Definitely not.

I'm pulsing, panting, pining for him. I can feel the slick desire pooling between my legs, my clit throbbing for attention, my walls already clenching, desperately aching for him.

"Come here," I grab the back of his neck and kiss him, hard and demanding, showing him how much I want this too. I rub his hard length over his boxer shorts, and his hands immediately go into my hair, angling me to take what he wants. His kisses move to my neck, hot, wet and frantic, dragging a whimper from my lips when his tongue flicks over my pulse.

I slip my hand into his boxers and stroke him slowly, his moans of appreciation filling the room, making me grip him tighter. My underwear clings to my pussy, wet with my arousal for him. Knowing I can affect him like this too makes me feel dizzy with power.

His hands roam my body as if he is discovering me for the first time and, in a way, I guess it is like that; ten years without each other is a long time.

His teeth nip a trail along my collarbone while his hands move lower. He reaches into my underwear, running his thick finger along the seam of my lips, teasing me. The thrill of us finally touching makes my skin erupt in goosebumps. The sensation of his fingertips on me travels everywhere, except where I need him the most; my clit beats against the ghost of his touch. A carnal need possesses my body, forcing me to arch my back, pushing into his palm, demanding more. "Liam, please," I beg.

When he grazes my entrance, we both hiss. "Fuck, Jess. You're so wet. I need to taste you." Before I can form a thought, he's pushed me further onto the sofa as he sinks to his knees. His head disappears between my legs, his warm tongue darts out, flattening against my thigh before he nips the skin there, making me shoot up the sofa. "Easy baby, I'm just getting started," he hums into my legs, pulling me back towards his face as he drops a kiss over my underwear.

"Oh, God." My hips roll towards him as he hooks his thumbs into my thong and drags the fabric down my legs. His eyes land on my pussy and his throat rumbles on a groan and he licks his lips, wetting them in anticipation. When he moves closer, my body opens for him, my legs falling further against the sofa. His stubble grazes my thigh as he trails kisses from my knee to my apex and I let out a desperate sigh at the contact. My whole body is a ticking time bomb that only he can diffuse as I lay completely at his mercy. "Liam, you're making me crazy... please, just fucking touch me already."

He laughs lightly against my skin, the huff of air leaving his mouth spreads warmth over my aching clit. "Such a needy girl. Since you asked so nicely." He smirks before diving forwards into me.

The pressure from his tongue covering my clit suddenly has my legs flying closed, trapping him against me. My body drowns in the warmth of him flicking against me before he sucks me into his mouth, making my legs shake around his head. I'm already so close, my body stumbling into the abyss of ecstasy as Liam consumes me over and over, daring me to fall.

"Don't... fucking... stop," I plead.

My hands instinctively go to his hair to hold him against me, the threat of oblivion too intoxicating. He pushes two fingers inside of me, earning a purr from my throat, frantic for him to find that sweet spot. When he curls and strokes me from the inside, my legs fly open as I gasp, "Liam!"

His eyes meet mine, still buried between my legs. "I want you to come all over my face, Jess. Give me what I want, and you get what you want." He growls between licks and his demands almost send me over the edge. *Who knew Liam had such a dirty mouth?*

He pumps me feverishly with his fingers, filling me so deeply while his tongue swirls around my bundles of nerves. "Oh god, I'm so... I'm so close," I cry.

Liam groans into my pussy just as his teeth graze my clit, pushing me over the edge. "I-I'm... fuck," I scream. My world shatters as I feel the rush between my legs; an explosion of pure bliss as my orgasm hits me. Liam finally slows his movements, alternating between licking and kissing as he eagerly devours every last drop.

My body is humming, floating, buzzing with my release as Liam slowly makes his way towards me until he reaches my mouth. Kissing me deeply, I taste myself on his lips when he sweeps his tongue over mine.

"See how fucking sweet you taste, Jess?" he mutters before he pushes his tongue back into my mouth, moaning as I suck my arousal from his tongue.

I'm in such a haze, so full of bravado and desire that I decide to stand and push him towards the armchair opposite us, removing his boxers as we move.

I kneel in front of him, taking in the sight of his silky cock as it sits against his stomach. He fists himself twice and hisses in approval at what I'm about to do.

"You don't have to."

"I want to... so much."

Eagerness flows like lava through my blood and sweep my hair to one side before leaning forward, replacing his hand with mine. Wrapping my hand around the base of him, I squeeze his thick length. My mouth waters and my stomach flips at the thought of having him inside of me. I run my hand up and back down, watching his jaw loosen and precum leak from his tip. My thumb smears his arousal over him and when he pushes his hips towards the ceiling, I dive forwards and circle my tongue around the end of his cock, making him moan. I lick away the saltiness and watch his eyes roll heavenward. I taste and tease his tip in shallow movements until he grabs my hair and forces our eyes to meet. The grip he has is gentle yet firm and I instantly feel another rush of wetness to my core.

"Don't tease me baby, I need you. Do you have any idea how many times you've done this in my dreams? Don't play games with me," he rasps.

I smile devilishly at him, keeping my one hand around him and guide him into my mouth again, sucking him deeply until he hits the back of my throat.

"Fuuuuuck. Your mouth is too fucking good, Jess," His words spur me on, begging for me to bring him to his climax. I drop my hand and reach for his balls as I cup them and softly roll them in my palm as I flatten my tongue against the back of him and drag upwards.

My eyes water as I double my efforts. Gripping his shaft, I pump him whilst hollowing my cheeks and moan around him.

"Jesus... Fucking... Christ... Jess," I surge forward, grabbing the base of him and I feel his body stiffen as he empties into my mouth, spilling a slew of inaudible curse words at the same time.

I swallow everything he gives me.

When I finally let him slip from my mouth and look up, I find him staring at me, his hazel eyes soft and sated. He looks boyish and vulnerable sitting in front of me.

"Fuck, Jess, your mouth..." He runs his thumb over my bottom lip.

Something passes between us as we are coming down from our highs. Something beyond a spark of lust. Something that I know he feels, too.

"I don't want you to go home. I want you to stay here tonight. I want to do that all over again and so much more, Jess. Please stay?" His big puppy dog eyes almost break my resolve. If that doesn't, then his cock, which is still staring at me, would. But I have to go home tonight. I can't stay because I know I don't trust myself not to fall into the abyss in Liam's eyes that is threatening to consume me. It's been one date and I can't fall in yet.

"I want to stay, but I think it's best if I go home tonight."

He sighs, obviously disappointed, but he stands and passes me my clothes instead.

"I just think if I stay..." *Fuck, I don't even know what I think.*

He turns to face me as he dresses. "I get it," he says. "It's fine." Even though it clearly isn't fine.

I feel a pang of disappointment at my own stupid decision and I bite my lower lip, wondering if I should stay after all.

When I'm dressed, I stand in between his legs, and he instantly pulls me towards him, sighing deeply. I brush my hands over his shoulders until his chin tips up and rests on my lower belly. "I had such a wonderful time tonight."

"Me too." He smiles, running his hands over the backs of my thighs.

"So, what do you think? Does adult Jess get a second date?" I muse, loving the way his expression softens.

"Adult Jess will be getting a second date whether she wants to or not,"

I smile broadly down at him. "I'll see you soon then?" I bend to kiss him when he whispers against my mouth.

"Wild horses couldn't keep me away, Scotty."

23

Liam

My mum fusses over dinner in the kitchen whilst me and my dad stand, watching her. She refuses to let us help every week, barely allowing us to even set the table. She says it's her favourite thing—making sure her boys are well taken care of. I agreed to let her on the condition that I always do the washing up and she grumbles every week when I insist.

"Okay, we're ready. Can one of you grab the bowl from the cupboard over there, please, for the chicken?"

My mouth waters as the aromatic steam rises from the chicken and vegetables that fill the bowl and my stomach growls, not realising how starved I was. Work was crazy busy today, so I only managed a very quick protein bar for lunch, but now I'm about to make up for it.

As we sit down and dive into our food, we settle into a peaceful quiet, just the three of us like it always is.

"So, sweetheart, tell me what have you been up to? I've missed you."

"Ma, I saw you three days ago when I came by with Dad after work."

She waves her hand dismissively. "I know, but this is family time. We don't get to talk much when it's not about work with you two," she points her knife between my dad and me and we look at each other and shrug.

I haven't talked to them about Jess and me reconnecting yet. When they recommended the restaurant, I didn't tell them who I was taking. Grayson is the only one who knows so far. "Do you both remember Jessica Scott?"

My dad coughs, almost choking on his dinner, so I slap his back to help him clear whatever that was. "You mean the only girlfriend you've had... that Jessica Scott?" he says between splutters.

"The one and only..." I bite into my food, ignoring the subtle dig. "Well, we've been seeing each other again."

My mum squeals a noise that I don't think I've ever heard her make before and I'm not sure I'll forget in a hurry either. "Jesus, Mum." I place my hand over my chest to steady my nerves.

"I'm sorry, it's just that you and her... Gosh, you were both so sweet. It was so sad that it never worked out."

Yeah, it was sad. I was sad, for months after we broke up. Not only had I lost my girlfriend, but my best friend too, and that stung more than I could handle. That's when I threw myself into dad's business. I worked until I was dead on my feet between college and the office, but it made me learn fast and I'm grateful for that.

"Thanks, Ma. I don't know what we are yet, so don't get excited."
Fuck, I probably shouldn't have told her because my mum has zero chill when it comes to me.

"Does she know her mum is in London, working for us?"

And there it is; the very thing I've been avoiding since I bumped into Jess. I can hear the tension in his voice as my dad speaks, but it's got nothing on the tension I feel in my body right now at his reminder.

"No. I haven't said anything." My lips form a frown, hating that I haven't said anything to Jess yet.

"Boys, I said no shop talk, please," Mum warns us both and I drop the subject for now, knowing that this won't be the last time we talk about it. "You must invite Jess over for dinner soon," she adds brightly.

"I'm sure she'd like that. She hasn't changed, still gorgeous and fiercely independent." I find myself blushing at the thought of her.

"I don't know if that's a good idea, Jessica coming here for dinner, until we figure out things with her mother," my dad adds.

Heat rises as I squeeze my knife and fork in my hands, forcing myself not to react.

"John, will you stop it," my mum interjects.

Dad sighs frustratedly, ploughing a hand through his thick, peppered grey hair. "Liam, all I'm saying is, I expect you to keep confidentiality with this. It's what any respected CEO would do, and you should do the same. You have a duty of care to Claire now. Think about your future with my company. You need to act in the interests of others, too."

I scoff, disbelieving the words he's saying or not saying. "*Our* company, Dad. You've spent my whole life preparing me for this, so threatening my future, when all I've done is dedicate my entire career to *our* company is... well, it's fucking low." I'm not backing down easily, but I will follow the rules for now, "I'm not going to say anything yet."

"You won't say anything at all," he booms.

"You know, you're acting like this is more important than someone I care about, but I know that can't be right," I say my chest rumbling with anger.

"This company *is* the most important thing. I need to see consistent leadership from you, and spilling something like this, without consent from Claire herself doesn't do that. It shows me you can't handle confidential matters and being a CEO comes with much more responsibility than what to tell your girlfriend."

I stand abruptly, rage simmering like a vast stormy ocean beneath my skin. "I'm completely capable as a member of *your* leadership team and you know it."

My fists clench by my side as I try and dampen my temper. I suddenly feel the need to be somewhere else. "I'm sorry, I'm heading out. Thank you for dinner, Ma. It was delicious as always. I'll see you in the office tomorrow, Dad."

I walk out into the cool October air and take a lungful of oxygen before blowing it out, releasing that conversation. My dad's always been a workaholic, but I don't need him riding me for this, not when I'm beating myself up enough about it.

When I get home, I see a text from Jess and my chest constricts.

Jess: Are you busy? x
Liam: Just got home from my parents, give me
five and I'll call x

Spoiler alert, I gave her two minutes, then couldn't wait and FaceTimed her.

"Hey," she says as her face fills my screen. She wipes crumbs from her mouth and chews softly through a smile.

"Hi, baby," I say and chuckle lightly. "What you eating?"

"Nora made some granola. I was just testing it for poison, of course."

"Oh man, I wish I had some of Nora's homemade granola."

"I'll save you some..." she says, shovelling more into her mouth.

"You sure there'll be any left?"

She smiles weakly and nods, humming her answer through her mouthful. "So, how are your parents?"

I omit the part of the conversation that I'm not allowed to talk to her about *yet* and settle on the easy answer. "Good. Mum overfed me as usual. My dad..." I run my hand over my face, "He was difficult tonight."

She tips her head towards the phone. "Difficult?"

The words burn my throat, my conscious desperate to break out and admit that I know where her mum is, but maybe she doesn't want to know. Judging from our conversation the other day when I asked, and she avoided it, I decide to listen to my dad's voice in my head and say nothing for now. At least, until we talk to Claire. "Yeah, difficult." I sigh, wanting to forget all about it. "We were talking about you tonight," I tell her, trying to change the subject.

"All good things, I hope."

"All good things. Kept it PG for them, obviously."

She dramatically wipes her forehead as she walks upstairs and throws herself onto her bed. "Thank god for that."

As I flop onto my bed, mirroring Jess, I pull off my t-shirt, needing to cool down a little. I hear Jess mumble something that sounded a lot like *holy fuck*, so I smirk at her when our faces meet again.

"Hi," I say.

"You're half naked, on my phone... again," she says as she gawks at me.

"Hm, and you're not. How disappointing... can I convince you to take a layer of clothing off too?"

She pauses for a second and goes bright red. "I'm not great at the uh, phone sex... I mean, I've never done it before."

"Me neither," I say, laughing lightly. "But since you brought it up, wanna try it?"

She laughs, it's nervous but also charming and sweet. She places her phone on her bedside and slowly reaches down, but I can't see what she's touching until she brings a sock into view of the camera. A fucking sock.

"Ha-ha, very funny."

"I thought so. You said a layer, you didn't say which layer..."

"Smart arse," I huff.

I scowl at her, but her smile just gets wider as she slowly unzips her hoodie, leaving her in a white sports bra and shorts. "Is this okay?"

I'm barely able to nod my head as I watch her nipples harden. My throat becomes thick with desire as I swallow and palm my hard cock underneath my jeans.

She smiles, as though she's seen the answer written all over my face. "Your turn then," she whispers.

Why do I do this? I go in all guns blazing without thinking things through. I'm literally sitting here with my dick in my hand–with absolutely no idea what I'm doing.

Is this hot?

I stand the phone on my bedside table as I walk backwards and take off my jeans, then my boxers and socks. I look at my screen and find her skin flushed from watching me undress, and my dick throbs in response.

Fuck it.

I'm not beating around the bush here; I've decided with every ounce of unwarranted bravado that I have that I want to pop her phone sex cherry, so I can't back out now. I hear a noise from her phone, a whimper or maybe a moan, and fuck, I pulse at the memory of her making those sounds, of her on her knees for me, drinking every last drop I gave her after our date.

I go from feeling stupid to ridiculously turned on instantly. That noise, the memory, Fuck.

Okay. This is hot.

"Strip for me, Scotty." I grip my cock and pump a few times to relieve some of the building pressure as her eyes widen and focus on my hand moving. When she removes her shorts, my body tenses at the view. "Naughty girl, Jess. No underwear." I lick my lips slowly. "I'm not sure if I want to spank you or praise you for that."

Her head falls back, whispering a moan at my confession, "I know what I'd want," she admits.

I lay back on the bed and adjust the phone so we can see each other better following her lead again. I want a front row seat for what is about to happen.

"Oh yeah, tell me. What do you want, Jess?"

She boldly moves her hands down her body, keeping one hand pinching her nipple and her breathing shallows. Her fingers find her pussy and her eyes close as her body quivers. "I want you to... spank me... then I want you to fuck me."

"Mmm," I hum as I fist myself slowly, not wanting to take my eyes off this stunning creature on my phone. Her hesitation makes it so much sweeter that she's trusting to do this with me. "So fucking needy for me," I praise her.

"Tell me what you would do to me if you were here," she breathes as her fingers slip inside herself, making her moan deeply and mumble, "fuck."

"I would fuck you with my tongue. Eat every single inch of you until you're screaming for me to stop. Your orgasms are mine, Jess, every... single... one." My cock is dripping with precum and I'm barely holding on, watching and listening to Jess lose control as she pants my name again. "Fuck, I want you so badly right now," I admit.

Her breathy moans drift through my phone as she says, "I want you to make me come, I want you in my mouth, I want you everywhere, Liam." Her back arches and I know she's close. So am I.

The sound of our moans, our hands connecting with our bodies and the primal need for each other fills my head. "Come for me. I'm right there with you. Fuck yourself like I want to fuck you, Jess."

Her whole-body trembles and she cries my name like a prayer, as we both reach our peaks. I don't close my eyes when I come. I watch her as my release spills into my hand and over my abs. I watch every inch of her sexy body curl and rise, then unfold on my screen. It's fucking mesmerising.

"You're so fucking sexy when you come." I stare at her beautiful, flushed face and her sated naked body as she hums under my compliments.

"That was fun." She glows and turns onto her side as she tucks herself under her blanket.

I pout. "I don't like you covering yourself. I like looking at you."

"Until next time..."

"I've got a surprise for you next week," I remember.

Her eyes sparkle with interest. "A surprise for me?"

I nod and she smiles broadly at me again, dimple intact. The sight of her happy makes me happy. I realise I haven't been this happy in a while, with anyone. I let the thought settle as she tries to dig for clues.

"Can you give me any hints?"

"Absolutely not. I'm really bad at giving hints. It's highly likely I'd come out and tell you the surprise by accident, so no, I'm not ruining this one."

"Is it a milkshake delivery?" she wonders.

I shake my head and store that idea away for another time.

"Well then, I'm not sure I want it, anyway." She teasingly crosses her arms over her chest and flips onto her back to pout.

"You're cute when you pout."

She turns to scowl at me. "I'm not *cute*."

"You really are," I taunt.

She grunts, making me smile even harder.

"Jess?"

She turns further away from the camera.

"*Scotty*?"

She peeks over her shoulder looking down at the camera at me but doesn't say anything, a scowl firmly in place, perfect pouty lips still pursed and so kissable.

"I really like you."

She huffs in defeat, knowing she can't keep this up and turns so she's facing the ceiling so I can see her side profile; she's fighting a smile, and something blooms in my chest as she mumbles...

"I really like you too."

24

Jessica

The next few days at work are busy; we have a conference being held all week, and the hotel is bustling with Italians. In truth, I'm grateful for the distraction, and it doesn't hurt to be called Bella by a sexy Italian man every now and again.

Although that is as far as it will go as my mind has been firmly on Liam. We've spoken every moment we can and I still tingle when I think of our video call the other night. My first attempt at phone sex was definitely a success.

Liam has a surprise for me this week, but he won't tell me what, when, or where. I'm not great with surprises, but I guess I'm starting to trust him because a surprise from him doesn't seem to spook me at all.

It's Thursday afternoon, and I'm closing the event room from the earlier conference. It's not that late, but my feet are killing me, and I'm dying to wander into my office for a moment of peace. The warmth from the radiator and the dark light in here are making me feel even more sleepy. My body sags into my winged office chair, letting the throb of my feet dull for just a second. A buzz from my phone brings me back to the present. I yawn loudly and stretch out my body as I reach for to check it.

Liam: Hey beautiful, how is working going? I'm headed to the gym after work. Call me later?

Liam: I hope you are working hard and not ghosting me because that hurts more than eating those seriously hot chicken wings from that place we went to when we were kids.

Liam: Don't tell me you don't remember. I definitely do. You were far too stubborn for your own good and then the way your head exploded because the sauce was so hot had me crying with laughter.

Liam: Not just me though, Nora too. So, you can't be mad at me.

Liam: Ok I get it; you have moved on. Probably with a man from the conference who is called something ridiculously Italian like Lorenzo and has swooped you off your feet already.

Liam: Fine, put me out of my misery, Scotty. Lay it on me.

Liam: P.S. I miss you.

The laughter that spills out of me is loud and carefree. I've neglected my phone a lot today, and it seems I've managed to make someone needy. I almost call him to put him out of his misery, but pining Liam is a very sweet version of him. I ponder my reply to him for a second.

Jess: If you must know, his name is Giovanni, and we are madly in love. He is whisking me away to his family home in Sardinia tonight in fact.

I bite my lip as I wait for his reply.

> **Liam:** Please tell Giovanni that he isn't allowed to have you because I want you far more than he ever will. I'm also sure that I can keep you satisfied for much, much longer.

I openly laugh out loud at his text. *He really could, though.*

My office phone rings as the red light flashes, telling me it's the front desk. "Hello?"

"Miss Scott, you asked me to call to remind you about the large booking tomorrow night."

I groan, "Yes, thank you, Matt. I'll be there in a second." I have to go through the room allocations to make sure the party booked for tomorrow is on the same floor. So, I begrudgingly put my tired feet back to work and walk back to the foyer whilst I text Liam.

> **Jess:** How sure you are of yourself Liam Taylor! Your ego won't fit into your fancy sports car soon. Also... If you boys can't get along, then I will have to punish you both and I'm very good at being stubborn and getting my own way.

I'm smiling from ear to ear as I wait for his reply. Matt at the front desk opens the booking, and we quickly allocate the correct rooms and ensure each room has champagne on arrival. It's something I could've let management organise but this particular booking is one of my wedding parties next month, so I always like to see things through.

I finish up with Matt as my phone buzzes again.

Liam: Firstly, let me say that any punishment you throw my way that doesn't include abstinence I'm happy to receive.
Liam: Secondly, you don't need to worry about me fitting into my car; it isn't my ego that is the biggest part of me.
Liam: Thirdly, you look adorable when you're smiling at my messages.

Oh, fuck.

I frantically look around and when I don't see anyone, I frown into my phone. As I turn towards the bar, I spy two familiar hazel eyes twinkling mischievously at me. He's casually leaning there, staring at me like I'm the most edible thing he has ever seen in his life.

I... am... screwed. Absolutely, utterly screwed.

Liam winks at me with a cheeky smile and lifts his hand to give me a little wave. My heart trembles and doesn't stop. In fact, it gets much worse when he walks towards me. God, even the way he walks is sexy. His six-foot-three frame looms in the vast foyer, devouring the space between us with his long strides. Suddenly he's right in front of me, all wide shoulders and thick thighs and... me, well, I'm an actual puddle on the floor at his feet.

His white work shirt is open a few buttons and I can almost see the top of his muscled chest. The sight of him sends signals directly to my core, pooling desire between my legs, knowing that I'm the one he wants. The one who was watching him touch himself just the other night over FaceTime.

His hair is slightly too long on top, and it falls forward just at the front, forcing him to move it out of his way as he stares at me.

"How did? What? When?" I can barely form a sentence, which is great for me right now.

"You're so fucking cute when you're flustered." He kisses my cheek softly as his large hands wrap around me, pulling me to his hard body. "I spoke to Nora, and she has rearranged dinner with Zoey. So tonight... you're all mine." He leans down and places a kiss as soft as cashmere on my temple. "And," he continues. "I called ahead and spoke to your friend behind you, and he's booked the rest of the day off for you." His expression changes to something much darker now. The light green that is sprinkled throughout his hazel eyes looks burnt with his desire for me. "There's a room waiting for us upstairs," he whispers.

I suck in as much air as my body will let me, for fear of never breathing around him again. I can't help it when he looks at me like that, but it wouldn't be fair to let him have all the fun though, would it?

"What about Giovanni?" I say, batting my eyelids. "He promised to whisk me away tonight." I smirk at him from underneath my lashes and he bites his lip. For a moment, he almost looks angry. It's hard to tell if he's acting or is just genuinely completely possessive of me. Either way, I'm loving every moment of it.

He steps toward me, so close I can feel his body heat. His chest rumbles with need. "Not a single person will be touching you from now on," he says, gently placing his finger underneath my chin so he can hold my gaze.

"Is that so?" I reply, wanting to coax him out even further.

Liam lowers his head, his breath brushing the tip of my ear. "You, Jessica Scott, are nothing but mine."

It really is cute, adorable even, how I thought I could gain the upper hand with Liam. Maybe I could have when we were younger, but this older, more self-assured version of him has my knees wobbling and my pulse racing when he takes control like this. I feel like I'm trapped in his orbit. Nothing makes sense except his need for me and mine for him.

When he pulls back, the look in his eyes consumes me as I whisper, "Yours."

I watch his expression change from lust to gratitude and I get another glimpse of that younger version of him, that always floors me, especially when two seconds ago, this new adult version of him was ready to throw me over his shoulder and ravish me.

We decide to have a quick drink at the bar because considering my plans have completely changed I need some time just to hand over a couple of tasks to my team.

When I arrive, Liam has ordered me a cocktail that looks very inviting and his face looks even more appealing, smiling at me as I sway my hips towards him. I also don't miss that he's picked the most secluded table in the whole bar that's half cloaked in darkness. Smart move, lover boy.

25

Liam

J ess sits beside me, tucked into the quietest part of the bar, her pencil skirt hugging her petite legs and showcasing some *fuck me heels* that I'd very much like for her to keep on later. She looks every bit the seductress that she doesn't know she is. The way her brown hair is neatly pulled back to show her beautiful face, her slightly bronzed skin, her big blue eyes, and the most perfect rose coloured lips I've ever seen.

I've never craved something more than I do her. I'm desperate to touch her, be with her, talk to her, and claim her, and tonight I plan on doing all of that.

"I know I might be at risk of sounding repetitive, but you look beautiful, baby." I take her hand and pepper kisses along her fingers, watching the way her body responds to my touch.

"Thank you." She blushes.

"I decided that you needed a cocktail. I don't actually know what you like, so I chose a Pornstar Martini..." I smirk because she knows exactly why I would choose a drink with a provocative name.

"Interesting choice. Are you trying to insinuate something, Mr Taylor?" She laughs and takes a sip. "That is pretty delicious." The way she licks her lips slowly sends messages straight to my cock.

I take a glance around, the darkness of the room covering us as I place my hand under the table on her thigh, just out of sight. Her pencil skirt has a slit that reaches midway up her leg. I let my fingers slip underneath the fabric as goosebumps erupt over her skin.

She inhales sharply, and I raise a brow at her.

"You okay over there?"

She clears her throat and uncrosses her legs, causing my hand to slip further up her thigh, dangerously close to her underwear. She's playing with fire and the look in her eyes tells me that she isn't backing down.

Game on baby.

I lean towards her, so our lips are almost touching, and her perfume invades my senses and I groan quietly, just enough for her to hear me. My hands slide higher, teasing the line between her underwear and her soft skin. My girl doesn't back down. She holds my gaze intently with a daring look on her face.

"There's my needy girl," I whisper near her cheek, and she shivers from my praise.

I smile to myself and wet my lips; she glows with lust from my attention. I dip a finger underneath the edge of the lace and pause just to make sure we are really hidden at our table.

Fuck, this is too much. I shouldn't.

Just as I think to pull away, she takes my earlobe between her teeth, nipping and winning a hiss from me.

The bold move surprises me and I instinctively move my finger lower to find her thighs absolutely soaking wet. "Fuck." I ripple with pleasure when I reach her core with one finger and I know this can't go any further where we are.

I need to get her upstairs now, so I withdraw my finger, watching the disappointment play across her face. I lift it to my mouth, with her watching my every move. Her jaw slackens as I suck off her arousal, making her eyes switch from a bright shining blue to a deep stormy colour.

Fuck, she is beautiful.

She doesn't say anything else, but she grabs my hand and leads me to the lift. As we reach our floor, I place my hand on her lower back and guide her to our room, locking the door behind us. She shoots me a sideways glance when we reach it. "You picked one of our most expensive luxury suites?"

"I want every moment to be special with you, with us." I cup her face with my hands, and she shines up at me. Those big, baby blue eyes kill me every time. "If you want to use this room to sleep, then we do that. If you want to fuck me until the birds are singing their morning song, then I'm down for that too. I just want to be with you, Jess."

Her blues flash at me, before she says, "I mean, sleeping seems a little... boring, don't you think?" Her face is coy and shy, fuelling my need for her. I immediately lift her up, wrapping her legs around my waist and push her against the closed door. My free hand runs up the side of her body until I get to her full breast, her breath hitching as I skim my fingers around where I can see her nipple pushing through her bra.

"You have no idea what you have just agreed to. I'll never let you go again, Jess."

My mouth takes her, swallowing her response before she had time to give it. My body pushing into hers, wanting everything she will give to me.

I walk towards the bedroom and place her legs down, whilst my hands trace down her arms, watching as her head lolls backwards at my touch, her skin flushing and her breath shallowing. I slowly undo each button of her blouse. Her chest rises and falls rapidly as she watches me with wide eyes. I grip the bottom of her blouse and carefully peel it from her, marvelling at every curve of her body as she stands in front of me. My index finger draws an invisible line down in between the valley of her breasts, watching her pulse with desire.

Her hand reaches for me as she unbuckles my belt and I reach around her back to unzip her skirt. It falls, revealing a white lace thong.

She pushes my trousers down, kneeling at my feet for the second time in two weeks, and I feel my heart stagger at the sight.

Her nails feather up my legs as she moves gradually upwards. I can feel the heat from her breath as she brushes past my cock, and it twitches in response. I pull her up to bury my head in the crook of her neck. I can smell her need for me on her skin. I can taste it as I suck on the most sensitive part of her neck. When I suck harder, her knees buckle and she moans in my ear, using me to keep herself upright.

"You fucking kill me, Jess," I growl into her neck.

Her breathy moan floats up to meet my lips and I take her mouth with mine. There's nothing soft about this kiss. It's the kind filled with desperation; teeth clash, our tongues battle, our chests heave with need. This kiss is us claiming something; something we are both willing to give.

I can't take anymore; I have to have her. I push her back onto the bed and pin her hands above her head as I lean over her. "Leave your hands there. You move, I stop and baby... you don't want that to happen," I warn, but in actual fact it would test all my restraint to stop once I have started to taste her again.

I slowly kiss her soft lips and run my tongue along her jaw and down her neck. She is warm and sweet; my favourite taste. I slip my fingers inside her underwear to find her even more wet than she was at the bar. Her hands move down to her nipples, and I remove my fingers in protest, shooting her a disapproving look. "Tut tut. Hands up.... Now," I rumble, and she raises an eyebrow at me.

I love her challenging me, so I rip her thong from her body and wrap it around her wrists before looping it around the bedpost in a quick, swift movement. Her mouth forms a perfect 'O' in shock as I run my nose along the curve of her jaw, whispering, "I'm going to make you scream, Jess."

I hover over her and sit fully up between her legs so I can marvel at the sight of her. The way her softly tanned skin glows in the light of the room, the way her chest rises and falls, causing her perfectly round breasts to bounce with each breath. Her arms are bound above her head, her pink pebbled nipples are begging me to lick them and her legs are spread open letting me see her need for me glistening.

"Christ, you are fucking beautiful," I purr.

My fingers feather touches down her neck, her collarbone, her breasts, her stomach until I get to the curve of her hips and I stop, watching her breath falter with anticipation. She whimpers as I ghost my hand over the spot she wants me the most. Her body pushes forward, silently begging me to touch her. I free myself from my boxers, unable to take the pressure and I fist myself twice watching her, enjoying watching her squirm for me.

Her wild eyes meet mine and she glances at my cock, hard, desperate for her. I lean forward and let my fingers gravitate towards her apex, gently massage her clit in light circles just enough to drive her crazy.

"Ohhh my... fuck." Her back arches off the bed with eagerness, pushing her chest towards me, and I suck in one of her nipples, tasting her again. I put one finger inside her, feeling how wet she is, and it near enough sends me into a frenzy. She's so perfect it's driving me crazy.

"More," she begs.

I push deeper inside her with two fingers and she groans with need, pulling on her restraint.

The slick sound of her arousal fills the room as she clenches around my fingers, and I know she's close. I draw back, teasing her, edging her, pushing her to her limits. She shoots me a look fuelled with lust and anger. "I told you I'd make you scream, didn't I?" I wink and start all over again with slow torturous flicks, licks and feather-light pressure on her clit. I edge her a few more times until she throws her fists into the bedsheets beneath her.

"Liam, I need to fucking come. If you don't let me, I'm going to do it myself," she blazes, propping herself up to look at me, her eyes full of that fierceness I love so much.

I chuckle, curling my fingers inside her. "You don't touch this pretty pussy, not when I'm with you. It's mine and I'll do everything to make her weep for me and me only."

She thrashes around on the bed, chasing her release as her walls grip me fiercely. I lean towards her and clamp my mouth around her clit before I nibble at the hardened bud, loving how responsive she is to me.

Her body grips me then shudders, signalling her peak. With one last suck, she falls apart for me.

"Oh... My... Liam..." She clamps down and I feel the rush of her release coat my fingers and soak my palm. I drag my tongue over her clit, lapping up her taste, and she bucks away from me, pushing my forehead away. "Liam, I can't," she squeals.

I instantly release the knot from above her head and pull her towards the end of the bed. Humming against her stomach as I move upwards, we lock eyes; hers shining brightly at me. "There she is. You did so well, baby."

She runs her hands over her breasts, purring with satisfaction, letting her eyes close, her eyelashes fanning across her cheeks. I sit up, resting my aching cock on her clit.

"I need to feel you, Jess." I shift backwards as I reach into the pocket of my trousers and pull out a condom.

She stops my hand. "Are you clean?"

I nod. "I've never had sex without a condom before."

"Me neither and I'm clean, too."

An understanding passes between us as I loom over her soft body again.

"Are you sure?"

She nods feverishly as my cock nudges her opening, her wetness already dripping over my tip. "I told you... I'm yours." Her voice is sincere and damn, if that doesn't make me feel like I'm floating on cloud nine. That and the reality of everything hits me full force. Jess is mine. Fucking finally mine.

I deliberately let my weeping cock slip between her folds, ghosting over her already sensitive clit as I watch her stomach contract at the movements until I can't take any more. I sink inside her warmth, making sure to move slowly, feeling every ripple of her around me. I push the head of my aching cock into her entrance, feeling her tight walls stretching for me. "Fuck... me." My eyes close tightly, and I groan as I feel her slowly sucking me inside. I pause for a second before I push all the way, feeding her inch by inch until I bottom out, my forehead falling against hers as we both pause for a minute while she gets used to my size. She whimpers as she takes all of me, opening her legs wider and rocking as she takes me deeper. "You good?" I husk, barely able to form my words.

"Mmm," she hums. "Just so... fucking full." Her eyes close as I slide slowly in and out, stretching her for me.

I grab her chin and her eyes open, "Eyes on me baby, you belong to me now and that means I get to see you when I make you fall apart. Every. Damn. Time."

Her breath hitches as I bend down, kissing her neck before pulling back to see her face as we take everything in for the first time. Her eyes fill with emotion, her hands trail my shoulders until they're at the nape of my neck, pulling me towards her. "Liam..." she whispers against my mouth, a sob threatening her voice.

"I know, baby." My throat fills with the same emotion I see in her as I stroke her face with my thumbs, getting lost in her gaze.

"I'm ready. I need you to move. Fuck me," she says, the fire reigniting in her beautiful eyes, making my cock pulse inside her.

I smile and pull back before impaling her again with one hard thrust, the sensation of her driving me wild. "So perfect," I groan.

With long, purposeful strokes, I move my hands to grip her behind, pinning her against me as I slam into her, tilting her until I hit her G-spot. "Oh shit," she screams, and I smile against her neck, sinking my teeth into her neck as I thrust against her sweet spot again and again.

I sit upwards, widening my knees for traction as her eyes devour my stomach as it tenses when I pull her down onto me, smiling as her eyes roll on a moan. "Mmm, do that again." She murmurs.

I adjust so I can slam against her, watching her body take all of me, my thumb coasting over her clit as I quicken my pace, the tingle of my orgasm sneaking up my spine, but I don't want this to be over yet. My eyes close, trying to keep my cool. "I can't hold on, baby; you feel too fucking good. Put your arms around me; I'm going to move us."

She grips onto me, and I flip us, so she is on top. Pushing into my chest, she takes me deeper inside of her sweet pussy. "Fucking... hell," I curse. Sixteen-year-old me is screaming in my head to keep it the fuck together and last for her, but Jesus she's so fucking perfect it feels like an impossible task right now. *Breathe through your fucking nose, man, you can't fuck this up.*

The sight of her on top of me makes me spiral. This was a fucking bad move. She looks like a goddess taking all of me, owning me the way I've dreamed about. Her hair is wild, her lips pink and swollen as she smirks, rotating her hips in slow circles as she gets used to the new sensation, knowing exactly what she's doing to me. I cover my eyes, desperate to claw back some control over my impending orgasm. "Jess, baby, move faster... ride me," I force out.

She licks her lips and parts them on an exhale. Following my instruction, she glides up and down my length, riding me like she's been doing it for a lifetime. Her head falls back as she grinds against me. My heartbeat rings around my head. My cock pulses inside her as she moves her hips faster and faster, her breasts bouncing every time our bodies slap together again, her wetness seeping onto my balls. My fingers dig into the skin at her hips, driving her deeper every time she comes down as I mark her as mine. Watching as she takes her pleasure from me, I need to be deeper. I want everything. I can't fucking wait anymore.

I place my thumb on her swollen nub and circle, edging her further, watching her writhe and shudder above me as my own release burns into my veins, the pressure too unbearable. "Now, baby. Come for me now."

She looks at me, her eyes searching my face for the same feelings she is having. Wild, fierce, and all consuming. *I feel it all, baby.*

"Ohhh, ohhh. Fuck..." she moans as she clamps down on my cock, coating me in her sweet honey.

"Jesus, Jess... fuck I'm gonna come..." I let out a throaty roar as I feel her release dripping down onto me. I grip her hips, slamming into her wildly, letting go of all the tension and pressure building in my body as I come inside her.

26

Jessica

As our haze subsides, we are caught in a moment of bliss and something intimate passes between us again. Something indescribable and potent. I'm lying on his chest and his arms are wrapped around me. And then it hits me. *Liam and I had sex. We actually did it and it was fucking amazing.*

We are a hot mess of tangled limbs and I break the contact because that unfamiliar feeling hits my chest, the one that screams, *I'm in over my head and I don't know how to react.* It was everything, and so much more. My thoughts are racing as his hands run aimlessly over my spine.

"Jess, you are fucking amazing." Liam squeezes me again and I feel something settle in me.

"You're not so bad yourself."

Not so bad? He is an absolute sex-god. The way he watched my body respond to his touch and knew exactly what I needed is like nothing I have ever experienced.

"Jess, I want to ask you something, but I'm scared you'll say no, and I really want you to say yes." His vulnerable tone has my head snapping up to see his face. His beautiful, sated, stubble lined face. His hands brush a stray hair and tucks it behind my ear.

"Ask me," I say, feeling brave. I cup the side of his face to stroke the short hair along his jaw.

He holds his breath, closes his eyes and then blurts out, "I want you to come to Paris with me."

I shift my body, and his eyes spring open when we disconnect. I stare at him for a minute, trying to figure out this wonderful man sprawled out inches from me.

I didn't think he would ask me that. I wasn't sure what he was going to say. His eyes tell me so much more than his words ever could. I can see the fear of me saying no, I can see the intimacy that we share, I can see how he feels about me; he makes me feel like I can do anything when he looks at me... like I'm the only thing in his mind. A big bubble lodges in my throat and tears threaten my eyes.

He wants me to go with him.

"Okay," I whisper, because anything louder will make me choke.

He buries his head into my neck and inhales in relief and I realise in that moment I never want him to let me go.

"You aren't just saying that because I made you orgasm today, are you?" He nudges me and then rolls on top of me, locking our eyes together.

"Guilty."

Liam beams. "If you come with me, I can give you French orgasms."

I laugh freely and loudly, vibrating against his chest. "What's a French orgasm?"

"I have no idea, but it sounds good, right?... You'll really come with me?" He strokes my face, staring deeply into my eyes, but it feels like he's searching deeper than that.

"You don't have anyone else you'd take?" I ask, half wondering if he does because we haven't talked about being together that much. I also want to give him an opportunity to change his mind in case he thinks he should ask me because it was my event that he won it at.

His eyes flash. "Jessica, if you think I'm asking you out of obligation, think again. I've never wanted to go anywhere with anyone. *You* are the exception. I want to make you feel like you deserve the world because you do. Whatever you're thinking, because we both know you're thinking something I can see it on your face, just... stop."

His head lowers to my lips.

"I want you."

Kiss.

"I want to take you away and do unspeakable things to this body of yours."

Kiss

"Come with me to Paris and find milkshakes, but fancy French ones."

Kiss

"And dandelions, but you'll need to wish in French because, you know... France."

Kiss

Kiss

Kiss

Honestly, this man.

"Liam... I..." He places a finger over my lips and continues to move down my body and once again, I'm lost in a sea of him, and right now I don't want to find the shore.

27

Jessica

*T*here are four doors in the hallway; a hospital or maybe a school. I'm alone, and all I can smell is smoke, the kind of smoke that I associate with my mother. Just as I think of her, she steps out of a doorway into the hallway with me. She is far away; her eyes are glazed and she is mumbling something that I can't hear.

I can't hear anything except a ringing sound.

She gestures to me. She wants me to go to her, but I can't. My feet are stuck and I can't make myself move. She starts crying and then disappears again, leaving me alone.

I still can't hear anything, and I can't move. My eyes dart around the hallway, desperate for an escape, for a way to move and go to my mother. I finally get one of my legs free and fall forwards into another hallway, but this time I'm facing a glass door. Inside, I can see Liam and his father talking. Liam is angry and shouting at his father. I can't hear anything, but then I spot my mother sat in the corner of their room. She has a syringe in her hand. I try to open the door, but I can't. It's locked, and she looks so sad.

I can't reach her, and I can't shout to get Liam to help me. I'm screaming without sound and banging my hands on the glass when it shatters...

I jump up out of bed, my ears ringing, and I can't quite get my bearings. The cool air in the room alerts me to my naked body and I press myself against a wallpapered wall I don't recognise. My eyes glance back to the bed to see Liam splayed out across it, the sheets half-draped over his legs.

Fuck, I'm in the hotel. I'm fine, I'm safe. I'm okay.

I take some deep calming breaths and blink a few times to rid my eyes of sleep and bring myself back to reality. It was just a dream, just a dream. The same dream I always have. I check the clock.

`05:35am.`

My heart hasn't got the memo that it needs to calm down yet, so I head into the bathroom and splash my face with water. I stare at my reflection. My hair is a tangled mess, my lips are swollen, and I have a small love bite on my collarbone. I look thoroughly *fucked*. Memories of last night fill my consciousness, helping me relax against the counter.

"Scotty girl?" I hear Liam call out, breaking my trance in the mirror.

I peer through the doorway. "I'm here."

His broad shoulders are flexing in a stretch, his tall body reaching far past the bedposts. My insides clench at the thought of this man being mine. I like it.

"I thought you'd left me for a second." He rubs his cute, sleepy face and tries to sit up but fails miserably and flops back down, pulling the blankets over himself again, groaning.

I shake my head. "No, I just..." I don't think I want to tell him about my nightmare. "I just used the bathroom when I woke up is all."

"Come back to bed. It's too early and I have something for you here."

God, it isn't fair that he is somehow sexier when he's just woken up. Even if he does look like a giant burrito, the way he has wrapped himself up in the blanket. I happen to love breakfast burritos.

I throw open the door so he can see my naked body and I get exactly the response I wanted.

His eyes widen when I whistle to get his attention. "Well, good morning to you, too. Get your sexy ass over here." He pats the bed. "Or I'll come and get you." He raises a challenging eyebrow at me, and I go to close the bathroom door, smirking at him. Having this Adonis of a man chase me could be pretty fun.

"You're getting it now," he shouts, padding towards the door before it flings open. I can't stop the squeal that leaves my mouth as much as I can't stop my body's reaction to seeing him completely stark naked stood before me.

Lord have mercy. This man doesn't belong on earth.

"You've backed yourself into a corner now, baby. How *will* you get away from me?"

He stalks forwards.

I step back.

He stalks forwards again, but he isn't the first thing to reach me. No, it's another part of him that touches me first...

"He looks energetic this morning." I glance down at his huge erection that is now resting against my lower stomach. "Who said I want to get away from you? I'm all yours, remember?" He licks his lips hungrily as his cock pushes against me again.

I turn, letting his length rest against my arse as I step into the shower and turn it on. He groans as he squeezes both cheeks and gives one a sharp slap before rubbing the same spot, sending pulsing shockwaves to my clit. I inhale, let out a soft moan, and turn to see his face beaming at me.

"Oh, you like that?" His breath is hot on my neck as I feel arousal spike through my veins.

He roams his hands to cup my breasts and pinches my already hard nipples. I can't help but moan again and push my chest forwards into his hands. "You're so greedy," he says, his smile evident in his voice.

I try to turn to face him, but he stops me, holding my shoulders with one hand while running his fingers down my spine. He pauses at the very bottom of my back, and he pushes his fingers between my cheeks, his finger drifting over my hole before he dips his thick fingers into my core, purring in approval when he feels how wet I am for him.

"I need you," I tell him as the hot water runs over our bodies. "Fuck me." I push backwards into him and he barely hesitates as he pushes into me, filling me completely.

28

Jessica

I didn't want to leave the hotel room but if I didn't, I know with a hundred per cent certainty that I will be walking out with a limp, because Liam Taylor is insatiable. He's also sweet and caring and so stupidly adorable, things that I guess I'd forgotten about, but he's definitely reminding me.

The sun beams down on my face as I walk the streets of London, heading back to my house. My shoulders are back, my feet feel light as a feather, I feel *good*. I want to hang onto this feeling because I haven't felt it in forever.

I open our front door and shout to see if Nora is home. I hope she is because I have a surprise for her. I find her in our lounge reading with her black rimmed glasses, and she immediately wiggles her eyebrows at me. "You're back and you look... fucked and happy." She laughs.

Nora listens to me word vomit about Liam without giving her too much detail, because even my best friend has limits. Meanwhile, I keep rubbing my chest because there's a hollow feeling that creeps in when he isn't with me, and I don't know what to do with it just yet. I swallow thickly and focus on Nora.

"So, I have a surprise for you."

"A surprise?"

I nod. "We are going to a club opening with Zoey tonight."

"Cocktails and dancing?" She looks at me hopefully and clasps her hands together.

"Exactly that! I figured we could go to a few of our favourite places that we've neglected lately. Oh, also Zoey has put our names on the VIP list for the new club on the Southbank."

Nora squeals when I finish, then her face pales as she grasps my arm.

"Oh God, what the fuck am I going to wear?" Her eyes are wide and scared. I have to stifle a laugh and she swats me. "This is serious. I need to attract someone of the opposite sex and to do that I need to not be wearing my work clothes or pyjamas."

"Sorry," I chuckle, then deadpan my face, fighting a smirk. "You're right. Serious face now. I have plenty of clothes you can wear. Slutty, not slutty. You can pick anything."

"True, you do have too many clothes. Let's go find something. What time are we going to go out?"

I look at my watch, "We have an hour and a little bit to get ready."

She groans and mumbles something about not having enough time.

We head upstairs to my room, and Nora makes quick work of going through my wardrobe. She pulls out three options; one is a black, strappy, cowl neck dress with a low back, another is a sheer black dress which I would usually wear hotpants and a bra underneath. The last one is the one I think she will pick; a short, satin, baby blue, strappy dress with adjustable ruched sides. It will make her dark hair pop.

She tries on all three and looks incredible in all of them. I tell her the blue is the one, and she agrees. She picks out her strappy white heels to pair with it, and if she doesn't get anyone's attention tonight, I'll be very surprised. She looks insanely hot.

She then, in true Nora style, picks my outfit for me. She's so bossy.

I don't mind because I'm distracted by texts from Liam telling me he misses me already.

She throws a white dress at me and insists I wear that with a bright orange coloured cutch bag and shoes. The dress has long sleeves, a cut out underneath my boobs and another just above my hip bones and my body in all the right places.

"You ready? I'll call us an Uber. Wait, what's our first stop?" Nora asks whilst opening her phone.

"I'll sort the Uber. Zoey texted me the address." I pull out my phone and order one. When I lock my phone, I notice Nora staring at her reflection in the mirror, tugging the length of her dress down unsuccessfully. I slap her bum to get her attention. "Don't overthink that dress. You look great," I say as she shrieks. "Really, you look stunning. Let's go, before you put on those awful granny slippers with the bows again."

"Those slippers are comfortable, and you know you want a pair."

I definitely don't. In fact, I'm going to throw hers away because if there is one thing that would scare anyone off it's those ragged slippers. Really, there have been nightmares about them.

We head downstairs to get a shot of tequila before we leave.

I pour us a shot each and Nora has sliced the lime. "Ready?" she nods and we both down the shots like the pros we are, sucking the limes after.

Delicious.

Just before our Uber arrives, we take some pictures together in our large mirror that hangs in our hallway. I decide to send them to Liam because we don't look this good every day, and I like the thought of him getting bothered by them.

Nora looks over my shoulder and laughs at the caption on my text to Liam. I decided to go with 'Girl's night question -are these dresses too short?'.

Liam immediately replies,

Liam: Jesus, don't do that to me. You both look stunning. Jessica Scott you better remember that you are mine and that hot as fuck body of yours should not be touched by anyone but me... and yes that dress is too short, and I'll be punishing you for it later.

I'm grinning ear to ear with his possessiveness because I haven't ever seen this side of Liam. I like it.

Jessica: Yes please, sir.
Liam: Noted. Enjoy your night x

An hour later and two delicious, fruity cocktails and Nora and I have put the world to rights.

The low thumping of the music is rising throughout the bar, making me check the time.

"Zoey says the club is open, but she's going to be another twenty minutes," I tell Nora. "We absolutely have time for another cocktail. I'm going to get them." I wander over to the dimly lit bar, lean my arms on the hardwood and try to get the attention of the bartender.

I bring our drinks back to our table and find Nora talking with a man. He is handsome, younger than us, with black thick-rimmed glasses. I glance over at Nora and I think she is flirting, either that or she's trying to do some sort of rain dance with her arms flailing around.

She's blushing and giggling and he is eating up her words. Well, this is adorable.

I reach our table and the guy she is with looks at me and says, "Oh we didn't order anything yet; we were just talking about our favourite cocktails. Can you come back in like five minutes?" He looks at the cocktails in my hands and then at Nora, and she bursts out laughing.

My brows have met in confusion. *I look like a waitress tonight?* I glance around and notice that all the waitresses or shot girls are wearing white. *The actual fuck?* I hadn't even noticed.

When Nora finally stops laughing, she says, "This is my best friend and sister, Jessica. We live together. She isn't a waitress here." She stifles another laugh, which gets me laughing too, and I watch as the guy turns an amusing shade of red.

"Oh, bloody hell, I'm sorry. I stole your seat. Here sit, please." He gets up quickly and awkwardly and we both laugh as he grabs another chair from a neighbouring table to sit with us.

"So, Nora, I can see you have a drink now and don't need me to buy you one..." The guy pauses, rubbing the back of his neck. "This is a long shot, but can I get your number? I owe you a drink now." His boyish grin charms Nora and I can see the blush spreading across her cheeks.

"I guess I could give you my number." Nora puts her hand out as a gesture for him to give her his phone. He obliges with a great big grin on his face as she types in her number.

He leans into whisper something to Nora, kisses her cheek and then leaves. My head spins to my best friend. "He was hot. You should have invited him to the club," I tell her.

"No way. This is girls' night. There is a code with girls' night. Rule number one being no guys." She winks, and we both laugh.

The club is heaving when we arrive, the buzz of the crowd competing with the music that dominates the atmosphere. It smells new and expensive, like leather and expensive champagne, as we walk towards the VIP area.

Windows run along the one side of the dancefloor, giving a perfect view of the River Thames. On the opposite side, there are leather booths and the entire place is decked out in navy and gold with white flower accents. The bar itself is lit up with warm, white lighting, showcasing the spirits available.

Dua Lipa plays through the sound system, and I scan over the dancefloor at the few hundred people moving their bodies to the beat as the bouncer at the VIP area lets us through to the upstairs.

"This place is awesome," Nora shouts.

Zoey comes flying over, all platinum blonde hair and high heels. "You made it!" she squeals, throwing her arms around us. "Come, meet some people." She drags us past couples dancing together, businessmen in designer suits and lots, and I mean lots, of women wearing a whole lot less than we are.

Thankfully, Zoey settles us into a booth in a quieter area, tucked in the corner with the perfect individual dancefloor in front of us.

"So, do you know the owner to get a VIP spot?" I ask.

"My brother owns it. He has this as a side business with a friend of his. Good to know people in high places." She winks. She's not wrong. There are a lot of people who look like they are dripping with money. For a second, I feel self-conscious but quickly brush it off when a waiter approaches us.

"What are we drinking, ladies?"

Nora and I look at each other, smile and both shout, "Tequila!" at the same time, throwing our hands in the air, making us all laugh. Zoey orders three shots and a bottle of champagne, and before we know it, we are sipping on chilled bubbles.

"So, Jess, spill. Tell me all about Liam." Zoey remembers us being together in school, but she doesn't know everything about what happened, so I keep it as current as I can.

"God, Liam... he's so..." A delicious shiver racks my body whilst I think about him. "He's all man, and we're having a lot of fun together." What I want to tell her is that he spent a whole twenty-four hours railing me into a headboard, wall, shower, sink, foot of the bed... but I keep those delicious memories just for me.

"I'm dead jealous," Zoey pouts.

"Jealous? Zoey, you get more attention than Minnie Mouse at Disneyland. Girl, why are you jealous?" Nora asks incredulously.

"Because… it's adorable. The whole love story of it all."

Nora side eyes me, knowing I won't want to dig up what happened. "They're adorable."

I smile a grateful smile at her, thanking her for having my back as always.

"Girls, the dancefloor is calling my name. If you don't follow me then… well, I'm going regardless, but dancing with my girls is way more fun." I stand stepping towards the dancefloor, only feet in front of us.

The floor is black with pink lights along the edge, giving the space a funky vibe. We pick a spot close to the windows. Zoey is ninety-nine per cent wild energy, so we both end up pulling out some cheesy dance moves, never taking ourselves too seriously, whilst Nora laughs at us both. After dancing and drinking for a few hours, I realise that this is the most fun I have had in a long time. I glance at my watch, and it is close to midnight. Nora catches my eye and looks at her feet and pouts. I nod my head and point to my feet too, both of us feeling the pain of our heels. We look over to find Zoey whispering to the tatted guy she has picked up just as he grabs her hips and pulls him into his broad chest. I think it's safe to say Zoey has scored.

Nora laughs and shouts over the music, "One more for the road?"

"Hell yes!"

At the bar Nora orders our last tequila shot of the night, bringing the total to… well actually I can't remember. Likely too many. When the spicy liquid slides down my throat, I wince. *Definitely too many.* "I should book an Uber," I announce as Nora shivers away her tequila shot.

When I open my phone, Liam's name pops up.

Liam: If you need a ride home, I have excellent Uber ratings and I only had one beer with dinner so I'm good to go.

I let out a laugh and show Nora Liam's message and she whoops, fists in the air and all.

"Yesssss, get him here to pick us up. That way we don't have to wait ages. That saying 'these boots are made for walking', well, these shoes are not made for all night dancing." She fake cries and I text Liam back.

Me: Pretty sure most Uber drivers aren't as hot as you. We're at Southbank if your offer still stands?

Liam replies almost immediately.

Liam: I'm blushing baby. Be there in 20 x

We collapse into a booth to wait for Liam while Nora texts Zoey to tell her we're leaving and Zoey replies with a series of rude emojis, which is very on brand for her. Within minutes, my best friend is snoring next to me. Also, very on brand for her.

When Liam calls me to tell me he's here, I wiggle Nora to wake her. "We're good to go, babe. Wake up." She mumbles a few words I can't even begin to decipher, so I haul her up into my side and stumble out to Liam's car.

Nora manages to find her feet again once we hit the fresh air, which is a good thing because when I spot Liam, leaning against his Tesla, I immediately want to run to him and claim him as mine. I've never appreciated a fancy sports car and a lean male physique more than I do right now; seeing him leaning against the sleek lines of his car with his long sleeved white t-shirt is sending all sorts of dirty signals through my body.

Down, girl.

He smiles broadly when he sees us and I can't stop myself from running to him. Call it liquid confidence, but I know this giddy feeling is a natural high from him and not a tequila one. I jump into his arms, wrap my legs around his waist as his enormous arms scoop me up, holding me tightly against him.

"Hey, Scotty. You miss me?" The feeling of his face buried against my neck, his stubble brushing against my skin gives me shivers.

"I did, lover boy. I missed you a lot," I admit.

"Owww! These shoes were made by the devil." Nora approaches us slower because she didn't run at Liam like a woman possessed. I lower myself from his grip and he pecks my cheek affectionately.

"Did you ladies have fun? You both still look amazing, by the way." Liam smiles his charming smile, turning my insides to mush, but I appreciate his lie because both Nora and I are borderline dishevelled after a night of dancing and drinking.

"We had the best night, dancing, drinking... and dancing. Wait, did I already say that? Oh, and Zoey was there. She met some guy on the dance floor and they were dirty dancing all over the place. We left them to steam up the windows. Also, a cute guy gave me his number, and he had glasses. He also thought Jess was a..." and that is the exact point I slap my hand over her mouth. Nora sniggers beneath my palm but then tries to lick my hand like a child.

"You licked me!" I shriek, wiping my freshly licked hand on her dress.

"What did he think you were?" Liam asks dubiously.

I roll my eyes at the ridiculousness. "It's not a big deal. He thought I was a waitress. All the waitresses were wearing white... yay for matching!" I say sarcastically.

Liam stifles a laugh and just as he bends to kiss me, we spot Nora wobbling around like a *Weeble*, laughing and stumbling. *Good lord alive, am I that drunk too?* I don't feel that drunk, but then Nora has always been a lightweight.

"Woah there, Nelly." Liam dives to grab Nora before she eats the pavement. "Let's get you two dancing queens home, then. Cuppa before bed?" He guides Nora to the passenger door as she nods her head sleepily. His front seat folds forwards and Nora jumps into the backseat with a squeal of excitement that makes us both laugh.

I wrap my arms around Liam, stroking the soft hair at the nape of his neck as I look up at him. His body moulds into mine easily, his hard lines discovering my soft ones.

"Thank you for coming to get us." I peck his cheek softly as he nods. His eyes burn into my own, his hands drift around me, soothing any soreness my body accumulated from dancing tonight. It takes all my strength not to let out a satisfied sigh from the feel of his hands on me so, instead I settle into staring into my favourite pair of hazel eyes.

"You're so good, Liam Taylor." I end the sentence with a drunken hiccup and a rumbling laugh leaves Liam's chest. He pulls me in closer and kisses me with such passion that forces out that involuntary moan I'm trying to suppress.

"You taste like limes and sin, Scotty." He licks his lips and opens the door, gesturing for me to get into the car. "Come on, baby. You need sleep, otherwise you'll feel like shit tomorrow." He closes my door and before I know it, we are outside our house and Liam is waking me up to come inside.

29

Liam

I wake and check my watch to see it's 8:05 am on a Saturday. I stayed at Jess' after picking her and Nora up last night. Watching the two of them drunkenly dance around to Abba once we got home was definitely one of the funniest things I've seen in a while. They both got a second wind after I made them tea and toast and ended up dancing until around half one in the morning.

I may or may not have got some video footage of them both being dancing queens and telling me that I was also a dancing queen. Highlight of the night for me.

I glance over at Jess, who is asleep on her front, her dark brown hair splayed across her pillow and her lips parted as she breathes deeply. I take in every curve of her face as she lays peacefully. I desperately want to touch her and trace the outline of her lips, her nose and her chin, but I let her sleep.

When we came to bed last night, she tried to seduce me by stripping, but she ended up getting tangled in her dress whilst trying to get it off. I've never seen someone be so confused by removing a piece of clothing.

She was drunk enough that she mostly found it hilarious and damn, did she look adorable, laughing and carefree like that. We ended up cuddling until she fell asleep, which was about two seconds. I didn't know how badly I craved just being asleep with her. The way her body moulds so perfectly into mine. Every inch of her was made for me and I plan on keeping her for as long as I can.

I decide I want to get the girls a decent coffee and breakfast and give them a chilled day and for that I need supplies. I make quick and quiet work of getting dressed and leave a note for Jess on her bedside table.

Gone to get supplies to fight your hangovers.
Back soon, Your lover boy x

I find a café open down the street and grab some pastries, plus three americanos. I head back to the house whilst most of London is just beginning to wake up.

As I open the door quietly, there's still silence throughout the house.

Knowing they are both going to be suffering today, I head to the kitchen to set down the pastries, find some paracetamol and water. I put Nora's breakfast and hangover remedies on a tray outside of her door, so she doesn't have to go far for in search of anything.

As I head back into Jess' room with her breakfast tray, I see her stir slowly and grumble. I sit on her side of the bed, brushing some hair from her face, looking down at my brown-haired beauty. There's that tug in my chest again, telling me that I don't ever want to lose her again.

Her skin is flushed from sleep and her hair looks like it has been attacked by birds overnight. I chuckle and that makes her eyes spring open. She looks at me, shocked for a second, and then a warm, familiar smile spreads across her face.

God, I can't get enough of her.

"Good morning, baby."

"Were you laughing at me just now?" Even though her voice is hoarse, she still manages to sound musical. She moves her hair from her face and pouts at me. That bottom lip has my crotch twitching.

"Not exactly laughing at you. I was laughing to myself at how adorable you look." She jabs my ribs and I laugh again at her fake annoyed reaction.

"Lies. I do not look adorable." She buries her head back into her pillow and curls up into a ball.

"Well, I happen to think you do. Even when you are hanging out of your arse." I peck a kiss on her forehead. "I got you some breakfast, coffee and, most importantly, water and something for your head," I say, whilst trying to move her hair from her face again.

Her head perks up, assessing me. Almost as if she can't figure out something. "You really are too good."

"So you told me last night." I smile, opening the lid of her coffee cup, letting the smell drift towards her and she hums in appreciation.

That noise definitely sends another direct signal to my cock, who was already trying to get in on the action this morning.

"I was thinking... we could have a chilled movie day today?"

She nods her head, sipping her coffee, "That sounds perfect."

Jessica

My brain is turning to mush. We're on our second film of the day. All three of us are snuggled on the sofa, blankets and all, whilst we finish watching Nora's film pick. Mine is next though and I'm ending it all on a classic.

Liam had first pick because he set us up this morning with his breakfast delivery, so he chose *The Shawshank Redemption*. I may have had a nice nap through most of the second half and woke to Liam scowling at me because I missed his favourite bit of the movie. My justification was that the nap was really good because he was my pillow.

He's cute when he scowls.

Nora's pick is *Father of the Bride* because she's a romantic at heart and we both grew up watching it. Nora made me watch it with her non-stop when we were kids and yes, fine, okay, I secretly love it, too.

Every party has a pooper... you know the rest, right?

Just like clockwork, whenever we watch this movie, Nora is sobbing and laughing simultaneously.

I'm definitely not crying too. Nope, not me.

Lies.

Nora is, though. I had to pull her closer to me to make sure she didn't start sobbing uncontrollably. Then Liam pulled me in closer, too.

"You're just a big softie, aren't you?" He kisses the top of my head, so I scoff because if I make any other noise, it'll sound like a sob and I'm *not* crying.

"I'm not crying. I'm... I'm..."

Nora looks up at me, tears still streaming. "Crying, you cry baby." She sobs again and Liam shakes with laughter.

"Don't be a little shit or you don't get any of those brownie points from this morning that I know you're saving for later," I tell him.

He zips his mouth shut and grins at me. *God, he shouldn't be this cute.*

The movie ends, and everyone gets up to make some snacks. Ours seem to have run out and that just won't do for my movie choice.

I make more popcorn and Nora grabs the M&M's from the cupboard and mixes them in.

I load up my choice—*10 things I hate about you*. A solid choice, if you ask me.

We watch the movie in silence, or what I thought was silence, until Liam leans towards me and whispers, "You're miming all the words."

I am? *Huh*

"I like this movie, so sue me." I shrug.

He nuzzles into my neck. "I remember. You're cute."

I hum as goosebumps scatter over my skin. "Tell me more…"

"You're hot."

"Uh-huh…"

"Delicious."

"Oh?"

"My favourite flavour actually."

"Interesting…"

"And you make me wild for you." He growls into my neck, and I almost pass out from the instant heat travelling around my body at lightning speed. If I didn't love this movie so much, I would've dragged him upstairs and shown him ten things I want to do to him. But I *really* love this movie.

Have I seen it a thousand times? Yes.

Do I need to watch it once more? Also, yes.

Is it more fun seeing Liam battle with wanting to throw me over his shoulder and drag me upstairs caveman style or let me watch my favourite movie? One hundred per cent, yes.

He nods to Nora, and I spy her mouth open, deep breathing, fast asleep. He winks at me in suggestion.

"She's cute when she sleeps." I pat his arm, letting him know that I'm still planning on watching the movie and not having sex with him whilst Nora sleeps.

He flops back onto the sofa with a huff that makes me grin like a Cheshire cat.

"I know you're smiling." He tugs me back into his arms.

"I just really love this movie, you know."

I hear him mumble something about little five-foot women, but I let it slide.

He's even cuter when he's grumpy.

30

Jessica

"I hope you know that you owe me for this, Jess." Nora sits beside me on the bench, shivering and clutching a hot chocolate like her life depends on it.

Liam asked if we wanted to come and watch his Little League rugby team play. The only drawback is that it's 8 am on a Sunday and we've been up for hours already since practice was on the other side of London.

I yawn loudly. "I know, I know. I owe you a big, fat burger after this. Promised, didn't I?"

"Damn straight. It's so cold even my hot chocolate is barely hot." She shoots me a scowl, while puffs of air stream from her mouth, but I ignore her. Mostly because she's just not a morning person and it's easier to let her be grumpy sometimes. I'll feed her and she'll warm up and be good as new.

Liam and another guy walk out of the clubhouse laughing. They both duck through the doorframe of the rugby club, wearing black jumpers that say *Coach*. Their long strides confidently eat up the space between the club and the bench we are sitting on.

Liam walks straight up to me and leans in to kiss me, giving me a peck that's seemingly so insignificant, yet has my heart doing a little happy dance in my chest.

"Nora, Jess, this is Grayson."

Grayson rubs his tattooed hands together like he has just been given the keys to a sweet shop. He smiles at me and then extends his hand to Nora. None of us miss the blush that creeps across her cold cheeks as he kisses the back of her hand. "You must be Nora. Liam's told me all about you." He winks, and I'm surprised to see Nora temporarily speechless.

She pulls her huge parka coat towards her blazing cheeks, puts her hood up, and smiles a forced smile as she clutches her hot chocolate. "I'm not a morning person." She states it like it's fact.

Liam huffs a laugh next to Grayson and slaps him on the back and Grayson removes his hand, shaking off her chilly mood this morning.

"Sorry about her. She'll warm up, I promise." I look at Grayson, who is still staring at Nora as she scoffs at my comment and mumbles something about her warm bed.

He finally looks at me and smiles. "So, you're the wife to be? Come to check out if he's father material too?"

My face blanches at his comment, and the laugh that barks from my mouth is scathing. When I get a confused look from everyone standing in front of me, I swallow thickly, unable to formulate an appropriate response that isn't followed by me fleeing the pitch. My eyes flick over the field, hoping for a distraction from my lack of response to Grayson's comment.

Liam's brows pinch as he looks at me, hurt flashing across his eyes. *Fuck.*

Grayson taps Liam's shoulder, telling him the kids are done with their laps. He jogs off but turns again to say, "Oh, and Nora, if you need warming up, I'm available to help in any way I can."

Nora barks a laugh and Grayson winks at her.

Liam eyes me for a second longer before dropping my gaze, his head shaking slightly before he turns and walks onto the pitch.

Shit, shit, shit. Why do I have to be so fucking stupid?

I groan and throw my hands into my glove covered hands when Nora's hand comes to comfort me. Not that I deserve it. That was a dick move.

"You okay?" she asks.

No. I'm stupid and not okay, but I bury that shameful feeling coursing through me and nod. "Yeah, I was just... surprised at what Grayson said."

Nora nods. Knowing when I want to talk about something, I will, but right now I just want to crawl away and hide. Liam and I have only been seeing each other for a month, so kids... marriage? Well, fuck, that shit is scary, and I freaked. Stupid really, because all I ever wanted when we were younger was to marry him and have a family of our own. But we're not those kids anymore and things *have* been happening really quickly between us. *Does he want all of that still?*

I settle into the bench next to Nora and watch Liam and Grayson warming up with the kids. Grayson is setting up cones and Liam has the kids huddled up in a group, talking to them, but I can't hear a word. All the kids start to laugh and Liam taps every other boy's head, telling them they are either team mouse or team cat. He then yells 'go' very loudly and all the team who are mice run around like looneys as Liam chuckles at them. He brings the team cats in and talks for a second before telling them to run too. The field is a mess with kids squealing, laughing, dodging one another. The game of cat and mouse is in full swing and I watch Liam as he yells compliments at the mice who haven't been caught yet.

Seeing him do something he loves makes my chest tight. He would be an amazing dad, but I just didn't think we were anywhere near there yet to even discuss it.

At half time, Grayson sends the kids over to their parents to get water and a snack. Liam jogs over to me, an unreadable expression on his face. When Nora realises he's coming over, she stands. "I'm going to the bathroom real quick."

Liam's breath bellows out as he stops a few feet away from me. "You okay?" he asks with none of his usual warmth.

I nod my head robotically, unsure what to say.

Liam downs some water, keeping his eyes on me, assessing every micro expression I'm sure my face is giving him right now. When he twists the lid back on his bottle, sucking the moisture from his top lip, his sharp inhale slices through the tension building between us. "Look, he didn't mean anything by what he said earlier. Grayson likes to shoot the shit and get a rise out of people."

I nod again, still not sure what should come out of my mouth.

"It's just... Jess, you looked... fucking shit scared and I'm trying hard to read you, but you're not giving me much right now." He runs a hand through his hair.

"Liam, I don't want to talk about this here."

He scoffs. "We're back to that?" He turns full circle before holding my eye contact again. "Is this what it's going to be like forever?" he asks, frustration lacing his voice. "We have all this sexual chemistry, but you won't talk to me about anything." His eyes blaze with hurt and it pushes a lump into my throat.

"I didn't say that, but I don't want to talk about it here," I plead.

"Okay, fine. Then when?" he asks quietly, contrasting his earlier mood.

I hesitate, unsure how to tell him that I'm scared to bring up anything about the past or the future. Years of therapy have prepared me for this moment to face my fears, but right now I just want to run.

"I don't know... later?"

Liam nods, frowning at the floor now. When he looks at me again, his vulnerability almost floors me. "Okay... later then." And he walks back to the pitch.

I let out a long, draining sigh as he leaves. Realising we didn't put a time or place on when 'later' was.

31

Jessica

"Please make sure that the event today has all the tables set, and the kitchen is fully prepared an hour earlier than normal. I've had confirmation that they will be here in two hours, so that gives us enough time, but I need you to take point on this one because I have a meeting in twenty minutes with a potential wedding. Any questions?" I ask Kylie, who is quickly becoming my right hand.

She smiles and stands. "I'm on it, boss." She collects the documents she needs from my desk and walks out of my office.

I just about have time to drink my not so hot coffee when I hear a knock at my door. "Come in," I say, not looking up as I finish writing out the final quote for a wedding.

When my eyes snap up when I sense someone looming over my desk. "How can I..." My face stills. "Liam?" My brows crease with confusion. "You're here..."

He nods, whilst tucking his hands into his suit trousers. "I wanted to talk if you have a minute."

The look on his face tells me something is bothering him and I'm betting it's what happened yesterday. "I have a meeting in twenty, but what's up?" I ask, trying to keep my tone neutral, gesturing for him to sit opposite me.

Liam undoes his jacket and fiddles with the button for a second longer than he needs to, making me frown. His mouth opens and closes several times before he makes eye contact with me and finally sits in the chair. "I have to tell you something..."

I nod cautiously, "Okay..."

Just then, my office phone rings, making me wince at the sharp, shrill noise. "Hang on one second," I say to Liam, who looks like he's sweating now.

"Hello?" I pause as I listen to Jean-Pierre have a meltdown over the fact that there's a typo on the menus for an upcoming event. "Okay, Jean-Pierre, it's no problem. I'll get it fixed before my next meeting." Looking to Liam, I flinch with an apology. "I'm sorry. I have to deal with this before my next meeting." We both stand and I notice how pale Liam looks.

I round my office desk, suddenly unsure if I should kiss him or not. "Come over for dinner tonight and you can tell me then?"

He nods, touching my elbow and leaning down to kiss my cheek.

I want to apologise too, but I don't have time to get into anything right now. Whatever is bothering him is obviously something important for him to be this stiff with me. He's always so cuddly and right now, it feels like he's the opposite.

I smile at him, and when I receive one back, my shoulders loosen a little.

"See you tonight, Jess.".

Liam

I tried to tell Jess about her mum, but the words just wouldn't come, but I had to try. Grayson's comment about our future might have freaked her out initially, but it made me realise that I'm keeping this from her, and I hate it. But when it came down to it, my dad's voice echoed in my head, telling me that I'm making a mistake and jeopardising my future, and fuck, I froze. I'm currently on my way back to my office to figure out why my dad is so hellbent on making my life difficult, or more correctly, for how long.

As I round the corner to his office, I hear voices from the other side.

"Things have got more complicated, Claire." My dad's voice booms. Standing with my hand on his door handle, I wonder if I should listen or interrupt. Deciding I have a right to be involved in this discussion, I raise my hand and knock twice before my dad bellows for me to come in.

Claire sits opposite Dad's desk, her face paling when she sees me. Claire looks a lot like Jess. They have the same golden skin and brown hair, although Claire's is much more unruly than Jess'. The only difference is Claire's eyes are grey, the kind of grey that reminds you of a dark cloud looming. Jess' eyes are bright blue, like the ocean in the Bahamas.

"Hi, Claire." I offer my hand for her to shake.

"Liam." She nods, accepting my hand.

A beat of awkwardness looms between us before my dad clears his throat.

"Liam, I was just filling Claire in with some company protocols, since she'll be working with our cleaning team from now on."

I scoff at my dad for lying to my face. "Dad, come on." I say openly, giving him the chance to be honest with me.

"Okay. We were talking about you and Jess."

I knew it.

"What about us?" I ask as I take a seat next to Claire.

It bothers me more than I'd like to admit that the person who left Jess years ago is fishing for information about her because she can't find the courage to face her. But I keep that to myself.

"Claire asked if you were together still." My father says confidently, as though that is any of his business to share. I swallow my anger towards him and turn my attention to Claire.

"We are together, and I plan on keeping her so maybe we should all figure out this issue we all have. I want to protect Jess, but I'm not okay with lying to her."

My dad goes to speak but Claire beats him to it.

"I've been clean for six years." She blurts out, hesitating before she continues, "I moved to Newcastle after... well, everything. I lived there for around a year, hit rock bottom." Her eyes flit nervously to my dad before landing on me again. "I moved back to London, still a mess, but that was six years ago. Then I lost my job a few months ago, the company went bust, and we all got laid off, so when I reached out to your dad, he offered me a job."

I take a minute to process her words and look at my dad for confirmation. "Is that true?" I ask him. He nods his head, a shadow of something flashing across his face before he schools his expression again. "I'm glad to hear you're sober. That's really great news." I smile a genuine smile. "Do you have any intentions of talking to or seeing Jess?" I make sure my voice is even and the words I say are calm because if there is something that is standing between me and Jess, it's trauma that the woman in front of me caused, so if I can help fix that, then I'm going to give it a good fucking go, but I need to figure out what she's willing to do here as well.

Claire hesitates, chewing her lip. "I haven't... I'm not sure."

I hide my frustration. "Can I ask why?"

"You don't have to answer that Claire," my dad interrupts. I shoot him a glare as guilt flashes across his face.

I haven't forgotten about his threat to my future and why he doesn't want me telling Jess. We've skirted around the awkwardness at work, but I need to hear it from Claire now. I need to understand why I'm going to lie to my girlfriend.

Claire runs a hand through her unruly curls, "No, it's okay... I don't think she would want to see me. I'm not sure I'm ready to see her."

Inwardly, my body rages for Jess and how much more she deserves from this woman. Outwardly, I nod and stay completely calm, knowing that any form of anger will make the situation worse.

"Okay," I say calmly before rising from my seat and fastening my jacket. "Jess and I are going to Paris next week. I don't like keeping this from her. I'd like you to consider what you would like to do about this. When we are back from Paris, perhaps we can talk with Jess. If she wants to, of course."

Claire's expression is unreadable as she flicks between me and my father. "Okay," she says meekly.

I take one final look at my dad. "Dad, can I have a word?"

I ignore the claw of pressure that's lodged itself around my gut and continue back to my office.

As I walk into my office, I take a deep, calming breath. Two minutes later, my dad appears, still with the same expression on his face that he had in the room with Claire. The one that I can't fucking figure out.

"Okay, what is going on?" I ask, wanting to clear the air.

He doesn't answer, instead he walks over to my window that overlooks the busy London streets and lets out a heavy sigh. "There's something you don't know about me."

My skin prickles, as I move my feet so I'm nearer to him, both of us staring out of the window. My pulse racing, teetering on the edge as I wonder what he's going to say.

"Before you were born, I was an alcoholic."

My head snaps over to his, eyes wide, as he continues to stare blankly out the window. "I'm sorry. Did you just say you were an alcoholic?" I ask, needing the words repeated.

He nods, flitting his dark stare over to me briefly. "I was. It started innocently at school parties, when me and your mother were young. Then somewhere between school and trying to build a life, I realised I couldn't go a single day without a buzz. The kind of buzz that only alcohol could give me." He shifts to face me, seriousness etching across his face. "We wanted a family, so your mother helped me. She took me to AA meetings. I got clean for her, for you. She was... is my rock and I wouldn't be here without her." Shame fills his voice. I've never heard him this way before, vulnerable. I had no idea.

My heart hammers against my ribcage as I try and accept this piece of information he's suddenly divulging to me. Shaking my head, I push my brows together. "Dad, I don't know what to say. Jesus, I'm sorry. I wish I knew," I say honestly. "But wait, why are you telling me this right now? Does it have something to do with Claire?"

He swallows. "It does. She came to one of my meetings a few years ago, newly sober and I guess we became... allies in this world of temptation. And now, I'm her sponsor. I have been for the last three years. I wanted to offer her security to help keep her sober."

I blink. And blink again. "Dad..." I say, running my hand down my face. I really wish I'd known more about this. I feel weirdly guilty that I didn't know something so big about my dad.

"I have a responsibility to her as a sponsor and now as a boss. If I sense that she might spiral into addiction again, then I will prevent that. I think from what Claire's told me, she isn't ready to see Jess yet."

I run my hands through my hair, "Fuck." I mutter. I understand that, but I never expected it. "This makes everything... fuck."

"I'm sorry I didn't tell you. Until you and Jess reconnected, it didn't matter that I was her sponsor, but now it does, and I can't let her down."

I think for a second about how we got here and what went on at dinner recently. "So, at dinner, you weren't being serious about me losing my job?"

His head hangs low, slumped between his shoulders. "I'm sorry I said those things. I wasn't ready to tell you about my past and what loyalties I had to Claire, and I acted out. This company needs you, and I shouldn't have made you feel any different."

I let out a long breath, feeling relief but still so much confusion. "Dad... why didn't you tell me?" Concern lacing my voice. "I feel like I should've been supporting you or doing... something."

"That life was before you. It wasn't exactly something I was proud of admitting, but I am proud that I've been sober since before you were born. Which is why I help people like Claire, too."

"What do we do now?" I ask.

"I'll talk to Claire again. We'll figure it out, son."

"Jess and I leave for Paris next week. I hate lying to her, Dad."

"I know, I promise we'll sort something, but you have to trust me."

I nod stoically. My mind blank as I stare out of my office window as my dad thumps me on shoulder before he leaves.

My dad was an alcoholic, and now he's Claire's sponsor. What the hell is this alternate universe I've stumbled into? I try to rack my brain over the years, where my mum would have a glass of champagne or wine with dinner, and I can't recall a time when I've seen him have a drink. Ever. It never crossed my mind as strange either because my whole life he's never changed.

I think about Jess and how she might react when she finds out we've hired Claire, and my pulse picks up at the realisation that I have no idea how she'll feel.

Grayson knocks on my door. My glass hangs loosely from my fingers as I focus on the swirl of the amber liquid, I poured it once my dad left, but in reality, I don't want it, I've been nursing it for an hour, wondering about addiction and how it affects so many people so easily.

"Mate, bit early isn't it?" He moves into my office, closing the door behind him. When we lock eyes, I know my expression is anything but friendly. I watch him frown at me. "I was going to see if you fancied getting dinner tonight, but the look on your face tells me you'd rather be alone."

That gets a little laugh from me, but it's empty. I place the glass on my desk, having never let the liquid touch my lips in the first place.

"This must be serious shit if you've got the booze out," Grayson observes. "You gonna tell me what's wrong, or are we going to sit and brood together?"

I sigh loudly as I rub my hands down my face.

"We hired Jess' mother. They've not spoken for years. Claire doesn't want Jess to know she works here, at least not yet, and my dad agreed he wouldn't divulge that information to Jess. Of course, it never mattered until now. My dad doesn't want me to say anything yet, and I didn't understand at first, but maybe now... maybe I do. My head's a mess."

"Would she freak if you told her where her mum is?"

"I think she'll freak if she finds out I haven't told her something like this, but it's complicated..." I pause, unsure how much my dad would want Grayson to know, considering he also works for us. "It hasn't come up in conversation yet, so I maybe have some time, but I hate the thought of lying to her. Fuuuuuck." I exhale loudly, feeling frustrated with myself for this situation.

"I'm sorry, mate. I wish I had the answer for you. Just see how things play out first with her mum and then hopefully things will work themselves out."

"Thanks, man." I check my watch realising the time. "Shit, I've gotta get to Jess'."

"Can I come?" His eyes twinkle with mischief.

"Not a chance, mate. Also, if you think I'm going to let you fuck my girl's sister, then you are seriously deluded. I've got enough problems without you getting involved. Nora isn't a fuck around type of girl, so back off, ponyboy."

Grayson laughs and stands with me. "But she's hot, man..." When he pouts at me, I shoot him a *don't even think about it* look, to which he sighs. "Fine, I'm out. Catch you later, mate."

Just over an hour later, I'm knocking on Jess and Nora's door with Thai food in tow.

Nora answers the door eagerly. "Thank God you're here. I'm starving." She does grabby hands to the food and leaves me in the doorway.

"Good to see you too, Nor. I'm glad we have established that you only need my friendship for food deliveries," I say wryly.

She shouts a half-hearted apology, but I can already hear her rustling through the food in the kitchen. I close the front door and when I turn, Jess is coming down the stairs dressed in grey shorts and a white, off the shoulder t-shirt covered in holes.

Her brown hair is in a bun on top of her head with some strands framing her face, and *fuck,* she looks good. I rub my chin, feeling the stubble that she told me she likes, and look up at her in awe.

She walks over to me without saying a word and slides her hands up my chest, cups my face and kisses me like she hasn't seen me in months.

She tastes like sweet mint and smells like clean cotton. It's a heady combination when combined with the softness of her lips against mine. I bite her bottom lip and part her lips to taste her again, groaning with need. All the earlier stress suddenly drains from my body at a single touch from her.

"What are you doing to me, baby?" I mumble against her mouth.

I needed that. She has, without a doubt, got rid of any bad energy I was carrying without saying a word. My chest swells being near her. I can feel her letting down her walls for me, letting me in, kiss by kiss. It makes me really fucking happy, but I also have so much confusion from the events of earlier wrapped up in that joy, too.

She smiles and pecks me one last time before leading me to the kitchen, where we all eat so much food we are almost comatose.

"Thank you for bringing dinner over," Nora says as we all amble into the living room. Nora sits in her reading chair, Jess flops onto the two seater with a grumble and I follow suit.

Jess starts running her hand along the back of my head affectionately. I lean into her hand and groan. "That feels amazing," I confess as she hums next to me, that noise stoking the fire that burns for her deep in my body.

We stay like this for a while, in comfortable silence, and I almost nod off until Jess whispering in my ear brings me back to reality.

"Baby, before you fall asleep on me, we should have a look at flights for Paris." She nips my earlobe gently, but I don't want to move yet, so I snuggle into her warm chest, not wanting to break this relaxed feeling.

"Mmm, I like it when you call me baby. Did you get the time off?"

"I did. Next Thursday for a week."

My head perks up. "Grab your laptop and we can book it now."

She goes to stand, but I hug her tighter. "Uh-uh. Stay," I pout, clinging to her.

"But you said... my laptop is in the kitchen." She strokes my head, but I'm still clinging to her.

She chuckles and it's a light sound; one that I love to hear. "I don't wanna let you go, though." I pout again, and she smirks, sighing as she looks at me.

"Then let's use my phone or yours to book things. That way, you can be hanging off me the whole time." She shuffles back in between my legs.

I nod and squeeze her behind. "Much better."

"You're impossible."

"Impossibly cute?"

"Impossibly something, that's for sure," Nora mutters with a chuckle under her breath.

Jess' snigger vibrates through her chest as I squeeze her again. "Get your phone, baby." She pats my hands and I reluctantly let her go, but only for the two seconds it takes for me to reach my phone.

"Do you have the details?"

"Let me log into my emails and I'll send it to you." She takes my phone to find what she needs and passes it back to me.

I scan over the website, opting for the more ornate hotel of the two offered via the travel company. Le Meurice hotel is a mile or so outside of the city and from what I can see, I know Jess will love it.

Once I've chosen our flights, I email the hotel and ask them to upgrade our room.

"Go get your passport," I nudge her, letting her finally break free of our cocoon.

By the time we've finished, we're both yawning. Nora snuck off to bed earlier, taking one of her many books and crossword puzzles with her.

"Time for bed, lover boy." Jess pecks my lips; it is the sort of kiss that shows me she is happy. Those moments where she unconsciously holds my hand, strokes my head, kisses me quickly; those are the moments I want to keep forever.

"Damn, I didn't bring a suit for work tomorrow. I don't know why, but I didn't think about staying here. I just wanted to get to you."

"That's okay," she hums, "I understand if you have to go."

I shift my body to get more comfortable on the sofa. Lying flat on my side, I stretch my legs out and Jess sits up slightly, so her body is higher than mine. It just so happens that it's the perfect height for me to rest my head in between her boobs. So that's exactly what I do.

I mumble something I know sounds completely incoherent to Jess. She pulls my head back and says, "I got none of that. One more time for the back row."

I grumble because she moved my head out of my favourite place. "If I have to die, I want to die right here." I bury my head between her boobs again and she chuckles.

"Okay, I'll be sure to make sure it says you died between my boobs on your headstone." She pats me, and I know she's joking, but I'm not.

"Oh, add a picture too, you know, for the heaven spank bank," I say, lifting my head.

Her laugh rumbles in her chest and my head shakes because I'm still buried between her beautifully soft bosom. *Yeah, I could definitely go out this way.*

"It's cute that you think you'll be going to heaven. You're far too naughty to be walking around with the angels."

I look up at her and grin widely. "Yet here you are, with me."

She rolls her eyes with a smile. "Okay, Casanova, let's get you home."

When I make no motion to move, Jess continues stroking my hair. Her breath hitches for a second as she says. "Hey, can I talk to you about something?"

"Yeah, of course."

"I want to apologise for the other day. I'm sorry."

"Listen, you don't have to—"

"I do. I'm not used to being open and honest with people. It feels... weird. But you've been so open and honest with me, and I want to give you that, too. When Grayson said about marriage and kids, I panicked. Forever just felt like a big word, but it's not, especially when I think about spending it with you."

"Scotty..." I say, willing the emotion to stay out of my voice.

"You don't have to say anything. I just wanted you to know that this feels right between us, and I don't want to lose it again."

I feel the moment that my heart stutters and stumbles into the palm of her delicate hands. The realisation hits me full force. I'm falling for her all over again. Maybe I never actually stopped. She remained in my heart even though it broke for her; it healed the moment I saw her again. It feels right being with her too. It always has, even if we spent ten years apart. None of that matters now that I have her again.

"This feels right to me, too. And that scares the shit out of me. I want you. I'd like to keep you, Scotty. Forever *is* a big word. But I'd be

ALL OF MY LASTS

lying if I said I hadn't thought about it." I admit, giving her a snippet of how I'm feeling.

Her eyes shine. "You feel like family. Like home. I need that."

Another wave of emotion ripples through me. I'm getting everything I've ever wanted. Jess is opening up to me and now I'm keeping secrets from her because of my dad.

I need to tell her about her mum. I want to tell her.

I grab her wrist and pull her towards me. "You know I came to your office to tell you something?"

She nods her head.

"Well I... there is something..." Fuck, guilt slams into me, I can't betray my Dad but I hate not telling Jess. I swallow the razor blades lining my throat as her hands cup my face softly.

"Hey, you don't have to tell me right now. It's okay, we're good. Come. Let's go to bed."

She gives me a big smile, my favourite one where her dimple shows. I rub my thumb over the spot where it appears and I sigh. "You're making me a wet blanket, Miss Scott. What am I going to do with you?" My nose grazes hers as I inhale my favourite smell... her.

Her eyes twinkle. "I think if anyone is wet here, it's me." She grips the back of my neck and pulls me to her.

"S-Sorry," I stutter. "I think my brain just short circuited. Say that again."

Her breath skates across my neck, our bodies still pressed together, making me instantly hard. "I'm wet for you, Liam."

Knowing that she's wet and wanting me right now has all the hairs on my neck prickling. I push it away, because there's something I need to do first.

"Scotty, that is music to my ears. You have no idea, but... " I say, almost drooling.

"Something more pressing than this?" She presses her hand to my erection, rubbing slowly.

Fuck me, if I wasn't hard before, I'm made of steel now.

"Christ Jess..."

Trying to regain some control, I slide my hands around to her bum and squeeze hard and she gasps, looking at me from under her lashes. Her eyes glint; feral and all fucking mine. My need for her overtakes every thought I've had in the last five minutes. I can barely form a sentence, let alone talk to her about everything right now. She grinds down onto my waiting erection, and my throat rumbles with desire. I'm shelving this conversation again, but right now my world is being rocked by a temptress that I have no business resisting.

I lean into her ear. "You'd better get that sweet arse upstairs, Scotty, because I need to sink my cock into you right fucking now."

Standing us both upright, Jess looks at me and smirks like the little devil she is. She casually turns her body and rubs her arse against my cock, which is straining to break free from my chinos. I grip her chin, holding her back against my front.

"You playing with me, Scotty?" She doesn't answer, she just bends over in front of me to pick up a pillow. "Fuuuuuuck, that's it. You're going to get it." I tap her arse one more time and chase her up her stairs. When we get upstairs, she squeals in excitement and jumps onto her bed, legs wide open, eyes wild. She crooks a finger telling me to come to her.

And who am I do disobey my girl?

32

Jessica

I wake slowly from my dream; a memory of the night Liam and I broke up. My eyes blink softly as I remember it. The thick fog of that night stayed with me for a long time. I'd go as far as to say that a part of me held onto it because I never wanted to say a final goodbye to him. I threw myself into everything except relationships instead and shut the door to my heart.

Today, waking up, I realise that I no longer hold on to that feeling anymore. The fog has gone, and all that is left is me and Liam. Together.

I don't want to say that this is it or we will be together forever because nothing is guaranteed. I, of all people, know that, but what I do know is we were meant to find each other again. I needed to apologise to him the other night and as much courage as it took for me to face it, now, I know I did the right thing.

It's freeing, letting myself feel so much, especially after spending so long with my heart tucked away.

Every second around him has me wanting more. I can feel myself slipping down a slope that only he has carved for me. Except this time, I'm aware and I'm beginning to let myself feel everything... and feel it deeply. And the biggest thing is that he is right there with me.

My alarm blares on my phone next to me, pushing me into a fully conscious state. I force myself to get out of bed and jump in the shower. It's early, 5 am, but I want to go to the gym before work. As I'm drying off, I'm distracted by thoughts of what to pack for Paris as we're leaving in the morning.

Reality hits me again and I can't stop the huge grin spreading across my face. Not only am I going to Paris, but I'm going with Liam. Jesus, a few weeks ago if someone would've told me this would be happening, I would not have believed them at all.

I grab my suitcase and start to pack easy items: underwear, toothbrush, pyjamas. I may have chosen my lace and satin ones just for him, although I secretly hope I won't get the chance to wear them. I choose a few easy to wear items: my converse, mom jeans, a midi skirt and some basic t-shirts, and I place some dresses that are dressier for evenings on hangers before deciding that I'll pack the rest after work.

Heading downstairs, I see that Nora isn't awake yet. She rarely wakes up before 6:30 am, so I move around my kitchen finding granola and fruit. I sit and enjoy breakfast with the sunshine peeking through the kitchen windows.

I have this urge to call Liam; I know he usually runs before work, so before I overthink it and talk myself out of it, I drop him a text to see if he is awake and he calls me back almost instantly.

"Hey Scotty." His breathless voice does things to me.

"Hey, are you running?"

"Yeah, just a quick one before work," he says, panting. I hear a knock on my door, so I tuck the phone between my ear and my face to free up my hands.

"Well, I just wanted to say good..." I open the door awkwardly and then I see him, standing in my doorway sweating in his t-shirt and running shorts, that are so short they should be illegal. His skin glistens, like he doesn't actually belong on earth with us mere mortals. He has the biggest grin on his face as he finishes the sentence I've long forgotten I was saying.

"Morning?" he smirks, taking out his earphones and walking past me.

"You ran to my house?" I ask, disbelieving he's actually here.

He smiles, panting in my hallway. "I ran to your house." He smirks that cute smirk again and my knees weaken at the sight of him. "I'm desperate for water because that run has me blowing out of my arse. You are my only cardio lately and I've been slacking with my running." He swats my behind as he walks into my house like he has lived here forever, leaving me with my mouth hanging open.

Oh, sure he's the one desperate for water? My mouth is drier than a Rich Tea biscuit right now.

When I follow him into the kitchen, he's glugging water. I've never noticed how sexy the simple act can be... until now. The way the water escapes from the side of his mouth and drips down onto his now naked chest. *When did he take his top off and God, he looks edible.* I follow the drip as it settles onto his peck and slowly creeps down towards his nipples, and I have to fight with every single cell in my body not to chase it with my tongue.

Jesus Christ alive.

He catches my eye, letting out a low rumble. "Enjoying the view, Scotty?" I definitely am. I'm also not doing a good job at hiding it, apparently. I'm nodding my head far too eagerly whilst knowingly eye-fucking him.

It's that smirk again that makes me want to play with him, so I saunter over to him, without breaking our gaze. The energy between us zaps around the room like fireworks because I want him and I know he wants me.

As I get close enough to touch him, I lift one finger and lazily trace his abs, running from the top of his pecs all the way down to the waistband of his shorts. His breathing filters through his nose as he tries to remain in control, but he gives himself away when I hear a rumble in his chest as I reach his shorts. God, that noise sends all kinds of naughty messages directly to my core.

I grin, loving how affected he is by my touch and just when I believe I'm in charge, Liam grabs my wrist and places my hand behind my back which forces me forwards into his chest, drenching me in the smell of his arousal and sweat from running. The worst part? I'm not even mad about it. He smells like the most delicious snack right now, all man and desperate for me. I smile sweetly up at him. "Yes?"

The look he gives me tells me that he's right on the edge of control; exactly where I want him. He leans down to brush our lips together but doesn't give me the satisfaction of a kiss.

"Shower. Now," he whispers into my mouth.

"Maybe I'm not done teasing you yet." I wiggle out of his grip and, to my surprise, he lets me. I take the opportunity to move around his body slowly until I'm standing behind him. I run my hands around his hips and down the outside of his shorts, feeling and needing his muscular thighs, the sweat making me stick to him as I move over his skin. His body sags against me, his head lolls backwards and he lets out a breath he was holding. I love the way he reacts to my touch. It makes me feel ten feet tall. Wanting to see him react again, I flex my fingers gently, dragging my nails up his thighs again and ghost over his bulging cock, and I watch as the six-foot-three man crumbles beneath my fingers.

"Fuck, Jess." He hisses as I move my hands to cup his arse over his shorts. I give it a little squeeze and bring my hands back to his front, using one finger to trace the outline of his length. His abs flex and tense as I circle the tip and run down until I palm his balls through the thin material of his shorts. His breathing stutters as I remove my hands altogether, loving the deflate in his body. My fingertips lift and drag along the side of his arm. I reach on my tiptoes as I lick along his collarbone, up to his jawline, humming as the salty taste of his skin covers my tongue.

"Do you want me?" It's barely a whisper and I already know the answer, but I also know he is letting me tease him right now and I'll willingly pay for it later.

His head tilts and his grin tells me I've just lost all my power in this little game. "You have no i-fucking-dea, baby." He grabs me roughly underneath my thighs and wraps my legs around his waist and I go willingly. "You're lucky I don't just take you here in your kitchen. Fuck, I want to bury my face in your pussy and taste you, but I don't like to be interrupted, and I want you all to myself this morning. I'm feeling selfish."

His eyes threaten to drown me with pure, unfiltered desire as he eats up the distance between the stairs and my bedroom before dropping me onto my bed. His eyes watch as my breasts bounce through my top, at the impact and his tongue darts out to lick his lips before he asks me, "If I put my fingers inside you, baby, are you going to be wet for me?" His words scatter over my skin, releasing tiny fireworks in their wake. I can feel my clit pulsing, needing to be touched... no, begging, as I close my eyes on a moan.

"What do you need, Jess?" he rasps, looming over me, desperate to consume me.

I've gone from teasing to being beneath him, begging him to touch me in a matter of minutes, and I don't care in the slightest because I need him more than I need my next breath.

"Please," I whisper as my body arches towards him, urging him to give me what I need.

"Tsk tsk, baby. I need to know what you want. Tell me." He knows he has the power now, and it's driving me insane.

"I need you to touch me. I need your fingers inside of me. I want you all over me... I want to come for you," I pant, completely breathless and now unashamed at how strong my craving is for him.

A growl forms in his chest as he bares his teeth in approval, and he doesn't disappoint when he pushes my sleep shorts to the side and sinks a finger inside of me. He buries his head into the crook of my neck, causing goosebumps to burst across my skin. My body is screaming for more as he lightly brushes over my clit with his thumb.

"More, Liam. I need more." He grins and the desire rolling through me forces my eyes to close.

He pushes in another finger and curves them skilfully until he finds my G-spot, then he pumps them, filling my room with the sounds of my arousal. He pulls out his fingers and glides them over my clit, making my legs shake with need. "Let it go, baby. Give me everything."

I want to give him everything. I grip his shoulders, clawing into his skin as he stretches me once more. *Oh, God.* My hips move on their own accord, shuddering against his palm as his thick fingers work me. "Fuck yes, ride my hand like the needy girl you are." he growls.

"Ohhh, fucking hell." My body teeters, shudders and pulses at his words as he moves his thumb and presses on my sensitive clit again. "Fuck, yes." I mutter as I grasp onto him harder and grind my hips to the rhythm of my thrashing heartbeat.

My whole body quivers and shakes as he draws out my orgasm until I'm gasping and dripping on his palm, but he doesn't stop, eagerly wringing pleasure bursts from my body. When I lock eyes with him, his head dips low and he licks me from my ass to my clit, as I writhe beneath him.

"Give me another one." His voice demanding and full of lust, his fingers dig deliciously into my hip bones, fuelling my high. Before I can breathe, my body falls apart, completely at the mercy of his devil tongue.

"Liam, I ... Oh my God. I'm coming..." I scream.

Liam

As I come out from the bathroom, Jess is still sprawled out on her bed, now sleeping peacefully. I could watch her sleep all day; the way her soft lips part, the gentle rise and fall of her chest and the almost undetectable snore that escapes every now and again. I feel that familiar squeeze in my chest. The way she moves, laughs, blushes, smiles, has me sporting heart eyes for her.

I want to lay down next to her and feel her warm body against mine, but I also don't want to wake her. She looks happy, like she's dreaming. I grab my phone and set an alarm for thirty minutes to wake her, so she isn't late for work.

I pull on my t-shirt and jeans I left here for emergencies after last time, and quietly make my way downstairs to find Nora in the kitchen making breakfast.

"Hey, Nor."

"Hey." She gestures to the granola she is making. "Do you want some? Wait, did you stay over last night? I don't remember seeing you come in." Her brows furrow.

"I'd love some, please. And no, I ran here this morning. She fell asleep whilst I showered and I didn't want to wake her." Nora pours me some granola and yoghurt, and I dive straight in.

The sweet and crunchy taste makes me nod in approval. "This is good. Did you make it?"

Nora nods as she crunches through her mouthful too.

We eat in comfortable silence we have always had.

"Hey, can I ask you something?"

"Sure."

"Do you think Jess and her mum will ever reconcile?"

She stiffens slightly at the question, tension rolling off her shoulders. "That... I can't say."

"Okay." I reply, not really sure what to say next.

"Why?"

"Just…. I'm not really sure what the situation is there. I don't know."

"Well, listen. That seems like more of a question for her, you know?" Nora says.

"Yeah. I guess… she's just so…"

"Flighty? Absolutely terrified of talking about her mum? A nightmare to get to open up about anything actually important?"

"Right." I force a laugh. Ignoring the guilt clawing at my throat.

"Honestly, Liam, I don't know what she wants… She's a closed book when it comes to her mum, even to me."

I lean over the counter and hold Nora's gaze. I hope this comes out right, but with my track record, it's possible it might sound weird.

"Thank you for protecting her and looking after her all these years."

Nora nods her head, smiling softly. "She's my best friend, as well as my sister. I'd do anything for her."

I know the feeling.

"Shoot, I've gotta go. See you later." She places her bowl in the sink and just as she heads towards the door, she turns to face me again. "Try talking to her. Even if she's scared to open up, you can plant the seed for the future. Let her know you're there for her, no matter what."

I nod my head, silently thanking Nora as she disappears, leaving me with completely conflicting emotions, swirling around like a problem in my head that I can't solve.

I'm not sure how long I stay downstairs until I hear familiar footsteps padding towards me. I feel her before I see her.

"Hey, you." She wraps her arms around my waist and kisses my neck as I sit at the breakfast bar.

"Hi, Scotty. Did you have a nice nap?" I turn so she is nestled between my legs.

"I did. Thank you for setting an alarm. I feel very relaxed." She smiles a devious grin that makes me chuckle. "I'll get you back though. You don't get to win all the time."

"I'm pretty sure you were the real winner on a count of the orgasms; plus, I like to keep my girl satisfied." I kiss her soft lips as her arms wrap around my neck, pulling me closer. I lean into the kiss, letting go of the anxiety I felt earlier, just focussing on her and us for now.

"You all packed for Paris?"

"Mostly. I'll add a few things after work. What time are we leaving tomorrow?"

"I was thinking... because I don't have work today, I'd go home, pack and then come back here. It makes it easier to leave at 9 am for the airport if we're in one place."

"Okay." She stares at me for a minute, studying my face, running her fingertips along my temples. I move a strand of her hair from her face and tuck it behind her ear, and she turns her head to kiss my palm. Such a simple gesture and yet I feel my heartbeat faster in my chest but what I can't quite figure out if it's beating for her or because of my fears of losing her again.

33

Jessica

We arrive at the airport in Paris without any setbacks. Liam spent the whole flight with his hands on my legs and at one point I thought he was going to get me on his lap when he tried to manhandle me, whispering about joining the mile high club. I pointed out it wouldn't happen, not until he got his own private plane anyway, to which he replied, "challenge accepted."

It's an easy drive to our hotel, but when we pull into the grounds, nothing could quite prepare me for the beautiful building standing in front of us. The perfectly primed green lawn sprawls out like a blanket in front of the building that is as wide as it is tall. The cream stone is amplified by the beautiful detail in the carvings and gargoyles that sit watching on the top of each gothic peak. The windows are laced with gold and the door looks like the entrance to another world.

"Oh, my God. This is..." I can't even finish my sentence because there are no words.

"Wait until you see inside." Liam beams as he urges me through the arched doorway. I'm sure as soon as I step through I'll be transported into the past where everyone is wearing huge ballgowns and corsets and men have coattails and swords hanging from their waist. Sadly, that doesn't happen, but I'm far from disappointed when I'm greeted with the most beautiful array of creams and golds that complement the outside of the building.

The dark oak flooring sweeps silently across the grand foyer, accented by luxurious art that looks like it's been painted directly onto the walls. Abstract strokes pick up the antique gothic vibes from the carvings outside, creating an elegance that takes my breath away.

"I... this is... beautiful." I try to think of a better word to describe it, but I can't. Everything comes up short, even beautiful doesn't cover it, but it's all I can say.

"I have seen far more beautiful things."

My eyes snap to Liam to protest, but he is already staring at me. Not the beautiful, French gothic décor, but little old me. I can't help the blush that stains my cheeks when he says things like that to me.

We walk over to the reception desk that sits modestly in front of beautiful, sheer white drapes and a single lamp lighting the area. The desk is surrounded by washes of cream, blush, terracotta, and brown that sweeps across the high ceilings and walls. I walk gingerly, wondering when I'll wake up and realise that this really is all just a dream.

"Liam Taylor s'enregistre dans la suite de luxe." *Liam Taylor checking into the luxury suite.*

Stick a fork in me, I am done. He speaks French? Fucking French? Pinch me before I pass out.

He needs to stop unless he wants to be jumped right here right now.

He catches my eye and winks as I mouth, *what the fuck?*

The receptionist nods and speaks to Liam in fluent French and he *casually* nods along, laughing at something she says. I'm flabbergasted at the knowledge that he speaks French and I had no idea about it.

"À quelle heure le petit-déjeuner est-il servi?" *What time is breakfast served?*

Swoon. I don't even care what he said; it sounded sexy. He could talk about politics in French, and it'll be the most interesting thing I hear all day.

When we get into the lift, alone, I immediately put my body in front of Liam, and he looks at me deviously. "You okay there, baby?"

"No. You've made me all hot and bothered with your speaking French. I had no idea you could speak another language." My arms flap dramatically at my sides.

He runs his index finger across my collarbone in excruciatingly slow strokes before he moves over my shirt and down to the waistband of my jeans. He undoes the buttons and slips his hand into my underwear as we climb the floors in the lift, my body temperature rising with every floor we climb. My breath hitches in my throat when he grazes my damp underwear.

"Hmm, this won't do. I need more time." He reaches behind me and slams his hand to the emergency stop button, and I gasp as he pushes me against the back wall. He lowers his hands back into my underwear, to find my slickness waiting for him, and dips his head into my neck, groaning like it is taking all of his self-control not to devour me right now.

I suck in a sharp breath as his fingers expertly circle my throbbing clit as my back hits the wall of the lift, his body covering mine.

"C'est le mien, oui?" *This is mine, yes?* He whispers and I let out an involuntary moan as my knees buckle below me. I have no idea what he said and I couldn't care less right now, the words pushing me to crest the wave of my orgasm.

He pinches me once, thrusting inside of me, fucking me with his hand in the lift. God, this is so bad, but so fucking good.

"Liam, I'm coming. I'm... fuck." I pant as he mumbles more sweet nothings in my ear in French. I tense and pull him closer before my legs buckle underneath me as I come hard against his fingers. "Fuck."

I pull away from him to find him looking at me like I'm on fire and he's the Firestarter. "I think that might be the easiest orgasm I've ever had," I say, surprised at the newfound capabilities of the body I've lived in for twenty-six years.

He smirks. "I'll take it. I've been waiting all day to do that." He turns to release the emergency stop button and we ascend two more floors in glorious and somewhat damp bliss.

The doors open, and Liam grabs my hand, pulling me toward our room. Apparently, the effects of the orgasm induced haze are multiplied when someone gets you off in a lift.

"What did you say to me?" I say, a huge smile on my smitten face.

"When?" he asks, turning so I can see his face as he backs me against our door.

"In the lift, in French."

I see that flame in his eyes again, and I know I'm going to love the answer.

"I said, this is mine." He cups my pussy over my trousers. With the other, he turns the handle of our door and opens it. "Get in there."

Well, fuck. Don't mind if I do.

As I walk into the room, if you can even call it that, it's more of an apartment, judging by the size, I gasp. The same colours from the foyer are echoed in the walls here too, except this room has the most exquisite gothic windows framing the entire space. I spin to face Liam, who has the biggest smile on his face. "Nothing but the best for my baby." He sweeps me up in a kiss that is so full of emotion and something else, something that tells me what he can't say. I pull away, searching his eyes, that are staring at me with the same softness.

"I feel like I'm in a dream." I sigh as I cup his beautiful face. His eyes are sparkling down at me all the colours of amber with moss green fireworks bursting through his iris and in this moment, I feel everything. Our connection goes beyond physical, beyond emotional. It feels as though I exist for him. To be near him is my only purpose. The connection I feel between our souls is something I've read about in romance novels, and only now do I understand exactly what they mean. He dips his head to kiss me and my heart flutters.

"We have reservations in around an hour at my favourite place in Paris." He says as he walks his case to the bedroom.

"You have a favourite restaurant in Paris?" I ask, following him.

"I have one favourite. My dad and I came here a few times last year on business and we found this place that is... incredible. So go, get changed, shower, do whatever, because we have somewhere to be soon."

I smirk to myself, seeing an opportunity as I take off my t-shirt and throw it at him. He laughs and then his eyes darken and that look is exactly the response I wanted from him.

"Oops," I shrug. "My clothes keep falling off."

I slowly unbuckle my jeans and slip them off too, watching his gaze follow my fingers as they move down my legs. His throat bobs as he swallows. Need is emanating from him, slithering around his body like a creature ready to pounce.

He licks his lips and hums, sending lightning bolts through my skin.

I throw him a wink over my shoulder as I walk straight past him to the shower, where I strip out of my underwear, too.

He bites his whole fist and groans, looking up at the ceiling as if saying a silent prayer. "I can't resist that arse, baby." He follows me. Follow maybe isn't quite the right word because he all but sprints towards me like a man starved. Luckily, I have just the thing to satisfy his hunger.

"Something you need, lover boy?" I ask innocently.

He tips his chin. "You," he rasps.

He undresses at lightning speed as I turn the shower on, water splashing onto the floor echoes around us. Just as I'm about to step under the hot water, he grabs my hips and hoists me onto the sink. Dropping to his knees, he spreads my legs, and my body shivers in anticipation. I love this version of Liam. He is so gentle and sweet normally, but when he has this fire in his eyes, I think I'm learning that he needs to have control and I'm willing to submit.

"See something you like?" I wink.

"My favourite meal." He dives forwards and licks through my slit, groaning when he tastes me. "You taste like honey. So fucking sweet." My whole body opens for him as he sends rockets through my veins. He softly bites the bundle of nerves begging for his attention and my hips buck, desperate for more.

I thread my fingers through his hair, and he looks up at me, lips glistening with my arousal. "Ride my face and scream my name, baby. Take what you need."

"Oh, fuck." My jaw goes slack at his words. I can't control the noises coming out of me, the same way I can't control the way I grab his hair and hold him right where I need him.

He makes good on his promise and eats me like I really am his favourite meal. The kind where you'd lick the plate, not wasting a drop and God, does the man know how to clean his plate.

"Who do you belong to?" He looks up at me, pushing a finger inside me, making me gasp at his intrusion. "What was that, baby? I didn't catch it." He pushes a second finger in and my back curves, my body sucking him deeper.

"Who. Do. You. Belong. To?" He works his fingers in and out of me in a steady rhythm that makes my toes curl. Each movement rubs deliciously against my G-spot, making my legs shake as I slowly lose control.

"You... fuck... I belong to you." I force out between pants.

His head dips back between my thighs and he barely touches me again before my world shatters around me. Birds fly around my head, fucking singing, because *Jesus*, Liam, can seriously worship on his knees.

He removes his fingers, stands, but not before he kisses a trail up my thigh, nips my hip, reigniting my need for him. He moves all the way to my neck, never letting his hands wander away from touching me.

"I fucking love your noises you make." He lets me down, stepping back slightly. Wrapping his hand around his now engorged length, smearing my arousal still on his fingers, all over himself as he thrusts into his hand a few times, his head rolling backwards in pleasure. He is a sight to be seen; all rippling muscles in his arm as he moves his hand from base to tip, precum collecting on his head. *Good fucking God alive.*

"On your knees, Scotty. You made me dirty, lick me clean."

I look at him with heavy eyes. "Say please."

His eyes hood as I wrap my hand around his cock, still standing in front of him. His breath shudders as I tease him by breathing on his chest, licking his nipple one by one but never giving him what he so desperately wants.

"Fuck this," he growls. Watching that rubber band of control snap for someone like Liam, who is always so gentle and sweet, *does things* to me.

In a split second he's turned my whole body around, "Hands on the wall, now," he growls, his cock resting between my cheeks making me flood with desire again. As soon as my palms connect with the slippery tiles, he's bent me over and thrusts inside of me, filling me to the hilt. A sharp slap on my arse makes my knees weak.

Fucking hell. My body sings under his control.

His fingers grip my hips, enough to leave a mark, but the pain and pleasure is everything we both need. He moves inside me at a piston pace, taking no prisoners. One of his hands brushes up my body, pinching my nipple on the ascent, pulling me upwards against his body. His hand settles around my neck, my pulse thrumming under his touch as he tightens his grip, taking away my air, my whole-body purrs under his touch. The heat of the water thrashes against my back, making me feel delirious, like an awakening, a baptism of him, of us.

"Harder," I beg, forcing the words out as he grips my neck.

Liam grunts, slamming into me. It's wild and animalistic, and I fucking love it. My body gives in to his touch as my fingers ghost his hand wrapped around my throat. My vision blurs, my body goes numb just as my orgasm devours my entire being, pushing me into ecstasy with a hard shove. Liam releases my neck as I slap my hands onto the wet wall in front of us, steadying my wobbling legs, and comes with me, slamming me hard, then stilling inside of me with a guttural groan. I have never felt so full of him, of us, of everything we needed and took together.

34

Liam

The top of the Arc de Triomphe isn't the highest point in Paris by a long shot, but it's spectacular, especially on a day like today. The sky stretches out above us like a clear, endless blanket of blue; not a single cloud blemishing it. Paris is laid out at our feet, twelve roads all starburst out in every direction; everywhere we turn we're greeted with French history and coffee-stained buildings that hold the test of time. Whilst below us, traffic hustles with no idea how we are marvelling at their city.

"The Eiffel Tower isn't as big as I thought it would be. It looks like a little toy version of itself from here."

"That's usually how distance works," I tease.

She playfully taps my chest as I pull her into a kiss. "Also, why was the Mona Lisa so tiny? How did I not know that?"

I laugh against her, my shoulders bouncing up and down. "It was pretty small, especially for a small person like you."

"Not all of us can be giants, you know." She pouts, barely reaching the top of my chest when she rests her chin against me, her hair softly blowing around her face.

"I like you tiny. Means I can throw you around and put you in my pocket."

"The feminist in me hates that... but also I love it," she beams. "Can we stop for coffee and ice cream?" She points towards a little café on the corner of the cobbled street below us, before twirling to meet my eyes again, her mid-length skirt flowing around her. "Maybe they'll even have milkshakes." I'm mesmerised by the way the peeking sun makes her eyes twinkle that little bit more, as though she's lit from within.

"Sure." I smile in reply, leading her back down towards the café.

Spoiler alert: they didn't have milkshakes. But Jess isn't deterred, especially when she sees the pistachio flavoured ice cream. It's green; the kind of green that looks like it should contain spinach or kale. But if she's happy, she can eat all the green ice cream she wants.

Jess enthusiastically licks her cone, its seductive without trying to be and when she leaves a drop on her bottom lip, I lean towards her smiling.

"You've got a little something..." I use my thumb to wipe it before licking it off while she watches me intently. *Green ice cream isn't so bad actually.*

We find a seat outside the café and sit in comfortable silence, our feet brushing one another every now and again. The rush of the day has passed and Paris is more peaceful now. The cool autumn breeze dances around us, making a mess of Jess' hair as it gets stuck in her ice cream. When I laugh, she scowls her famous scowl, and it makes me laugh more. My chest swelling at the sight of her.

My mind drifts to Claire. I'd be lying if I said this was the first time I'd let my mind wander to her since we arrived, because I love being with Jess, but I don't want to hold back anything anymore. I called my dad earlier whilst she was showering; he said that Claire needs more time but that she's reaching out to Cam to mend bridges first. I guess that's something better than nothing.

I look over to Jess who looks as lost in thought as I was. "What are you thinking about?"

She shakes her head and looks at me sheepishly. "Nothing important."

"It looked important. You had your cute little frown between your eyes. Right... here." I lean froward to smooth the place where the line is and her face relaxes.

"I was just watching a family over there. The mum was doting on the little girl, hugging her, holding hands, making her laugh... sometimes I forget things are the way they are, other times my mind won't let me forget. I'm not sad because I don't feel like I missed out on anything in life. Cam and Harriett are amazing..." she drifts off, her eyes cloudy with thoughts as she picks at the cone of her ice cream.

"But you feel like you still want to find out about your mum?" I offered the answer she couldn't say, and she nods looking down at her hands.

"Sometimes... I think it could give me closure, other times I wonder if we would have any sort of relationship. Is that even what I would want? I don't know."

I don't say anything else. I can't. I'm stuck between a rock and a hard place. I know where her mum is and could easily get them talking, but it's not my place.

We sit quietly again for a while; I'm lost in a turmoil of thoughts again, desperate to give her some semblance of peace from years of pent up trauma that I see in her. After weeks of trying to tell her and being interrupted, I have the perfect opportunity, but I physically can't tell her.

"Are you okay?" Jess asks. "You're all sweaty," she says, patting my damp brow.

I clear my throat a few times and take a deep, cleansing breath. "What if... what if I told you I could find her?"

Jess' eyebrows shoot to the sky. "You can do that?" She tilts her head. "I can."

Jess pauses, looking out over the Seine before turning back to me. "Okay, yes. I'd like your help." Her eyebrows meet at a thought.

"How *can* you help exactly? Do you have a stash of secret MI6 agents underground somewhere just waiting for your command?"

I laugh but it's emptier than usual; there's no depth to the tone of it. The noise even sends chills down *my* back. "No, baby. I'm no James Bond... or M for that matter."

I shake off the uneasy feeling running over my body. It must be because of the cool air. I wrap my arms around myself, shielding my body from the chill before smiling up at Jess. "If I can help you, I want to, and I may have the means to find her for you, if that's what you want."

She nods, and then the frown is back again. "But seriously, how can you do that?"

"I'll explain more when we get back to the UK, but my dad will be able to help us. Help you. Think about it some more and if you still want to see her next week, then we can talk to him."

"Your dad?" she asks, scrunching her nose. "Now you really are making me think there's a lot more to you both than you're letting on. I don't understand."

Heat crawls up my spine, spiderwebbing across my shoulders as I think about what to say without giving away my dad's position in all this. "I promise as soon as we get home everything will make more sense. Do you trust me?" I ask, hope lacing my voice.

Her brows push together, and then instantly soften when I pick up her hand and kiss her knuckles, "I trust you." She says.

I exhale, hoping that I've just done the right thing.

I watch her breasts bounce as she rides me hard and fast. Sweat glistens over her body as she desperately searches for her peak.

Her hips are meeting mine with every thrust. "Oh God, yes, don't stop," she pleads.

Every breath we breathe is in sync, so when I know she is close. I go deeper, harder, forcing our orgasms to explode together. We are a mess of moans and heavy breathing and I can't take my eyes off her.

The moonlight is pooling in through the window and the cool evening air seeps through the small, open window. Jess is still laid, draped over my body and we are both quiet.

I stroke her face and she sighs, looking at me longingly. "I'm so fucking hungry right now."

I laugh at the intrusion from her stomach.

"What? I was hungry before the sex and I'm pretty sure my stomach is eating itself now."

"Then we better get you food before you release that hangry beast."

I stand and grab a snack bar from my suitcase. She forgets how well I know her, so I came prepared.

I toss her the bar and she smiles a beaming grin at me before opening it and chomping down.

"Now, go get the room service menu and pick something. I want to watch you walk around naked," I say, lying back down on the bed.

As she comes back into view, I can feel my cock threaten to come to life again. Her eyes are shining, her soft natural waves hang messily around her face with that just fucked look I love so much. I move my arm to prop my head up so I can watch her better as she sways her hips towards me, her breasts bouncing as she moves. I smirk because that beautiful creature is all mine.

She smiles brightly at me, dimple and all, and my chest constricts in the most familiar way. In the way I've only ever felt with her. It's how I knew I loved her when we were kids, because I felt like my chest was a constant thunderstorm, and now that feeling is back.

We spend ten minutes animatedly discussing what food to order. Jess insists that she won't steal my chips if I get the steak, but I know her, so in the end, we both order the steak and chips.

There's a knock at the door half an hour later and the smell of our dinner has me salivating. Jess comes into the living area in one of my t-shirts after the staff has delivered our food and if I wasn't so hungry, I'd want to eat her for dessert first.

"That smells so good. I think I've gone to heaven."

You and me both, baby.

Before I even lift the metal cloche from my dinner, she is already scoffing her food, moaning in appreciation.

My cock twitches involuntarily at the sound. The side of my mouth tips up as I take my first mouthful and the explosion of taste now has me moaning too.

She looks at me triumphantly. "Right? It's incredible, isn't it?"

We eat mostly in silence, apart from our odd moan of satisfaction, and once we're done, I search my suitcase for something I have planned for our trip. "I want to do something tonight. Get dressed. Put something warm on. It'll be cold out."

Jess looks at me with a confused look. "Wait, right now? It's practically midnight Liam, and my tummy is so full. Look." She pats it affectionately and pouts at me.

"I know, but get dressed, baby. It'll be worth it. Promise." I get dressed and Jess follows, grumbling and every now and again, throwing glances my way to see if she can figure out what I'm up to.

Ten minutes later, we're outside on the chilly streets of Paris, heading to a place I've never wanted to take anyone before.

We arrive at the bridge. The moon is dancing on the surface of the Seine like a bubble dancing in the breeze. The water looks inky black under the night sky, twinkling with the reflection of the streetlights that line the riverbank. The autumnal breeze picks up a faint smoky aroma from the bar across the street where people sit, laughing and drinking.

"So... you brought me to a bridge." She says, half smiling and frowning at the same time.

"This is the Love Lock bridge or *Pont des Arts,* as is the French name. Do you remember years ago people would put locks on this bridge with someone they love?"

Jess nods and turns her head slightly. "I'll never get used to you speaking French, but yes, I remember," she says as I kiss her cold, pink cheek.

"Do you know the story behind how it started?" Jess shakes her head again, so I continue. "The story goes that a woman who lost her love in the war would place a lock onto any bridge she visited around Europe to show they were never really apart and always unbreakable."

I place the lock in Jess' hand and she twirls it around, staring at the space that is engraved with our initials. She brushes her thumb against the letters, tracing them slowly, before she locks eyes with me. The look on her face is one I haven't seen since we were kids, and it almost floors me. The honesty blaring in her blue iris' is so bright it makes the moon look dull. I want to capture this moment and remember it for the rest of my life, so I wrap my hands around her face.

"Jess, I want to be there for you. I want to see you happy. Be there when you're sad and comfort you when you're sick. I love the way you pretend to be strong, but secretly love the soppy parts of a movie. I love snarky Jess, hangry Jess, hungover Jess and happy Jess, and I'll damn sure love any other versions of you that pop up in the future because..." I pause, sucking in a deep breath before I say the words that have been on the tip of my tongue for longer than I care to admit. "I love you and I don't want to be without you."

A single tear falls from Jess' eye. She turns her head slightly to kiss the inside of my palm and when I drop my hands, she launches herself into me, burying her head into my chest.

"I love you too. I'm scared as hell to admit it, but I don't know how I could ever love anyone that isn't you."

The honesty in her voice. It's unravelling me. Making me want to be anything and everything for her. I make the decision there and then

ALL OF MY LASTS

to talk to my dad as soon as we are back in London to figure this out for her.

She scans the rails of the bridge then looks up at me, confused for a second. "I don't see any other padlocks. Are we allowed to do this?"

I smile at her and show her the key. "We can't leave the padlock, but I thought we could keep it and throw the key in the river."

Her face is full of emotion and I run my knuckles across her chin and lift her lips to meet mine. "I love you," she whispers before she kisses me.

35

Jessica

As I pack up my desk for the day, I place all my pens neatly in their pots again. My assistant, Kylie, used my office whilst I was away and she and I have very different ideas of what tidy is. Once my laptop is closed, I stand, brushing the creases from my pencil skirt and call an Uber to take me to Liam's office.

It doesn't take me long to get there and I walk towards the front desk, admiring the space that I knew so well. The light that filters into the lobby area still beams down like sunshine and the glass doors that still create tiny little rainbows on the floor that still make me smile when I see it. The front desk, all clean white lines and potted plants courtesy of Helena, and that is where I spot her familiar face. "Helena?" She looks up, eyes wide and mouth slightly open as she takes me in.

"Jessica Scott?" She rounds her desk and throws her arms around me. Her wild, curly hair tickles my nose as I return the hug, basking in her familiar cinnamon scent. "My word, you are beautiful. I haven't seen you since you were yay high." She gestures to her shoulder height, as her big brown eyes look me over again.

"It's so good to see you, Helena. You haven't changed a bit. How is Anne?"

"You are too kind, my darling. Anne is good, driving me crazy as usual... I hear you and Liam are dating again." Her elbow gently nudges my side, an impish smile gracing her lips. "He is quite smitten, you know. Humming tunes and letting me get away with murder." She winks, and I can't help but smile at the thought of him singing around the office.

"Liam singing, how do you cope?" The man has many graces, but unfortunately singing was never one of them.

"It's sweet really." The shrill ring of the phone cuts through our conversation. She rounds her desk, pausing her hand over the phone before locking eyes with me. "He's in his office. Second on the left. Come back for coffee soon, yes?" I nod and smile as she picks up the phone.

Memories of a young Liam, Nora and I flood my head as I tiptoe through the familiar hallway.

We played marbles over there in that corner, we did our homework sat on the floor of the kitchenette. It didn't matter that we were uncomfortable, we were together and that was our favourite place to be.

As I walk towards the door, muffled, raised voices permeate the air outside the door of Liam's father's office. I take one tentative step closer so my feet are almost touching the door frame as I zone out any other office noises around me to focus on the conflict on the other side of the door.

"Liam, this isn't our choice to make. It's hers," I hear his father boom.

I can't actually hear much, but what I do hear stops me in my tracks "... I can't keep this from her anymore," Liam declares, but it seems to fall on deaf ears, as his father's voice offers a muffled response that I don't catch.

What the hell are they arguing about?

My heart jumps when I hear a loud bang from the other side of the door. My body involuntarily leaping backwards as my hands fly to my chest.

More muffled voices sound out and that's when I hear Liam's dad say, "We need to wait for Claire."

Claire.

Claire.

Claire.

Her name echoes in my subconscious as it repeats relentlessly.

My hands go numb, my mouth is dry, my heart is beating uncontrollably fast just at the mention of her name. White noise is rushing in my ears, bile rises in my throat as I fumble my steps backwards. I don't know where I'm retreating to, but I'm hoping I find a surface to lean on soon.

Fuck, fuck, fuck. I can't breathe.

One-one thousand.

Two-one thousand.

Three-one thousand.

Hearing her name has all the blood rushing in my ears, unable to think straight from all the memories that are flooding back to my subconscious. I thought I was ready, but right now I know I'm not. I can't come face to face to the one part of my past that I so desperately wish wasn't connected to Liam at all. I break out into a cold sweat that makes me shiver.

I need to run. I need to move, but as I turn to stumble back to the front foyer, Liam's voice filters into my reality.

"Jess?" His face pales when he sees me. "What are you doing here?" he asks with an unusual shrill in his voice.

I try to get words to form in my brain, but all I can manage is a string of vowels and consonants that don't make any sense. I don't know what they were talking about, but I want to know... or do I?

When Liam steps closer, I step backwards until my back bumps into something else. Someone else.

My body shakes as I swirl around, an apology on the tip of my tongue, but it dries up fast. My skin goes cold and clammy when I focus on the storm clouds blurring in her eyes and her untamed brown hair wisping around her face.

Mum.

She looks older. Obviously. It's been ten fucking years. But she looks... weathered. As though it isn't just age that's made her skin sallow and wrinkly.

I hadn't expected to see her here. I'm not prepared.

What the hell am I supposed to do? As much as I told Liam I wanted to find her, I want it to be on my terms and my heart hasn't had time to prepare. My pulse quickens at the thought of bolting out of the door I came through, but I'm rooted in place, staring at her, wishing this was all just another bad dream.

My eyes flick around the space that suddenly feels emptier somehow. I glance at the end office, Liam's office, officially abandoning my plans to wine and dine him tonight as I turn back to her face. Adrenaline pumps in my blood like lava when I remember that she is the one who abandoned me and left me without any parents all those years ago. My body shakes and tears prick at my eyes, but before I can let myself fall apart, I scramble towards the door.

"Jess, I can explain. Please just wait," Liam cries, but I don't stay to hear his explanation. Instead, I push past them both and burst through the door like a bat out of hell.

Outside, the world spins. I can't remember which way is home. I don't even know left from right, but I don't care. I just need to keep moving. I duck around the side of the building, immediately out of view, in case anyone chases after me.

My body is filled with fire and ice, simultaneously melting and burning with rage as I wring my hands together to try and temper some of my nerves.

I see Liam rush out of the revolving doors, shouting profanities and running his hands through his hair. I know he said he could find her, but I didn't think it would be that fast; I didn't know exactly how he would find her, but she was there in his office. I feel guilty for running from him, but I panicked and I couldn't face whatever that was. He grabs his phone, and I feel mine vibrate in my handbag, but I ignore it. Tears well in my eyes as I try to swallow them back, but it's no good; they fall, one drop, then two, until my cheeks are wet and I have to cover my mouth to stop the sob that's rising in my throat.

Eventually, he turns to go back inside and I slip from the side of the building and hail a taxi. I call Nora unable to hold back the sobs. I know I'm barely making sense, but she tells me to go straight home and she'll meet me there.

The taxi driver pinches his brows, as he turns to look at me as I sob into my hands. "134 Victoria Park Avenue... please," I manage to say. He pauses, a question ghosting his face, but I'm grateful when he silently drives away without asking anything.

When I pull up outside my house, the tears have dried a little. I apologise to the driver, pay him and he says something that I can't hear because I'm already walking, hoping that behind the door will be my sanity, a time machine or maybe just a really big bottle of tequila. *Yeah, tequila would work.*

The chill from the outside follows me in, making my skin shiver. I wander aimlessly to the kitchen and grab said bottle of tequila to take the edge off my nerves. I swig it back, my eyes squeeze closed at the burn from the warming liquid, but I shake it off and walk into the living room. Just as I'm about to take another swig, I hear the front door open and close.

"Jess?" Nora shouts.

"In here."

Nora comes bustling through the hallway and into the living area where I'm slumped on the sofa. "Honey," she says sympathetically, before taking the tequila and pulling me into a hug.

I burst into tears again, letting them fall freely and messily down my cheeks and onto Nora's shoulder. It feels like hours pass before I can gain any sense of composure. Sobs still threatening to start the whole ordeal again.

"Liam called me." Her words snap me back to the moment. "He told me everything."

"What, what did he say? You know more than me, I'm guessing, because... I ran."

Nora gives me a look that I know all too well is her, silently chastising me for running rather than talking. She doesn't press it but instead tells me everything Liam told her.

"He told me that your mum has been working in his father's company for the last few months. Her job only just became permanent. She's clean. He said she has been for years now. This afternoon, Liam was fighting with his dad about the fact that Claire had said she wasn't sure if seeing you was a good idea." She sighs deeply. "Please don't be mad at Liam, Jess. He's tried to keep you from getting hurt in all this."

"I'm still hurt though... and confused. I told him in Paris that I wanted to find her, and he said he could help. I didn't once think that meant he could find her on his payroll. I thought he meant he knew a guy. God... I'm such an idiot."

"No, you're not. And neither is he. He's not to blame here. I think... I think Claire pushed them not to say anything. Liam said he needs to talk to you about something else, too. He wouldn't tell me."

"I-I need a minute before that happens."

Nora nods. "Don't be mad at Liam for this... please. He was so upset when I spoke to him."

"I'm not... Well, I am a little," I admit, wanting to be honest with her. But I don't want to be. Something has shifted between us after Paris. Now I'm not sure I'll ever be able to lose him because no matter what, I fucking love him with every fibre of my being.

36

Liam

I wake feeling like I've been hit by a truck; little to no sleep will do that to a bloke. My eyes are heavy, and I want to punch my past self for not closing my blinds last night. The morning sunshine is far too bright for my mood.

I texted Jess last night and I saw the bubbles appear like she wanted to reply, but she never did. Nora texted me to say she went to bed early, but without much else to go on, I've spent most of the night assuming that she's going to leave me, or that she's going to run again. History repeating itself and the catalyst for all this is Claire again.

Jesus, I don't want to lose Jess.

Dragging myself out of bed and into the shower is purely fuelled by the fact that I'm going to see her today. One day, less than twenty-four hours, is probably not enough time for her to deal with everything, but today is the picnic event for her charity and I'm not letting her down any more than I have.

I stare at my reflection in the mirror; the black bags under my eyes have black bags and my skin looks dehydrated, sallow and grey from lack of sleep. My body is cursing me for only letting it drink whiskey for dinner last night, but when you feel like you've potentially fucked up the one thing that mattered most to you in the world, it's going to mess with your appetite.

I quickly text Grayson to come and meet me at my flat in half an hour, and like the best mate he is, he arrives promptly and with coffee.

"I figured you'd need this today," he says, passing me the cup.

"Thanks man," I reply and grab it. "You're the best."

Unfortunately, a lot of people at the office saw and heard the commotion yesterday. Grayson included. He was the one who took the second bottle of whiskey away from me last night before he headed home.

We head out across town and say a grand total of zero words to each other.

When we arrive, Nora greets me at the edge of the tree lined park where the picnic is taking place.

"Morning, Nora." I hug her and turn to Grayson. "You remember Grayson?"

Nora smiles. "Yeah, I do. Hi, Grayson. You're over with the football net, please. Goalie gloves are on the floor. And Liam," she says, pointing to a table across the field. "You're on drinks."

Despite Nora's clear instruction, Grayson makes no attempt to move. Instead, he stands and takes Nora in, staring at her curiously. "You're not so grumpy this morning," he says.

Nora laughs. "Give me time, sir. Give me time."

"Sir," he says, folding his arms and smirking like the cocky bastard he is. "I like that."

Nora is blushing, actually charmed, and I can tell Grayson notices. *Well, this is an ego boost he really doesn't need.*

"Right well, Grayson, behave," I say, leaning into him. "Like, seriously. As though your life depends on it, mate."

"Pric—"

"And Nora," I continue, cutting Grayson off before he can say any more, "I'll see you later."

Before I witness anymore of Grayson being Grayson, I make my way over to the drinks table, telling myself that I don't think I want to know what the fuck that was.

Multi coloured balloons line each table, blowing in the light breeze like giant lollipops. We're surrounded by several tall trees that are decorated with homemade banners and rainbow ribbons. The park is busy. Maybe forty people fill our secluded space with families and children. Laughter buzzes around me as I scope out which table I've been assigned to. Then I see her. *Jess.*

She doesn't look my way, but I can see her profile. Her shoulders are slouched, her hair is pulled back from her face when she usually wears it down and natural. Her usual aura that vibrates through her isn't there today and fuck, if I didn't feel bad before, I sure as hell do now.

Rubbing my hand over my face, feeling the scruff of my beard under my palm, I shuffle over to the drinks table that has a homemade giant rainbow sign that says, 'Drinks on me'. I smile at the sign that I'm guessing might've been made by one of the kids here judging by the backwards 'e'.

I settle behind the table, checking over what there is to offer, and when I look up, I notice that this table gives me a direct view of Jess, which just about kills me.

She glances over to me and at first she looks surprised, but I swear I see the side of her mouth tip up in a tiny smile making my battered heart perk up in my chest. I want to wave, but that feels anticlimactic. I want to scoop her up into my arms, but that feels over the top. Instead I smile ... and wave. Awkwardly. *Good one, loser.*

The picnic goes by excruciatingly slowly, even though I'm kept busy handing out drinks. Every now and then I hear Jess laugh and my eyes instantly search for her so I can catch a glimpse of her happy. I swear I heard it just a second ago, but she's moved out of sight and my line for drinks has just got even longer so I need to focus. Just as I hand over a lemonade to a little boy with his dad, a balloon swipes me across the face for about the millionth time today, I throw a punch at the wayward balloon and mutter a curse under my breath just as Jess steps in front of my stall.

"Hi." She offers a small smile, looking between me and the balloon that's got it in for my face.

"Hi." I swat the balloon once more, hoping that it says away from me.

"The balloons causing you trouble?" she smirks.

"It's like I've offended them and they are out to punish me," I deadpan, but when she gives me another glimpse of her full smile, I let my own take over my face. "You think Nora would cover me for a second so we can talk?"

She nods, and before long, Nora appears to take over my stall.

Jess and I stroll over towards a shaded part of the park. The tree branches swish above us, letting snippets of autumn sunshine fall over Jess' hair as the warmer auburn strands glimmer in the light, making her glow. My hand twitches to hold hers, but I need her to listen to everything, so she understands, so I force them into my jean pockets.

"Jess, I know Nora told you everything already, but I want to explain myself." Unable to resist touching her, I hold out my hand in the hope that she takes it. When she does, my entire body sings at the contact. I steady my breathing before I continue. "My dad..." I pause to swallow. "He's Claire's sponsor. I found out just before we went to Paris and he promised me this would all be sorted once we were back, which is when you walked into the office."

Her eyes widened at my words, her mouth slightly open as I continue. "I'm sorry Jess, I tried to tell you so many times. I've tortured myself about whether it was the right thing... I know how you feel about your mum and I didn't want to make that worse for you, but I also hate keeping secrets from you. I hated every second of not telling you. I never want to keep anything from you or lie to you again."

She chews the inside of her lip. I can't tell what she is thinking, and she stays quiet until I can't take it anymore.

"Jesus, please talk to me." My voice cracks on the last word.

Her eyes snap to mine, flaring before they soften instantly. "Liam…" her hands fly up to her face, shielding her emotions from me. I instinctively step forwards wanting to give her comfort, my hands cup her face as she leans into me ever so slightly.

"Talk to me, baby. Let me in, I've got you," I whisper, my words being carried off in the breeze that whips around us.

She sniffs and straightens herself, pushing her shoulders backwards. When her glazed eyes meet mine, my chest seizes at seeing her so broken again. "I didn't mean to run yesterday, but I couldn't stay there." She pauses, eyes flitting around the strings of my hoodie. "I thought I was ready to see her again, but as soon as I did, I just felt… scared. I wanted to be in control and suddenly… I wasn't." She exhales, the air whooshing into my chest as I pull her in, wrapping my arms around her. "I'm not mad at you, or at least I'm trying not to be. But your dad is her sponsor? I had no idea." She buries her face once more and I pull her into my chest.

"I was shocked too. He's supported her for the last three years."

Her head jerks up. "Three years? Jesus," she shrieks. "I-I don't know what to say. I'm glad she's got help. I never thought it would be from your dad, but… you said she's sober?"

I nod my head. "She's sober, has been for at least six years."

Her expression changes from confusion to hurt. I can practically feel the memories swirling around her, the pain from her past. I want to take all of it away. Her eyes connect with mine, filled with unshed tears. "I need you to know that you're one of the only people who can keep me from falling off a cliff right now. I *need* you," she whispers. "That pain from years ago is still very much a part of me, but I can't let it win. I won't."

My arms strengthen around her as the air escapes my lungs. I swallow heavily, unable to clear the frog in my throat from her words. Ten years ago, she asked me to leave and now… she's telling me she needs me. Hot prickles burn behind my eyes as tears threaten to escape.

I've only ever wanted to be there for Jess. She deserves to be treated like she matters. It's all I've ever wanted to do.

She rests her chin on my chest, "I'm sorry for pushing you away when we were kids. I know I've said it briefly before but I… I don't want to push you away again."

My pulse races as emotion floods my bloodstream, rushing it fast around my body. I swallow thickly, trying to clear the frog in my throat. "Jess, that means so much to me. You have no idea."

We stand in each other's embrace for God knows how long. I never want to let her go and I never will. Jess' feet shift beneath her as I reluctantly release one arm from around her, holding her chin in place, making sure she hears everything I'm about to say. "I need you to know that if you ever feel like you're broken, you lean on me from here on out. I'll take all your broken pieces and spend a lifetime putting them back together because you deserve that and so much more. You mean more to me than anything, Jess, and I refuse to give you up again. I want to be clear because you need to know I'm all in. I've been all in since the moment I saw you again." I pause, sliding my hand to cup her cheek. "How could I ever belong to anyone else when I left my heart with you all those years ago?"

I guide her mouth to mine and press our lips together in a kiss that is branding, her body immediately gripping onto mine. She is mine and even though, deep down, she always has been, it took us both time to get here and that's okay, because I've got her now.

She breaks the kiss, her eyes shining up at me. "I'm all in. Liam, I never want to be without you again."

37

Jessica

It's been two weeks since I saw mum. I've taken some time off work, and considering I never take a holiday, Jean-Pierre had no problem letting me take some time. Time I needed. A lifetime of grief has hit me like a freight train. My eyes sting from crying and lack of sleep. My more frequent nightmares are to thank for that one. My body feels weary, like it's finally trying to figure out how to find the closure it needs. That *I* need.

It hurts to deal with all these emotions, ones that have bubbled around my body for years but have never surfaced until now, and now they're pushing to be acknowledged, ready to burst out of me. Therapy helps, so does my newfound love for journalling, but it doesn't completely prepare you for the good things to blindside you, too. I keep fielding all the bad things and dealing with my reactions to those, so when the good and the bad collide, I find myself in a state of constant overwhelm. My rational brain tells me how to deal with things whilst my heart thuds in my chest, telling me it's confused. I've spent so long protecting myself that I never fully considered what it might be like to let someone in again and what I'd be able to offer that person in return.

I think a part of me has always grieved my mum. The part of her that I lost to the addiction and now, as an adult, I've spent the last ten years grieving for the life we never shared as mother and daughter. I've been coasting, taking each day, never planning ahead, never getting attached because of that fear of loss overwhelming me. It all felt too much, so I hid in the shadows of my mind for such a long time. But not anymore. Liam has been so patient whilst I try and figure all of that out and it's been tough. But I'm not giving up. I'm dealing with things, *with* help from people who love me.

I let out a long, calming breath, finding solace in the ocean before me. I tuck my journal back into my tote bag before padding my feet, feeling the soft sand beneath them. I spot Cam walking towards me with a hot chocolate in hand. My head tilts with a smile at his gesture.

"It's set to be colder tonight, so I brought you something to warm you up. I didn't know how long you'd be out here." He comes to sit next to me. "That and I wanted to spend some time with you. I know we talked about your mother last week, but I wanted you to know that I saw her today."

My heart stills and a whisper of fear snakes around my neck at the thought of her being back into my life so easily. He's her brother, though. He has every right to see her; I tell myself, trying to dampen my worries with rational thoughts.

I bite my bottom lip but release it as soon as I exhale. "And how did that go?"

He sighs heavily. Steam bellows from his cup like the top of a volcano as he blows the hot air away. "It's never going to be easy with her."

I let out a quiet laugh that feels bitter on my tongue. "No shit."

Cam joins my sentiment, whilst he takes a sip of his drink. "Do you want to see her?"

It's the question I've been asking myself for the last two weeks. *Do I want to see her?* If I'm being truthful, the answer is yes, the same answer I had in Paris. I need to see her to figure out how I can move on from this limbo of emotion I'm stuck in. My therapist agrees I need to see her, too. However, a really small part of me doesn't want to give her the time of day, because I don't feel like she deserves it. If I see her, I'm giving her the power to destroy me again, as much as I want to be in control I'm not sure I ever will be with her and that's scary as hell.

"It's okay if you aren't sure, kiddo." He sips his hot chocolate. "For the record, she would like to see you."

I slowly nod my head, not entirely sure if it *is* okay that I'm torn between yes and no.

"I'd hoped coming here would give me a little clarity or something profound like that. But all I've gained is sand in my bum from sitting out here." I admit. Cam's head whips my way, an amused look plastered on his face, then he throws his head back and lets laughter erupt from his throat.

A cackle bursts from me too and my shoulders shake with the rattles of my laughter as it turns hysterical. I wipe the tears pooling in my eyes, my mouth wide, as I let out big, obnoxious bellows, clutching my chest, feeling the freedom of it all. It feels nice to laugh this way. God knows I haven't done a lot of that lately.

The laughter settles like dust on a windowsill as we both slowly come down from our high. "I do want to see her," I say out loud, realising that it is something I need to do, especially if I want to feel as free as I did a second ago.

My eyes open slowly and I blink the sleep from them rapidly, letting my mind wake up when I take note of my body… and to try figure out why I feel like I'm on fire right now. Looking down at myself, I quickly take in the 6-foot-3 man wrapped around me, who has the body temperature of a furnace. I'm sticky, hot and sweating from being tangled together all night in my small double bed at Cam and Harriet's house.

Liam grumbles at the loss of me as I deftly untangle myself from his long limbs. I lean down to kiss his forehead. "Sshh, go back to sleep, baby."

As I sit on the edge of the bed, my body chilling with the settled sweat from the night, I look around my room. Nothing has changed and I love that it's been kept the same. The light blue walls are faded in places, the fairy lights no longer light up, but all my fake plants line the room like a picture frame. I smile at the memories of Nora and I trying (and failing) to hang these and how Cam ended up doing it all for us.

I stretch my arms up, revelling in the feeling when my body burns for just a second. I twist my body side to side when I come face to face with my polaroid wall that is littered with pictures from when we were growing up. I see baby faced Nora and I posing at a music concert. Cam and Harriett holding hands, walking somewhere in London. There are lots of pictures of Liam and I but one image catches my eye and has me moving closer. I think it was taken when Liam, Nora, and I were on the beach when we were fourteen.

In the picture, I'm lying on a towel and I'm guessing Nora is the one who is taking the picture. But what has my heart beating out of my chest is Liam. He's propped up on his elbow, staring down at me like I hung the moon and the stars. *Did he always look at me like that?*

I trace my fingers over the edges of the photo before propping it up on the bedside table so Liam can see it when he wakes up. I scribble a little note to go with it and head to the bathroom.

When I finish in there and step back into the bedroom, the cooler air caresses my slightly damp skin, causing goosebumps to scatter along my bare arms as I wrap the towel tighter around me. I hate being cold, so I quickly get dressed in Liam's hoody and a pair of old shorts I found in my drawers when I hear my phone buzzing on the floor. I grab it, immediately answering before checking who it is.

"Hello," I whisper, not wanting to wake Liam, as I duck into the hallway.

"Jess? Why are you whispering?" Nora's voice filters through the phone.

"Oh, Liam is still sleeping. I've moved now though. Are you okay?"

"I'm good…" she pauses.

"Why does there feel like there's a but at the end of that sentence?"

"There's not. Ignore me. I'm just calling you back. I saw I missed a call last night from you."

My eyes squint at her avoidance of my question, but I'll let it slide for now. "Oh right, last night. I…I want to talk to you about my mum."

"You?" she asks, her voice almost a squeak.

"Yes."

"You want to tell me how you feel?"

"Yes."

"About your mum?"

"Yes, Nora." I tap my foot against the hardwood floor.

"You, Jess, queen of the repressed shit, opening up to me?"

"Yes."

"Not the other way around?"

"No."

"And you're a willing participant?"

"My God, Nora…" I huff, my free arm being thrown in the air.

"Halt the presses! This truly is a momentous day."

"I'm already changing my mind…" I shake my head, regretting all my decisions.

"No! Don't. I'll shut up. I'm all ears. Give it to me." She clears her throat.

"I'm going to see her today." I bite my bottom lip until I begin to taste metal in my mouth, "And… I don't know how I feel."

"Okay."

"Well, I guess I feel… Nervous."

"Nervous?"

"Yes." I nod, even though she can't see me.

"Anything... else?"

"I think not knowing how I'm going to feel when I see her is making me want to run a mile and I need you to help me not do that." My earlier thoughts about not running away from my problems come to my mind, full force, as I admit my fear.

"Well, that is totally understandable." She pauses, taking in a deep breath the way she always does when she's turning on her 'therapist' voice. "Here's the thing. Any reaction you have, it's fine. I mean, maybe try to avoid flipping tables and causing any sort of violence, but anything else goes. You will feel how you feel, and it's okay."

I release the breath I'd been holding. "Yeah?"

"Yeah."

"But you can't run this time."

"I know."

She pauses. "I'm very proud of you, Jess. For all of this." Emotion laces her voice.

My heart swells at her support. "Thanks, Nor. I love you."

"I love you too. So much."

An unknown voice sounds out through the phone. "*What self-respecting household doesn't have eggs!*"

My mouth opens on a laugh. "Is someone at the house?"

"... No," Nora whispers, sounding flustered.

"*This is the saddest fuckin' fridge I've ever seen. And why do you have so much pasta...*"

"Oh, my God. You have a guy over." My hand flies to cover my gaping mouth and to stifle a laugh. Nora rarely has guys over and I can't decide if I want to ask her if she's okay or high five her.

"Don't be ridiculous," she says, far too squeaky for her normal voice.

"*A guy puts out and you can't even provide eggs?*"

"... he's not talking to me."

"*Nora!*"

I hear muffled sounds, as though she's covering the mouthpiece, before she yells, "*Oh my God, shit for brains, stop talking!*"

My smile is huge. I've decided she deserves a high five for getting some. "*So...* who's the lucky guy?"

"Some absolute egg-obsessed loser, apparently... Ugh. I hate myself."

"You do know how to pick them. He better be giving you a *really* good time. That's all I'll say."

"Eh... I can't complain too much."

"Well, you better get to finding eggs for your fella. Gotta keep that protein up... "

"Jessica!" she giggles into the phone.

A quiet beat passes between us before she says, "Hey. You'll be great."

I nod, accepting her words. "Thank you. Enjoy your man."

"Ugh, I hate you."

38

Jessica

For mid-afternoon on a Tuesday, the café is busy. People sit at tiny square tables, blowing their hot coffee aromas around the room, laughing, chatting, and generally displaying every kind of happy emotion that I'm *not* feeling right now.

I glance at my watch. It's 1:45 pm and she's officially late. My leg jitters underneath the table, my nerves growing larger with each passing minute. I pick at a tiny piece of skin on my thumb that's been bugging me since I sat down, trying to distract myself. Cam sits beside me, casually reading the newspaper he brought. A sharp, shrill bell rings through the room again, alerting everyone that another customer is coming in, but every time that's happened, it's not been her and I'm beginning to think she might not show.

Just as I turn to ask Cam how long he thinks we should wait, she hurries in behind the person who opened the door and frantically searches the room for us. Her short messy hair tumbling around her face as the wind pushes the door closed behind her. She's dressed all in black; jeans and a long sleeve t-shirt with black, chunky boots. If I didn't know anything about her, I'd say she looks normal, stylish even. What gives her away, though, is her eyes. They look tired and worn, like she has to battle through every day. When she spots us, my leg jitters even harder. Every noise in the room feels like it's echoing right next to my head.

How are you supposed to greet your mother who abandoned you after years of not seeing her? *Hi Mummy dearest, how've you been? I've been great, you know, only spent the last ten years feeling abandoned by you but, no, let's talk about you.*

When she stops next to our table, my body turns to lead, unable to move or utter a single word because all the hurt that I've ever felt in her presence comes hurling back to my reality like a smack in the face. I hate the way my chest feels like it's bruised and the way my breathing stutters, I'm trying so hard to keep it together.

I feel Cam's hand reach for mine, the anchor he likely sensed I needed right now, and he squeezes tight enough for me to focus on something else for a second and not spiral into a panic attack.

After a few seconds, she sits down and my breathing evens out. Although, when her scent hits me, I have to squeeze Cam's hand once more, gripping it like I might disappear any second. Notes of orange and lavender flood my brain, making me feel foggy. I shake my head, willing it away, needing to keep as clear a mind as I can to get through this.

I straighten my shoulders and clear my throat, the sides of my mouth lift stiffly.

"Claire."

"Cam, it's good to see you again." I don't miss the slight malice in her tone, especially since I know their last meeting wasn't easy.

Cam stands and my body leaps. *He isn't leaving me, is he?* I look up at him, only to feel his hand gently hold my shoulder. "I'm going to get a few coffees. I'll be right there." He points to the counter and I hesitate, my head turning towards the counter to see just *how far* he'll be from me, then I nod, letting the death grip I have on his wrist loosen so he can leave.

"So... how are you doing?" my mum asks, nerves lacing her tone.

I resist the urge to scoff at the mundaneness of her question and her attempt at small talk, even if it burns my throat not to say anything spiteful. If she really wanted to know how I was doing, she would've contacted me before now. A bitter taste coats my tongue as my mood sours, but I swallow it, not letting myself be controlled by my wayward emotions.

"I've been better. You?" I cross my arms over my body protectively, leaning back in my chair.

She pauses, her eyes downcast and unreadable. When she finally looks up again, she's steeled her emotions, and I want to applaud her for being able to turn it on and off so easily. "Jessica, I need to be honest with you"

My pulse hammers like a drill sergeant in my neck. My body twitches at the urge to run away from what she's about to tell me, knowing that it isn't going to be all sunshine and rainbows, but I resist with everything I have because I'm done running from her. I'm fighting for me now. I fill my lungs until they feel like they might explode and tapper my breath slowly, counting backwards from ten, and then I nod my head, wanting to hear what she has to say.

"I need you to understand that I'm sorry. Being high was my priority for a really long time, and I'm truly sorry for that. After my accident, I felt as though I'd failed at everything; my ability to look after you, to provide for us. Nothing felt attainable except the control I had with the drugs. They made me feel… better. That control I had, it felt easy, and I didn't recognise the slope I was falling down until it was too late. When Cam and Harriet took you to Kent your child benefit payments from the government stopped. I wasn't your mum anymore, officially. I needed money to keep the only thing I had control over and you were the way I got it, so that's why I came back for you that New Year." She pauses, as she bites her cheek while furious tears fall down my cheeks. I swipe them away, forcing myself to stay and listen to her.

"Go on." I say, my voice wobbling.

"Listen, I know that sounds really shitty, and it is. I'm not excusing my behaviour. When I finally got clean, six years ago, a big part of my recovery is to apologise to those I may have hurt in my life and I almost did once. I found Nora's social media and I saw a few posts with you, and you looked so happy." She quickly wipes away a stray tear before it falls on her cheek, "But that was enough for me to know that I wasn't going to ruin your life again. Then, as time went on, I didn't think you'd *want* to see me, so I stayed away for good."

More tears burn my eyes and tiny flames of hurt spill down my face. I can see that she's sorry, I can hear it in her words, but as much as I want to understand her behaviour, I'm not sure I ever will.

"Okay," I manage to force out. I don't know what else to say. Years of dealing with a nagging feeling that I have no idea where she is... if she's even alive, are drowning me. I clear the tears from my face as I look at the woman who made me. The sweet memories we shared before her accident, when it was just us against the world, slam into me. I spent so long clinging to those memories, hoping that I could get that version of her back. But I didn't, and now, I'm here, I'm trying to heal from that loss. I *need* to heal from it.

Then it barrels into me like a meteorite tumbling to earth. My mother gave me the best gift she could without even realising. She gave me to people who would love me, care for me, and treat me like I matter. She might've been acting selfishly, but I suddenly can't bring myself to rage and scream at her because I'm too thankful for the choice that was taken away from her. I'm grateful for my Uncle Cam and Harriet. I'm grateful for Nora, Liam, and Zoey... all these people love me unconditionally. All of them have brought me so much joy in my life when it could've been filled with sorrow. They are the ones who have picked up my pieces and made me feel whole again. I know my mother still loves me, but that love has consistently been pushed to the bottom of her priorities and for *that*, I'll never understand her. But I can forgive her, because if I don't accept what I can't change, how can I move on with my life?

All the anger I've been carrying with me for all these years starts to lift. My shoulders relax, my chest expands evenly and with ease, my pulse is a steady silent beat as I look at the woman I thought held all the answers for me. When it turns out, I had them all along.

"You gave me everything by giving me up. I'm grateful that you left me alone all these years. I am the woman I am today because of those who fought for me. But I never stopped hoping that I was going to be enough for you to be better." Her grey eyes darken as they fill with tears and her lips purse as I continue, "I forgive you, though. I can't understand you, but I can forgive you and that's enough for me for now."

A tear falls freely down her face before she swipes it away as though it never existed. "I never meant to hurt you, Jess. You were my everything." Her eyes dart away and land in her lap, where she is twisting her fingers.

"I know I was your everything... until I wasn't."

Cam and I fall into step with one another as we walk back to the beach house. I focus on the crunch of the autumn leaves underneath my boots, and the distant squawk of a seagull and even the cool, salty sea air that fills my lungs. Before I know it, I look up to see we're home already.

Cam smiles at me. "Harriett is home early from work, so I'm going to head up to the house. You stay out here if you want. I'll let Liam know we're home."

"Thank you for today. I really mean it." I pull him into a hug as his clean cotton scent surrounds me.

"Anything for you, kiddo. I'm proud of you. Last year's Jess couldn't have done that. Look how far you've come." He releases me, flicking his long, greying hair behind his ears before he walks to the porch, tapping the kitchen window as he approaches, making Harriett jump. I stifle a laugh, watching her clutch her chest and point her finger at him before he ducks inside.

I kick off my shoes and let my feet carry me to the ocean. The firm sand is cold as the ocean kisses the very tips of my toes and then retreats, teasing me with the cool foam it leaves behind. The air smells like seaweed; earthy, sour and a little damp, but weirdly, it gives me a sense of peace, knowing that I can come here, and everything is the same as it always has been. The beach doesn't change, the tides stay the same, it's a constant in a world that changes so quickly. I like that.

Soft padding of feet rushing towards me snap me from my daydream and then two familiar, strong arms wrap around me from behind, while my favourite scent that is indescribably *him* assaults my nose.

"You're back," he breathes into my hair, inhaling me as much as I inhale him.

My hands grip his arm where it wraps around my stomach. "I'm back," I echo.

We stay huddled into each other, surrounded by the sound of the ocean swooshing in front of us and the seagulls cawing above us. I lean my head back into his chest, feeling content for the first time in a long time.

Liam drops his hand and reaches between our bodies to pull something from his hoodie. He places the polaroid I found this morning in front of us and rests his head on my shoulder. "You left this for me today and asked me if I loved you even then." I nod, swallowing a few nerves. He spins me to face him, his eyes searching my face, cataloguing me like they always do, and I can't help the way my lips purse into a smile for him.

"I've always loved you, Jess. From the minute you and Nora introduced yourself at the park where we met when we were, what ten? It was instant. I'd never met anyone like you..." He pauses, remembering the day we met. "You were full of moxie and *such* a control freak, but you had this softness that you only showed to people you cared about and when I became one of those people, I knew… I wanted you to be mine." He looks down at the picture again and laughs. "At some point, I got really bad at hiding it. Judging by that picture, anyway. Your boy has zero game with that poker face." He laughs deeply, the sound settling somewhere in my soul.

"You looked at me like I was your world even when we weren't together," I say, emotion wobbling my voice.

Our noses touch. The zap of energy between us feels potent, like a living flame.

"You *are* my world." He breathes and I capture his exhale with my lips, pushing myself into him, pouring my emotions into our kiss, because he's chosen me all these years and even when we weren't together, he still somehow gave me strength I didn't know I needed.

Our lips consume one another's, teeth clashing and hands gripping until we're both breathless. When we break, our foreheads remain connected, neither of us wanting to lose the other yet.

"Trust me, you had plenty of game. Still do."

39

Liam

From the moment I met Jessica Scott, I understood the feeling of never wanting to let something so beautiful slip away. To be determined enough to go after it. The truth is, I always knew I loved her and I would never find another person who matched my soul exactly as she does.

She's like waking up on Christmas morning to find a fresh blanket of snow outside. She makes wishes on dandelions because she thinks they'll come true like it's some sort of magic; she loves milkshakes like no one I've ever known, she's the other half my heart and no matter how much I tried to fill a void that was Jess shaped, no one ever fit the same.

We've been sitting on the beach for over an hour now. After a heavy kissing session that almost ended indecently, we've settled into a comfortable silence watching the sun disappear.

"I want to tell you everything that happened today."

"I wanted to ask, but I needed my girl to know I was patient, too." I press a chaste kiss to her temple.

She looks down at our hands and looks up at me with her big blue ocean eyes. "My girl," she whispers, smiling to herself whilst mindlessly tracing patterns on our connected hands.

I move closer to her and place my hand gently on her face. "Always my girl."

"Liam, you've given me back a part of me that I thought I'd lost. A part I never knew I needed back." She says as she shines up at me, "You make me happy, and you bring light back into my darkest places. Places that I've hidden in for too long. I'm so sorry that I ever made you feel like I didn't want you in my life. I wouldn't have been able to get through all of this without knowing you care about me." Her blue eyes blaze with determination and love. "You don't question my moods, you accept them; you don't walk away from troubles, you want to help me find ways to fix them and I know I've said it before but I'm so fucking sorry that I pushed you away when we were younger. I was weak, but I don't want to be weak anymore. You have and always will be my best friend and I can't live without you. I don't want to."

I smile at her, loving the way she's opening up to me.

"I love you, Jess. Just like I told you I did at the beach years ago. If it's possible, I love you more."

"I'm ready for you, Liam Taylor. All of me is ready," she whispers.

Her words echo through me and if I didn't know it before, I know now that my heart belongs to her. I want to keep her forever. I pull her closer and I never plan on letting her go.

"I hope you don't mind, but I booked us a hotel not far from here. As much as I've loved spending the last two weekends with you here, I want us back in London together. Well, that and I need to fuck you so hard that we break the fucking bed and that isn't something I've been able to do in your uncle's house."

"You are something else." She turns and wraps her arms around my neck, seating herself on my lap as she pulls me into a deep, demanding kiss and I put my hands on her waist and slowly squeeze, enjoying the feel of her beneath my touch. A soft moan falls from her mouth as she grinds against me. "Yeah, we should go... Now." Her eyes darken, and before I can agree, she's pulling me to my car in the driveway. Not even sparing a glance back at the house where Harriett is waving and laughing at the window. I wave back and then focus on the little firebomb that is dragging me to have her way with me.

She stands by the door of my rented 4x4 and I raise a brow mischievously. "In such a rush, baby. What do you want to do to me that has that sweet, peachy bum bouncing so fast? Hm?"

Her lips part and her breath shallows as she steps into my space, pushing me back against the car. My heart thrums under her fingertips resting on my chest.

"Come on, don't make me say it." I smirk at her whinging, not letting her get out of telling me what she wants. "You know I want you, lover boy. So, show me how you live up to your nickname. Love me the best way you know how." Her tongue darts out to wet her lips before they ghost across my cheek, making my cock harden painfully for her.

She slips into my car with ease, smirking at me through the tinted windows. My mouth gapes and my cock swells for the woman who absolutely floors me. I swallow hard and practically speed out of the driveway and into the hotel carpark in record time.

"Fuck, I've missed you so much." I slide inside Jess hard and fast for the third time tonight, and she groans into my neck as I fill her completely. Her warmth clenches around me, teasing me, the urge to slam into her overwhelms me as I growl, "Hold... the fucking... headboard," through clenched teeth, holding back my orgasm for dear life.

She does as she's told and my hands dig into the perfect soft skin of her hips as she arches her back, pushing her arse into the air, begging me for more.

The taste of her on my tongue lingers, fuelling my desire for her. Her vanilla scent invades my senses and her tight, hot centre squeezes me again, almost making me see stars.

"Liam... baby... I can't hold on. I'm..." Her whole body vibrates as she comes all over me, her sweet as honey nectar spilling down my cock. I push into her two more times as a guttural groan rips from my chest while I empty myself inside her, before falling bonelessly onto her back, where we stay for a while as our breath settles and our bodies recover.

I somehow manage to make my legs move and walk to the bathroom to run a warm bath. "Come, get in here, otherwise you'll be sore tomorrow," I whisper to a sleepy Jess. She moans and opens her clear blue eyes before she slowly gets up to follow me into the tub.

As she sits between my legs in the warm bubbles of the bath, I run my fingers up and down her arm, watching the goosebumps come and go at my touch.

"I feel so relaxed. I could fall asleep right now." As she leans back and tips her head up to kiss my neck, I hold her gently against my body, letting my hands slip all over her skin. I watch her chest rise and fall, her nipples peeking in and out of the bubbles as she moves. I'll never get my fill of her.

"It was strange today..." she says quietly. "I thought I would feel angry. I thought I'd *be* angry with her. But I wasn't. I thought I needed to interrogate her to find out why she left and get some answers, but... all I really did was forgive her." She plays with some stray bubble clusters in her hands as she talks. "I hadn't planned to say anything like that to her, but I had this overwhelming urge to just let it all go. So, I did."

I nod and continue moving my fingertips up and down her arm.

"How did you leave things with her?"

"I left it at that, mostly. I don't have the same need for answers anymore. I don't *need* anything from her and realising that was... freeing."

"I'm proud of you, baby." I kiss the top of her head that rests on my chest.

"I'm proud of me too."

40

Jessica

On the drive back to London, Liam's hand rests on his favourite place when we travel together, wrapped around my thigh. It's the sweetest thing and I'd be lying if I said I didn't love it.

A loud bang and a drawling sound shakes the car and I sit rod straight. "What was that?" Just as Liam shouts "Shit!"

"I'm pretty sure that is a blown tyre." He slowly pulls over and tells me to stay put, the hazard lights clicking in the car as he checks. I can see it in his face as soon as he sees the tyre on my side is blown. He looks at me and makes a neck slice motion, telling me it's a goner.

I wind down my window when the smell of burning rubber fills the car. "Have you ever changed a tyre, lover boy?"

"Define change a tyre…"

I laugh loudly. "If I need to define it, you definitely haven't done it." I jump down from the car and look down at the shredded tyre. "Yeah, that is completely gone. Let's check the back for a spare."

I move to the boot and dig around until I touch the compartment where the spare tyre should be. "I never asked, but why do you have this car anyway? Where's your fancy Tesla?"

"It needed some work doing on it, so I rented this car. Fancied a change for a while."

I nod, whilst rummaging for the latch to open the compartment. "Aha!" I shriek, opening the hidden layer beneath the car. "Here it is and here are all the tools we need."

Liam looks at the tyre, tools and back to me, completely confused. "Don't worry, city boy, I'll show you what to do with your tools." I pat his shoulder whilst picking up the box.

"Oh yeah, I bet you'd like to show me what I can do with my tools." He stalks towards me and I laugh, stopping him with my palm flat on his chest.

"You, Liam Taylor, are about to be schooled. Grab the tyre and bring it around to the side of the car."

His mouth remains mostly unhinged as I walk around the car and loosen the wheel nuts. I wait for him to join me because I want him to learn. He eventually stops gawking and places the tyre down by the side of us.

"Okay, this is the tyre iron, and this is the jack. It lifts the car. I've loosened the wheel nuts, so now we need to jack up the car. You then remove the wheel nuts and make sure you keep them somewhere safe, switch the tyres over, put the wheel nuts back on, tighten them and then the car comes back down." I realise he is staring at me, licking his lips like he wants to eat me. "Are you even listening?"

"You are so fucking hot right now. I can't tell you how much you are turning me on."

I swat his arm. "Behave and listen. Then if you're a good student, maybe I'll give you a reward after class."

"Yes, ma'am." He smiles like a giddy schoolboy and I can't stop the chuckle building in my chest.

It takes us over thirty minutes to change the tyre because Liam couldn't keep his hands to himself, constantly pinching and groping me all over my body. We're both covered in black grease. Liam stands, sweat covering his brow as he wipes it with the back of his arm, smudging more grease over his face and I smile. All his touching has done is ignite that fire deep in my belly that's just for him and seeing him dirty and sweaty *does* things to me.

"So, what's the verdict, Miss Scott? Was I a good student or do you need to punish me?" His arms slowly snake around my waist and he jerks me forward, forcing a gasp from me. A car driving by beeps his horn, snapping me out of my Liam-induced haze and I smile at him knowingly.

"Let's go home, lover boy, so I can show you how I want you to use your other tool." I slowly and purposefully trail a finger down his front until I reach his belt buckle and I tug him closer so I can bite his ear playfully. His body is throwing sexy pheromones at me like I've won the jackpot. I smile, sauntering past him as I climb into our newly fixed car.

As we drive, Liam stops at traffic lights while a few parents walk across the road holding the hands of their children. I watch as they dote on the mini versions of themselves, smiling and laughing, looking really bloody adorable. Something hits me square in my chest as I realise that I want that. Not right now, but the thought of being married and having little Liam's running around doesn't terrify me like it used to... like it did a few months ago when Grayson mentioned it. In fact, I even *like* the idea of being Liam's wife. Actually I'm lying... I *love* the idea.

"So, I was thinking..."

"Uh-oh, that's dangerous," Liam scoffs.

"You're awful, you know that?" I smirk.

"Go on..." He tilts his head, encouraging me to continue.

"Well... I know we talked about forever, but what does that look like for you?" I wring my hands in my lap.

Liam's eyes dart to mine before returning to the road, his arms flexing against the steering wheel as he kneads the leather beneath his palm. "I guess, for me, that means I'd like to marry you and build a life together, a home, and if we want children, then we cross that bridge when we come to it."

My hands immediately calm and stop twisting as I take in Liam's profile. Imagining a life together is something I haven't let myself do since we were sixteen, but the difference is, I'm not afraid anymore. I'm... excited. For the first time since my mum's accident, I feel lighter. I've gained a part of me that I thought was lost. The part that makes plans for the future I deserve.

"I think I want that, too." I smile. The feeling of joy overcomes me. I'm getting everything I ever wanted with the boy I've loved since I was sixteen.

Liam's hand reaches for mine and as he brings it to his lips, his stubble grazing against my skin before he presses peppered kisses along my knuckles. "I love you," he says against my hand.

"I love you more."

"Not like I love you."

For once, I'm not falling, I'm soaring.

41

Liam

I tap my pen on my desk.

One, two, one, two, one, two.

The low light of the sun blares through my office windows, burning my eyes as I stare directly into the beam that's projecting onto my desk. My hand drops the pen and assaults my hair instead, tugging the strands backwards and forwards.

A knock on my door has my eyes focussing again. "Come in."

Grayson appears with a cup of coffee and places it on my desk in front of me. The nutty aroma steaming from the cup as it drifts up to my nose. "What's with your hair?" He frowns as he looks at me. I bet I look like a mad-man from the way I've been running my hands through it.

"Nothing. What's wrong with yours?" I retort, snapping the cup from the table.

"Oooo, someone's touchy. Wanna talk about it or just ignore the elephant in the room, that seems to have taken up residence in that nest on your head?"

"Elephants don't live in nests, dickhead."

"Okay, well then, enjoy your coffee. Don't say I didn't offer." He turns and spins on his heels, his fresh white trainers squeaking against the wooden floor. Before his hand reaches the doorknob, I grumble to myself then shout, "Wait." When he turns wearing a cocky smirk, I almost want to change my mind, but I know I need to vent for a second.

Grayson strides over to the chair opposite my desk as he settles in and sips his coffee. "Talk to your agony aunt."

I laugh heartily for the first time today. Scrubbing my hand down my face, I take a deep breath. "I need to talk to Dad about Claire again. he..." I pause, contemplating if I should tell him, but decide I trust him. "He's her sponsor and I don't know... when he told me I feel like I was so shocked that I didn't actually process it properly."

He nods thoughtfully. "I had no idea, man."

"Yeah, it's been a whirlwind." I shake my head. "Jess is doing so well with all of this, and I don't want to complicate things for her."

"And your dad might do that?"

"Maybe, I don't know..." I trail off. "I'm just..."

"Procrastinating?"

I nod, fiddling with my pen again.

"Want my advice?"

"Like you're going to leave here without giving it to me anyway."

"Rude." He adjusts his black tie that's blended into his black shirt. "But you're right. You need to stop letting your dad control so much of everything. I've seen the hours you put in here. I've seen your plans to expand, Liam, and they're fucking good. Not just that, they're just what this place needs. So, if anyone deserves more respect around here it's you. Talk to him, sort it out and get me promoted whilst you're at it." His wide grin has me mirroring him.

"Thanks man." I say, grateful for him.

He hikes his sleeve up, his silver watch catching the light. "I'm out. Got a meeting with a client over in the wharf."

"Don't think you're getting an easy ride to a promotion just because you think you're my best mate."

As he opens the office door and walks away, he shouts over his shoulder, "Admit it, you're obsessed with me."

Cheeky bastard.

Grayson's words resonate with me. He's right. Not about the part where I'm obsessed with him, but the part where I work hard for this place. I push my rolling chair away from my desk as I stand and button my suit jacket and stride over to my dad's office, counting my steps as I go with my heart beating in my ears.

Knock knock.

"Come in," my dad's voice bellows from the other side of the door, and I take one last deep breath in. I've never been so nervous about approaching my dad. I mean, he's my dad; the guy who taught me to ride a bike, but right now I need to see him as the CEO so I can take all this emotion out of the situation.

When I open the door, I see him in his usual spot, on the sofa in his office. He hates desks and has always worked from a low sofa onto a coffee table, despite my many attempts to tell him he'll end up with a broken back. The man's a creature of habit.

"Liam, everything okay, son?"

My hands find my pockets as I hover in front of his black, glossy coffee table. "I'm good. I wanted to talk to you about something. Do you have a minute?"

He nods, as his hand gestures for me to take a seat in one of the wingback chairs surrounding the table.

I hesitate. "I want to talk about Claire first."

He shifts in his chair. "What do you need to talk about?"

"I guess I want to let you know that Jess is doing really well. She met with Claire last week and I think she got the closure she needed. I don't know if they're going to have a relationship yet. I guess I need to know where you stand, too."

"I'm still her sponsor. I also plan to keep her working here, but she'll be based with the site teams rather than in the office," he says.

"Okay, that makes sense." I rub my hands over my trousers to rid myself of the damp feeling coating my palms. "I feel like I need to do something to support you. I've missed out on something big and I can't shake this feeling." I stand, needing to move.

"There is something you can do for me." He says confidently. I turn my gaze to him, trying to read his face before he says, "I'd like to take a step back, spend more time with you mother. I know you have plans and I've been ignoring them, but I want to hear them."

I stand tall, letting his words soak over me. He's finally letting me take on more. I'm more than ready. I know I am. "The company does need an overhaul. We're in desperate need of new IT systems. We need to hire more upper management and if I were you, I'd be looking to push more of the smaller properties into a separate division from the larger corporate companies." I wait, trying to figure out if the frown he's giving me is good or bad. "It doesn't make sense to not use the revenue we've generated in the last two years alone to expand and evolve the company. We'll be washed out of the water soon with all these new kids on the block. If we act now and re-brand with two divisions, then we'll be setting president for other companies instead of following."

He's still frowning, staring at me blankly. He shifts his weight, leaning his elbows onto his knees. "Who will run the divisions?"

"It's something we would need to decide."

"And you said something about new IT systems?" he questions.

"Yes, Grayson has a contact who is leading the field for office software."

He nods, looking down at the scattered paper in front of him. "What's the timeline for Grayson's contact to install it and run some training for the staff?"

"I'm guessing a couple of weeks."

"Okay."

"Okay?" I echo his words as my feet fidget inside my shoes. I have zero clue what my dad is thinking right now.

"You'll take point on this. This is a great way to introduce you as CEO. Start the division of the company and work out what the cost is for expansion and how many staff we'll need, in addition to who will be allocated new roles within each division."

My whole body vibrates with excitement. I want to fist punch the air. I want to whoop like I've just won the world cup. "Okay. I'll get started." I stand and turn, dazed from my dad agreeing to my ideas. My head is awash with determination and elation. My hands clench at my sides with excitement as I nod to my dad. "Thank you. I mean it."

"Liam?" He pauses. "I'm sorry for what I said before about your abilities. I was wrong and I'm sorry."

"Thanks, Dad," I croak, my emotions getting the better of me.

"I really hope things work out with Jess, too. I like seeing you happy." He says with his eyes glistening.

"I am happy... In fact, I'm going to ask her to marry me."

His whole face softens as he stares at me. "Son, that's..." he clears his throat, "I'm really happy for you."

"I'm happy too." I say as I round his desk to give him a hug. Not something we do often, but it felt like the right time.

As I walk out of the office, I may as well be prancing, singing a fucking *Disney* song, whilst riding a sugar high because my body is bubbling with opportunity.

I pass by Grayson's office with the biggest grin on my face. "Mate, about that promotion."

42

Jessica

New Year's Eve-Eve

"Here you go, one coffee for my girl." Liam passes me my drink as the earthy, sweet aroma floats around me and I hum. We've found a new routine that we've fallen into in the mornings since he pretty much lives here now. He makes coffee after giving me an orgasm or two and I can't say I'm hating it because it sets the world right every day.

"What would I do without you?" I sigh fluttering my eyelashes at him as I rest my chin in my hand.

He smirks. "You'd probably get more sleep without me, but have a lot less fun."

"Morning, lovebirds," Nora sings as she walks around the kitchen island, grabbing her morning coffee that Liam makes her too.

"You're awfully chirpy today. That wouldn't have anything to do with a guy, would it?" I sip my coffee, raising a brow over my mug.

She meets my stare. "I'm just in a good mood. My best friends are here. It's my last day of work today for the year. It's New Year's Eve tomorrow, my favourite time of year." She shoots a look to Liam that I can't figure out but immediately flicks her attentions back to me. "There's a lot to be happy about."

Just as I'm about to ask what that was passing between Nora and Liam, his phone cuts through my plan. As he swipes his screen to answer it, he quickly pecks my temple. "G-man, what's up?"

I narrow my eyes as I watch him walk away, then suddenly I'm appreciating how he looks in his chino suit trousers and white shirt. *Ooof that man does things to me.*

Nora snaps her fingers in front of my face. "Earth to Jess."

"Sorry, it's hard to pay attention when he..." I shake my head. "What did you say?"

"Just that you guys seem good. Is it after New Years weekend that Liam is actually moving in?"

I nod my head. "Yeah, and you're sure you don't mind? It's temporary until we can find something together that's close by."

Nora smiles. "I'm happy if you are. Stay here as long as you need. I just need to invest in earplugs."

"We won't... I mean, we'll be quiet." I bury my face in my hands as heat creeps into my cheeks.

"Oh please, you do you, honey. I'll get you back one day."

Three loud knocks at the door has both of our heads snapping up as Liam comes back into the kitchen and places his phone on the kitchen table. "That's Grayson, he's giving me a ride to our first meeting today, but I told him to come in for a coffee first, if that's okay?" He strides over to me, placing a kiss on my head as he reaches me.

"Yeah, sure." I smile.

Liam disappears around the corner just as Nora leans into whisper, "Grayson, how do I...?" her eyes widen. "Ohhh right. Flirty playboy, Grayson. I remember."

I nod my head, sipping my coffee. "The one and only."

Nora's eyes roll just as Grayson comes into the kitchen. His all-black suit is tailored to perfection and his black hair is wavy and still damp from his shower.

"You remember Jess and Nora?" Liam gestures to us, and Grayson's lips twitch devilishly.

"How could I forget the woman who stole my wingman?" Grayson moves over to hug me, but Liam bats him away before he can get too close.

"Get your own. She's off limits."

I chuckle and grab Liam to kiss his cheek. "You're so cute when you're jealous... It's good to see you again, Grayson."

Nora passes him a cup of coffee and eyes him suspiciously. I watch her eyeing him as his tattooed fingers wrap around the mug and he sips the hot liquid, all the while not taking his eyes off her.

"Damn, that's good coffee."

"You look like you need it today. Busy night?" Liam asks.

Grayson rubs a hand through his hair, his biceps flexing under his suit jacket, and I know I definitely don't miss the way Nora averts her eyes. *Interesting.*

"You know me, man. Sleep is for the weak, sex is for the wicked." He steps closer to Nora, making sure he's got her attention, "And I prefer to be wicked all the time." He winks hoping to charm Nora and it might be working as the stain of pink on her cheeks is definitely not blusher.

Hmm very interesting.

"Does it get boring? Being a fuck boy?" Nora asks, surprising us all.

Someone get me some popcorn, Nora just opened the show.

Grayson lowers his eyes over her, trying to suss out her question. "I'm never bored when I've got a woman riding me or when she screams my name over and over and—"

Liam interrupts. *Oh, that was just about to get good.*

"Dude, we get it." He slaps Grayson's shoulder, but he still doesn't stop staring at Nora. Fire burns in her eyes as she takes on a silent challenge and one thing I know about Nora is that she's insanely competitive.

"Hmm, I'm trying to see things from your perspective, but I can't seem to get my head that far up my own arse." Nora pushes Grayson backwards without touching him as she sways towards him, leaning down to get her keys and handbag before she walks out without saying another word.

My mouth hangs open, I don't think I've ever seen Nora behave like that. The sass alone was top notch. Again, I kind of want to high five her.

When Grayson finally closes his mouth, his steel exterior is back in place and he turns to Liam. "She's smoking, man. Uptight as fuck, but hot all the same."

"Not happening, Grayson." I wag a finger at him. "She's way out of your league."

He mumbles something under his breath and drinks his coffee as Liam laughs at him, "Come on *fuck boy*, we are going to be late to do the... meeting." His eyes widen when he says *meeting* and my head tilts, watching this interaction unfold in front of me.

Grayson immediately remembers something, and his body straightens as he avoids my eyes. "Right the *meeting*. Don't want to keep them waiting. Let's go mate... See you soon, Jess."

Liam kisses me quickly on the lips. "I'll be home around four. Love you."

Well, that was fucking weird.

43

Liam

New Year's Eve

My palms are slick and sticky and I'm pretty sure I've looked for the ring a thousand times, only to find it in my pocket every time. Every noise has me on edge; party poppers explode and I almost duck from the adrenaline rushing around my body. The music is loud and voices cheer and sing from the other room as I pace the kitchen with Cam, trying desperately to calm my nerves but failing miserably.

"How did you do this and keep cool? I feel like my lungs are about to explode."

When we were here a month or so ago, I asked Cam if I could marry Jess and he said he couldn't think of a better person for her. It's always been my plan to propose on New Year's Eve at midnight, I want us to see the new year in with her as mine, with a ring to prove it, and I want to make sure that Jess has re-written New Year with good memories.

"I wasn't calm, I was exactly like you are now. Probably more jittery actually. You need another shot of liquid courage?" He gestures to the multicoloured rainbow shots that Nora made for everyone earlier and I wince, shaking my head. "I don't want to throw up on her. I'll pass."

Cam chuckles and slaps my shoulder as he walks back into the party. "Just breath, Liam."

Just breathe. Solid advice, except I feel like I've got an elephant sitting on my lungs right now, so breathing is more difficult than usual.

I pace the kitchen alone, thinking over what I might say to her again. I'd planned a speech, but I threw it out because no one wants to see something that rehearsed. Then I wrote another one, and threw that out too. I know what I want to say, but I'm worried it'll come out wrong; a lot like the first time I told Jess I liked her. Between the fear, the boob grab and the stumbling mess I was, I'm still surprised she kissed me back that day.

Jess bounces into the kitchen and when she spots me, her smile widens. "Hey, lover boy. Why you in here all alone?"

"I was just... getting a drink," I say with an empty hand. I don't think she buys my lie, so I grab her to wrap her legs around my waist and she squeals, kissing me as we move. I lower her onto the kitchen island and settle between her thighs. She surprises me and opens them wider, giving me access higher underneath the short blue dress she's wearing and leans in to whisper in my ear, "Put your hands on me."

My eyebrows meet my hairline. When I'd hoped for a distraction, I never guessed it would be as good as this. I run my hands slowly up her smooth, tanned skin until I reach the top of her thigh. I watching her breathing stutter and her skin pebble from my touch. I reach the apex of her thighs, expecting to find underwear and when I find nothing but her bare pussy, I let out a deep groan that makes my cock harden instantly.

"You are a naughty girl, Miss Scott." I brush the tips of my fingers through her lips and gently pinch her clit. She moans into my ear and her body bucks forward, searching for my hand.

"I want you, now. I need you to touch me." She breathes out the words and I dive my head into her neck and bite gently as she arches her back again, my fingers still torturing her underneath her dress.

"Scotty, you're so bold. What if someone walks in?" I ask, amusement lacing my voice. When she gasps in my ear, it sends another bolt of lust straight to my cock. "Oh, you want that? You want to be caught, you want everyone to know you're mine?"

She nods, breathless as I graze my stubble over her skin and I can feel her body shudder at the contact. I push a finger inside of her and she whimpers at the intrusion. "Oh, God, Liam," she purrs against me.

"Is that why you're so wet? You're thinking about me fucking you?" I don't wait for her answer as I remove my hand and bring my finger to my lips and suck her taste off, "Mmm... you taste so sweet; I'll never get enough."

Her eyes are the darkest shade of stormy blue, full of desire and thoughts of what she wants me to do to her. She swallows hard as her gaze drops to my lips. The power she gives me surges through my body like fire ripping through a forest; it's wild and untamed and makes me desperate for her.

Looking into her eyes, I whisper, "Do you want me to fuck you? Right here?"

Her eyes dart around the kitchen as though she realises where we are again, the music still echoing from the other room filled with people, but she doesn't back down. She nods her head shyly.

"Don't go shy on me now, Scotty." I grip her chin and hold her stare, loving the shiver of desire she gives me.

"There you guys are!" Zoey shouts as she stumbles into the kitchen. I shield Jess from view as I pull her dress down her legs and help her off the counter.

Lucky for us, Zoey is drunk and completely oblivious to what she just walked in on, and heads straight to the other side of the kitchen island to grab some of the truly disgusting rainbow shots. "Jess, you have to try every colour. Taste the rainbow," she slurs.

"Zoey, how many of those have you had?" I ask, not taking my eyes off my girl. Jess isn't a big drinker and Zoey knows that Jess is sober right now, thank fuck, because for what I have planned later, I need her to stay that way.

Zoey does a pretend thinking face and shrugs. "I can't remember, but it's a lot." She hiccups, then squeals and jiggles on the spot when she hears a song blasting in the other room. "This is my jam. Come on Jess, you have to dance with me."

Jess reluctantly groans against me before she is dragged out of the kitchen and I'm left with her sweet taste on my tongue and cock as hard as steel. *Fuck, I need to chill out*. I grab a red coloured shot, knock it back and wince, as I mutter, "The fuck is in that shit." I grab a beer instead, just to take the edge off my fraying nerves.

An hour of watching her move her hips to the music has been slow torture, but I'm also enjoying the show. Damn, that sway of her hips, though... that has me weak. I would love nothing more than to throw her over my shoulder right now and drag her arse upstairs, but I practice restraint because she's happy, dancing carefree and having the time of her life with her friends.

I glance at my watch. 11:29 pm. I've got thirty minutes.

Another song comes on that has her grinding into Zoey, and I find myself losing all the restraint I swore I'd show her. So, I stalk over, making sure she sees me coming, and I watch as her whole body pauses and comes alive under my gaze. Her lips part, her body screaming in anticipation. Just perfect.

I tilt my head as I reach her and I can see a glisten of sweat on her skin from all the dancing she's been doing. I devour the space between us, bending to her ear, letting my warm breath affect her the way I know it always does. "Come for a walk with me, baby."

Her eyes dart to mine in a silent question, but it quickly fades and she nods, licking her lips. *Damn, my girl is hungry tonight.*

I smirk and lead her by hand to the patio doors and down towards the beach front. As our feet touch the cold, damp sand, our eyes lock and we shiver together, letting the chill settle over us both.

"Let's go over there." She points to the water's edge.

"You want to go in the water? It's December, Jess."

"What's the matter, lover boy? You scared?" She tilts her head and purses her lips in a ghost of a smirk.

"Don't play games, baby. You know I'll always win in the end." I wink, and before I can catch her between my arms, she kicks off her heels and runs off towards the water, her hair bellowing wildly behind her. I peel off my shoes and follow, padding along the sand as I chase her, the chill of the breeze rushing past me. Jess' eyes glisten in the moonlight as she turns to see if I'm following her, shrieking as she runs faster, slapping her feet across the sand.

I catch her around the waist and spin her around, her laughter filling my ears with sweet music as I slowly put her down. "You thought you'd run from me? No chance. Not going to happen."

"I like when you chase me, though." She beams, lust shining on her face. I pin her to my front, growling in her ear and walking together until our toes touch the freezing water.

The moonlight gives the metallic look as it ripples in the waves. We stand watching the waves meet our feet and then disappear just as fast, listening to the soft roars of the water as it greets us and the smell of cold winter air and sea salt surround us.

I check my watch and it is almost midnight. Jess notices the time too as she turns towards me, her chin resting on my chest. "Maybe we should go inside to see in the New Year with everyone." She pecks my lips softly and I move quickly back for another kiss; one that is more demanding than hers... more needy and one that I hope is a perfect prelude to everything that is about to come next.

My hands tremble as I pull away. I mindlessly run my thumb over her lower lip and catalogue every fine line, every freckle and my favourite... the dimple.

"Jess, I love you. More than anything or anyone..." I pause, trying to remember one of my discarded speeches from earlier, but I suddenly can't remember anything. *Fuck, why didn't I plan better?*

"I love you too. Are you okay? You're shaking. Let's go inside." She tries to angle us towards the house, but I stop her.

"I mean it. I never want to be without you again." I lean in to needing to feel every inch of her, holding her close.

"Sometimes you need a second chance because you weren't quite ready for the first," she whispers, almost to herself. I look down as her head is buried into my chest, her brown hair catching the moonlight and I move my hand underneath her chin to face me. Her eyes are full and ready to burst. She's right—we weren't ready for it all back then, but I damn sure know that I'm ready for her now and I want all of her, forever.

I inhale the biggest breath, filling my lungs until they're bursting.

"I want you to be all of my lasts, Jess. My last kiss, my last dance, my last happy memory, my everything. Are you ready for everything, Scotty?"

My heart thrums against my ribs, waiting for her words that will calm its chaotic rhythm.

Her lips tip up in a little smile. "You've always called me Scotty, but you are the only one who ever did. I like that. It's like a part of me always belonged to you."

"You've always belonged to me... with me." I cup her face between my hands, loving the softness of her cheeks as I gaze deeply into her baby blues. "I guess I'll have to start calling you by your first name anyway, if you take my last name."

Her eyebrows rise, and suddenly cheers and laughter echo behind us in the distance. It's midnight.

I drop on one knee to the sand, pulling out the three carat diamond and sapphire ring I picked for her, and I look up at my girl; my forever. Her eyes fill with tears and her hand covers her mouth. I extend my hand and she immediately fills it with hers.

"Jessica Scott, be mine forever. Marry me?"

She collapses to the ground with me as she pulls me into a kiss, wrapping her hands around my face.

She pulls back only a little to stare at me. "Is that a yes?" I ask, shakily.

She nods, tears falling freely down her face. "Yes, Liam Taylor," she cries. "I'll marry you."

I go to say something, anything, but the words catch in my throat. Instead, I pull her into my lap and we both fall into the sand and we seal our connection, more deeply somehow than ever before. I feel her everywhere.

She encompasses every inch of my soul, my heart, and my everything. She's going to be mine forever.

Epilogue

Liam – 7 years later

The most beautiful thing about loving a guarded girl is that she lets you in because she wants you, not because she needs you.

J essica Taylor is still as strong as a hurricane and as warm as the sun. But now she is *my* sun and *my* hurricane and I am happy to be swept up in her every day if it means I can be soothed by her every night.

She's standing on the porch in our house in Kent, five months pregnant with our second child, and I'm in awe of her.

Her long brown hair is blowing in the breeze as she rubs her growing stomach. She's watching our daughter, Poppy, run around in the grass just outside the house. Poppy is three, and the image of Jess. My heart swells in my chest as I watch them both laugh around the dandelions and make wishes in the wind. When Jess told me we were pregnant again, my heart near enough exploded. This life is everything I ever dreamed it would be, and sharing it with my best friend is the icing on the cake.

Jess and I got married the year after we were engaged, neither of us wanted to wait. Then, five years ago, I bought The Clover Hotel and Jess became the manager. Six months later, we fell in love with a run-down B&B here in Kent and we bought it on a whim. It took us another six months to open and by that time we were pregnant with Poppy.

When Poppy turned two, we made the move to Kent to be nearer Cam and Harriett and, believe it or not, also Jess' mum, who we see a few times a month. Their relationship will never be the way it was before, but Jess has worked hard to heal from it all, and that included having her back in her life when she was ready. Nora now runs the charity full time, and she is the best aunt to Poppy, who adores her.

I still can't get enough of my wife. She gives me everything I need and more in a friend, a confidant, lover and soulmate.

Fuck, whatever I call her can never justify how incredible she is.

"What are you staring at over there, lover boy?" Jess gets my attention and smiles widely.

"Oh, just checking out my insanely hot wife." I move towards her and wrap her in my arms, placing my hands on her beautiful swelling belly.

She hums as I stroke her stomach over her t-shirt. "Insanely hot or insanely huge. I feel the size of a hippo right now. I swear this time round I'm so big."

I turn her to hold her face in my hands and kiss her deeply, leaving her breathless. "No, baby, you're wrong. I've never been more attracted to you than I am right now. You are seriously rocking this hot Mama body and I want to eat you up." I lean in and growl into her neck, making her squeal with delight.

"I don't know what I did to deserve you, but I'm glad you're mine." She pushes onto her tiptoes and kisses me softly.

I'm just about to drag her inside and lick her from head to toe when Poppy appears next to us and tugs at my t-shirt.

"Daddy, my hungry. Can I have snacks now?" Her big, blue eyes shine up at me and her caramel hair wildly flops into her face, just like her mother's. My girls have me wrapped around their little fingers and soon another one will make me even more outnumbered.

Jess and I laugh as I scoop Poppy up into my arms and kiss her cheek. "I can do that, baby girl. Actually, you want to help Daddy make some dinner? Mummy is going to put her feet up and read her new book, so I need a sous chef tonight."

I take her hand leading her to the kitchen at the front of the house and place her on the kitchen worktop, and she looks at me confused. "What's a Susie chef?"

I chuckle. "A sous chef, baby. They are the second in command in the kitchen, which means you are technically one of the bosses tonight." I nudge her and wink making her chuckle.

"Daddy, you're silly. Mummy is bossy, not you. I like to be Susie-chef though. Can I pleeeeease?"

Her little voice and her Poppy-isms have me melting. How we made her so perfectly, I'll never know.

"Pops, you're so funny and so right. Mummy is the boss," Jess shouts from the lounge.

"I'm pretty sure she said Mummy is bossy, but you keep reading, baby. Me and my Susie-chef have work to do," I shout back and hear Jess snigger.

An hour and lots of deep breaths later, Poppy and I are serving pasta and roasted vegetables.

"Mummyyyy, dinner's ready," Poppy shouts from the dining room. "Come onnnn, my hungry," she whines. She definitely inherited her mum's hangry trait too.

"I'm coming baby. It just takes Mummy a little longer to get anywhere with your sister in my belly."

Jess comes slowly into the dining room. Her eyes are sleepy and she's wearing her glasses; I love this relaxed, natural, barefoot and pregnant version of her.

"Hey, mama," I say, giving her the once over, biting my lip.

"It smells so good in here. Did you have a good time being Daddy's Susie-chef?" Jess moves to Poppy and kisses her head then to me.

"I like it, but my so hungry now." She rubs her tummy and licks her lips looking at the food in front of her.

"Here, baby girl, let me help you." I spoon some pasta and vegetables onto her plate, and she dives right in, then I plate up Jess' food too.

Sitting around the dinner table eating with my girls has my heart beating fast. I'm so fucking happy. I wish I could go back in time and tell 16-year-old me that he gets the girl in the end and she's worth every single day of the wait.

Jessica

Liam stumbles sleepily into our bedroom, after falling asleep with Poppy in her bed. The fact he is so enamoured with our girl makes me love him on another level.

I sit on my side of our bed, rubbing my stomach, feeling like the luckiest woman in the whole world.

The mattress dips as Liam gets in, kissing my forehead before lying down. His body glows with the small amount of light peeking in through the curtains, and I run my fingers over his stomach and watch his abs flex under my touch. The need for my husband has not gone away and I know it never will. He grabs my wrist.

"Are you teasing me, baby? Hm? Something you need?" His voice is laced with amusement and *God, that's turning me on more.*

"I want you," I say breathlessly, desire pooling at my core.

"You want me to what?" He lets my wrist go, only to run his fingertips slowly up my arm, making me tremble.

"I want you inside of me."

Liam hums and I can't stand the distance anymore. I sit up carefully, my leg over his waist, his dark, tempting gaze locks with mine, "Kiss me," I breathe out as he moves upwards to meet my mouth in a searing kiss. I push my tongue in, invading his mouth, taking what I need and loving that he gives it to me willingly.

He pulls away, breathless. "Fuck me then, Scotty," he rasps, pushing up his t-shirt I stole and digging his fingers into the skin on my hips.

I lift his t-shirt over my head, and he groans at the sight of my naked body. I lift my hips from his. "Take them off," I demand, and he deftly pushes his boxers and pyjama bottoms off, freeing his cock.

I sit back down, grinding myself onto his hard cock, teasing him with my wetness as his head falls back in bliss. "Fuck, I want you so bad. Sit on me now, baby Mama."

I smile at the nickname as I wrap my hand around the base of him, lining his cock to my pussy lowering myself down slowly, sinking deeper, inch by inch, torturing both of us. My eyes close and my head tips back as I begin to rock slowly, letting the burn of his stretch fill me. Needing more, I lift my hands to my nipples, palming my breasts and pinching the sensitive peaks as they harden from my touch. "Mmm, such a good fucking girl, taking all of me like that. Now bounce, baby. I need you to ride me."

I lean back, bracing my hands on his thighs as he bends his legs, his feet flat on the mattress, so he can fuck me harder and deeper. I start to ride him as his hands roam all over me. My skin explodes with pleasure as his touch moves from my breasts, to my round stomach, down my thighs and eventually to my clit, circling and teasing until I'm so wet, I can hear my arousal as loudly as I can hear our frantic breaths..

"Fuck Liam, you're going to make me come," I pant, grinding myself against him.

He pushes up, leaning on his hands and takes one of my nipples in his mouth, twirling his tongue, sucking and nipping until I tumble over the edge of the abyss I've been circling, my orgasm ripping through my body.

"Oh, fuck. You look so hot coming for me like that. You're so wet. Fuck…" Bucking harder into me, my body vibrates from the aftershocks of my orgasm and the force of his release makes me come again, my walls clamping around him like a vice as I bury my face in his neck and cry out his name.

Liam collapses back down onto the bed, running his hands through his hair. "What are you doing to me? I can never get enough of you, especially like this." He rubs my stomach affectionately and my chest tightens.

"I love you." I say, still trying to catch my breath.

"Not like I love you."

THE END

Thank you to....

My husband – You have listened to me talk about these characters as though they are real and sometimes it does feel like they live with us. You understand me when I dive into conversations that start in my head. I am forever grateful for you and your patience. I love you always and forever.

Debbie – My person the universe knew I needed. I genuinely couldn't have got this far without you. Thank you for putting up with me blowing up your phone with voice notes every second of every day. You make me smile more than you'll ever know. I'm forever grateful that reading Say You Swear led me to you.

Amy 'Check your welly' – My wifey for being the first person I spoke to about this mental journey. The one who would cheer me on when my fears choked me. I think it might be time to get the pompoms out now!

Sam – Thank you for finding all those Goograysonumps. That will never not be funny. Thank you for telling me when you needed Liam to be sweet, he will always be your book boyfriend.

Adi – For being my official alpha reader and for never being too busy for me, even if I do pester. This book is better because of you. You helped me breathe life back into it and for that I am forever grateful!

I'm so grateful I met you in this crazy bookstagram world, you are a true friend. Thank you, a million times, over. <3

Cygnet ladies & T L Swan – Being accepted into this community and learning so much in the last year has been incredible. I'm so lucky to have a platform of knowledge from you all as a reference to navigate this new writer world. You're all a huge inspiration to me x

My beta readers – Nicole, Tash, Allie – you all got a very rough version of this book, and you were all so very kind to me as a new writer I had no clue, but you all helped me more than you'll know. Thank you from the bottom of my heart x

The Rare group chat ladies – I don't think I would've made it through edits had it not been for you all cheering me on. Love you all immensely – Daily dick pics for life <3

FINALLY... to everyone who shares anything of mine on Instagram or TikTok, I'm in your debt. You're all wonderful people who give up your time to help indie authors like me and I'm so happy to be a part of it with you xx

About Author

Meghan lives in rural England with her family – husband, two children and a yappy dog!

She works in Education by day but writes smutty romances by night.

There are lots of plans for Meghan to write more books so if you enjoyed this one there are more on the way!

Follow Meghan Hollie on Facebook, Instagram, TikTok and Goodreads.

If you enjoyed this book, please consider leaving a review on amazon and you'll be thanked in virtual hugs forever!

Printed in Great Britain
by Amazon

23784943R00182